Scorpio Moons

Scorpio Moons

Helen Noble

Winchester, UK
Washington, USA

First published by Soul Rocks Books, 2014
Soul Rocks Books is an imprint of John Hunt Publishing Ltd., Laurel House, Station Approach,
Alresford, Hants, SO24 9JH, UK
office1@jhpbooks.net
www.johnhuntpublishing.com
www.soulrocks-books.com

For distributor details and how to order please visit the 'Ordering' section on our website.

Text copyright: Helen Noble 2013

ISBN: 978 1 78279 566 7

A CIP catalogue record for this book is available from the British Library.

Design: Stuart Davies
www.stuartdaviesart.com

Printed and bound by CPI Group (UK) Ltd, Croydon, CR0 4YY

We operate a distinctive and ethical publishing philosophy in all
areas of our business, from our global network of authors to
production and worldwide distribution.

CONTENTS

1. Brigit 1

2. Welcome to the Juggler's Arms 19

3. Broken Smile 36

4. Radio Grandma 65

5. Elena 83

6. Moments of Truth 116

7. Goodnight Girl 143

8. Vanquished 166

9. The Magic Works 185

10. Lady Magpie 230

11. The Glass Cliff 249

12. Secret Powers of the Silence 268

Acknowledgements

For Donna, a brave, honest and beautiful spirit;
Imelda for her inexhaustible optimism, patience and proof
reading;
Jordan for the unique art work;
John, with whom the metaphorical head-banging helped to
create some of the crazy scenes;
and for Gareth with gratitude for his encouragement and
support.

Brigit

"Scaredy-cat! Pussy boy! You're afraid of your own shadow, Brian Bovary!" The leader of the bullies shouted. His followers chimed in, collectively backing the young boy into a cubicle. Brian closed his eyes and drew a sharp breath as his soft, golden-red hair was grabbed from behind and his face plunged into the toilet pan. As the flushed water battered the back of his head, he heard the usual eruption of spite-laden laughter, and felt a sharp kick to his rear end. He lifted his face and gasped for air, but dared not move until the boys were finished with him, knowing that he would be rewarded with yet another thump. A pivotal moment in the young boy's life; he had slunk away, unseen, out of school for the last time. Never again would he experience the pain and humiliation of a sodden head and dripping shoulders; the awkward questioning from staff members, or satisfied smirks from the perpetrators. Upon reflection, this was the start of many years of social isolation as Brian crawled inside his self-spun chrysalis, in the hope that one day he could safely emerge into a kinder world.

* * *

On a sultry, August night Brigit was woken up from her light sleep by the sound of muffled voices and scuffling in the alleyway beneath the balcony of her holiday apartment. She had chosen this secluded location to ensure her privacy, now compromised by the couple in the throes of passion beneath her window. Wrapping a sheet around her naked shoulders, she stepped onto the balcony and peered over the rail. The couple were in full view; the young woman's slim legs wrapped around the hips of the man. He was holding her wrists above her head and pressing her back firmly against the wall in rhythm with each passionate kiss. His mouth was devouring her naked breasts, their pinkness peeping through her long, raven hair. Brigit watched for a moment, until her eyes connected with those of the young girl; she hastily pulled herself back out of view, and continued to listen from behind the drapes. She heard the sound of the man's moans increasing in tempo as he thrust his way to his release amidst the gasps and groans of the ecstatic girl. A momentary silence ensued. She hovered a little longer to hear them exchange a few words, trying to figure out in which language the couple were conversing. It sounded like Greek, maybe with an Eastern European intonation. There was the sound of cigarettes being lit and the voices faded away, leaving behind a faint trail of laughter. Brigit waited a few moments before stepping out from behind the curtain. She looked out over an empty alleyway filled with the scent of tobacco and sweat. Aroused, she caressed her own nipple and stepped back into the room, where she dropped the sheet and stood facing her own nakedness in the mirror. It had been a while since she had experienced such sexual passion to which she had just borne witness. It was a strong reminder of her deep desire to be possessed, if only momentarily, by the all-consuming love of another. She was looking for a relationship, for commitment. However, for the first time in the thirty-six years of her life, she now felt entitled to go out and find it.

Although unable to deny the arousal she was feeling, Brigit steered away from relieving herself and, lying down on the bed, she waited for the pressing moment to pass, just as it always did.

"Soon," she reassured herself, *"soon I will have passion and love, in the way that feels right for me…"*

The following morning, as the sun was still rising, she rose early to go for a swim in the inky, Aegean Sea. Slipping through the cobbled streets, she dropped her sarong at the tide's edge and glided into the clear waters. This was the best time of day to be immersed in the cool, salty waves of the sea, as few other swimmers had yet surfaced from their beds to face the day. After an initial splash around to warm up, Brigit increased the power of her strokes and swam out towards the large rock, which emerged from the sea, to sit majestically against the distant skyline. Each morning she argued with herself whether or not she could make the distance and every day she arrived back at shore with a wide grin of satisfaction on her face, emerging from the waves cloaked in the fresh, tingling drops of healing water.

Brigit had chosen this particular Aegean island as it was believed to be the birthplace of the goddess Sappho, Greek muse and lyrical poet, whom she had discovered during her literary studies. One of her few surviving great Odes, 'Hymn to Aphrodite,' resonated deeply with the student for whom a whole new world was opening up. In stark contrast to her harsh upbringing and unhappy childhood, Brigit was learning how to live with love and care. She sought to change the habits of criticism and condemnation heaped on her by her own parents and peers, and to treat both herself and others with tenderness and compassion. The hours she spent reading the loving words of others helped to fill her moments of loneliness and the dark hours of doubt had lessened.

Following a reinvigorating shower at the apartment, Brigit dressed and made her way to her favourite beachfront café for breakfast. Taking her usual seat in the corner, from where she could see the passing crowd yet not be interrupted by its flow, she perused the familiar menu and waited for a member of staff to spot her. Her clothes, although clean and colourful, always contributed to her dishevelled look as she habitually wore her blouses two sizes bigger than she needed; she was confident in the knowledge that very soon her enhanced breasts would fill the empty space. Her once greyed-out complexion, now tinged pink by the daily exposure to the early Mediterranean sun, spoke of a more relaxed, recreational lifestyle. However, it was the way in which she shook free her damp, golden-red locks from the green dragonfly clip, allowing it to dry in the warmth of the sun, which suggested that she was finally comfortable in her own skin. Lifting her sunglasses to greet the waitress as she approached, the young girl noticed something unusual about Brigit's eyes. They were coloured jade green. However, her left iris tinted mauve as she smiled. The waitress wondered as to the story behind her eyes. Ignoring her stare, Brigit placed her order for a sweet Greek coffee, a fruit salad, and a slice of spinach pie. She had worked up an appetite with her early morning swim and was eager for some wholesome food. This was her only concern.

Happily eating alone, she eased into the day, listening to the conversations of the people sitting around her and watching those passing through. She loved to speculate about the passions and problems of others, using the newfound insight she had developed about herself, and some general knowledge of human behaviour that she had picked up through years of psychotherapy. Each time she felt that she could identify with a character, even if their life story was merely a work of fiction, courtesy of her imagination, Brigit still felt more comfortably affirmed in her own choices in life. Since learning how to express herself through her own poetry, she had found that focusing on the minute details of life had helped her to more fully appreciate its beauty and truth.

* * *

A week later, a wakeful Brigit had stepped out onto her balcony into the cool night air. The temperature having peaked at thirty-nine degrees earlier that afternoon, the stifling heat of the apartment was preventing her from falling asleep. The atmosphere was still and closing her eyes she listened to the faint, rhythmic sound of the sea breaking on the distant shoreline. She imagined the spray from the waves showering her in the hope she would feel refreshed. Her trance was broken by the sound of voices as two people entered the alleyway beneath the balcony. Brigit had only a side view of the man. She recognized his wavy, dark hair and the strong arm muscles visible beneath the short sleeves of his white shirt. Again she listened to the sounds of their passion until it was spent. She felt like a player in the erotic scene, strong feelings of desire welling up inside. It wasn't until the couple crossed the alleyway in front of her that she noticed a girl's fair hair shining in the moonlight. This wasn't the lithe, raven-haired beauty who had been enraptured in the alleyway the previous week. For a split second, Brigit felt betrayed. Somehow, the moment had lost all of its magic for her and what she believed to have been a beautiful expression of love between two people now appeared tainted and tawdry.

I guess he conducts all of his casual conquests here, she thought as she stepped back into the apartment, her disappointment palpable. She felt like a teenager trying, but failing, to make sense of the behaviour of those around her. Puberty had been a particularly confusing time for Brigit. She had spent many hours alone, shunned by the awkward, adolescent boys. She had always felt more comfortable in the company of girls. The sense of belonging for which she had yearned in her younger years continued to elude her, despite her best efforts to assume the role for which she had appeared destined in life. She had both played the field and the faithful boyfriend, actively worshipping some of the girls in her younger life. The love had just never seemed to last.

In later life she had been fortunate to have engaged the services of a talented therapist who had asked her to recall all of the poignant incidents in her childhood; thus helping her to understand the social dynamics of the threatening situations in which she had found herself. The wise woman had helped her to conceptualise the realities and close the chapters on her past so as to disempower the memories and limit the continuing hurt. In response, she had taken a major step forward by signing herself as 'Brigit Bovary' on her application for gender-reassignment surgery.

Now her post-erotica-viewing erection persisted, as if out of a sense of spite. Again, she resisted the urge to manipulate her own release, telling herself that she would soon be free of this cruel grip. After all, there were only another few months to pass until she would finally start her schedule of operations after which she could finally live and love in a way that would snugly fit.

The following day proved to be the hottest of the holiday and Brigit decided that she would need to drink some alcohol if she had any chance of sleeping that night. Although happy to be out alone during the day, she always felt more lonely and vulnerable in the evenings. On the few occasions that she did venture out, she looked for places where lots of people congregated, in the hope of blending in with the crowd. Tonight, there was a party happening in a bar along the beachfront. She squeezed through the crowd on the sands to order herself a Bellini. Manoeuvring herself towards an empty shelf under the thatched roof of the temporary wooden structure, she stood sipping her drink from a tall cocktail glass and resumed people watching. There was a warm energy circulating through the gathering. She felt quite safe and welcome in the friendly crowd which was mainly female. Young, vibrant women were dancing in a space on the sand to the loud music coming from a makeshift deck. Older, bright-eyed ladies sat serenely sipping their drinks and some couples had paired off to kiss and caress each other on the beanbags in the corner. Brigit was surveying the scene when she recognized in the crowd the face of the raven-haired beauty from the alleyway. The laughing girl was wearing a revealing black dress and holding a pair of black high-heeled shoes in her hand, the shiny, thin straps wrapped around her elegant fingers. She was enjoying attention from a variety of admirers. Brigit's attention was drawn to her smooth, olive skin, taut across her elegant bone structure, and the soulful expression of her ebony eyes. She felt a sense of urgency, a need to catch the attention of the beautiful girl, but Brigit knew that she had nothing to say and had to content herself watching the interactions from a distance.

On returning from the bar with her third cocktail of the evening, she felt a little perplexed at no longer being able to see the face of the beautiful girl in the crowd. The music playing was much louder now and the atmosphere had heightened to one of a late-night party, with much laughter and some horseplay on the sand. One group of women had removed all of their clothes and had ventured into the sea, accompanied by whistles, cheers and clapping from the crowd. Feeling isolated and despondent, Brigit decided it was time for her to head home. However, before making the long walk back along the dark, cobbled streets she needed firstly to visit the toilet. Stepping into the darkness of the convenience located at the rear of the bar, she fumbled around on the wall for the light switch. Suddenly, she sensed movement close by and she froze. She caught a whisper and the sound of a gentle gasp. She flicked on the light and she saw the raven-haired beauty reclining on the top of the hand basin unit, with the face of another woman buried deep between her splayed legs. As the startled couple parted in response to the unexpected intrusion, Brigit caught a glimpse of the glistening, crimson interior of the woman's body and in that instant she recognized the truth.

In her mind, and in her heart, she knew she was a woman. She thought, felt and loved as a woman and soon she would have a woman's body in which to live. All fears and doubts melted away with the moment and, for the first time, Brigit understood exactly what it meant to feel free. Although she had long been able to intellectualize the idea, having discussed all of the issues at length with her therapist, she now physically experienced the reality. The thoughts had been unlocked and their power translated into the feelings running through her body, waking up each and every cell to its core. With a heartfelt apology, she turned and left the toilet, flicking the light switch off and closing the door behind her.

"Sorry, that one's out of order," she explained to deflect the intrusion of another woman approaching the building.

Later that night, as she lay down to sleep in her hot, stuffy and silent room, Brigit drifted off to sleep with ease, picturing herself in the muscular arms of the alleyway lover, intimately merging amidst the pounding of their passionate hearts. She imagined the urgency of his hands grasping her generous breasts and the moist sensation excitedly emerging from between her legs. In her mind's eye she could see the intensity in his eyes and feel his warm breath on her neck as their bodies melded into one. On waking, she knew that she would return to this place that had inspired her passion.

* * *

"Welcome back, Brigit. Are you with us yet? Can you hear me?"

The recovery nurse's tone was calm, yet concerned. Brigit opened her eyes and blinked in response to the blinding strip lighting on the ceiling.

"How are you feeling?" asked the nurse in a more relaxed manner now that the patient was conscious.

"Do you have any pain, Brigit? No? Okay, just lie here for a moment. Are you experiencing any nausea?"

Brigit tried, but failed, to shake her head in response. Although awake, she felt disembodied, as if her mind was swaddled in some alien substance. The anaesthetic-induced imagery was still looming large in her mind's eye and she wasn't sure if the voice she could hear was just another feature of her weird experience.

"Would you like a sip of water, Brigit?"

Brigit wondered how she could drink water without the use of her mouth. She closed her eyes against the harsh light and was once again wrapped in the warmth and comfort of the other place. Here, there was the golden light of gently dancing flames and the cadence of a distant chant. She bathed herself in the caress of the flickering light and fell into the soothing rhythm of the sounds. Here she felt protected, safe. Drawing nearer, she found herself focusing on the pale blue centre of the largest flame. Reluctantly, she felt herself merging with the light, fearful of the all-consuming power of its intense heat. However, all she felt was the warm kindness of shelter, as the flames rose up around her.

"Wake up again, Brigit! Wake up! I swear she opened her eyes," said the desperate nurse, whilst a doctor filled the syringe from the vial. He quickly checked the measure before squeezing the contents into the tap on the back of Brigit's hand.

"Replace the IV rehydration pack," he ordered, reaching for her arm to take her pulse and leaning over to look into her face for signs of response.

Within a few minutes, Brigit once again opened her eyes. At first it felt as if she had been hurriedly pushed through the wrong door into an echoing, cold room. However, this time there was no going back. Slowly the numbness faded as the first sharp, post-surgical pains cut their way across her torso. Even to the blurred vision of the sleep-deprived doctor, the discomfort on the patient's face was prominent.

"Where's the morphine?" he asked irritably before turning to address his patient. "Brigit, you are back with us. We are doing all we can to make you comfortable. In a little while you can drift back off to sleep, but for now I want you to stay awake. Do you understand?"

Brigit managed a slight nod and, opening her eyes wide, she tuned in to the sounds around her. Gradually, she turned her head to watch the fraught movements of the medical staff in the recovery room and she began to hear quite clearly the sounds of the heart-monitoring equipment beside her bed.

"I'm just going to perform a few tests, Brigit. There's nothing to worry about, just relax."

The doctor gently pulled aside the single sheet protecting her modesty and scraped the soles of both her feet. Next, he carefully bent her legs and tapped each knee, nodding to himself in approval at the responses. Flashing a narrow light into her eyes, he suddenly stopped to speak directly to his groggy patient. "Have your eyes always looked like this, Brigit? It seems that the iris in your left eye has been damaged at some point. It's somewhat cloudy in appearance and the pupil is less responsive to the light."

Brigit gingerly nodded her head and struggled to speak as the vivid memory burst through the confusion in her brain. She spoke in short bursts, "Since childhood; accident at school." Once more in her mind she tried to bury the scene where, as the young boy, Brian, she had tried to resist the attempts of the bullies. She jerked suddenly, reliving the pain as her delicate cheek bone was smashed against the unforgiving porcelain of the toilet pan, wishing only to drift off once more to the place of warmth and safety.

"She's fine, just a bit disorientated," the doctor informed the nursing staff. "She'll probably sleep well into the evening. You don't have to wake her when taking your observations, but do make sure that you check on her regularly."

* * *

During the six-week recovery period following the breast-enhancement surgery, Brigit had plenty of time to reflect on her surgical experience. She found that she was able to relax into her newly shaped body and her scars healed very quickly. She took to bathing in milk, where she enjoyed watching her new soft curves rise to gently break the surface of the liquid, and reported back to the doctor that although she felt rested she was having strange dreams. Sophia, her psychotherapist, was also very interested in her client's experience of these vivid dreams.

"Dreams can act as a metaphor for something happening or troubling us in our life," Sophia explained when Brigit raised the subject.

"I'm being called back to that place, I am sure of it," Brigit reasoned aloud. "I'm lying down, surrounded by a ring of fire. There is chanting, a chorus of female voices and I'm being told that I'm safe. Then something else will happen in the dream. On one occasion I was back in school; a place of bad memories for me. However, it felt different. It felt good. I was not Brian, the sad little boy who got bullied. I was Brigit, the little girl with the golden-red hair. In the cloak room, I was no longer fearful of being shoved into a smelly, damp cubicle by rough boys. I was breathing in the fresh, meadow air, surrounded by the chat and laughter of my friends, where I hung my school coat on a sunbeam. It was like I had been given a second chance."

"Tell me more..." The interested therapist sat forward in her chair and started to jot down some notes.

Brigit continued, "In another dream, I found myself in the circle and was told to close my eyes and listen. I heard the sound of running water and I opened my eyes to see myself standing alongside a river that ran red. There were people there; sick people who were asking me to put my hands on their bodies to heal them." She fell silent.

"How did you feel about that?" asked Sophia.

"It felt perfectly natural," Brigit responded. "I was looking at people with all sorts of deformities and yet I wasn't scared or repulsed. I just knew what to do. I closed my eyes and wished them to be well. It seemed as though the hands of another person were actually touching them."

"So all of these dreams that you experience are pleasant and affirming experiences, where you feel supported and loving?" the therapist suggested, pressing for some further insight into the dreams.

Brigit hesitated before replying, "There was one dream. I tried to forget it, but I might as well tell you about it now."

Sophia nodded her support and listened carefully.

"I was with a group of people – women – alongside a fire. They were playing a game where they stepped in and out of a hoop made of straw. It was some sort of festival or celebration, but it was spoiled by a man who stumbled into the fire. The women shouted a warning at him to stay back but he insisted on going too close to the flames and as they dragged him out I could see that his right leg and his penis had been charred by the fire. I awoke from that dream feeling nauseous and the image of the man kept reappearing in my mind for a while."

"How are you feeling about the next stage of surgery?" asked the therapist.

Silently, Brigit made the connection between the dream and the impending procedure which would transform her from this in-between state, allowing her the complete female shape.

"The vaginoplasty procedure has been fully explained to me," she replied slowly. "I know of all the possible complications and risks and the aftercare which will be necessary. I have a realistic idea of how my body will look when the work is finally finished." She paused, before continuing:

"I'm living for that day. At the moment, it feels as if I merely exist in some in-between world. I'm still technically a man, although I now look more like a woman and, as you know, I have always felt female. The day I become a woman in the full sense of the word, I'm sure my life will begin."

Another few moments of silence followed before a thoughtful and composed Sophia replied, "You have such a rich inner life, Brigit. From what I've heard today, I believe that if you turn to what is inside you, rather than relying on everything you can see around and outside of you, I think you will feel much more contented. It sounds as if you have enough sense of your inner self to start living today, right now. These dreams, these details, they have been generated from your own experiences; your own personal history. Some believe we can also tap into our collective consciousness and that we are able to tap or tune into the lives of others that have existed before us, or maybe the lives that we have lived in other times. I believe that dreams are an illustration of the rich tapestry of our own unconscious realms. Perhaps the childhood we have experienced in this lifetime can be seen as just a tiny part in the whole of our existence. As just a small part of a much larger picture, we can reframe the extent of these early experiences; the significance of the negative influences can be lessened and sometimes disempowered. This leaves the space free for us to fill our own existences with our choice of pictures, sounds and stories which hold some meaning for us. Ultimately, Brigit, you will have to accept yourself before you look to others for recognition and appreciation."

* * *

"Brigit, love, how are you feeling?" The friendly nurse's face loomed large as the newly conscious patient squinted her eyes against the harsh lighting of the recovery room. It was a rhetorical question; Brigit was now familiar with the post-operative procedure. She nodded her head to signify she had heard him. Soon she would be back in the side ward where she could sleep off the anaesthetic.

At the end of his shift, the surgeon appeared at the door of her hospital room to speak with his groggy patient. "How are you doing? Is it sore? You can expect the swelling to persist for a few more weeks but when it subsides we will have a better idea of how successful it was. Then we can look at the possibility of labiaplasty. Of course, anything further will be purely cosmetic but otherwise the transition is complete." Although Brigit was still numb, she knew that the irreversible change had been effected and she was now, finally, female in every aspect of her being. "We'll keep you under observation overnight," the soft-faced man continued, "so use the self-administering morphine drip as much as you need and try and get as much rest as you can. I'll be back tomorrow to check in on you."

As much as she appreciated his friendly, caring manner, Brigit was relieved when he left her bedside. There had been no welcoming lights or warming scenes prior to her recovery on this occasion. She had emerged from a boundless, black silence with a fearful sense of dread. She had spoken about the possibilities of an adverse reaction to the surgery with her therapist and had been sure that she held steadfast in her decision to undergo the irreversible surgery. She had thought of little else for years now. *Perhaps this is just a reaction to the anaesthetic?* Time would tell and all she wanted to do was drift back off to sleep, to conserve her energy to deal with the pain which would inevitably make its presence known soon.

Her drug-induced sleep was uncomfortable and restless. In her dreams she was lying frozen in a dark cave on a bed of the crushed heads of wild poppies. She was being shown two gateways: one fashioned from ivory, another from ebony. A voice from behind her was urging her to choose a gate to walk through. It was warning her that one would lead to a life of truth and fulfilment, whilst the other would lead her to a place where she would stumble over falsehoods, lose her footing and fall to an early grave. However, she was unable to move or speak. The voice became angry at her failure to respond and she felt its presence closing in on her from behind. A sudden gust of frozen air chilled her to the core and she was deafened by a violent clatter and the pounding of heavy daemon wings. As the heavy shadow hovered overhead, her pulse pounded through her veins. As it swooped down to engulf her petrified form, her fear rendered her conscious. Panting, Brigit opened her eyes to scan the dark room. Shaking, she fumbled around on the bedside cabinet for the emergency call button. Within minutes, there was a nurse at her bedside. As soon as she could breathe steadily again and speak coherently, Brigit explained, "I was in a dark place. It was icy cold and I was scared. There was some sort of creature, a winged creature that was going to hurt me."

"It was just a dream," the nurse reassured her gently. "Morphine can have that effect sometimes. Do you have any pain?" Brigit replied that she was not in any pain. The nurse switched on the light above the bed and took Brigit's pulse. Next he fixed the blood pressure reader to her arm and took two readings.

"Your pulse is racing, but your blood pressure is falling back towards normal. We expect it to be slightly raised, but yours is well within the normal range for the post-surgical period. I'll get you some more water. Drink some and try to get some more sleep. And don't worry; we're here if you need us." Brigit sipped the fresh water, feeling grateful for the nurse's kind words.

* * *

On returning home from hospital, Brigit searched for the elation she believed would be awaiting her at the door. Instead, she found herself languishing in a strange, unknown state of mind. Even her previous, liminal stage now seemed somehow more appealing. Standing naked in front of the mirror, she tried to see beauty and feel love, and yet such happiness eluded her. In desperation, she forced out a laugh to be sure that the image reflected back at her was indeed that of her own body. Perhaps she had made a huge mistake. Brigit began to question her own convictions, to doubt her own judgement. *What if there are no second chances?*

Her doctor readjusted her levels of hormone therapy, prescribed some anti-depressant medication and advised her to resume sessions with her therapist.

Brigit became a brave intrepid explorer seeking to establish herself in her newfound existence. Throwing herself deeper into her studies, she had illustrated the barren walls of her mind with the art works of the ancient Greeks, filling its corners and spaces with their white marble Kore sculptures and black silhouette pottery. She immersed herself in the love and emotion of the Archaic Greek melic poets, absorbing the beauty and truth of their words. From within the privacy of her home, her studies took her over land, sea and centuries to places of great wonder and romance. How simplistic the lives of the ancient Greeks seemed to her. How rewarding a quality and pace of life which allowed the time for the delightful pursuits of poetry and the music of the flute, where hours could be spent in a true and full appreciation of the shapes and colours of nature. Revelling in the words of the poet Sappho, she became filled with the notion that everything in existence emanated from a point of desire.

* * *

"Hello, Brigit. How are you feeling today?" The weekly visits to Sophia had now morphed into monthly meetings.

"I'm sick of being asked that question. I'm sick of examining my thoughts, feelings and behaviour. In fact, I'm sick of this whole process. It seems as if all I've done for the past few years now is to examine, analyse, rationalize how my life could be, how I could be happy in the world." Brigit spoke not in anger, but with passion. "I want to stop thinking about it and talking about it and start living it!"

"Well, you're free to start as soon as you like," replied Sophia. From that point onwards Brigit knew that something had shifted within her. It was as if she had been given permission to open the front door and step outside the castle walls of her recovery. During her work with Sophia, she had found her freedom from the darkness of her self-imposed dungeon. For the very first time, she had become aware of a new source of light in her life. Yes! Of course it was entirely up to her to take the first step into the world. It was time to take her place in the grand order of things and make of it what she could. With a tentative sense of pleasure, Brigit was finally able to grant herself permission to go back out into the world, just as she stood, just how she looked, just as she felt. It was her right to claim her own space in the mad maelstrom of the world, and she knew exactly to where she would head first.

* * *

Passing through the quiet courtyard of the hotel, Brigit's hand gently brushed the leaves of a faded rose. The delicate pink petals fell, silently cloaking the shoulders of the naked stone figure, so alluringly outstretched in the bubbling fountain. The heat from the Mediterranean summer sun now pleasantly muted by the seasonal change, the late-September evening was the perfect time to walk along the shoreline in search of its refreshing breeze. Exchanging a few shy smiles with friendly, passing strangers, she crossed the cobbled path and headed towards the beach. The sun had started its descent into the distant horizon and she exhaled deeply, releasing the day's tension from her shoulders.

It was then that she saw him: the white-shirted waiter, chatting congenially with a group of diners just taking their seats at a table on the veranda of the restaurant, overlooking the beach. Brigit fixed her look just long enough for him to sense her gaze and as their eyes met she quickly looked away. She was in no hurry.

With her golden-red hair trailing behind on the cool breeze blowing in off the sea, she continued to walk along the deserted beach. She gazed at the bay stretching out in front of her, enveloped by the vernal hills which sloped gently to the sea. It suddenly occurred to her that these were the same rocks which had so lovingly protected the ancient Greek poets and artists who had dwelled here centuries before her.

As she strolled barefoot and wrapped only in an aqua silk sarong, she traced the curve of the inky sea soaking into the golden sands. Brigit knew this was the same ocean that had been undulating here with the same, gentle ease for centuries. She smiled at the realization that she now inhaled the same air from which the ancients had drawn their breath; that everyone who had ever lived here had existed amidst this timeless and eternal inspiration. Stretching her arms to soak up the warmth of the burnished gold rays, she absorbed the intensity of the setting sun. Sighing deeply she sensed a profound contentedness welling up within her.

The goddess had returned home.

Welcome to the Juggler's Arms

Ed's trance was broken by the creak of the rusty old sign, caught momentarily by the gentle sway of the summer breeze. The bored agent, weary from waiting for yet another prospective purchaser of the abandoned pub, was really hoping for a no-show so that he could leave without even having to step once more inside the Jugglers Arms. He was feeling despondent, desperate to find other ways of scratching a living. There seemed little hope of an upturn in the property market any time soon, and shifting a turkey like this was proving impossible.

After a further, painful five minutes, he glanced at his watch and prepared to leave. It was then he heard the short, fast footsteps in the gravel and raised his sunglasses to see a petite, smart, suited woman approaching across the rough ground of the car park.

This looks promising, he thought to himself. *Perhaps I can finally make a sale here.* He would feel very pleased to finally offload this place, which had taken up too much of his time and advertising budget. There was just no market demand for this sort of business these days. He remembered visiting the place with his parents many years previously, but as an adult it was not the sort of establishment he had chosen to frequent. Cranking up the charm-o-meter he soon realized he couldn't recall her name, so he swung out a handshake and beamed a wide, toothy welcome.

"Hello! You must be..."

"Here to see the pub, shall we go inside?" Silenced by her

straightforward manner, he fumbled in his pocket for the keys to the front door of the rustic, old country pub.

"Uh, oh, of course, where would you like to start?" he mumbled. "It's been empty for a while," he explained, opening the heavy oak door and gesturing for her to step inside. "The décor is looking a bit drab and dated, and some of the paintings and ornaments are rather, um, eclectic, shall we say? Not everyone's cup of tea." He grimaced, pointing to a large oil painting of a loin-clothed warrior standing against a vast African plain, brandishing a spear. "Structurally, I believe the building itself is sound. It's been standing for as long as I can remember." The truth was that Ed didn't actually know what he believed anymore. He had been in this game for so long that he now had great difficulty in distinguishing the salience from the sales pitch.

Ignoring his comments, the viewer continued through into the lounge area. Ed made sure he got a good look at the slim woman's rear view, from her neatly pinned-up hair right down to her sharp and shiny three-inch heels as she walked purposefully into the building. *Nice!* He was smiling to himself as she turned quickly on her heels, just inside the door, once again catching him off guard.

"Is the kitchen equipment still in working order? When was the central-heating system serviced? What about the bar, is it fully stocked?" She fired each question at him with the force of a handbag pistol, and suddenly he was on notice.

Looks and brains, eh? Ed thought to himself. This was not the usual mix of personal qualities of the women in his life. He might need to use a slightly different approach…

"This place has been on the market for quite some time now. It eventually closed down, as in ceased trading, about eighteen months or two years ago, I think. I'm not really sure when the owner actually moved out though." Ed stumbled through his words. What was wrong with him? He was failing to deliver his usual, sleek performance. There was something about this situation, or the woman, that was unnerving him, but he couldn't quite put his finger on it. Taking out a tissue, Ed quickly patted his perspiring hairline; as the woman took herself off into the kitchen, he checked for signs of sweat under his arms. He spoke sharply to himself, in an attempt to get back on track with his sales spiel. Then he took a deep breath and followed her.

"All the kitchen equipment is included in the price, but I would advise you to have it checked out, of course," he added, watching her scrape a layer of dusty grease from around a hob ring with a perfectly polished finger nail. Realising how thorough this viewer was, Ed prayed that the refrigerator wasn't harbouring any mouldy food offerings. "Of course, any of the national restaurant chains would be interested to include this place into their franchise portfolio, once it's up and running again. Countrywide Steak Houses, for example, they are success-fully expanding at the moment."

Ed found himself talking to the back of the woman's head just before it disappeared through the swing door of the kitchen and back into the restaurant seating area. He wondered what, if anything, he could do to get her to show the slightest interest in the property. Starting to feel stifled in the interior of the heavily draped building and thinking it might be cooler outside, he suggested that they take a look at the garden. He couldn't under-stand why he was sweating so profusely. It was a typically English summer day, cool and breezy, with an occasional shaft of sunlight breaking through the cloud. Perhaps he was coming down with a seasonal cold? Well, he had to hold it together for this viewing if he had any chance of getting to the ker-ching part of the deal. They both headed towards the rear doors of the bar, situated just past the abandoned pool table and the dusty, empty space that had once housed an array of gaming machines.

"I'm sure the previous supplier would be happy to re-stock this area, if that's what you are interested in, I understand these gambling machines can prove quite lucrative in local pubs..."

Ed's voice trailed off. He really could not get a handle on this one, she wasn't giving him any clues, no comments, offering absolutely sweet nothing in response to anything he was saying. "There is living accommodation on the first floor, which could be used for bed-and-breakfast bookings," he continued and then pointed outside to a disused building. "I understand that at one time some sort of beer was brewed here, on site, but we don't seem to have a key to that door, although I suppose we could try to gain access through one of those broken window panes." Watching his comments appearing to float, unheard into the ether, Ed was seriously thinking about giving up.

"That's a nice feature, the well under the willow tree there." He played his final card and was about to throw in his hand when his viewer finally spoke, her timing making it seem as if she had actually heard his thoughts.

"Yes, at least the garden has been maintained. It's a great place for children." She smiled up at him as they stood in the garden of the pub, and he squinted at the bright reflection from her unusual, aqua-coloured eyes. Fumbling to retrieve the sunglasses perched on the top of his head; Ed saw this as his moment and homed in.

"So you're thinking of a family-friendly establishment? I'm sure that's exactly what's needed in this village, well in every village really. The traditional community spirit is being lost in this recession, through all of the local business closures, don't you think? Is that more of the sort of thing you had in mind?" He checked, unable to conceal his surprise. It had been the furthest thing from Ed's mind. He lived with his discontented wife in a sterile, characterless house on an estate, recently built on the edge of an out-of-town retail park. No kids, no pets, no mess, which, up until this very moment, had been exactly what he thought he had wanted.

"Hmm, sort of," she replied. "I have some ideas. How about I send you a copy of my business plan?" Ed was confused and excited at the same time,

"Well, there isn't really any need, and my role is largely to pass on your offer, if you intend to make one, to the seller, but of course I would be interested in hearing about your business plans," he lied. Was she intending to make an offer? It was certainly looking promising! How was he going to handle this? Ed's thoughts began to race. After two years on the market this was the first sniff of an offer on this property, his commission on this sale could be the biggest invoice he'd posted in the previous six months.

"In view of the upgrading work necessary on this property I know that the seller would be interested in any sensible offer you might want to put forward at this time. And I will probably be able to get an answer for you later today, if you can let me know what sort of figure you have in mind." Ed tried to stop his gaze creeping down towards the subtle cleavage of her petite frame as he spoke.

She beamed him a wide smile. "So you have a hot line to God? Or maybe it's the Devil?" Laughing out loud, she explained her amusement. "I'm sorry, I should have said, the owner, my grand-father, died last month and left me this place in his will. I thought you knew. When I called your office asking for the only key to the pub, your young assistant said that you would be more than happy to accompany me on a viewing for a valuation."

Dammit! He knew he'd done the right thing by letting his assistant go at the start of the week. She had been costly and clueless, and even now he was still paying the price for her mistakes. In an attempt to regain some sense of professionalism, he coughed that there must have been some cross-communication but that it wasn't a problem and he would be happy to sell the pub on her behalf if, and when she decided what she was going to do with it. Now she was looking him up and down, taking in the width of his chest and the cut of his suit. He found himself hoping that the collar of his crisp, white shirt hadn't curled up, and that his stay-hard hair gel hadn't melted into a Mohican in the heat of the afternoon's events.

"I spent much of my childhood here," she continued. "My parents worked abroad and I was at boarding school from the age of nine. My grandparents entertained me during school holidays. I loved coming here. I spent hours in the kitchen with my grandmother, learning how to cook, and I enjoyed listening to my grandfather's tales as he chatted to the customers across the bar. He had lived in Africa for a large part of his life and he had many amazing tales of African magic to tell. When families with children came in I was allowed to play in the garden with them. I have many happy memories of throwing coins into the well and making wishes with the water spirits." She paused before continuing, "My grandmother passed away some years ago, but my grandfather kept this place open until he became too ill to stand behind that bar. He employed a manager to take over the business, but it looks as if the place has been neglected for some time."

Ed looked around aimlessly for a chair to take the weight of his feet but instead he leaned heavily against a wall, alongside a display of fierce faces carved into wooden masks.

"Are you feeling okay?" she asked. "You're looking a little pale…"

"I'm just tired," was the only response Ed could muster.

"You should go home and get some rest," she said in a softer tone. "I have your number, I'll be in touch when the probate papers for my grandfather's will are granted and you can hand me the key," she said, turning to leave.

"Wait! I don't even know your name…" Ed called after the woman as she disappeared through the front door, amazed at the words he could hear coming out of his own mouth.

She paused momentarily and laughed before answering. "I'm Jude, you can call me *the Juggler*," she replied, pointing to the sign hanging above the pub door, before disappearing across the car park and into the road beyond. Ed fished in his pocket for the keys and locked the door, reassuring himself that she would have to be in touch as there was only one set of keys for the pub. He would be keeping them firmly about his person, as he was keen to meet up again with this curiously alluring woman.

Jude felt sure that she was doing the right thing. As she drove home to her small, sparsely furnished flat, she decided that she would give notice to the landlord as soon as she received the papers from the probate registry. She had been named as the sole beneficiary in the will and knew its contents. The practical young woman had already assigned her capital inheritance for the refurbishments needed to improve the pub, and at the end of the month she would be leaving her job as a hotel chef, to become a country publican.

That night, Ed's sleep was restless, dominated by distorted dreams of his visit to the Juggler's Arms. Ella, his wife, complained of his thrashing about and calling out, and said she was going to sleep in the spare room.

"I think I have a fever," Ed groaned. "I've been feeling offish all day." With an impatient flick of her hand on his forehead, Ella huffed that he felt perfectly fine to her and left him alone with his troubled thoughts. Every time he dozed off to sleep, Ed found himself dreaming he was back at the pub. However, on each occasion, the interior of the pub had changed in appearance and he experienced an overwhelming sense of guilt at just being present. This was followed by a sense of urgency that he needed to leave before he was discovered. It was at this point in the dreams that he would wake up, drenched in sweat.

At breakfast, Ed's wife was staring at him over the rim of her coffee cup, tapping out her irritation with brightly varnished fingernails on the white marbled breakfast bar.

"You look like shit," she stated without an ounce of sympathy.

"Perhaps you have picked up some nasty virus. Make sure you change the bed clothes and go and ask the pharmacist for something." She lifted Ed's half-full mug of cold tea and squirted some anti-bacterial spray to the surface beneath.

"And don't forget to wash up before you leave," she ordered. "I'm going to work now and then around to Aimee's this evening. She's just had a new sofa delivered and…and I'm going to seduce her husband on it." Ella knew that he had switched off long before she had finished her sentence. Ed had other things on his mind; Ed always had other things on his mind. In the hallway she rifled through his jacket pockets to see if there was any money that she could take. Indiscriminately emptying the contents of each into her handbag, she flounced out of the front door, cocking a snoot as she pulled it closed behind her.

Emptying an ancient aspirin bottle and washing down its contents with a cup of cold tea, Ed sat back and took a deep breath. He was feeling worse by the minute but he knew that he had to pull himself together. After a second cup of tea he struggled into the hallway, pulled on his jacket, grabbed his car and office keys from the hall table and headed into the office.

On arrival he started to look for any contact details on file for the deceased seller that could help him find the Juggler. Ed knew he was obsessing, but it felt as if he had no control over his compulsive actions. Furiously flicking through the filing cabinet, he quickly became frustrated when he couldn't find a file for the Juggler's Arms. What was the dead seller's name? If he could only remember the name of the guy, he might be able to find some information somewhere. Ed turned his attention to the computer database, but after scrolling through pages of entries he could find no trace of the property. He racked his memory trying to recall when he was first asked to market the property. Inexplicably he was struggling to remember anything. He knew in his heart that not many properties on his books had changed hands during that time. So what was going on? There was simply no record of him ever having anything to do with the Jugglers Arms, not even an email exchange. What about the phone records? His initial joy at the thought of finding a telephone number was quickly crushed at the realization that trawling through the last two years' call log was just not practical. Ed couldn't even recall the old man's face or his instructions for the sale of the pub. The aspirin had done nothing to improve his fever and this goddamned virus was gradually turning his mind into mush. He knew he should stay in the office to prepare the quarterly VAT return; after all, with so few sales it wouldn't take long. However, he found himself scribbling a 'closed' note to pin on the door, and heading out to his car. He just had to take another look inside the Jugglers Arms. It was a compulsion that he could not overcome. Approaching the pub, Ed knew that something was wrong. Quickly scanning the building, he couldn't see any obvious changes; yet he intuitively sensed that the goalposts had shifted. Patting his inside jacket pocket, he felt a shock wave wash through him at the realization that the keys were not there. He was sure he had secured them in the inside pocket, with that meagre fifty quid the cashpoint had allowed him to withdraw on the previous day. What had happened to the keys? Was he losing his mind? Ed's sweating suddenly turned to icy shivers. He realized that this flu virus now had a strong grip on him and he needed to get home.

* * *

At lunchtime, Ella put a pencil line through her appointments diary on the desk. There would be none of her sparkly gel-tips embellishing the fingers of the local girls for the foreseeable future. She was so pleased to be taking a break from the salon; the house and her husband. With only a fleeting sense of guilt as she said her goodbyes, she smiled as her colleagues expressed their envy at the notion that within hours she would be enjoying a couple of cocktails at the beach bar with her girlfriends. After a quick application of her 'all day stay' gloss lipstick, Ella curled one of her latest lock extensions around finger, and smiled at herself in the rear-view mirror of her car, before starting up the engine and driving over to Alan's house. Checking on the contents of her bag, she counted out the five ten-pound notes she had helped herself to out of Ed's jacket pocket. She also picked out a small set of strange keys.

"Tosser!" she exclaimed, throwing the keys out of the car window in contempt, watching in satisfaction as they slipped between the spaces in the grill of the curb-side drain. By the time Ed got around to missing those keys and calling Aimee's house, later that evening, Ella and Alan would be halfway to Marbella. Their affair seemed to be reaching a serious stage, at least in Ella's mind. She felt sure that this holiday on Alan's yacht in the Spanish marina was a sign that he was ready to commit to her exclusively, and she was more than ready to leave Ed. The balance of her secret savings account was steadily rising as her husband's estate-agency business was nose-diving straight down the pan.

Meanwhile, convinced that he might die, Ed had taken himself home to bed. Sleeping deeply through the afternoon and late into the summer evening, he woke feeling relieved to be alive. It took an hour or so for him to wonder about Ella. She would be home soon and pleased to find him feeling better, he was sure. He knew things had been very strained between them lately, but finally he had an idea for a new business venture and was sure that she would be thrilled with the news. He would sell the agency and take on a pub, something like the Juggler's Arms. He wasn't quite sure where the idea had come from, but the notion had gained a firm foothold in his imagination and his ideas for the development of the place were flowing freely in his mind. The change of pace would be good for his health and his marriage. Ed envisaged a stress-free existence filled with delicious food and laughing families. Every time he closed his mind he could see golden-lit scenes of adults relaxing at a large table filled with platters of brightly coloured foods and interestingly shaped bottles of wine. The doors to the garden stood wide open and some children were running around; whilst others sat picnicking under the tree. Ed knew none of this was real, probably an hallucination caused by his ever-increasing temperature, however he liked what he was seeing and even if he closed his eyes to the imagery he could still hear the clink of glasses and the sound of laughter.

At ten o'clock he tried to call Ella on her mobile phone, only to hear a recorded message informing him it was switched off. Although he momentarily thought of calling Aimee's house, instead he found himself dozing off on the lounge sofa, leaving the closing theme-tune to the nightly news programme playing in the background.

When he woke, cold and crabby, at four o'clock the following morning, Ed felt a mild panic. Ella still wasn't home. She had stayed over at friends on occasions, but never without telling him beforehand. Should he try her mobile again? He couldn't call Aimee's house at this hour, he might wake her husband or their new baby. After the initial fear that something awful had happened to her, Ed rationalized that Ella never ventured very far. She had probably had one glass of wine too many and decided not to drive, he thought. She wasn't working this weekend and would probably be home in a couple of hours full of remorse for the unnecessary calories she had consumed. As a result, Ed thought he would find himself having to eat salads all weekend, but he was happy as there were new opportunities on the horizon. He decided to send her a text telling her all about the exciting, new developments going on in his mind and that he loved her very much. However, he received no reply.

Taking what he hoped was to be a final dose of analgesics to stop the pounding pain in his head, Ed snuggled into the duvet and continued to fantasize about the fresh, organic food and home-brewed beers that would be on the menu for the loyal customers. He was so looking forward to telling Ella all about his ideas for their new business venture. She was forever nagging him for spending so much time at the office, although perhaps a little less frequently as of late. He was sure she would be pleased that he had decided to wind up the estate agency and spend more time with her, as they worked alongside each other in their new life as country publicans.

Ed's dreams became even more vivid when he fell back to sleep, despite the dawn light gently filtering through the bedroom curtains. He found himself curled up on a soft sofa, side on to the open log fire in the bar of the Jugglers Arms, roused by the aroma of freshly roasted coffee from a large, steaming mug that had just been placed on the small table in front of him. The scene switched to one of Ed, himself, chalking up the specials on the board behind the bar. Double-checking the spelling, he was watching his own hand writing 'Melancholy Mud Pie with fresh Consolation Cream'; 'Cough-it-up Chickpea Curry' and 'Home-baked Cheery Tart,' with great amusement. Above the rear patio doors there was a sign saying 'Ginger Beer Garden' and wiping off the dusty panes, Ed found himself looking out to some smiling people sitting around a wooden picnic table, under the willow tree; whilst a group of small children tossed coins into the wishing well. Walking back towards the bar, he took a double-take at the console standing alone in the corner. On the screen he read 'Magical Muse-ical Juke Box, playful Inspiration, never the same tune twice.' However, it was clearly a lie, as he could hear the same tune playing over and over…

The door to the kitchen opened and Ed saw Ella carrying a tray with plate of paella and two glasses of sangria. He called her name and held out his arms to embrace her as she walked towards him. Placing the tray on an empty table, she gently wrapped her arms around him and held him for a few minutes in a warm embrace. However, as she gently worked herself free from his hold, it was Jude's face there in front of him. With a seductive smile she intimately murmured into his ear, "Welcome to the Juggler's Arms."

Jude stood before him, rhythmically throwing a series of brightly coloured balls into the air. He watched open-mouthed, in awe of her skill. She gestured to him before throwing the balls, one by one, in his direction. In the dream he stumbled, falling to the floor, feeling helpless as he failed to catch any of the balls, rapidly increasing in both number and speed as they pummelled him into unconsciousness.

* * *

Ed woke in a hospital bed amidst the indignity of having his stomach pumped.

"No! You don't understand!" He kept trying to explain that the overdose was not intentional, his high temperature must have made him delirious and he simply took too many pills. Yes, he was very sorry to have given the cleaning lady such a fright and he was very grateful that she had called for an ambulance. However, he really did not need a referral to for counselling or the local branch of NA. Signing himself out of the hospital, Ed limped home to find an answerphone diatribe from Ella in response to his earlier text message.

"No! I'm never coming back to that tired little town, Ed, not ever. What planet are you on? Alan and I are making a life for ourselves here in Marbella. The salon knows that I'm not coming back and, anyway, there are loads of nail bars here, if I have to earn some money, not that we need much. Alan and I are staying on the yacht, yes Alan the property developer, that's right, you sold his mother's house in Manor Park back last year. We have been seeing each other ever since. I'm sorry, Ed...sorry that business is not going well for you, but did you really think I would want to spend my days serving pints to lecherous old men and smiling at snotty customers while they complain that the food is cold? Get real, Ed. Wake up and the smell the coffee. Oh and Alan says that if you need somewhere to rent when the house is repossessed, his old flat above the butcher's shop in the High Street opposite your office, is empty at the moment. The house is three months into mortgage arrears, Ed, I just couldn't afford the payments once I decided to start saving for the summer in Marbella. I have to go now, Ed, Alan and I are…" The recording ended with a series of giggles and a shriek of delight, after which Ed heard sound of the dropped phone clattering to the floor.

He had nothing better to do than replay the message, over and over, wondering how in God's name all this had been going on right under his nose. He really had no idea. He had lost his wife, and was about to lose his home. Shortly, when he opened his mail he would also realize that he was about to lose his livelihood. The VAT man was simply not prepared to wait in line for his dues and Ed was going to be forced to wind up the company before the administrators were called in to take control over what little assets were left over from the failed business venture.

* * *

Ed laid low for a couple of months. He gave up wearing pristine shirts, as they smelled of raw meat, whatever detergent he used. Instead, he found himself wiping the fresh blood from the cleaver on a blue-and-white striped butchers apron, as he helped out in the shop below the flat; taking a leftover cut upstairs as dinner-for-one each evening. He let his soft brown hair grow out into its natural curls and became keen to learn as much about the hospitality industry as possible, honing his customer-service skills behind the butcher's counter. When the owner wanted to take a winter holiday in Thailand, he was happy to leave his clientele's Christmas orders to Ed, who was rewarded with additional responsibility for sourcing good meat for the shop. Ed used his newly found power to buy produce from local organic farms. Surely and steadily he was increasing the quality and variety of the stock and soon the butcher began to notice a significant increase in the profits of his business. He asked Ed if he, himself was interested in training to become a butcher and investing in the business. However, as the spring approached, Ed's thoughts focused once more on the Juggler's Arms. He still harboured the desire to return, just to see if anything had changed. He knew it was crazy; he had only ever been inside the pub on that one occasion, the day when he had met Jude. And yet, through the visits he made in his dreams, Ed believed he had an intimate knowledge of the place. In the latest dream, he had found himself revelling in the luxurious, velvet softness of the newly upholstered, fireside sofa and eating a rich, organic beef-in-red-wine casserole.

It was the mention of that very dish, in the butcher's shop a few days later that caught Ed's attention. He tuned into the conversation between two women who had almost collided in the doorway and chosen to continue their conversation beside the herbs and spices section of the shop.

"I always use organic wine for the casserole," one of the women was saying. "It's a bit more expensive, but then you don't have to use as much, so it evens out the cost, in my opinion." The other woman smiled and Ed noticed the curious light reflected in her unusual, aqua-coloured eyes. Her shiny brown hair bobbed gently over the top of her shoulders as she reach up to the shelf for the Manuka honey, and placed it in her basket. Ed spoke up when the shop queue cleared leaving her alone, looking intently at the shelf stacked high with grains.

"Can I help?"' he asked.

"I'm looking for some hops and yeast," she replied.

"Ah! Yeast is there, bottom shelf, left of centre. Hops? Not sure if we've ever stocked any..." There was something vaguely familiar about her, Ed thought. No doubt she was a regular in the shop. "Excuse me, but have we met? I mean somewhere else, apart from in this shop?" The woman simply smiled knowingly in response to his question. *Damn!* Ed thought. *She thinks I'm hitting on her.*

"Can you point me in the direction of somewhere to pick up some hops?" she asked, looking carefully at his face before finally responding to his question.

"Ah yes! I remember…you were the estate agent with the keys to the pub. You look so different! I called around to your office a few weeks later to pick up the keys but you were closed…down," she said.

"Are you Jude, from the Juggler's Arms?" Ed asked in disbelief. "I have been thinking about you, well about the pub, and what happened to it," he corrected himself. "You look different from how I remember you."

"It's been a while," Jude smiled. "I do like your longer hair. So, you are working here now?"

"Yes, it's a long story," Ed said somewhat apologetically and hastily changed the subject. "What's happening with the pub? Did you manage to sell it?" Ed listened as Jude told him how she had taken on the business and was running it herself.

"It's hard work, especially as there is only me, but my grandfather always said that if you create the space then people will come to fill it." She smiled, her compelling eyes fixed firmly on Ed's face as she gently leaned her head to the left. "He was right. It is a very busy place and I have been looking for a manager, and someone to help with the business," she continued. "So, if you know of anyone suitable, please ask them to contact me at the pub."

That night in his dreams, Ed found himself in a disused brewery. It was small space crammed with a full complement of brewing kit; including a host of dusty demi-johns and a hydrometer, suggesting that the previous owner had been experimenting with original recipes. As he reached for the handle to the door he noticed a pane of broken glass and realized he was in the disused brewery in the garden of the Juggler's Arms. Wiping the dust from the pane he could see a small figure outside in the garden. It was a little girl. She was leaning over the wishing well and appeared to be talking to someone. In the dream Ed's vision became blurred and in an effort to see more clearly he wiped the dust from a second pane of the window. There were now two figures around the well. The second was that of a little boy, with wavy brown hair, who reminded Ed of himself, as a child. On looking more closely he could see that it was him. Ed was looking at himself as a child, leaning over the wishing well, smiling and laughing with his friend.

On waking he knew exactly what he had to do. He called the pub and asked to speak to Jude.

The following day, he made his way out of the town, wearing once more a crisp white shirt and smart, casual trousers. His hair, now far too long for the gelled look, was neatly brushed into its natural wave; and for the first time in many months his face wore a genuinely relaxed smile. As he crossed the pub car park, excited at the thought of what the future could hold for him, Jude caught sight of him from her bedroom window and hurriedly scooped up the small figurine from her dressing table. Kissing the head of home-fashioned male figure with soft, wavy hair, she whispered "Welcome home," before carefully placed it into her pocket and running downstairs to let her prospective new beau into the Juggler's Arms.

Broken Smile

Jennie's chest constricted with every narrowing of the country road, her blood pressure increasing at every blind curve. Fumbling through the stash of paperwork in her bag, lying open beside her on the passenger seat, she realized that her inhaler must have fallen to the bottom of the pile. She would just have to continue to breathe slowly and deeply to safely navigate her mud-splattered car along the lonely Cornish lanes, to her destination, the picturesque fishing village of her childhood memories. As she neared the secluded cove, the landmarks became increasingly familiar. She realized that little had changed since the fateful summer of her thirteenth birthday in the cottage holiday, at this quaint, cobble-fronted harbour. Remembering that vehicles were not allowed over the stones, she thought it best to use the National Trust car park, located close to the harbour entrance. After choosing her space and parking up, she emptied the contents her bag and self-administered a few shots of salbutamol, neatly replacing the paperwork and pocketing the inhaler. Feeling some respiratory relief, she scraped together some loose change to hand over to the old man, watching a portable television in the attendant's cabin. Noting the fees on the tariff board, mounted on the wall of the cabin behind his head, she realized that long-term parking arrangements could prove costly and so it was important to put some permanent plans in place.

Jennie was grateful for the short walk along the harbour front, finding the late-afternoon sea air most re-invigorating. At the sign of the Contented Sole, she stopped and opened the grimy, net-curtained door. Stepping through, the sound of the ringing bell alerted the elderly lady, dressed in a navy dress and white apron; she looked up from behind the serving counter to say, "Good afternoon, dear. We're not serving at the moment. We're waiting for the fat to warm up, it has to be the right temperature to fry the chips. It should be ready in half an hour, if you'd like to call back?"

"Oh I'm not here to eat, not yet anyway," replied Jennie. "I was told that a key for the cottage would be left here for me."

"Fuchsia Bank Cottages?" asked the lady, the smile lines from her eyes and lips disappearing into the wrinkles at the edge of her face. "Just one moment, dear, I have it here, somewhere..." She reached out to a handful of keys suspended on a rusty old hook in the wall behind her. "I was told to give you this," she said picking out a green plastic fob with the number '3' written on it in bold, indelible ink. "The place has been empty for a while," she advised as she handed over the fob with two keys affixed. "It's still early in the season and I think you're the first person to visit."

"Thank you," Jennie said, gently accepting the keys.

"You're welcome. Will I see you later?" the friendly old lady asked. "We have some lovely large cod, caught locally. My husband is just mixing up the fresh beer batter." The old lady gestured behind her to the kitchen door. Following her hand, Jennie's attention was drawn to a notice which read: 'Free WI-FI service for paying customers. Please ask waitress.'

"Yes, I'll be back in half an hour," she confirmed as she stepped out of the café and back onto the cobbles.

A few metres along the front, she took a right-hand turn into a narrow lane, from which she approached the cottage; the first in a row of three traditional, single-storey fishermen's abodes. Despite being extended over the years, it still retained the essence of its original, nineteenth-century design. Stepping inside the wrought-iron gate, she closed her eyes and listened to the silvery plink of the underground stream as it emerged from its source, softly muffled by the large fuchsia bush draping the bank. She slipped effortlessly into the familiar rhythm of its gentle flow, which rose to a heightened rush as the stream flowed past the cottages, picking up pace as it headed along the lane towards its outlet into the harbour. Jennie recalled racing along the harbour front and around the headland to the sheltered beach, where she had played with her cousins. A safe, secluded cove with a modest waterfall and rock pools, the perfect scenario for an idyllic childhood holiday; now the sole remaining memory of her innocence and trust, before it was so cruelly shattered.

Opening her eyes once more, she followed the well-trodden path to the cottage door, keys at the ready in her slightly shaky hand. One forceful turn of the stiff Yale lock, and the lifting of the creaky, wrought-iron latch opened the door to release the stale air of the musty interior. Standing just five-feet four inches tall, Jennie was still forced to bow her head beneath the engraved stone plinth above her head, dating the building to the year 1898, as she entered through the white, wooden door of the old cottage.

The dark, dingy interior appeared untouched for some time; she felt the dampness on the curtains, as she drew them back to let in some light to the cottage. Looking around, she recognized the same heavy, dark dresser and awkward wooden table that had stood in the corner some twenty years previously, now bare except for the cobwebs and dust.

She had scoured the internet in the hope of finding this place on a holiday cottage website. With just the one external photo-graph posted to entice the searcher, Jennie could see why few holidaymakers had clicked to book this place. The arrival of spring has been a sluggish affair this year; and there were numerous offers and deals on holiday accommodation being advertised. This humble offering was clearly outshined by the newer properties, full of technological gadgets such as games consoles and DVD players to entice young families.

The slate hearth of the open fireplace was littered with dry sticks, bird droppings and the skeleton of a small mouse. Catching a glint of something amidst the debris, she bent down to look more closely and she retrieved a tiny bent and tarnished ring. On further inspection she could see that this was a child's signet ring. Yes, this was her ring! It was her lost, childhood treasure, now so small she could only just squeeze it onto her baby finger. Jennie was immediately transported back to the day of her thirteenth birthday, during that fateful summer, when she was on holiday at the cottage with her family. She had been very pleased with the present from her parents, a heart-shaped and golden signet ring, engraved at the edges with a flowing pattern. However, her adopted cousin, Monica, three years older than Jennie, and far more streetwise and self-assured, had experienced pangs of jealousy over the treasured gift. Monica's feigned disinterest in the ring, and critical comments left Jennie herself feeling very small and insignificant, undeserving of receiving anything of real worth; a feeling which had had insidiously pervaded her to the core, throughout her adolescence and into early adulthood; no doubt reinforced by her choice of intimates and companions.

"You best not wear it when we go crabbing, you might lose it in the sea," Monica had advised her younger cousin, whilst positively relishing the idea of the disappearing ring. The spiteful girl had watched closely as Jennie had anxiously removed her treasured gift, and placed it on the kitchen sink for safekeeping. It wouldn't be there when they got back from their venture into the rock pools, of that Monica was quite sure. Both of the girls' parents were spending the day sailing on a friend's boat in and around the harbour. However, Monica, who suffered with sea sickness, had sulked until it was agreed she could stay on dry land. At her insistence, it had also been decided that

Jennie should stay with her, even though it meant that the young girl would be separated from her family on her birthday. Not wishing to make waves, a reluctant Jennie had agreed to stay ashore, despite her feelings of disappointment and sense of injustice at missing out on an exciting event originally arranged for the celebration of her birthday. Such was the power of Monica's persuasion; or maybe her parents were secretly relieved to have a day free of the manipulative, demanding teenager. She was so unlike her twin brother, Tom, who, also adopted at the age of six, had instantly fitted so comfortably into their family life.

An innocent Jennie had been blissfully unaware of Monica's intentions when her treacherous cousin had slipped back from the beach that afternoon, under the ruse of a need to use the toilet. With the sound of the adults laughter echoing from the yacht afloat in the harbour, Monica was confident that there was no one else at the cottage, and in a fit of jealousy, she had thrown the ring from the corner of the sink unit onto the flagstone floor of the kitchen, stamping on it until its fine, golden roundness was all bent out of shape. In the spirit of triumph the spiteful girl had then carried it out through the kitchen door to the old shed and dropped it in amongst the dusty logs and pieces of coal, believing it was unlikely to ever again see the light of day.

Upset and bemused, Jennie had no idea what had happened to her ring, other than it had mysteriously vanished from the kitchen; she suffered a most unjustified scolding for her carelessness, from her annoyed mother. The fact the dressing down had taking place in front of her older twin cousins Monica and Tom, and Matt, the handsome son of the yacht-owning friends, had only served to intensify her frustration and embarrassment. Red-faced, she had run out into the garden to hide her tears whilst Monica had looked on, unable to stifle her own self-satisfied smirk.

Now, with the ring fixed firmly on her little finger, Jennie smiled, reliving only the joy and excitement of receiving the gift.

This was a good sign, she was here on a childhood reclamation exercise, and finding her beloved birthday ring was a great start. From here on in she would always keep it on her person.

She continued to explore the scenes from her young, summer days. From behind the lounge she located the door to a fusty bedroom with one small, netted window, instantly recalling her childhood anxiety of the darkness. As her eyes adjusted to the dim light she could make out the shape of a large, wooden four-poster bed. She remembered creeping in there when no one else was around, enjoying the challenge of jumping up onto it, and spreading herself out on the wide mattress and running her fingers over the quilted satin cover. At home as a child, Jennie's bed had only ever been dressed with plain cotton bed linen; and although faded and worn at the edges, she had loved the luxurious feel of lying on this great big, soft and silky bed. Now, almost twenty years later she felt no fear of the dim atmosphere and no allure of the four-poster bed. Life's experiences had taught her that the dark, in itself, was not anything to be feared. The things in life to watch out for were the actions of humans who intruded into your life, usually when you least expected it and yet almost in broad daylight. However well-dressed their intentions, their true feelings were always betrayed by their cruel and hurtful behaviour.

Gently closing the bedroom door behind her, Jennie walked back through the lounge and into the kitchen, noting that there was still no washing machine or dishwasher in place. Next, she stepped through to the recently installed bathroom. The year they had stayed at the cottage there had been an ancient, outside toilet and she had been fearful of using it at night. Her fears of spiders and moths were greatly amplified by the dark; and with her mother's screams at discovering a grass snake in the garden of the cottage, shattering her senses, Jennie had flatly refused to use the toilet at night. Even now she shivered at the thought of the lurking snake.

There was now just one area of the cottage for her to check out. To the left of the kitchen door was the foot of the stairs leading up to a galleried area, which had served as a bedroom, her bedroom. This had been her haven, her magical place where on her first visit she had looked out over the lounge, from the balustrade, imagining it was the helm of a ship on the high seas. However, when Monica had arrived, she had implored her parents to let her share the space with her cousin. From then, the dream turned dark as an unexpected encounter on the gallery served to obscure her vision of life. The shock of the scene she witnessed manifested inside her as a sense of self-doubt that was to last for twenty years.

As she now climbed the stairs, the unwanted memories flooded her mind. However, as was her way, she quickly committed the unwelcome images to the bottom of a very heavy trunk and watched it sink to the bottom of a distant ocean. Standing once again at the helm of her imaginary ship, Jennie told herself this was not the time to face this demon; there was some further action required if this scenario was to run exactly as she had planned. There would be time for every piece to fall neatly into place, providing she got her timing right.

As the cottage had no wireless internet access or mobile signal she would return to the harbour-side café to send the required emails and text messages from her smartphone.

Once more descending the gallery stairs, she freshened herself up from the journey and headed once more for the harbour front. Despite the notice on the door reading 'open all day', Jennie was still the only customer of the twilight zone. She suspected that the popular place would be busy with hungry diners later on and was happy to take the opportunity for an early dinner.

"Hello again," smiled the friendly waitress, taking a small paper pad and pencil out from the pocket of her white apron. "Will it be the fresh cod in batter that you'll be eating?"

To Jennie it felt as if nothing in this place had changed in decades. Flicking through the plastic-coated menu on the table by the window, she could see that the traditional fayre on offer had remained constant over the years. Agreeing to the old lady's suggestion she also requested a portion of chips and mushy peas, with a pot of tea.

"Can I also have the wireless key?" she asked. The elderly waitress nodded in agreement as she pencilled down the order and walked it to the kitchen, reappearing minutes later with a tray of condiments, a pot of tea, cup and jug of milk, and a plate with one bread roll and a solitary packet of butter placed neatly on a serviette. From behind the serving counter she also retrieved the mysterious piece of card that was kept alongside the payment till. She had no idea what the customers wanted with this number, although she found so many of them requesting it. Walking over to where Jennie was sitting, she placed the card on the tray before placing all of the items on the table.

"Your meal will be ready in a few minutes, my dear," she advised. Jennie nodded and took out a mobile phone. Once connected, she waited patiently for the received messages to fill up her inbox. Meanwhile, opening up the envelope-shaped packet of butter she started to spread its contents whilst composing in her mind the messages she needed to send. She intended to say as little as possible, so that she, alone, could orchestrate the moment of revelation. She did not want anyone else to get wind of her plans and so the timing was crucial. With the buttering of the roll complete, Jennie wiped her hands on the serviette and attended to the phone. Firstly she would read the inevitable question from her husband, Paul. Scanning through the text messages she clicked on his name, which appeared on the list in bold, and opened the message. It read: *'You weren't here when I got home. Where are you? Why do you need to be away, on your own, on your birthday? I think we need to talk about this. Please call me as soon as you can.'*

Ignoring his message she clicked on the name 'Monica' in the contacts folder of her phone and selected the 'compose email' function. If she texted, Monica might try to call in response and Jennie did not want to speak with anyone at this point. Biting her lip, she took a deep breath and wrote: *'Monica, I am here at the secret weekend getaway. If I mention 'cottage' and 'harbour' I'm sure you can work out where ;-) I can't wait for him to arrive! I have been cleaning up the place, have wine in the 'fridge and fresh sheets on the bed...will keep you posted as to developments... Jx'*

Jennie smiled knowingly as she pressed the 'send' button. She was not expecting any immediate response from Monica and would give it about five minutes before she received the antici-pated text from Paul. Sure enough, a loud ping announced the arrival of another message from him: *'I still haven't heard from you and am getting concerned. Where are you? Let me know and I will come to you. I don't know what is going on but I need to see you.'*

"Well, you can jolly well sweat it out, you bastard," said Jennie under her breath.

Emerging from the kitchen with a large plate of fish and chips, the look on the face of the waitress suggested she had overheard the last part of the sentence. Placing the meal on the table in front of her only customer, she tentatively asked, "Is that everything now, dear? Just call me if you need anything else." Jennie smiled and thanked her before devouring the food. She was hungry and needed the extra energy to see herself though the events of the evening.

Wiping up the remnants of tomato ketchup with the last chip, Jennie took the last mouthful of her meal and placed the cutlery neatly on the empty plate. She drained the last drops from the pot and with a satisfied sigh she took a final sip of her tea.

"Was everything alright with your meal?" the waitress asked as she cleared away the used crockery.

"Yes, thank you. Everything was fine," replied Jennie.

"Would you like to see the dessert menu?" the old lady asked.

"No thank you," Jennie responded. "Is there any chance of a top-up on the tea?"

The waitress said she would fetch a fresh pot and Jennie looked at her watch. Twenty minutes had passed since she received Paul's second text. She clicked on the blue and white icon on the screen of her phone and logged into the social network as her alter ego, 'Betty Woo'. Betty and Paul had struck up an online friendship some months previously, their exchanges mainly taking the form of flirtatious messages and dubious photographs. Betty's profile picture was downloaded from a website offering free photographs of Asian models. The face Jennie had chosen for her character was of a beautiful and provocative woman in her early twenties, with generous, pouting lips, painted pillar-box red. To create a life for her character, she had detailed on her profile that Betty was a personal assistant to the chief executive of a fictitious graphic design company called *'Hothouse Floral'* which specialized in imagery of exotic flowers. Betty also had a penchant for provocative poses, which littered her page at frequent intervals. Jennie had enjoyed learning about yet another secret aspect of her husband's behaviour. He had engaged most enthusiastically with this fictitious character, happy to describe his most intimate sexual fantasies and proud enough of his physical manhood to take and send photographs of himself online. She quickly typed a message,

'Hello Handsome! What's happening in your world at the weekend? x B'

Within moments a response was received: *'Hey Beautiful, bit busy this weekend, working late tonight and sailing on Saturday. Will be around for some slow-and-easy Sunday morning sex if you're online.'* Paul finished his message with a typed wink and some kisses. Jennie laughed out loud. Sailing? Paul had never set as much as a canvas shoe on the deck of a boat in his life. She could vaguely remember some early incidents of eroticism with her husband on the weekends, but that was actually before they were married. Ever since, he had apparently spent quiet Sunday mornings checking the sales figures on his weekly spreadsheets. As for 'working late', she had long recognized that particular euphemism. In Paul's language it translated to time out with his latest tart.

Having blown off Betty and bought himself some time to find out exactly what his wife was up to, Paul called Jennie's phone. The ringtone sounded just as the waitress was placing a second pot of tea on the table and Jennie quickly reached to turn the phone to silent mode. She knew it would switch to answerphone after forty-five seconds. As she poured the milk into her cup, a red light flashed, signifying the receipt of another message. The screen was displaying a 'missed call' message and the icon to signal the recording of a voicemail message had appeared in the top right-hand corner. Slowly stirring her hot tea, Jennie listened to the message.

'Jen, it's me, Paul. Where are you? Why haven't you called? I want to see you. We need to speak. If you tell me where you are I will come to you. Jen, darling, I don't know what's wrong but we can sort it out. Call me.'

Placing the handset on the table, Jennie pursed her lips as she tried to work out the tight time schedule. The journey to the harbour would take him a minimum of one hour and ten minutes, depending whether or not he got caught up in the Friday evening rush-hour traffic. She needed to time her response carefully. Switching to email she checked the time of the message she had written to her cousin. The 'sent' box said the message had left her phone at 17:24. That was forty-two minutes ago. It was time for the next message.

'If you've worked out where I am, perhaps you would care to join me? I'm so excited! I will be waiting for him in The Fisherman's Rest from 7 onwards. J x'

Jennie knew that Monica would jump at the invitation, and

would leave immediately, if she wasn't already en route to the harbour. She allowed a further fifteen minutes before texting her husband, certain that he would have also heard from Monica during that time.

Firstly she responded to his last text message, saying: *'I thought the time apart and space to think would be good for us both. I am quite safe. You do not need to worry about me. I'll be home on Sunday night.'*

Almost instantaneously she received a reply: *'I am coming to find you, leaving now.'*

No! Jennie did not expect him to be on his way quite yet. She needed Monica to arrive first. She would have to speak with him to slow him down. She called him: "Paul? It's Jen. Yes, I'm fine. I'm on my own. Who did you think I would be with? … Of course not! … If you really want to come then I guess we could use the time to sort some things out. Meet me at the cottage. It will be quiet here. Come straight here, I'll get a takeaway from the local café. No, I don't know the postcode for SatNav, let me give you directions…"

Jennie gave her husband travel instructions which included a short, scenic detour to ensure he could not arrive before 7:30. She ended the conversation by arranging to meet him at the cottage. The minutes were ticking by and there had been no response yet from Monica, she needed to call her.

"So you're already on your way? You remember the route? That's great! Yes I'm a little nervous but very excited. So what time will you arrive? Okay, shall we meet at the Fisherman's Rest at seven? There's great food there. Yes I'll be sitting by the bar. See you later." A satisfied Jennie smiled widely as she ended the call, glancing in the direction of the waitress who was staring quizzically at her. She had just watched the young woman eat a large meal and then overheard her arranging to eat with two other people, at different times and places, yet all within the space of an hour or so. Had she heard correctly? Shaking her head, and muttering under her breath, the confused woman continued to wrap the clean cutlery in paper napkins and lay them on the freshly wiped surfaces of the café tables in readiness for the evening custom.

Jennie asked for the bill and secreted her phone away in her bag. She needed to get back to the cottage to set the scene. Crossing the cobbles, she turned into the lane once more; her heart rate increased and she started to feel breathless. Despite a shot of the inhaler and her attempts at slow breathing, Jennie found her pulse racing as she once again turned the key in the lock. As she tried to banish the images from her mind, the memories served only to further fuel her emotions and for the millionth time she became locked into a cycle of anger and hurt. As her thoughts raced, and the blood pounded through her veins, she had to remind herself that she had to keep her cool if she was finally to dismantle this destructive dynamic. All of the events which made her feel this way were now in the past. She needed to shake them off, to disempower their hold over her, if she had any hope of finally moving on with her life. She was sick of making the same mistakes and having to jump through the familiar hoops to make amends; tired of finding herself in the same old situations, with people who would inevitably let her down. She knew that she deserved better treatment from people, she wanted more from life and the time had come for her to take back her power. To do this she knew she had to revisit the scene of the original sin – the first time she gave away her power to people who could not be trusted with it. It was only by returning to this moment that she could reclaim her personal control.

It had all happened the summer when she had fallen in love for the first time. Matt was the handsome, sixteen-year-old son of the friends who moored their yacht at the harbour. Jennie had been especially excited at the prospect of celebrating her birthday afloat, secretly hoping she would get some time alone with the handsome boy. Although three years older, he enjoyed teasing the young girl and they had developed a genuine friendship; both loved to dive from the boat into the sea and snorkel amongst the rocks. The boy, enjoying Jennie's playful nature and their mutual sporting pursuits became very attentive and Jennie was soon smitten. However, Monica, just few months younger than Matt, was also very interested in him and jealous of the attention her younger cousin was receiving. On the day of her birthday, Monica had successfully separated the two by feigning seasickness, and insisted that Jennie accompany her for a picnic in the secluded cove. There had been no cake or sandwiches on the sandy rug. All that Monica was really interested in doing was sunbathing topless to even out her tan. When she had been left alone on the beach that afternoon, a strange feeling of loneliness had set in, and she wondered why her cousin had taken so long to return to the cottage. Her sense of uncertainty had increased on Monica's return. The girl had seemed smug and triumphant. Later that evening, when Jennie was still smarting from the humiliating admonishment she had suffered as a result of the loss of her birthday ring, Monica had made a move on Matt; the two had disappeared from the Fisherman's Rest where the families were all enjoying a beer-garden barbecue. Finishing up her game of table tennis with her cousin Tom, Jennie had acted on a hunch and headed back to the cottage to find them. The front door was locked and so Jennie tried her luck with the kitchen door. It was open. She stepped inside and stood to listen. There were voices coming from the mezzanine. Quietly mounting the steps, the young girl froze in horror as the scene so cruelly unfolded before her innocent, young eyes.

Monica lay topless on the bed, her short, denim skirt hitched up around her waist. From her side view, Jennie saw a red-faced Matt, with his jeans around his ankles, grinding his naked groin against Monica's partially clad body. Resting his on one hand firmly on the bed for balance, she watched his other hand eagerly grasping at her cousin's bare breasts. Catching sight of Jennie out of the corner of her eye, Monica raised her knees and pressing the sole of her feet into the mattress, thrust her hips upwards towards the young man. With eyes closed, Matt's face had flushed a deeper shade of crimson red and an involuntary groan of pleasure had emanated from his generous, young lips. Monica threw her arms around him and pulled him down, pressing his face into her chest. Turning her head to smile triumphantly at her devastated young cousin, she let out a loud, lascivious laugh.

Jennie had run from the cottage, the sounds of the laughter and pleasure of the couple amplified in her ears, tears blurring the vision from her baby blue eyes. Not seeing the motorbike which had unexpectedly turned into the lane, she stepped straight into its path, blackening out at the searing pain in her leg upon impact. The rider, who had been thrown from the seat, suffered a broken arm and cuts and bruises.

Jennie regained momentary consciousness to hear the clatter of footsteps and shouts of people calling out for someone to call an ambulance. Then there was silence. She had spent the next forty-eight hours in the accident and emergency department of the local hospital, whilst the doctors waited for test results to rule out concussion. It was a subdued Monica and Matt who visited with flowers, their tryst remaining a secret, despite the crashing interruption. Jennie's parents cut short their stay, and the family ended the summer holiday at home, under a cloud of sadness.

Although the most hurtful, this event was only the first in a long line of conflict which unfolded between the feuding cousins. Even Jennie's broken leg served to provoke a poisonous jealousy in Monica, who used the opportunity to interlope with the friends who came to visit. She wrangled for the visitors' attention, whilst Jennie lay immobile, cast in a heavy plaster from her left ankle to her thigh. Despite the patient's protestations to her parents, they refused to see that Monica was doing anything than helping out and once again, Jennie was left crying, alone.

A determination now welled up inside her. Today the clock

would be turned back; it was time to release the hurt and frustration that she had previously carried around inside of herself, weighing down her soul and casting a cloud of sadness about her demeanour. This very evening, she would, for the first time, walk away from a situation of conflict as the victor; the prize being the restoration of her own sense of self-esteem and self-worth. Glancing at her watch, Jennie knew that she had now to set the scenes in motion. Monica would not believe she was meeting a man for illicit purposes if she saw her dressed this way. She changed into a clinging sweater and retrieved a bag of cosmetics. Applying mascara and lip-gloss to her lightly powdered face, the soft-featured woman stood in the bathroom mirror, deciding what to do with her sandy-coloured, shoulder-length hair, before deciding simply to brush and leave it to hang in its natural curl. Spraying a hint of Chanel, she smiled tentatively at herself. Pulling the red cashmere sweater off one shoulder, she pouted provocatively at her reflection and felt a surge in confidence. With a wide smile now masking her face, and close-fitting jeans skimming a pair of shiny three-inch heels, she knew she was ready to face her nemesis.

Jennie positioned herself at the bar, just inside the Fisherman's Rest. Feeling rather conspicuous she ordered herself a large Pinot Grigio and stood with her back to the room, sipping constantly until she drained the glass. The attentive barman quickly returned with an offer to refill the glass, and she gratefully accepted. Glancing at her watch she noted there were ten more minutes to wait. She would have to make this second glass last a little longer than the first. She needed her wits about her. The vibration of her phone in her jeans pocket told her someone was trying to contact her. Jennie read a text from her husband informing her that he seemed to have lost his way, but was now back on the correct route and would be arriving at the cottage, as scheduled, in about half an hour.

As she closed the message, Jennie heard the pub door open

and heard Monica's breathy voice. "Jen! Hi, how are you? I had to go back to the Trust car park. I forgot the harbour front was a no-traffic zone! It's been a while! You are looking good."

Jennie watched as her cousin eyed her up and down, from her recently highlighted hair to the steely points of her new heels.

"So who's the mystery guy?" Monica asked beckoning to the barman.

"I'll have whatever she's having," she said. "And please do have something yourself," she flirted shamelessly with the man who seemed not at all impressed.

"No thanks, not when I'm working," he politely declined.

"Is it anyone I know, Jen? How long has this been going on? You are a dark horse!" Monica said turning her attention back to her cousin. Jennie laughed silently to herself. Monica knew all of her male friends and ex-boyfriends on an intimate basis. It seemed she had made it her mission in life. Monica's husband, Mike, had been a student in the same shared house as Jennie during their time at university. They had developed a close friendship over the three years, which Jennie always hoped would develop into something more serious. However, the friendship had fallen apart when Monica turned up uninvited at their graduation party and had left with Mike on her arm. He apologized to Jennie a few weeks later, claiming to have been exceedingly drunk and unable to resist. However, the two quickly morphed into a toxic pairing, each forever cheating on the other. There was an exhausting cycle of dramatic outbursts and accusations, followed by predictable episodes of grovelling apologies and declarations of undying love. Jennie had extracted herself from the centre of the drama.

From that point on she had been reluctant to involve her cousin in any aspect of her life and had navigated her way through a number of superficial relationships, always avoiding the question of commitment, her fear of betrayal constantly floating perilously close to the surface. That was until the wedding of Mike and Monica. It was at the reception that she, the most reluctant maid of honour was introduced to Paul, the best man, a work-colleague of Mike, who was more than happy to escort the attractive woman for the day, and into the months that followed. Everything seemed to finally have settled down with Monica and Mike, and Jennie most foolishly felt it was finally safe to fall in love and marry Paul.

Their wedding had taken place some fifteen months previously and for the first nine months Jennie had actually believed that her popular, wide-smiled, husband was playing squash with the competitive head of department, at impromptu sales meetings, or working evenings on a time-sensitive project at the office, when he was late home from or heading into the office at weekends.

"So what time does he arrive?" Monica asked, interrupting Jennie's reflections.

"Any time now," her cousin responded. "In fact he's already late." She watched as Monica's eyes widened.

"I wonder what Paul would make of this, if he knew," Monica ventured provocatively.

"What Paul doesn't about know about can't hurt him," Jennie replied.

"I have to say I am rather surprised," Monica continued. "I never thought you were the type…"

"…The type to get what I want, for a change?" Jennie finished her cousin's sentence. "Shall we have another drink?" she suggested.

Monica nodded and ordered two more glasses of wine. Jennie allowed her cousin to pay for the round, knowing that she would not be drinking hers. She excused herself to the bathroom to check for any more messages. When her watch displayed twenty-five minutes past seven, she relieved her wheezing chest with an inhaler and returned to the bar.

"I have just received a text from him, saying he's making his way to the cottage. He sounded lost. Can you hang on here for a while? I'll find him and bring him here. I'll be as quick as I can," she assured her cousin. Looking at the full glasses of wine standing on the bar, Monica agreed.

Jennie walked briskly to the cottage. On arrival, she left the front door ajar and checked her bag to ensure its contents were intact. Taking out a large, brown envelope addressed to her husband, she placed it, unsealed on the first shelf of the dusty, old wooden dresser. Next she needed to find the best place to position a phone. Looking around the cottage, she had to guess where the conversation was most likely to take place and hide a handset to secretly record the exchange. Walking up the stairs to get a bird's-eye view of the room, she decided to place it against the open balustrade of the steps, some halfway between the ground floor lounge and the mezzanine. She laid it in the corner of the step and pressed the record button. Just as she reached the bottom step, so the front door opened and Paul appeared.

"Hi, Jen, I managed to find the place!" he announced, walking over, holding out his arms to embrace her. "Wow, you look great!" At her refusal to engage, he dropped his arms and tried to take her by the hands. "Jen, what's wrong? I know I've been working a lot lately, but we've got the weekend, and this place," he said looking around dubiously. "And it's your birthday! Let's take some time together. I think it's what we both need right now."

"Do you?" Jennie responded tartly.

"Yes, Jen. All we need is some time together. If you wanted a holiday, why didn't you just say so? We could have put our heads together and come up with something better than this!"

Jennie bit her lip. There was so much she wanted to say and yet it would serve no purpose at this juncture. It would only waste valuable recording time.

"Are you hungry?" she asked. "There's a café on the harbour front. I can get us a takeaway meal."

"I'll go, if you give me directions," Paul volunteered.

"No you wait here, I won't be a minute," she insisted. Leaving through the front door, she slipped past the lounge window and around to the side of the cottage. From here she slipped easily through the dilapidated garden fence and made her way around to wait outside the back door of the cottage.

Inside, Paul took the opportunity to check out the accommodation. He opened the doors off the lounge to look inside the bedrooms, looked in the kitchen fridge in the hope of finding some beer and relieved himself in the bathroom. Next he took himself upstairs, and cast his eyes around the galleried space before leaning to look over the dusty, old balustrade. He wondered what Jennie had been thinking to book this place. It was hardly set for seduction. How could Monica have got it so wrong? He remembered some reference to a childhood holiday cottage but this was not what he had expected.

Surveying the scene from above, he noticed the large brown envelope on the dresser shelf below and headed down the steps to check it out. The toe of his of his shoe accidentally caught the corner of the phone, sending it flying off the step. He watched it skim through the air and cross the lounge floor, clattering to a halt on the slate hearth. Recognizing the device as belonging to his wife, he walked over to the fireside, picked up the pieces and tried to fit them back together. Replacing the SIM card, he tried to reboot the phone with the intention of checking her contacts, messages and call log. However, the display was darkened and the buttons proved ineffective. Placing the damaged item on the table, he reached out for the brown packet, surprised to find it addressed to him. Paul emptied its contents on the table and picked out a covering letter. It informed him that included amongst the enclosed documents was a divorce petition, issued from the Plymouth East County Court. It named his wife, Jennie, as the petitioner and him as the respondent. It cited the reason for the petition as being on the grounds of irretrievable breakdown of the marriage, partly due to his 'improper association with others,' including one identified as 'Mrs Monica Bradford'. Scanning the detail of the accompanying documents, he read a list of the times, dates and places of his meetings with Monica which had taken place during the previous six months. Additionally, some of the entries referred to photographic evidence. It was stated that these could be made available on request.

Paul was stunned. Dropping the paperwork on the table top, he took a step back and raised his eyes to heaven. He had no idea that he was being watched, or filmed, over the preceding months. His mind started to race at the possibility of all aspects of his private life being recorded and subject to scrutiny. Who else knew? Mike? What if his friends and work colleagues found out... He cast his gaze to the floor.

Outside the back door, Jennie looked nervously at her watch. There was no sign of Monica yet. Perhaps she had got it wrong. She was sure that her cousin would have not have been able to contain her curiosity and keep her distance. The woman had never respected anyone else's boundaries, and Jennie believed she was not about to start now. As another few moments passed, Jennie considered returning to the pub to invite her back to the cottage. After all, the outcome of the situation would be the same. Venturing from around the side of the cottage, Jennie was about to head into the lane when she saw the glossy dark hair of Monica, as the woman walked past the mossy stone wall. Edging back, she heard the clank of the heavy, wrought-iron gate and crept back to the kitchen door. She took advantage of the noise occurring at the front entrance to open the back door and slip inside the kitchen, where she stood silently, listening to the unfolding drama in the lounge.

Paul looked up at the opening of the front door. He wanted to explain, to apologize, to beg for forgiveness and to persuade Jennie to withdraw the petition. He was prepared do anything that she asked of him. However, it wasn't the face of his pretty blonde wife which greeted him. He was fixed by the equally surprised stare emanating from the large brown eyes of Monica.

"What are you doing here?" he blurted out. Monica, equally as shocked, explained that Jennie had called her.

"She asked me to come around, said she was expecting some trouble and wanted my help," she lied. She walked towards him holding out her arms, but Paul pushed her away.

"Paul?" She was confused at his response. They had been secretly meeting for months. Monica knew all of his sexual proclivities and had arranged many an interesting scenario to entertain him during their lunchtime hotel rendezvous. She certainly had imagination and Paul had fully appreciated her efforts; however he had to admit that lately the excitement seemed to be bottoming out, as he struggled to find the time and effort to keep up their erotic games. Monica could be a very demanding lover, yet Paul had never viewed her as anything other than a source of entertainment. The thrill was in the power play between them. She was a worthy adversary. In his mind this was not the same thing as love and as in any game, one player inevitably tired before the other. In an attempt to inject more excitement into the arrangement, Monica had started to book lunchtime hotel rooms closer to Jennie's office. She had 'accidentally' crossed paths with her unsuspecting cousin on more than one instance, as she was en route to meet up with her husband. On these occasions, her passion had been a little overwhelming for Paul, whose discomfort at being in close proximity to discovery merely served to dampen his ardour, much to Monica's frustration.

"Jennie's here alone. There is no one else, no man with her, as you said there would be," he now stated coolly.

"But there soon will be," Monica explained. "He just hasn't arrived yet. Jennie asked me to wait in the pub in case he turned up there. He got lost and so she's out looking for him."

"Jennie has gone out to fetch supper for us," Paul contradicted her. He wondered what conflict his wife was anticipating. Was she fearful of his response to the petition? What on earth did she think he would do?

"She was worried you would show up and there would be a confrontation," Monica said boldly. It was Paul's turn to raise his voice.

"That's funny, because when I got your message I texted her and she told me straight away that she was here. She wanted some time and space apart to think about our marriage. I told her that as far as I was concerned there was nothing to think about and that she should come home. When she said that she wanted to stay for a few days I asked if I could come down and she agreed, said she would be happy to show me where she spent a childhood holiday. This place is hardly the inspiration for a hotbed of passion with an illicit lover, Monica."

"So you didn't believe me? You didn't come here to catch her out?" Monica asked accusingly.

"I don't believe that she was here to be with someone else. I think she had other plans..." Paul replied.

"Are you calling me a liar?" Monica shouted.

"No, I'm just wondering where you got such an idea from." Paul's suspicions were aroused. Not wanting to expose her true motive, Monica suggested that perhaps her cousin had found about their affair and wanted to get even. It was Paul's turn to become animated. Gesturing to the paperwork spilling out of the envelope on the table he shouted, "Oh yes, she knows all about us. She has done for months, judging by the evidence of the private investigator that she hired to follow us. How the hell did she find out, Monica? Did you let something slip?"

Smirking, Monica replied, "Of course not! I never said a word, but she is definitely here to meet someone. I've never seen her dressed up like that before, she looked hot!"

"Is that why you told me? In the hope that I would come

down and catch her in the act, see her in the arms of someone else? Was that your plan? Why would you do that?" Paul was bemused. Of the many faces of Monica to which he had been privy, never before had he seen this spiteful side of her.

"Look, Paul, you might as well face it, your marriage is over and it's about time that Jennie found out, anyway, it's only fair; now's the perfect time for you to leave her." Monica spoke in a cool, emotionless manner. Soured by the suggestion, Paul looked closely at Monica's expression, seeing for the first time the cruelty in her thin, pursed lips and sensing the coldness in her dismissive manner. He was appalled at the apparent lack of concern she seemed to show for anyone except herself.

"I can't believe you would talk about your cousin, my wife, in this way. Have you no concern for other people's feelings? How would Mike feel if he found out about us? I have never seen this side of you, Monica, and I really don't like it. In fact I'm starting to wonder what I ever saw in you." Paul was flooded with fear at the thought of the exposure of his sleazy sessions with the woman and the corresponding reactions from both Jennie and Mike.

At the mention of her husband's name Monica tossed her head.

"Why bring him into the equation? What he doesn't know won't hurt him. Especially if we are no longer going to be together, there's absolutely no need for him to know anything about this sorry little affair."

"I think it's a bit late for that," said Jennie, who had had been listening intently to the conversation, as she stepped out from behind the kitchen door. Monica's jaw dropped.

"You knew?" She made it sound as if Jennie was the guilty party.

"Jen, I'm sorry. I don't know how it happened. It's over anyway. I don't want a divorce. Can we talk this over?" A desperate Paul stood in turmoil between the two women in his life.

"Yes it's over!" exclaimed Monica; red-faced and furious at the rejection. "You two deserve each other anyhow," she spat out the words.

"Do you think Mike will take you back when he hears about this? Quite frankly I think he deserves better." Jennie spoke provocatively, feeling she had the upper hand for once in her life.

"He's not going to hear anything about this," Monica retorted. Jennie watched as once more the bully inside her cousin rose to the surface. "I'm not going to tell him and you two had better keep quiet," she threatened. "There's no other way he could find out."

"He might be interested in playing back this recording," Jennie announced as she moved to the bottom of the stair to reach for the phone she had placed there earlier.

"Are you looking for this?" Paul asked, retrieving the device from beneath the paperwork on the table. Jennie held out her hand and he passed it over.

"How did you get this?" she asked, checking to see if it was still recording.

"It was an accident, I…" Paul started to explain, but Monica intervened to snatch the phone away. With a scream she threw it against the old stone fireplace.

"That won't work for you!" she sneered. "You bastards, thinking you can set me up!"

"This has nothing to do with Paul," explained Jennie. "I have set up both of you. I'm sick and tired of you, Monica. You have ruined every chance of happiness with everyone I have met. When you settled down with Mike I thought you would finally stop interfering in my life. But I was wrong." Turning to Paul she continued, "Don't think for one minute that this is about you. She was only ever interested in being with you because it she knew it would hurt me." She delivered the calculated blow to his ego in a slow and deliberate manner, reaching into her jeans pocket and holding her other phone.

"And as far as Mike is concerned, he knows all about the situation. I called him from the kitchen and he has been listening in to our conversation." Jennie placed the handset to her ear and proceeded to speak.

"Have you heard enough, Mike? Do you want to speak with your wife about this?" Monica's face crumbled as Jennie held out the phone. "I'm sorry, Monica. But enough is enough. Everyone has their level and as far as I'm concerned you've had your last chance with me. I never want to see or speak to you again."

Paul looked on as the once confident, self-assured Monica shrunk before his very eyes. Her bold stare and cruel sneer faded, leaving just a pale face and broken smile. In contrast, Jennie's presence appeared to increase in stature. Rooted in right-eousness, she stood upright holding her nerve. Monica cast her eyes to the ground and started to snivel.

Desperate to disempower her nemesis once and for all, the bluff was Jennie's final attempt to put an end to Monica's inter-ference in her life. If her cousin had taken the handset, she would have discovered that Mike was not, and had never been, on the other end of the phone.

Conversely, for the first time, Monica felt a complete loss of control over the people and events in her life. In a last-ditch attempt to manipulate a response she sent a final, pleading look in Paul's direction. It was steadfastly ignored.

"And don't worry about Paul, Monica, he's already got Betty lined up to help him fulfil his sexual fantasies. Tell her, Paul. Tell her about Betty Woo and how the two of you engage in online sex when Monica's not around. Now you'll have the free time to meet up in person and perhaps put all the details of your sleazy desires into practice."

A sunken Monica slunk out of the door, leaving the estranged couple immersed in a strained silence.

"Good, I hope that's the last I see of her," Jennie was first to unmute the moment.

Weakly, Paul asked, "How do you know about Betty Woo?"

"I am Betty Woo," the determined woman replied, fixing her gaze squarely on his face.

"Jen! I've never seen you like this!" a shocked Paul was wondering what else could possibly be revealed.

"Well you can get used to it," she replied in a matter-of-fact tone. "There's no way I'm taking you back, Paul. You never gave this relationship a chance. I trusted you and you cheated on me from the outset. I did nothing to warrant that treatment, I deserved better." The beleaguered man had no choice but to admit defeat. Jennie continued, "This mess can be cleared up quite quickly, from a legal standpoint. It was a short marriage; thankfully we have no children, and apart from the joint mortgage on the apartment there no other liabilities. It can be a clean break, Paul, if we agree terms, and we will never have to see each other again." Paul stood in silence. His wife, once warm and welcoming, was now forever lost to him. Faced with the strong and determined female, he knew there was no point in arguing any further. His character and his actions had been laid bare and Jennie's contempt was reverberating furiously around him. He knew that any further pleading or apology would only serve to deepen her hatred for him.

"I have spoken with the estate agents. The flat will be on the market as soon as you sign the consent form. They have been instructed for a quick sale. I have arranged for my belongings to be collected on Monday and I have authorized my solicitor to sign the contract on my behalf." She gestured to the partly viewed packet of documents on the table. "It's all in there. I have also contacted the bank and my name will shortly be off the mandate of the joint account. If you're thinking about emptying it, just know that I have already transferred half of the current balance to an account in my sole name. In a couple of weeks' time it will be as if we were never together. As soon as you respond to the court agreeing to the petition and sign the financial consent order I will file for the order of decree nisi. Six weeks from the granting of that order, I will apply for decree absolute and you will then be out of my life, forever. Please be advised that if you cause any unnecessary delay, in any aspect of the process, it will be you who pays for it in the long run." Paul was astonished. He had no idea that Jennie was capable of such skilled organization.

"I can see you're surprised," she continued. "But I had many lonely hours in which to plan all of this, Paul. When you were playing sex games with my cousin, and wife of your best mate, I was planning for my future."

"I had no idea that you could even think of all of this," Paul confessed.

"How could you?" Jennie asked. "You never took the time to get to know me. You even preferred spending your time online, with some fictitious woman. You're a joke, Paul, and I'm afraid the last laugh is on you. Oh and by the way, Betty Woo has now blocked you."

One hour later, Jennie, still high on the success of finally taking charge of her own life, touched up her lip gloss and straightened her sweater. She headed back to the Fisherman's Rest for a final glass of wine, to relax after the eventful evening.

"So you're the new owner of Fuchsia Cottages?" The barman smiled knowingly when the beaming woman told him her news. "Will you be renovating or renting them, if you don't mind me asking?"

"I intend to live in one and rent out the other two, mainly for holidaymakers," Jennie replied. "It may be a couple of months before I am able to start work on them as I have to wait for the sale proceeds of my old flat. All of them need some attention but I don't want to change the character of them."

"Yes, they hold a lot of valuable history," the friendly barman advised.

"They do indeed," Jennie agreed, turning the tiny ring on her little finger, happy in the knowledge that finally having faced and taken ownership of her personal history in the place, she had now cleared the breathing space in readiness for whatever the future may bring.

Radio Grandma

"It may feel unfair, but there's magic in the air..."

Megan removed her fingers from the 'select' function of the car radio and smiled at the synchronicity; the words of a song playing on a randomly selected radio station, which just happened to reflect the very thoughts circling in her own mind. Someone, somewhere, had submitted a request for Sunday morning's Secret Songs on 102.3 Magical Moments FM; an anonymous person, who would probably never know how their choice of words had reached out to affirm the emotions of a complete stranger, at such a poignant moment in her life. It was so unfair; her mother's life so cruelly torn away from her in such a short space of time. Megan knew that she wasn't the first person to lose her only living relative to the ravages of cancer. However, it felt as if her safety rope had been cut and she had been callously set adrift into dangerous, dark waters. It was just a short drive from the hospice where her mother, frail and weak had finally died in her sleep, just three hours previously, and for the first time in her life Megan felt completely alone, wondering how on earth she could continue to live in the world.

For the past few weeks she had been a round-the-clock visitor to the hospice having only the company of the nurses and Pete, a man she had met on numerous occasions in the hospice cafe. He too was the only visitor at his father's bedside, on a constant watch, not knowing how long the vigil was to last. They had chatted in a way which only two strangers, confronting the death of their loved ones could: open, emotionally, personally, and often with a touch of dark humour. It seemed strange to Megan that the dying should be segregated according to gender, in their last days. After all, they were headed, in their glorious nakedness, to the same destination. However, she welcomed the brief interludes in the cafe, talking, amongst other things, about property development and interior design which momentarily distracted them both from the grim reality of their respective situations. She was always pleased to find her new companion sitting alone and his face had always lit up on seeing her.

In the early hours, the sunrise shift nurse had checked on the patient and gently roused Megan, who was dozing in the chair next to the bed; she whispered that Maura had passed away. As the dawn light crept across the pristine hospice pillow, she had leaned over, casting a shadowed kiss on her mother's cold, wasted cheek for the last time. Then she had silently left the room, allowing the staff to remove the remaining intravenous equipment from her mother's childlike body. There had been some papers to sign in the office and Megan had returned one last time to the now-empty room, to pack up her mother's few belongings, which had been left in the bedside locker. Megan left the hospice, taking with her all the remaining traces of her mother. The next time she would see her would be in the chapel where her body would finally be laid to rest. In Megan's mind there seemed to be a huge, white space, a numbness that made everything else in the world feel vague and remote, until the words of the song had permeated her cold cocoon.

I'll get some sleep, Megan thought to herself on arriving home. *And then I will get on with the business of sorting out the house.*

Maura McKinley had been a feisty lady. Widowed young with a child to raise, she had worked well into her retirement, encouraging her only daughter to get out into the world, to travel and take the chances necessary to build herself a better life. Recently, Megan's visits to her mother's house had become very infrequent.

She had become absorbed by the demands of her interior-design business. She only learned of the advanced stage of her mother's illness, as the only next of kin, on her admittance to the local hospice. Megan had travelled to be close to her mother, staying in her childhood home for the first time in years. She was now alone, with each and every decision resting on her shoulders. The family home and its contents were her sole responsibility.

The house was a three-bedroomed, 1920s semi-detached villa in a tree-lined avenue, bordering a city park, in a southern suburb of London. It was here that newlyweds Maura and Jack had made their home amidst the optimism and relative affluence of the late 1960s, and where Megan had been born in the early 1970s. However, life for Megan and her mother changed when Jack left home one morning for work and never came back. Megan was too young to remember any of the events of the Underground tragedy when a power failure resulted in the collision of trains and the death of hundreds of people. Her father was, and always would be, the handsome, smiling, young man in the black-and-white wedding photo on the lounge wall. For Maura, life took a sharp detour and the housewife trained as a community-based physiotherapist so she could keep her home and raise her child. She never remarried and Megan had no memory of any male company in the house. Grandma May moved in to help out for a while and ended up staying until the end of her days, some ten years later. As Maura settled into her retirement, keeping active by cultivating a kitchen garden and maintaining her self-reliance, Megan had become increasingly entangled in the corporate world of her career. Their lives had drifted apart; Maura's life becoming more simplified and solitary, whereas Megan was constantly negotiating time limits and professional constraints, which left her little time for family or relationships. However, now a single woman in her early forties, Megan once more felt like a young girl alone in the house, just waiting for her mother to come home. Wearily, she climbed the stairs and fell asleep in her mother's bed.

* * *

On waking, Megan felt rested but still raw with the memory of her mother's death. She needed to make a list in order to help her focus and deal with all the issues in hand. However, she also needed to do something, to feel something, to somehow reassure herself that she was still alive. She wanted to sell the house as quickly as possible to get back to the city and get on with her life; Megan knew that she would have to get cracking on the renovation work. The place had some 1970s features which would not be great selling points, such as the wipe-clean wallpaper, linoleum flooring and Formica worktops in the kitchen. At least she could make a start by getting rid of this stuff.

Throwing on some old clothes that she found in her mother's wardrobe, Megan rooted around in the kitchen cupboards and the old larder, looking for some DIY tools which would help her to get started. She would strip the walls, rip up the old carpets and arrange for the old furniture to be taken away. Then she could arrange for some workmen to come in and upgrade the kitchen units and the bathroom. Megan had an image of a house where all the clutter was cleared and the orange-and-brown floral patterns were replaced with crisp, white walls and the simple lines of functional furniture. She intended to keep it as neutral as possible to maximize selling potential. Yes, she needed to create a fresh, new space for someone else's family to come in and personalize.

It was whilst she was rummaging through the larder shelves that she came across an old transistor radio. She recognized it as the one her grandmother had always been listening to in the kitchen when she, as a young girl, came home from school. Now slightly paint splattered and generally battered, she recalled that it had always sat on the kitchen table where she ate the warm muffins that Grandma May baked for her every afternoon. Most days, she would have to listen to end of the afternoon Radio 4 play before she was allowed to change the channel to Radio 2 for some popular tunes. It was a ritual that warmed her now as she recalled those safe and comfortable times. Megan placed the radio on the table and plugged it in.

Good! she thought to herself; it still worked. Tuning it to the frequency for receiving Radio 2, she decided that she would listen in whilst working on the kitchen and she spent the rest of the day balancing on a stepladder and various kitchen surfaces as she removed the faded paint and curling paper of her past. In-between the sound of the steam paint stripper and electric sanding machine she caught snippets of tunes, old and new, playing on the radio as she immersed herself in the refurbishment task. Stopping for lunch, Megan realized that the music on the radio had been replaced with the sound of voices in conversation. She hadn't changed the channel, however the dial had moved and she was now listening to a Radio 4 play. A strong image of Grandma May emerged from Megan's memory and, with a strange shiver she reached out for the knob and searched for more music.

* * *

The following afternoon, when Megan stepped back into the kitchen after accepting condolences from the neighbour, dear old Mrs Riley, she noticed that the radio station had changed once again. Feeling spooked, she hurriedly switched off the radio and sat in silence with her thoughts. Had she imagined this? Was she losing her mind? She had read somewhere that grief can have strange effects on people. Perhaps she needed to see a doctor, before the symptoms worsened and she lost her grip on reality? She brooded over a lonely dinner, a can of oxtail soup she found in the larder. That night Megan dreamed of Grandma May. They were both in the kitchen, Grandma taking the warm muffins out of the oven and Megan, wearing her old school uniform, was sitting at the table in anticipation. She awoke feeling comforted and warm.

The next day, when the radio seemed yet again to magically revert to its default setting of the afternoon play, she sat herself at the kitchen table with her paint-daubed hands wrapped around a cup of coffee, and listened. What she heard was her Grandma's voice talking directly to her, "Megan, now you're home it's time we got back down to basics!" May had always been a straight-talking sort of woman. "There are a few things you need to know before the funeral, so listen up…" Megan's trembling hands dropped the cup she was holding and reached out to snap the radio's switch to 'off'. She felt as if she had been enveloped in some kind of time warp, another dimension of reality. Had she been poisoned by the paint fumes? Opening the window above the sink, she took in a deep breath of the fresh air and closed her eyes. Then, feeling a little calmer, she braved the radio switch, just to reassure herself that she wasn't hallucinating any longer.

"Megan? There's no need to be afraid, child. It's me, Grandma May!" There was no doubting that voice; warm and authoritative, it had always made Megan feel safe and loved. The voice continued, "As I was saying, there are a few things we need to sort out in time for your mother's funeral. I want to make sure that everything left over there is laid to rest before she gets here."

"What do you mean?" Megan found herself saying out loud.

"There are some things your mother wanted to get done before she left but didn't have the chance to get around to doing. I promised her I would help."

"But you're dead!" Megan blurted out. "You've been gone for years!"

"Yes, but you, my dear, are alive and kicking and I promised your mother that in the space of time between her leaving there and arriving here, I would make sure that you would see to it that everything would be left just as it should be!" In a weird kind of way, this made perfect sense to Megan. Both May and Maura had been eminently practical women, both seemingly very concerned with the 'how' of getting on with things and less of the 'why'.

"So you've been in touch with Mum, ever since you died?" Megan couldn't help but ask.

"Of course! And so has your dad," May replied. Megan felt as if all the breath had been sucked out of her.

"Dad?" she gasped.

"Yes, Jack's right here with me now. Do you want a word?" said the voice from the radio.

This was a just a bit too bizarre for Megan. "Ever wondered why your mum never remarried, Meg? It was because your dad was still very much around; albeit not in a physical sense, you understand. Your grandfather's here too!" However, instead of chatting to her dead father, Megan panicked and picked up the telephone to call the local clinic. She booked herself an emergency doctor's appointment.

Later that evening, a rather distressed Megan found herself explaining apologetically to a registrar that she had been hearing voices and conversing with a kitchen radio and that she thought it best to seek medical help. After filling in the Silverman Scale Questionnaire, the young doctor advised her that the slight depression that she appeared to be suffering was probably to be expected, given the recent death of her mother. He advised her to make a further appointment, if she didn't feel any better in a couple of weeks' time, unless her symptoms worsened in the meantime, in which case she should come back sooner.

Megan returned home with a feeling of unease. She had been reassured that she wasn't losing her mind, but she had been hearing things. She decided to submerge herself in the practical-ities of the funeral arrangements, in the hope that things could return to normal as soon as possible. Tomorrow she would find out if her mother's will specified any particular funeral requirements and then she would get in touch with a local undertaker. Having completed the work in the kitchen, Megan moved the freestanding furniture into the hall for ease of access and arranged for a local charity shop to collect it. She replaced the old transistor radio back on the larder shelf and closed the door, reasoning with herself that as soon as this business was sorted out she could get back to her own life.

It was between the early morning hours of three and four that Megan was awoken by the sound of muffled music. She had realized that Mrs Riley was hard of hearing as she sometimes heard her TV through the adjoining wall in the lounge. However, this didn't sound as if it was coming from next door. Making her way downstairs, Megan found that both the door to the kitchen and the door to the larder were wide open and the sound was blaring from the old transistor radio on the shelf. This was getting out of hand! She knew she had unplugged the radio so she thought that it must be working on battery power. Megan removed the batteries and the radio fell silent.

That should do it! she thought to herself. Confident that she wouldn't be hearing anything further from that damned radio, she took herself back to bed. However, she was very restless and her sleep was disturbed with thoughts and images of her dead relatives.

* * *

The following morning, Megan picked up a copy of her mother's will from the family solicitors and stopped off at a local cafe to digest its contents over a creamy cappuccino. The house and its contents were being left to her and then there were a number of specific gifts, mainly to local charity concerns.

"No surprises there, eh?" On hearing the words, Megan coughed up the piece of iced carrot cake that she was just about to swallow. It was her grandmother's voice, again, loud and clear.

In vain, Megan searched the other tables in the cafe, looking for, but at the same time knowing that she wasn't going to see, the source of the comment. Everyone else seemed engrossed in conversations amongst themselves; she was the only person sitting alone. What was she to do? She couldn't speak out loud to her invisible companion. She would have to just talk in her mind.

"Can you hear me?" she heard herself say slowly and deliberately in her own mind.

"Of course I can!" Grandma May snapped back. "Now, can we get on with the business in hand?" Megan knew there was no escaping her now. Grandma May had connected online to her brain and there was no more switching her off!

"Our generation invented the concept of wireless, if you recall," Grandma May continued. "Yours has just extended the concept to transmit other information in addition to sound."

"So you can hear my thoughts?" Megan asked, silently.

"Yes."

"What, all of them, all of the time?"

"Well, it depends if I'm tuning in. Sometimes I have better things to do, you know! Although I quite agreed with you about the chap you met at the hospice. What a lovely man! And I didn't notice a wedding ring either…"

"Gran!" Megan heard the sound of Grandma May's laughter. It had always been rather raucous and generally infectious. *"Well, what do you want me to do?"* she thought to her grandmother when the laughter subsided.

"Your mother wants you to make sure all of those financial gifts detailed in her will, the ones to Age Concern, Barnardo's and the PDSA, are distributed as soon as probate is granted on the will."

"Okay." Megan nodded her head and got a weird look from the woman facing her from the next table.

"However," Grandma May continued, "in a small, brown, zipped case at the back of your mother's wardrobe there is some cash that she has left for you. This isn't covered in the will, and she didn't have time to write down what she wanted you to do with it. I don't think she really knew what she wanted you to do, until she went into the hospice. By then she was too weak to write down her wishes. That's why she asked me to get in contact with you."

"Are you in contact with her now?" Megan asked with her mind.

"No. We spoke just before she died, but I have to wait until she passes over before we can be in touch again."

"How come Mum never told me about you? I mean, that she talked to you?" Megan suddenly became aware that she had been sitting in silence, apparently just staring into space, for far too long now to be acceptable in a public place and so hastily she took a slurp of her cold coffee.

"I don't know," answered Grandma May. "Perhaps she wanted you to concentrate on the future, rather than the past? Whatever the reason, I'm sure she thought she was doing the right thing. It would have been different if you had heard me yourself."

"Will I be able to hear her too, when she passes over?" Megan felt a shot of warmth in her heart at the thought.

"I don't know. I don't make the rules, but I can't see why not!" Grandma May replied.

"Okay, what does she want me to do with the money?" Megan asked, again in her mind.

"She wants you to count out two thousand pounds and donate it to the hospice where she died. It's a thank you for the kindness they showed and the comfort they allowed her in her last days. Oh, and she wants you to take it in person, tomorrow at exactly 10 a.m."

Megan was just about to ask why it had to be that particular time, when her grandmother pre-empted the question, "Don't ask me why, just do it!"

Megan gathered herself together and returned home to look

for the case and the money. True enough, just as Grandma May had described it, there was a brown, leather, zipped case stuffed with cash wedged behind some boxes of old photographs on the shelf at the top of the wardrobe. It was crammed full of old five- and ten-pound notes, a total of five thousand pounds which Megan counted out into piles of five hundred each whilst sitting on her mother's bed. Separating two of the five thousand, she replaced the remainder in the case.

"Where did she get this money?" she asked out loud.

Grandma May replied that Maura had religiously saved something, however small, every week since Jack had died, for Megan's future. However, as Megan became more successful and independent, so her need for the money seemed to become less and so Maura had held onto it in case of an emergency. Now she had decided how she wanted her daughter to spend the money.

A little bemused, but also with an air of excitement, Megan found herself returning to the hospice. Maura's body was now in the care of the undertakers and as such, the hospice, whilst still retaining an air of familiarity, now felt much lighter to Megan. As she spoke with the ward sister, she felt a great sense of warmth and release. The tender-hearted nurse offered her a tissue and hugged her, whilst thanking her sincerely for the kind donation. As she turned to leave, Megan glanced for one last time into the cafe where she had recently spent so many hours. It was empty. Somewhere in her mind she heard a faint voice saying, "You've missed him..." However, it was with a lighter heart that Megan left the hospice for the last time and headed home. There was just the funeral day to negotiate and this phase of her life would be over. She could leave the house in the hands of estate agents and get back to her life in the city.

* * *

"What do you mean you've had to rearrange the funeral for a priority case? They're all dead! How can the burial of one deceased person be more important than that of another?" Megan was incredulous. However, the undertaker stood firm by his decision and so the funeral was rescheduled for three days later than the original booking.

"Your mother will be fine with us for a few days longer, here in the chapel," he reassured her in a deadpan, monotone manner.

Megan knew she would have to find something else to occupy her for the next couple of days and so decided she would start work on redecorating of the kitchen. Initially, she had intended to employ a host of carpenters, plumbers, tilers, painters and decorators for the job. As she was still here, she thought she might as well make a start by choosing the new fitments and colour scheme. However, flicking through the DIY catalogues she found herself drawn in by the detail. Instead of a neutral choice of bland colours, symmetrical shapes and standard sizes, Megan's own personal tastes were drowning out the sound of her professional reasoning and influencing her choice of fitments and textures. As she was measuring up for an expensive kitchen island, once again Grandma May spoke up, "You have great taste, young Megan. This kitchen is going to look amazing when it's finished! But don't spend all of your money on it. You've got a holiday to book."

"What do you mean?" Megan replied. "I have no intention of going away. As soon as this work is finished, I'll be heading back to work in the city."

"Listen to me," Grandma May's voice said, taking on a more serious tone. "It's your mother's wish that you go to the travel agency and pick up a brochure. She wants you to book two weeks away to start in exactly three months' time. She said she liked the idea of you flying long haul."

"Well, that's a bit of a tall order!" retorted Megan. "What if I don't want to fly halfway around the world on my own?"

"It's a booking for two..." came the short reply.

"I must be hearing things!" Megan said out loud. "This is madness. I need to go back and talk to that doctor." Grandma May tutted impatiently before responding,

"It's your mother's wish. It's what she wanted for you."

"How do I know? If it was written in the will, I might not doubt my own sanity right now. But I only have your word for it, and how do I even know if you are who you say you are and that this whole thing is not just a symptom of my sick mind?" Megan was beginning to panic. Was she going mad? What would people think if they looked through the window and could see her talking out loud to herself? She rummaged around in her bag for the number of the local clinic, with the intention of calling for a further appointment with the doctor. She was stilled by the sound of her father's voice:

"Megan, it's me, Dad."

Her grieving heart lurched. It had been so many years since she had heard his voice yet it felt as if she was a small child again, safe in his arms.

"Your mother only wanted what was best for you. We all want what's best for you, so please don't think this is about anything other than that."

"Dad?" whispered Megan. "Dad, is this real?"

"Yes," the calm, male voice replied. "We're all here, waiting for your mother to arrive. What you are being asked to do, just know that it's all for a good reason. Darling, we love you and we just want you to be happy." A single trail of tears pooled softly onto the dark circles under Megan's eyes before silently dripping down her cheeks. She felt so very tired. The tragic events of the past few weeks were now starting to take their toll on her emotional reserves and her feelings were now raw. She wanted to curl up under the protective cover of sleep and simply drift off to be with her family. However, those on the other side had different ideas.

"Megan, just book the holiday. What harm can it possibly do?" her Dad's voice said, low and hypnotic.

He's right, thought Megan. *It's only money. So what if I don't even make the flight?*

For some unknown reason, she was being asked to do this. It wasn't as if she would be causing harm to anyone else. After all, there was just her now...

'*Fourteen nights, island hopping around the stunning ten-island archipelago that is Cape Verde...we will fly you to the top of the Pico de Fogo volcano and drop you into the verdant valleys of Santo Antao. You can explore the bustling markets at Santiago and bliss out on the golden beaches at Sal,*' read Megan. Inspired by the scenery in the brochure she tried working out the cost, including the sale price discount. However, a booking scheduled for the end of November would still prove too expensive if she booked for two. Perhaps this was not the holiday for her? She closed the glossy brochure and rested her exhausted head in her hands on the kitchen table.

For the next few days, as the funeral approached, the radio remained silent in the house. Megan washed, dried and ironed her clothes, hanging them on the outside of the wardrobe in readiness for the service. The solitary funeral car was booked to arrive at 10.30 a.m. to take her firstly to the service at the chapel of rest before moving on to the crematorium. The idea of booking a car just for herself had seemed ludicrous to her and so she had invited the neighbour old Mrs Riley to accompany her. There would be some surviving associates of her mother at the service. However, Megan knew she would not be surrounded by friends and family. As she helped the friendly widow into the second row of the polished, black, seven-seater car, Megan felt grateful for her company and yet, paradoxically, she was also acutely aware of how alone she was in the world. Being hard of hearing, Mrs Riley attempted only the merest of pleasantries during the journey and was content to hold Megan's hand firmly within the grasp of her own. However, the silence was not to last for long. Megan soon sensed some disturbance in the rear seats behind herself and Mrs Riley. Then she heard them: the voices, they were back. Amidst a general sense of jostling, she quite clearly heard Grandma May's voice, "I think it should be me, after all she is my daughter. You men can keep each other company outside."

What on earth...? Megan had the uneasy feeling that her deceased relatives would be attending the funeral. *How bizarre!* she thought to herself.

The voices quietened down.

However, as the car approached the crematorium, Megan once again sensed an uneasy atmosphere.

"Yes, I'm going to do it now; as she steps out of the car," said her grandmother's voice.

And as she leaned over to help her elderly companion out of the car, Megan felt what only could be described as a deep but gentle penetration, a surge of energy that touched the core of her being. Whilst not unpleasant, it was very unsettling and, as she straightened up, Megan felt faint. The colour drained from her cheeks and she steadied herself with her hand against the roof of the car.

"Are you all right, dear?" Mrs Riley asked, was most concerned. "You look as if you've seen a ghost!"

Regaining her balance, Megan took a deep breath and answered that she was fine. "It's time to go inside," she said softly to her apprehensive companion.

Taking their seats at the front of the chapel, the two women stared at the coffin laid out before them. Megan could hear the hushed movements of others entering the building from behind them, but she kept her focus firmly in front of her. However, she was struggling to sit still. Waves of strange energy seemed to be washing over her and for a moment or two she felt as if her body was moving independently of her mind. Then she felt it: a great big sigh of relief, emanating from low in her abdomen and inflating her chest.

"Ah! It feels so good to be embodied once more," announced Grandma May in a somewhat muffled tone. Megan frantically looked around. No one else seemed to have heard the voice.

"*Where are you?*" Megan asked with her thoughts, fearing that she already knew the answer.

"I'm inside you," whispered Grandma May, as the hum in the room quietened and the service commenced. Megan's mind was in a whirl. Although her body was present in the room, her thoughts were spiralling into unknown territory. She could not deny the sensation of her grandmother's spirit within her and as a result her own mind had become open to a myriad of possibilities. She smiled apologetically as her grandmother insisted on using her eyes to stare intently at the face of every person in the room, commenting on how well, old or ill they were looking.

A closer gathering at the crematorium enabled Megan to listen a little more closely to the internal dialogue between her grandmother and her mother. May then announced to her granddaughter that she would be leaving her body to help Maura pass over into the spirit world, and as the curtain closed on the flower-clad coffin she heard the reassuring words of Grandma May to her daughter, "Welcome home, my darling Maura. We are so pleased you are finally here with us."

"Thank you, it feels so good to arrive," the recently deceased Maura replied.

On feeling the spirit leaving her own body and hearing her mother's voice, Megan wept. The rest of the afternoon remained something of a blur in her memory; however, she recalled one event. It was through her tears that she saw the face of Pete, the man from the hospice, as their respective funeral cars crossed paths at the entrance gate to the crematorium.

* * *

Three days later, Megan awoke with a mission in mind. Rifling through the week's mail which had gathered on the welcome mat at the front door, she found a flyer advertising the services of a local building contractor. Leaving a message on the voicemail of the mobile number on the page, she requested a call back explaining the possible opportunity for a house renovation project.

"Who knows? Perhaps he might even want to buy the house..." she mused.

Next, she telephoned the travel agents and, using her credit card, booked a two-week holiday to the Cape Verde islands. She decided that she would use the stash of cash left by her mother to pay the balance in six weeks' time.

* * *

Three Months Later...

"Well, you could have given us a bit more notice," huffed Grandma May inside Megan's mind as she excitedly unzipped her bulging suitcase on the king-size bed in the luxurious hotel room.

"You didn't have to come!" Megan retorted.

"What? You, our only living relative, finally getting married, and you don't think we want to attend?" Megan knew by the old lady's tone that the spirits were secretly pleased.

"Well, you were so insistent that we met," laughed Megan, as she lifted a silky shift from the case. She held it up against the bright light streaming in through the hotel window, which revealed a sparkling azure sea set against the breathtaking backdrop of a volcanic mountain.

"Yes, and even with our help you couldn't get it right!" Grandma May laughed. "He left the hospice before you arrived to make the donation, and then the funeral car had to take a detour and so your paths failed to cross at the crematorium."

"So you had a hand in the rescheduling of the funeral?" Megan asked.

"I'm afraid so," answered Grandma May, a little subdued. "We try not to interfere, but sometimes…"

"And you orchestrated the flyer in the mail?" Megan was getting a fuller picture.

"Yes! We had a word, and as soon as he picked up the voicemail message he experienced an urgency to pay you a visit. We are pleased about your plans for the house. It will make a great first home for you two, together."

Sensing that something was happening in the bedroom, the subject of the conversation stepped out of the en-suite bathroom.

"This is amazing!" he exclaimed. "How did you find this place?"

"I had quite a lot of guidance," laughed Megan. "I think we're going to enjoy it here. It's the perfect place for the start of our life, together."

"Let's start now…" There was a twinkle in Pete's eyes as he gently steered her by the shoulders, towards the bed.

"The wedding ceremony isn't for another three days," piped up Grandma May.

"You spirits don't get to make all the decisions for the living," Megan replied with her thoughts. Smiling, she silently she advised her dead grandmother. *"And now might be a good time for you to tune out…"*

Elena

Each had been stealing glances at the other for over an hour, both abruptly averting their look upon the meeting of their eyes. She liked the bulge of his bicep, evident through the sleeve of his pristine white shirt, as he lifted empty dinner plates from the table. He enjoyed the curve of her breasts, the glimpse of her cleavage as he leaned over to pour the wine into the glasses of the beautiful woman and her companion. As their eyes met once more across the terrace of the traditional Greek restaurant, *Estiatorio Nikolaos*, the waiter knew that the inattentive man would be sleeping alone that night, even if the couple left the restaurant together.

Eyes shining amidst coy smiles, she settled the bill just before midnight, and leaving behind the handsome waiter, the attractive woman and her companion left the restaurant. The waiter checked his watch before turning his attention to the last remaining table of guests. They requested a glass of brandy each and toasted to the last night of their holiday. He charmingly obliged, knowing that within half an hour or so, the lively group would be leaving and he would close the restaurant and head out into the night.

Meanwhile, Elena had refused a drink at a late-night bar in the resort and feigning fatigue, she excused herself from the company of her date. He had proved a disappointment. So keen at the outset of the evening, his conversation had been full of compliments about her entrancing, ebony eyes and her shiny, raven locks. The woman had smiled with pleasure and offered affection by taking his hand in hers, over the table top.

However, the subject had soon lapsed rather boringly into a monologue about how well his portfolio investments were performing and where he was looking to make his next profit.

Elena had no problem with men or money; she found both useful for fun and entertainment. However, the mere notion of being concerned with the collection of money or items of worth and storing them for future use was alien to her. Life held a sense of urgency for Elena. She wanted to live now, to feel everything in the moment. Unable to consider what might or might not happen tomorrow, she lived fully in the present, constantly seeking out any pleasure and enjoyment that was available to her. Always the subject of attention at social gatherings, she knew that her youth and beauty would not last indefinitely and sought out friends and acquaintances with a similar outlook to her own.

Born the fifth of seven children to a Greek mother and a Spanish, Catholic father, the independent young woman had returned to the island of her maternal family to live, finding work in the local travel industry. She loved the transient nature of the job, meeting with so many new people and speaking a variety of languages. Each day was a new chapter for Elena; she rarely dwelled on past events, and the arrival of the new waiter at the restaurant in the Old Village was an interesting development in this summer's storyline. It was almost the height of the season and the astute woman was wondering how she had failed to spot the handsome man earlier in the year. However, she now recalled her occupation with Hans, her Danish lover, for almost three weeks at the start of the season. His energy had inspired her; their athletic lovemaking had exhausted her, flooding both her body and mind with ecstasy. Hans had a fascinating obsession with sex and water; Elena had found herself constantly in his arms, alternately immersed in salty seawater, saturated with chlorinated pool water or reinvigorated in the steam of the hot shower. Eventually summoned back to his suspicious wife in Copenhagen, Hans had vowed to return later in the season to continue with their lusty liaisons. She had particularly relished kayaking to the secluded beach, where they had made love under the sun; also enjoying their energetic poolside activities at the company's villa, hired as a perk for the high-performing sales personnel, such as Hans.

However, following his departure, Elena had not spent her evenings waiting in for him to call. During the week she would travel across the island, escorting visitors to and from the airport; she also led two weekly bus tours to local places of historical and cultural interest. Although she enjoyed the company of the energetic travellers who chose the resort for its array of water sports and beach activities, she also appreciated the interests of the independent travellers; most of who chose to stay in the traditional accommodation at the Old Village, and spent their days mooching around the monasteries and ruins of the ancient Greek world. There had been one such traveller who had recently caught her attention.

A literary academic from an Italian university, Vincenzo spoke four European languages including both Greek and Spanish, and had entranced Elena with both his mythological knowledge of the ancient land and his array of romantic skills. He had charmed her with sensual gifts of scent and flowers and entertained her with recitations of erotic poetry. Every meal they shared had followed an intriguing dance of the observance of etiquette, interspersed with the mutual sharing of their respective romantic aspirations. Each evening they had spent watching the sunset from the busy village square, sipping on rich red wine, their desire for each other had increased.

Their mutual passion was finally consummated on the last night of his stay.

On the small, secluded balcony of his village house room, Vincenzo had kissed her slowly and deliberately, whilst unwrapping her; allowing the loose, silken dress to fall silently to the floor, leaving her standing naked in the moonlight. He was gentle and precise with his hands and within minutes the aroused woman found herself flooded with pleasure. Their discreet lovemaking continued inside his bedroom in the shared house until just before dawn, when they both drifted off into a halcyon slumber.

Somewhat sad to see him leave, Elena had kissed him politely at the airport later that day and wished him a safe journey. However, before his flight had departed, a rugged-looking man carrying a well-travelled rucksack walked through arrivals and into her life.

Etienne was an artist from rural France who had tired of Parisian life and could not face returning to the farmlands of his childhood. The fields of sunflowers now held little allure for his artistic vision and he felt constrained by the stylized fashion of the art in the capital. The only way forwards for him seemed to be to leave his homeland and explore new territory. His choice of destination was determined by a random flip of a coin over a map of the world and Etienne had booked himself a one-way ticket to the Eastern Mediterranean. With little knowledge of Greek and limited Spanish, Etienne attempted to speak to Elena in broken English, whilst she struggled to recall her schoolgirl French. However, words proved of little importance to the couple who found themselves in a passionate embrace within minutes of arriving at his room in the Old Village.

Elena loved the hot smell from his long, curly, unkempt hair and the way his hands so urgently unzipped her fitted skirt, before slipping into her silken panties and squeezing the smooth flesh of her buttocks.

The young woman had lost herself in passion with this man to the exclusion of her interest in any others. For three days the two had remained in the dimly lit room, opening the window shutters only to release the stale smell of cigarette smoke and sweaty sex.

Erotically they explored every inch of each other's bodies and Elena knew that she had found a higher state of excitement and a deeper sense of satisfaction with this man, than she had previously experienced. She also knew that the intensity could not be sustained.

Showering off the grimy pleasure of the long weekend, she returned to work, with a renewed energy for life.

The couple had met up only once more after that weekend; both realized that their passion for each other had been spent and Etienne, unable to settle to any creative work, had booked himself on an island-hopping excursion, announcing his intention to return to the Old Village in ten days' time. Elena had not seen or heard from him since.

Knowing that they shared an exciting attraction for each other, Elena now headed back towards the village restaurant in search of the waiter. As she passed through the square in the sticky heat of the night, from the street below she noticed that the lights were out and the terrace of the restaurant was empty. Turning to leave for home, she heard a soft voice through the darkness and the click of a cigarette lighter. Looking back she could see his face, momentarily illuminated beneath a trail of fresh, grey smoke.

"Hello? Can I help you?" The waiter was leaning against a wooden post, under the vine-covered pergola in the restaurant garden.

"I wondered if you would still be open for a glass of brandy. I can see that you are now closed. It's no problem," Elena replied, reaching into her bag for a cigarette.

"Perhaps you could give me a light?"

The waiter nodded and Elena stepped into the garden, where he duly lit her cigarette. Elena thanked him, took her first inhalation and offered her hand.

"I am Elena," she volunteered, on breathing out.

"Adonis," he reciprocated, taking her hand in his and

squeezing it. "Shall we walk?"

Elena felt a flush of excitement as the two wandered into the deserted streets of the Old Village.

"Where do you live?" he asked, his muscular arm momentarily brushing her bare shoulder. He had noticed the smooth olive skin and high-arched brows of her beautiful face and now looked intently into her dark, shining eyes.

"I have an apartment just outside of the resort," she replied, gesturing further along the lonely road that separated the two distinct areas. The way ahead plunged into darkness.

"Should we walk along the beach?" Adonis asked and Elena agreed. There would be a breeze from the sea, and as it was a clear night the moonlight would be reflected on the waves. The two turned along a cobbled alleyway and continued to walk, both smoking in the silence until they reached the sand. Elena bent over to remove her pretty sandals and sunk her henna-tattooed toes into the cool sand.

"What happened to your friend from the restaurant?" Adonis asked, discarding his spent cigarette.

"He had to get an early night as he flies home tomorrow," she replied diplomatically, inhaling a final breath from her cigarette.

"And you are staying here longer?" he continued to question her, whilst taking the finished cigarette from her and disposing of it with his own.

"I intend to stay around for a little while," she replied and quickly switched the focus back onto him. "How do you like working at the restaurant?" she asked.

"Nikolaos is a fair man," he replied. "But he is old now and most of his children have moved off to the mainland to find work; he is grateful for the help." Elena was unsure as to the origin of his accent. Like her own, it was a Mediterranean mix, although she thought she detected an Eastern European intonation.

"How long will you work there?" she continued.

"Until the end of the season," Adonis replied.

"And then?" Elena looked directly into his eyes.

"And then I will go where the wind blows me," Adonis laughed. Elena was hooked. All she wanted to do was be with him, to feel the warmth from his smile and share in the excitement promised by his laughter. The two casually chatted and laughed as they walked the length of the deserted beach. They shared a love of freedom, of enjoyment and each felt enlivened by the other. Adonis traced the curve of her silky hair along the side of her face with his fingers and she looked sideways into his deep brown eyes, a playful smile escaping her sensual lips. As they stepped off the beach and once more onto the cobbles their pace slowed, until Elena stopped to say, "My apartment is just across the way. I can't ask you in, it is late and I don't want to disturb Maria, my flatmate."

"I don't want you to go in yet," Adonis replied. "Walk with me a little further."

Elena followed him to the end of the cobbles where the lane opened out into a small courtyard, housing some trees and surrounded by the shuttered windows and balconies of the traditional buildings. He stood in the shade of a large fig tree with his back against the wall and beckoned to her. As she approached him he wrapped his arms tightly around her and kissed her passionately. Elena responded with equal enthusiasm. He ran his fingers through her hair and along her shoulders. She broke away from his lips and leaning back, she guided his head towards her neck and onto her shoulders. Turning her head to feel the touch of his lips in the crook of her neck, she gasped with pleasure as his kiss turned into a gentle bite. Gently placing his hands on her lower back, he pulled her body in closer to him and Elena felt his arousal. He was licking and nibbling his way from her shoulder and onto her chest and his hands dropped to cup both buttocks. Elena reciprocated, placing her hands on his lithe torso, opening the buttons of his shirt and working her way down to his slim hips.

Suddenly there was the clattering of shutters opening and the sound of muffled footsteps on the balcony above. Adonis signalled to Elena to be very quiet and she stifled a giggle. The entwined couple remained still and silent, listening to the bickering of the people occupying the room, their discontent spilling out into the early morning air. The restraint served only to increase the passion brewing beneath the balcony. Adonis grabbed Elena by the hand and the two ran out from the courtyard and along a dark alleyway. Once they were no longer in earshot of the domestic discord, the couple stopped running. In the darkness, Elena felt her back pressed up against a wall, whilst her breasts were being freed from beneath her silken vest. Adonis' mouth was warm and wet on her firm nipples and his hands were now lifting her skirt. She fumbled with the button of his trousers before unzipping them and sliding her hand over the firm presence already finding its way out of his shorts. With only the sound of a moped engine fading into the distance, soon all the couple could hear was the fast breathing of the other. In the silence, the intensity of the heat between them and the increased rhythm of Adonis's movements caused Elena to gasp for air in the sultry night. As he neared climax, a few excited groans emanated from his chest.

Something told Elena to open her eyes and she saw the face of a woman watching from the balcony of an apartment above. The viewer quickly dropped her gaze and retreated back into the room.

"Adoni, someone is watching us," she whispered in her lover's ear. The thought served to facilitate the climax of both lovers simultaneously; as if in complete oblivion as to the nature of their surroundings, they continued to embrace, locked together in pleasure, smiles and laughter.

A few minutes later Adonis stepped back to zip up his trousers and lit two cigarettes, handing one to Elena. After hurriedly adjusting her clothes, she accepted and the two made their way out of the alleyway. Elena cast a glance at the open window from which she had seen the woman. She saw that the glass door was open and a faint light shined through the curtain. She felt sure that she caught sight of the shadow of a figure from behind the drape. At the end of the alleyway she bid her lover goodnight with a final kiss and walked the short distance to her apartment. Adonis lingered a while, watching her climb the steps to her apartment and waiting for her to close the door. With a feeling of satisfaction in his heart, he headed home.

* * *

The final weekend of August witnessed the advent of a unique event at the resort. An internationally renowned arts festival took place on the island over a period of five days, during which some of the street artists, storytellers and musical performers from all over the world descended on the Old Village. For this occasion, almost every house opened up its doors to offer a warm welcome and accommodation to the visitors, many of whom returned year after year. This year the Virago travel agency had advertised the event more widely and Elena was instructed to find suitable accommodation for the extra visitors expected. The resort was happy to assist, offering their empty rooms at a premium, however everyone seemed happy with the arrangements and Elena soon found herself at the centre of the festival vortex, surrounded by swathes of colourful people and swirls of lively music. She arranged locations for the events by day and attended a variety of post-event parties by night. The extroverted woman found something to appreciate in all of the traditional performances she witnessed and enjoyed every hour of her waking day, finding little time to sleep. She gazed at the bold colours of the artists whose work covered the walls and walkways of the beachfront and immersed herself in the sound of music playing in the open-air performances at the park. In particular she found herself drawn to a female theatre group who specialized in improvisations. In theatrical costume, representing fashion throughout the years, they played out a variety of comical scenes. Elena stopped to watch one where the players appeared to be depicting the absurdities of society's conventions and hypocrisies regarding forbidden love. She found the false moustaches, ostentatious outfits and exaggerated make-up of their unique performances highly amusing. At each subsequent performance she noticed how the characters' personalities changed and the storylines transformed. Her imagination captivated by the intriguing process, Elena found herself increasingly drawn into their company.

At a beach-front bar on the fifth night of the festival, she found herself the centre of attention of the vivacious troupe of women, celebrating the last performance of a highly successful season. Some of the players would be returning to their usual jobs and families at the end of the tour, others had made acting their life and would continue to promote and perform their art in other locations, throughout the winter months. All members were confident that they would be returning here to participate in the next year's festival; such were the positive accolades they had received for their performances.

Removing her strappy, high-heeled shoes, which were sinking into the sand, Elena shook out her long hair as if she was throwing off the vestiges of her working day and ordered a margarita. As the group rallied around, the artists, now free of their disguises, they embarked upon a debate as to which performance they regarded as the best well-received, and which of the skits they personally had most enjoyed performing.

One member of the troupe, who was particularly pleased to see Elena at the party, took the opportunity to engage her in conversation at this point. A mature woman – Elena had noticed her for her striking, unconventional looks and the ease with which she commanded respect from the rest of the group – Anya appeared to be the unofficial leader of the troupe; a dedicated actress, she featured as the sole remaining member of the original hub of individuals who had founded the group, some four years previously. The daughter of a Russian family who had emigrated to the United States of America when she was just five years old; she spoke English with an American accent. She entranced Elena with her knowledge of the ancient Greek god of drama and wine, Dionysus, and the fifth-century Athenians who were responsible for the creation of the concept of theatre. She described how the performers wore masks in the hope of protecting themselves from the fate of the characters that they were embodying. Elena marvelled at the notion that the art of acting had been practiced in Greece for thousands of years.

Anya also informed her that they were always looking for new members with unique ideas for the group performances. She also remarked on Elena's beauty and gently stroked her hand as it lay on the bar in front of them both. Elena laughed, feeling both pleased and a little uncertain of the nature of the unexpected compliment. She turned to look around the crowd gathered under the straw roof of the beach bar, as if to ascertain her social bearings. Her gaze alighted on the face of an attractive redhead who appeared to be staring at her, yet who looked away when their eyes met. There was something familiar about her, Elena thought before turning back to Anya, whose attention had not wavered. Elena was left in no doubt as to her intentions when the woman leaned in towards the dark beauty and whispered in her ear:

"I find you irresistibly beautiful and I want to be alone with you."

Her heart pounding with excitement, Elena found herself being led by the hand into the rest room. She had experimented sexually with other girls whilst growing up, however she felt exhilarated at being pursued in this manner and keen to find out what Anya had planned for her. In the empty toilet, Anya parted the long, elegant dress at the thigh, where it split, to reveal Elena's naked body beneath, as the young woman leant back over the wash-hand basin. Kneeling in front of her, Anya gently ran her fingers up Elena's inner thighs and gently parted her smooth, bare lips. Elena gasped as the woman's tongue flicked teasingly between her legs, the momentary connections flashing like lightning to her core. She groaned with pleasure, a milky moistness pooling within. Holding her breath in anticipation of the next tantalizing touch, knowing her empowered lover was making her wait a little while longer for the next lick, Elena wriggled in an attempt to initiate contact with the elusive tongue, but its owner, an experienced woman, was wholly in control. She sensed that the longer she withheld, the greater the climax on the final contact. Elena moaned, running her fingers through her lover's smooth hair, steadily tightening her grip on the strands in anticipation of the final explosion. Once Elena relinquished all sense of control, it was with the lightest of licks that her swollen pearl seemingly exploded beneath the gentle press of the tongue; the release of her satisfaction spilling over into the mouth of her lover. With an erotic shriek, Elena's tense body instantly relaxed and her lover momentarily retreated to take a deep breath. As Elena reclined further onto the cool tiled shelf between the wash-hand basins, her impassioned lover's tongue disappeared inside her, relishing the spoils of her skilful lovemaking.

Someone switching on the light interrupted the erotic coupling. Elena noted the arrival of the redhead in the ladies' toilet. She was sure it was the same woman who she had seen watching her in the bar, and something told her it was the same person who had been watching on the night she had made love in the alleyway with Adonis. The woman stood frozen in response to the act she was witnessing. Although Anya had withdrawn from her body on the arrival of the uninvited guest, Elena did not mind sharing the moment with the stranger. In her view, an act of love was a work of art, a manifestation of beauty, just like a painting or a film or any other performance, and as such was meant to be shared or viewed. She merely smiled warmly at the woman, who blushed and retreated, mumbling an apology as she switched off the light and closed the door. Anya, somewhat reluctant to continue following the disturbance, was soon persuaded by the alluring Elena to continue with her impressive performance.

Unsure whether it was the effects of the margaritas she had drunk or the high from the climax that now flooded her head, the young woman and her lover returned to the bar, both in high spirits, where they continued drinking and dancing into the night. However, from that point on, Anya only had eyes for Elena.

When the first rays of the morning sun rose over the hilltop behind the beach bar, the music wound down to a more chilled-out rhythm and people started to order iced coffees from the bar. Many were already laid out on the sofas occupying the corners of the makeshift bar, some wrapped in the arms of their lovers, whilst others slept alone. Elena explained that she needed to return home to shower and dress in readiness for the day's work. She was to accompany a party of holidaymakers to the Tsamtiki monastery that day. It was one of her favourite places, an ancient building in the most beautiful setting, high on a hill, sitting on a peninsula which stretched out over a breathtaking, turquoise bay. Anya asked if she would be out that evening, and kissing her goodbye, Elena agreed to meet her later, in a quiet restaurant in the Old Village. They exchanged telephone numbers and parted after a long embrace.

As she approached her apartment, the tired woman saw a bleary eyed Adonis on the steps of her apartment. She caught a glimpse of Maria's blonde hair as she hugged and kissed him goodbye and realized that they had spent the night together. As he approached her in the alleyway he spoke, "Elena, how are you?"

"I am fine thank you," she replied politely.

"Elena, I came looking for you, but you were not at home…" he lied.

"Yes I was out all night," she explained, "and now I have to get ready for work, so if you will excuse me, I must go home."

"Elena, I want to see you again," Adonis persisted.

"Okay, I will be in the Old Village tonight," she replied. "I will see you then."

Adonis smiled in surprise at the woman's response.

"Great! See you later," he agreed, lighting a cigarette before walking away.

Inside the apartment, Maria, part of the children's entertainment team at the resort, had taken herself back to bed. She worked shifts, alternating between supervising the younger children in the crèche during the mornings and working with the older children at the entertainment workshops during the evenings. Knowing that their paths were unlikely to cross that day, Elena scribbled a note informing her friend that she would be late home again that night and that they needed some milk and coffee for the apartment.

A refreshed Elena stepped out of the shower and looked for something cool and chic to wear. Bored with everything in her own wardrobe she spotted a subtle lemon-coloured shift dress hanging over the balcony of the apartment. Maria had obviously washed it and hung it out to dry. Although a couple of sizes too big for the lithe Spaniard, Elena added a brown leather belt and liked the line of the skirt as it fell in gentle waves around her hips; the colour complemented her olive complexion. She knew her friend would not object to her borrowing the dress. They shared most things.

On her arrival at the office, Elena found a message marked 'urgent', waiting for her on the desk. It read simply: *'I am back and need to see you. Please call me. Yours, with love, Vincenzo.'*

She noted down the number before asking her colleagues if they had seen the person who had left the message. Irina, a tall, slim, Czech girl replied that a handsome Italian man had asked her to pass the message on to Elena.

"When was he here?" Elena asked.

"He called around yesterday and asked for you," Irina explained. "I told him you would be in the office today and then he wrote the note and left it on your desk."

Elena was intrigued. *What is he doing here?* He had not said he intended to return and she had heard nothing from him since he had left some three weeks previously. Impulsively Elena tapped into her phone the number on the paper and pressed 'call'. When she heard the ringtone she checked her watch for the time. It was still early. The coach left at nine and she had to be there beforehand to carry out all of the necessary checks. She left a voicemail for Vincenzo, informing him of her whereabouts that day and stating that she hoped to speak with him later.

Counting the group of twenty-five travellers onto the coach half an hour later, she was still wondering as to the reason for his surprise return to the island. The party would stop at a café en route for refreshments. Elena decided she would then call him again. In the cool morning shade of the mountainside café, Elena sipped on an espresso and listened to a voicemail message from her Italian lover.

"Thank you for your call," Vincenzo had said in a polite manner. "I am so very pleased to hear from you. Can we meet up sometime today? I have something I must tell you. Ciao, Bella."

Shaking off an initial sense of unease, Elena assured herself that he must have some good news for her. She texted him a message in return, *'I will be at the Tsamtiki Monastery from midday and will return to the Old Village this evening. I hope to see you later, yours, Elena x.'*

The woman was not sure how she would manage to meet up with Anya, Adonis and Vincenzo all in one evening but she told herself that things would work out for the best, as they always did for her.

On returning back to the coach, she took the microphone and started to speak to the party of travellers. Animatedly, she told them the romantic history of the monastery, describing how it had served as a hideaway for the local people during times of Turkish invasion and she named the many monks who had chosen martyrdom over conquest by plundering forces over the centuries. In more recent times, the monastery had been inhabited by an order of nuns and had become widely known for its spring water, which was said to aid fertility.

Many pilgrimages were made to the garden of the ancient building, which was only accessible on foot. A steady climb of some three hundred steps led visitors to the spring water. Here, on firstly removing their shoes, people drank from the fountain in the hope of falling pregnant. Elena had spotted one such couple, over whom sadness hung, despite their youth and beauty and the fact that they only had eyes for each other. The girl was very thin and without any sparkle, yet the protective boyfriend seemed full of hope and expectation. Elena secretly hoped that the water would work its magic for them.

As the bus climbed to the summit of the hill, she put down her microphone and admired the panoramic view. From the windows on the right-hand side the travellers could see the high mountain ranges at the interior of the island; and from the left the view was of the deep blue Aegean Sea stretching as far as the eye would allow.

The tour guide took in a deep breath. This vista never failed to inspire her, especially on the most glorious of summer days. There was so much of the world that she had yet to explore; so many places to visit and people to meet. Here on the tip of the peninsula, on top of the world she was reminded of her freedom and the excitement resonated within every cell of her young body.

Before the travellers disembarked, their guide handed them each a leaflet containing a simple map of the modest monastery and its surrounding area, with details of the facilities on offer. She informed them that their trip would end at three o'clock and they should all meet at this same point in the car park. The eager visitors headed straight for the steep, worn steps that would take them to the summit. Waiting for the backs of her group to disappear from sight, Elena removed her shoes, not to be blessed with fecundity, but just to feel the heat from the ancient stones soaking into the soles of her feet; and she stepped her way to the pinnacle.

Despite having made this pilgrimage on many occasions, Elena still felt the need to pay her respects in the closeted silence of the small church, with its deep crimson embroidered cushions, tasselled, velvet drapes and stained glass window panes. She bowed her head before an oil painting of the Virgin Mary cradling the infant Jesus, mounted on a silver plate; she genuflected before a gold-painted effigy of Christ on a roughly hewn wooden cross, hanging on the whitewashed wall of the modest building. Taking a small candle, she lit its wick from the flame of another and placed it on the altar. Closing her eyes against the gentle golden lights, she quietly said a prayer for her relatives in Spain. Then making her way out to the brightness of the gardens, she sat in the shade of an old Cypress tree.

Spending her days at work and nights out at parties, the young woman needed a power nap to regenerate. From experience she knew that she would not be disturbed on the seat and so setting her watch alarm for an hour's time, she sat back and pulled her large straw hat over her face. Elena was a light sleeper and she drifted in and out of consciousness, the voices of passing people permeating her dreams, as they stopped to partake of the life-giving water springing from the garden fountain.

After an hour she was woken by the sound denoting the

arrival of a text message on her phone. It read: *'I am here, where can I find you?'*

Elena typed a reply, letting Vincenzo know that she was in the garden of the monastery.

She received a single word in reply, *'perfetto'*, and within minutes he was crossing the garden, brushing back his shiny, waved hair as he walked towards her. He approached with outstretched arms and she stood to greet him warmly.

"Vincenzo, this is a great surprise. What brought you back here?" Elena took in the crisp collar of his pristine white shirt, effortlessly presented under his grey linen jacket. Always immaculately groomed, the slim, Italian man was very pleasant on the eye and Elena wondered just how he had managed to keep the shine on his black leather shoes, when everyone else's feet were dusty and scuffed from the mountainous terrain.

"You, my darling," he replied. "I am back for you. Please sit." He gestured for her to sit back on the seat, joining her to sit alongside. Elena laughed nervously, not knowing what else to say or do.

"After I left, you were in my thoughts every minute of every day," he continued, as he turned to place his hands on the tops of her arms. "I was tormented. I could not sleep without dreaming of you. I saw your face on every poster in the city and heard your voice in every conversation around me. I embarrassed myself when I approached a lady in the street who I was convinced was you. I knew then that I had to come back for you, my beautiful Elena."

Elena shifted around uncomfortably in her seat. When she offered no response to his declaration Vincenzo persisted, "Elena, there is no one else as beautiful or as passionate as you." He lowered his voice towards the end of his sentence, whispering the word passionate, as if it was a secret. He continued to look directly into her eyes, as he announced, "I want you to be my wife." He let go of her to retrieve a small box from his trouser pocket. Opening the lid, he showed Elena the sparkling diamond-clad ring inside, before taking her hand and sliding it onto her left ring finger. It was a perfect fit.

"Your wife?" Elena blinked.

"Yes, Elena, there is no one else for me. I must have you." His gaze intensified as he spoke.

Wide-eyed, Elena spluttered her words, "Vincenzo, you are so kind, but I couldn't possibly accept this."

"Elena? Don't say no to love. We will live in my house in the countryside, just outside Urbino. You and me; we will drink wine whilst we watch the sunsets over the fields and make love until dawn." Vincenzo smiled at the picture of perfection he was painting with his imaginary brush. However, the image did nothing to enchant Elena.

"I'm not saying no to love, Vincenzo. This is a beautiful ring and you are a dear man, but I cannot go to Italy with you," she said gently.

"You say you cannot come with me? Why?" he asked in disbelief. Elena opened her mouth to explain but no words came out.

"You are in shock," Vincenzo smiled in relief. "You do not mean no, you just need some time to make sense of all of this. Of course it must seem like a dream come true. But you have nothing to worry about, I will treat you as my principessa, I will give you everything and I will be always at your side." Elena felt the world closing in on her. She could not think of anything worse than rattling around in a large house in the country, playing the perfect wife to an Italian academic, hosting chic dinner parties where the people jousted with their intellects and expertise. No, that was not the life for her.

"Vincenzo, I cannot take this ring, I cannot marry you," she protested gently. However, the smitten man was refusing to take no for an answer.

"My darling, you must have known when you reserved our

room again for me, that I was coming back for you." Elena stared blankly at the man. She had made no such booking; surely she would have recognized the man's name? "I know this has come as a great surprise for you and you will need a little time to make arrangements," he accorded.

"I did not make the booking," she protested. "I did not know you were coming back and I have a job here, an apartment and friends." Elena's resistance was growing.

"Yes, yes I understand. I will stay here with you until you are ready to leave. I would not ask you to fly alone to Italy. I will be here to escort you. From here on in we will never be parted. I am devoted to you, dearest Elena." He smiled benevolently.

The woman's frustration heightened. In an exasperated manner she tried further to explain, "I am not ready for marriage. I still have so many things to do and places to see." She tried to remove the ring; however Vincenzo took her hands in his, to prevent her from doing so.

Unfazed by her protestations, he sought to smooth over the situation; with a kind smile, he nodded his head in agreement. "Yes, you are young and want to travel, I understand," he responded. "I will take you to see St Peter's Basilica in Rome; we will travel the Venetian waterways; you will visit the birthplace of Raphael, in my hometown of Urbino in Le Marche." For a second he engaged the young woman's imagination; however, she replied:

"I would rather go shopping in Milan with my friends or lie on a sunny beach somewhere in Sorrento." Taken aback by her response, he replied a little stiffly:

"There will be time for those places and pursuits also. We have many happy years ahead of us." At that moment, Elena heard the clank of the bars of constraint; she saw herself as a prisoner in a picture-perfect palace, with Vincenzo her gaoler holding diamond-encrusted keys. With her heart racing, she stood up to flee from the scene. As she did so, he threw his arms around her and kissed her passionately.

"I am so happy, Elena!" he exclaimed. Turning to face the small group of people who had gathered around the magical spring, he proudly announced, "I am the luckiest man in the world. We are to be married!" There was a small ripple of congratulations from the group, some of whom came over to shake the hands of the bride and groom-to-be. Elena smiled embarrassedly as her beautiful ring was admired by the women tourists. How was she going to get out of this? Not wanting to cause an unpleasant scene in front of her tour group in this sacred spot, she was forced into a polite silence, graciously accepting the congratulations whilst resolving to deal with the situation as soon as she and Vincenzo were afforded some privacy. Meanwhile the happy man continued to participate in the felicitations. Having ingratiated himself in with the tour group, he joined the bus load for the return journey to the Old Village. Elena believed that allowing him to travel separately, by way of taxi, would undoubtedly provoke unwelcomed questions from the tourists. She sat alone in silence, in the seat behind the driver, for the duration of the journey.

As the bus pulled into the Old Village, the passengers disembarked, thanking their tour guide and wishing her well for the impending nuptials. Vincenzo was last to leave the bus. He lifted her hand, complete with the sparkling diamond engagement ring, to his lips, and kissed the smooth olive skin on the back of her hand. Seizing the moment, she started once more to explain, "Vincenzo, listen, I'm sorry, I just can't..."

However, once more he interrupted before she could finish speaking her mind. "Shh, my darling! Don't worry. I will take care of all of the arrangements. We will talk about it later, over dinner at our favourite restaurant." The smile on his radiant face forced Elena to sigh.

"Yes, we will talk about this situation at dinner," she accorded. The bus driver was getting tired and testy after a long drive in the hot sun. He coughed and shifted about restlessly in his seat.

"We have to go now, the driver has to return the bus to the depot before five o'clock," she explained. Reluctantly Vincenzo stepped backwards off the bus, as if he did not want to lose sight of his loved one. The doors clattered shut and the bus pulled off, leaving the besotted man standing on the side of the road. Elena sat back in her seat and sighed deeply.

Most unusually, the grumpy driver broke his silence and spoke to the young woman. "You are in trouble," he said.

"I know," replied Elena. "What can I do? He just won't take no for an answer."

The driver merely shook his head and repeated, "You are in BIG trouble."

In the cool interior of her apartment, Elena changed out of her work clothes and stepped into a cold shower. She lay naked on her bed, directly under the air conditioning unit. The temperature had peaked at forty degrees Celsius that day and in the stifling heat of the coach her hands and feet had swollen; and her mind was swimming with the unexpected events of the day. What was she to do? In a few hours' time she would have to face Vincenzo once more and explain that she could not accept his proposal and his ring. She hardly knew him. They had spent a week, dining together at sunset. On only one occasion had they shared the intimacy of passion. Elena had heard nothing further from him. She had not expected their paths to cross again and had no idea that he would reappear so soon, and with such intentions. She would ask at the agency for the name of the agent who had taken the booking request. She had a feeling it was Irina.

Admiring the sparkling gem on her finger she had to admit she was enchanted with its beauty and impressed with the correct fit. However, that was not reason enough to enslave herself to this charming man. She resolved to return the ring as soon as they met that evening for dinner. She would place it on the table directly in front of him and then he could not fail to realize that she was not accepting his proposal. Surely his pride would prevent him from continuing with his pointless endeavours to win her affection in public.

Elena tried unsuccessfully to remove the beautiful object from her swollen finger. It was stuck fast. Searching through the bathroom cabinet she found and applied some moisturizing cream to her ring finger and squeezed once more. However, the struggling appeared only to increase the swelling of her finger, now bulging most unsightly in an angry shade of red. The ring was lodged halfway between her knuckle and the web of her fingers. There was no way she was going to remove it until the swelling subsided. What was she to do?

Her thoughts were interrupted by the voice of her friend, Maria.

"Hello, Elena? Is that you?" she called out, as she walked into the apartment. Elena replied from her room and a surprised Maria walked into her bedroom.

"I didn't expect to see you home this evening," she commented.

"Maria, I am in trouble," Elena replied. "You must help me."

Maria, who hailed from the Tuscan hills, listened intently to Elena's tale of woe

"This man is serious," she stated in response. "It will be hard for him to accept a refusal from you. Now that his mind is set and he has travelled here with a ring, he will not leave without you."

Elena resumed her vigorous attempts to remove the ring from her finger; her fear was compounded by the comments of her friend. The world was closing in on her. The thought of spending the rest of her life with Vincenzo was almost unbearable. She knew that she had to ask for help. Anya would know what to do. Elena called her and explained the situation. Anya's calm approach served to soothe her, momentarily. Anya advised her to text Vincenzo before the meeting to set his expectations accordingly, to 'soften the blow'. The mature woman assured the young girl that she would also be at the restaurant to provide assistance if it was required. Elena was not concerned that Vincenzo would hurt her in any way but she suspected he would be capable of creating an unwanted scene.

With her words carefully rehearsed, Elena composed the text message as if she was speaking it across the table to the besotted man. She wrote: *'Dearest Vincenzo, I am very flattered with your feelings for me and your proposal of marriage. However, as much as it hurts me to part with this beautiful ring, I cannot accept it from you. As I have explained, I am not ready to commit to marriage with you or anyone else at this time in my life. I will meet you as arranged for dinner but I will return the ring and you must accept it. I do hope we can continue to be friends, yours, Elena.'*

There was no reply. She decided to dress down for dinner, so as not to give the rejected man any false hope. She selected a plain black dress with a long, flowing skirt. She covered her bare shoulders with a decorative Spanish shrug and added only the lightest touch of moisturizer to her otherwise bare face. Maria remarked that she appeared dressed for a funeral.

Arriving early at *Estiatorio Nikolaos*, Elena was pleased to note that most of the tables were as yet unfilled by diners. Perhaps they could get this over with quickly and then she could meet up with Anya to enjoy the rest of the late summer evening. She was greeted by Adonis who was clearly surprised to see her there so early in the evening. He had been expecting her to turn up later that night. Heeding Anya's words that she should choose a table at the restaurant that was easily seen by the other diners, she scanned the room and chose to sit on the terrace facing the direction from which she expected her guest to approach the building. There was just one set of steps leading to the terrace and so she couldn't possibly miss his entrance. From the corner of her eye she saw that one table was already taken, by a solitary man, probably waiting for others to arrive. Elena overheard him ask the waiter for more time to peruse the menu. For a split second she thought there was something familiar about the man, however as he turned his head to look towards her, she quickly turned away. There was no room for any more complications in this evening's schedule. Taking a seat, she arranged the flowing skirt of her dress to sit respectfully over her legs and she drew the shrug protectively over her shoulders. As Adonis left the waiting man he approached Elena, switching on his charming smile. His daily activity of swimming showed itself in the form of his lean musculature, and as always his shirt was pristine.

"Good evening," he said with a slight bow. "Here is our menu. I recommend the grilled swordfish and the village salad."

"Adoni, I am waiting for someone," Elena explained. "I'm expecting to meet with a man who wants to marry me!" She showed him her red finger swollen around the sparkling diamonds. The waiter blinked.

"How old are you, Adoni?" she continued. "I am twenty-four years old and that's much too young to be considering marriage. What would you say if someone asked you to marry them?"

Adonis took a deep breath. "Marriage?" He looked startled. "No, I am not ready for marriage!" he exclaimed.

"That's my point too," a relieved Elena sighed. "Vincenzo is a lovely man and I am flattered but I cannot accept a proposal of marriage. And now I have to tell him."

"You need a drink," stated the waiter. "Just one moment, I will get you a glass and you must drink some before he arrives." He disappeared into the interior of the quiet restaurant and Elena cast a glance towards the steps, expecting Vincenzo to arrive at any minute.

Adonis reappeared a few moments later with a bottle of ouzo and two glasses filled with ice.

"Here, drink this," he said, passing a glass filled with the liquorice-flavoured liquid towards her across the table. "It will help to relax you."

Elena gratefully took the glass and beckoned to the young man to take a seat at the table with her. As he did so a family with two small children arrived at the bottom of the steps. They were reading the menu, which was affixed to the post at the entrance and discussing their meal options. Usually Adonis would encourage the people in to test out some of the great dishes on offer, making a friendly fuss of the children as he did so. However, he continued to sit quietly and listen to the woes of Elena as they both sipped the intoxicating spirit.

"We knew each other for only one week. How could I know he was going to come back for me?" she implored.

Adonis shook his head. As he started to speak there was a fierce rapping on the window from inside the restaurant. The elderly owner gestured towards the family still digressing at the foot of the steps. The waiter jumped to his feet and walked quickly over to the top of the steps but the family had already started to walk away. He turned to his agitated boss and infuriated him further with a casual shrug of his shoulders, before turning his attention back to Elena. Taking a seat beside her he took her hand in his and looking directly into her eyes he said, "You, beautiful Elena, are far too young to be trapped into marriage. You are like a butterfly. You need to spread your colourful wings and fly to distant places. It is not right for you to be caged, to become someone's pet. If that should happen, your wings would fade and become old and crumpled, until you could no longer fly."

"Yes you are right," Elena agreed, taking great pleasure in the view of herself as a creature of delicate beauty. "I must be free and travel to see the world," she agreed.

"Yes," agreed Adonis, taking her hand and putting it to his lips. "You must be free; perhaps to spend another night with me?"

At that moment a shout was heard from across the terrace. It was from Vincenzo. He had appeared unnoticed at the top of the steps, watching as Adonis had kissed the hand of his love. He rushed over to the table.

"Is this why you will not marry me?" he bellowed. "Is this your lover?" He looked at Adonis with contempt. Elena knew he had received the text message.

"No, Vincenzo!" she exclaimed. "I cannot marry you because I am not ready to settle down. I have to travel, to see places and meet people." Shaking in anger, Vincenzo took hold of Adonis; grabbing the waiter by the collar of his shirt he pulled the startled man towards him. Adonis raised both hands in submission but Vincenzo stared into his face and bellowed, "She is mine!"

Elena was on her feet and imploring the incensed man to let go of Adonis. She was shocked at the intensity of the outburst from an otherwise mild-mannered man. From inside the restaurant, Nikolaos, the aging owner appeared at open doorway and shouted Adonis' name.

"What are you doing?" he called out. "Come here immediately!" The command brought Vincenzo to his senses. He pulled back from the waiter's face, relaxing his grip on the shirt. Straightening his attire, Adonis turned towards his boss,

"It's okay," he assured the hoary man. "There's no problem here, nothing for you to worry about."

The stubborn old man frowned and stood his ground. Vincenzo switched looks between the two men. Adonis was torn between obeying Nikolaos' instructions and shielding Elena from the unwanted attention of the angry Vincenzo. Whilst the three men each continued to stand their ground, a fourth man present on the restaurant terrace also took to his feet. Elena became aware of someone standing behind her; a voice spoke her name and explained, "It's me, Anya, in disguise. I can get you out of this situation but you have to listen to what I say."

Whilst the three men were engaged in a face-off, the two women plotted their escape.

Quietly, Anya instructed Elena to walk away from the table. "Take your time," she whispered. "Walk slowly and they won't even notice we've gone."

She was right. The three men had reached ego deadlock. Adonis had bowed to the wishes of his boss and started to walk away. Vincenzo had once again taken hold of him, this time by the left arm, and Adonis had swung a retaliatory punch at him with the right. The unexpected move had caught the Italian man unawares and he stumbled backwards over the empty table. Regaining his balance, he staggered across the terrace towards the restaurant door in further pursuit of Adonis. It was Nikolaos' turn to raise his voice. He instructed his waiter to enter the restaurant whilst he stood in the doorway, preventing the incensed Vincenzo from following him inside.

"You have no business attacking my staff. You must leave my restaurant," he boomed. "Leave now, immediately, while you can still walk."

No one had witnessed such a powerful voice emanating from the old man for many years. The chef, who had been chopping vegetables, stopped and marched out of the kitchen, with his knife still in his hands. He wanted to know what all the noise was about. Dorothea, the wife of Nikolaos, lifted her head from behind the bar where she dutifully cleaned the imaginary dust from the spotless shelves, to gaze in astonishment at her husband's outburst. No one was sure as to what might happen next. Meanwhile, Elena, now arm-in-arm with Anya was headed towards the steps.

As the sound of shouting continued to ring out over the terrace, the two women reached the bottom.

"I'll never get away with this," Elena whispered to her escort. "He will find me. This is a small town. He will hunt me down. He won't give up, I know it."

"Trust me, I have thought of a way," Anya assured her young friend.

The chef, who now stood protectively at the side of Nikolaos, suddenly intervened. Pointing his knife, which still had a slice of beef tomato stuck to the side of its blade, in the direction of the absconding couple, he challenged the angry Italian.

"You want her so much, you go after her, now! She is leaving with another man." Instinctively the women ran.

"Follow me!" Anya panted, after they had been running for a few minutes. At first, Elena could not work out to where she was being led. Anya had looped back on herself to ensure that they were not being followed. Elena finally found herself at the entrance to the *Aphrodite Hotel*. This was the women-only hotel into which she had booked the travelling actresses, just one week previously.

"We will be safe here," a breathless Anya stated with confidence. "Even if he knows you are here, he will not be able to come inside the building. The rule against men is strictly enforced."

At reception, Anya removed her wig and fake facial hair to reveal her short fair hair and strong bone structure, before requesting the key to her room. Elena noted how well she wore the casual shirt and jeans, which suited her androgynous shape.

"They are used to seeing me in all sorts of costumes here," she explained, leading Elena to the first floor. "Even if he sees you here, he will not be able to reach you," she explained, once inside. Unsure, Elena walked over to the balcony of the room. Stepping out, she looked tentatively into the quiet street below. There was no sign of the angry man.

"But I can't stay here indefinitely," Elena exclaimed.

"You can stay until he leaves the resort," replied Anya. "Did he book a return flight?"

"I will contact the agency and ask," replied Elena. "But he did say he was prepared to wait for me, so perhaps he had a one-way ticket."

"Well he'll soon get fed up of waiting around if he can't find you," Anya reasoned.

"I can't stay here until he decides to leave," Elena thought out loud. "What about my job?"

"I have thought of that too," Anya replied with a smile. "Think of it as practice, as a form of training for your future career in improvisation theatre." The woman pulled out a suitcase from under the bed. As she unzipped and opened the lid, Elena saw numerous false hair pieces, of every style and shade. Underneath were layers of costumes and accessories.

"Every day you will be someone else," Anya laughed as she lifted a long blonde wig out of the case. "Of course we don't always use costume or disguise," she explained. "The real art is getting people to believe something that is not actually happening."

Elena recalled a street scene where one woman interrupted the sketch by raising her arms to the sky and appeared to be worshipping the sun. The other players started mirroring her action and changing the movements until it was no longer clear who was leading and who was mirroring. "I think I get it," she replied.

"You'll only really get it when you participate," Anya explained. "Anyone can learn the theory but you can only learn the practice by joining in and taking part. Every sketch we perform is unique because we ask the audience for a suggestion at the start. Their request is our starting point and none of us ever know how the performance is going to work out." Elena thought it all sounded like excellent fun. It certainly fitted nicely into the way in which she loved to live her life. Anya's descriptions of the various European festivals and events that the group had attended that summer had filled Elena's mind with excitement. As the two women relaxed onto the sofa, Anya explained that the core of the group would be heading Stateside within the next few days, flying into New York and working their way south, by way of performances and competitions, to the annual festival at Miami.

"Some of the girls are taking a break this season and so we are looking for new recruits, if you are interested," she planted the seed firmly in the young woman's mind. Elena reasoned that her seasonal job at the travel agency would soon be coming to an end and so she would need to have some other form of employment lined up or she would be forced to return to her family in Spain. In comparison, touring the United States seemed a far more appealing option.

"How much notice do you have to be able to leave your job at the agency?" enquired Anya.

"Just one week," Elena replied. "Could we both leave here in a week's time?"

Anya replied that it could be arranged.

"Then there is only the problem of this ring," Elena explained. "How can we return the ring to Vincenzo without having to meet up with him?" The swelling of her finger had now reduced in the cool autumn air. The two women worked on its removal with a few drops of essential oil.

"Tomorrow morning I will take it to the agency on your behalf and ask them to return it to its rightful owner," Anya explained. "At the same time I will tell them of your problem, and your intentions to leave. I will ask them to book flights to Athens and we can sort out our further travel arrangements from there. Meanwhile, we can lay low here until Vincenzo retrieves the ring and leaves the island."

* * *

Three days later, the excited women ventured out of the hotel room, both in disguise.

Anya looked very feminine in her wig of tousled red curls,

whilst Elena appeared as a striking young man, with her newly cropped hair, and breasts bound so as to give her a flat-chested appearance. She wore her jeans in a loose fit, belted at her slim hips with a distressed leather belt and large buckle. Practising her mannerisms in front of the mirror, she felt confident that she could pull off the disguise and the two excited women headed out to try their performance on an unsuspecting audience.

Having seen nor heard anything further from Vincenzo, Anya believed he had now left the island, leaving the coast clear for them to eat their final meal at the best taverna in the town.

At a rather busy *Estiatorio Nikolaos*, they selected one of the few remaining tables and anticipated the arrival of the waiter service. Minutes later, Adonis appeared, nodding an acknowledgement to the young man he saw seated at the far side of the table, before turning his charming smile on the foxy redhead. Anya summoned the remnants of her Russian accent to order meals for both her and Elena, who simply nodded in approval at her choice. The waiter collected the menus and advised them that the meal would be ready in about fifteen minutes' time. He announced that he would return shortly with the orders from the bar.

It was a Saturday night, nearing the end of the season, and the restaurant seemed surprisingly busy. It was Dorothea who appeared shortly after at their table, serving the couple their drinks and apologizing for the delay with the food. Anya reassured the old lady that they were in no hurry and she was not to rush herself unnecessarily.

Adonis brought the meals some half hour later and he caught Elena smiling at her companion. He felt confused. He had been around to Maria's place asking discreetly after the wellbeing of her friend, only to be told that Elena had left the island. Whilst reasoning that the boy sitting at the table could not possibly be the same beautiful woman he had known, he was more than a little perturbed at the likeness and disconcerted by his inexplicable attraction to the boy.

As the otherwise uneventful evening drew to a close and merry holidaymakers made their way down the restaurant steps, Elena caught sight of a tall young woman appearing at the top of the steps. She stopped and looked around the terrace, smiling and waving to Adonis. It was Irina, her colleague from the travel agency. She was about to turn away, when she noticed the intense sparkle from the girl's hand as it caught the light of the lantern hanging from the post of the terrace pergola. She was wearing the ring! Elena was in no doubt that it was the very same ring that Vincenzo has presented to her, just a few days previously. How had it come to appear on Irina's finger?

The Czech beauty must have felt the eyes on her and she turned sharply to her left. Their eyes met fleetingly, until Elena quickly dropped her gaze. Perhaps Vincenzo had fallen head over heels in love with her young colleague and proposed to her? Witnessing the greeting Irina received a few minutes later from the waiter, Elena felt sure that the two had recently become an item. She breathed a huge sigh of relief. Vincenzo was out of the picture and hopefully out of the country. She was now free. Perhaps he had left without his ring? It was looking suspiciously as if it was Adonis who was about to enter the dangerous arena of marriage. Her ex-colleague would be a formidable opponent and Elena did not like the odds of his survival. Irina was obviously a girl who got what she wanted. As they embraced, Elena saw an image in her mind's eye; it was of Adonis, caged like a bird. Silently wishing both of them well, and in eagerness to move on to the United States for the next stage of her life, she left the restaurant, hand in hand with her latest love.

Moments of Truth

Sophia glided beneath the surface of the cool water, stretching out the concertina of muscles in her midriff; her body flooded with the momentary relief of weightlessness. Surfacing, she squinted in response to the intense sparkle dancing on the watery ripples and took a deep breath before continuing with the movement. Slow, steady strokes carried her across the length of the pool, as she inhaled the fresh mountain air and soaked up the welcome warmth of the Cypriot sun. This was her second swim of the day. Counting a total of twelve lengths, she paused at the shallow end and called out for assistance with the steps.

"Alex! I'm finished," she announced.

A tall, slim man appeared at the doorway to the villa, holding a towelling wrap.

"How was the water?" he asked, throwing the soft, white item over his left shoulder and holding out both arms to assist the glistening Sophia, who paused to ensure her balance before taking three tentative steps out of the pool.

"Very invigorating," she replied. "I could have stayed in for hours, but I can already feel my shoulders tingling."

Helping her into the wrap, Alex gently patted her back. "Shall I fetch the aloe rub?" he asked.

"Yes, please," she replied gratefully, as the two entered the villa. Sophia showered and changed, pinning up her damp, shoulder-length brown hair and wrapping a fresh white towel around her lightly bronzed body, before calling the young man into her room to moisturize her naked shoulders and upper back.

"Your sternocleidomastodius muscles are still very tight," he commented whilst applying the lotion to the top of her shoulders. "I will massage you later, this evening, if your skin is not too sore." Sophia lifted her chin to look up at the ceiling, before gently dropping it again to look at her chest. Tentatively she turned her face, first to the right and then to the left. As she tried to lean her head into her left shoulder she cried out in pain.

"Take it easy!" Alex exclaimed.

"It's so frustrating," Sophia complained, rubbing the taut muscle. "I have been conscientious with my daily exercises. Why is it taking so long?"

"It will take a little time!" Alex reassured her. "You will get there. You just have to do so slowly. There is no need to rush things." Sophia looked in to the earnest face of her handsome young assistant and smiled apologetically.

"Yes, of course, you're right, and I would love a massage," she said.

"Now it is time for you to relax," he instructed.

"Now I am going to sit in the shade of the fig tree and work on the book," Sophia announced in mild defiance.

Alex sighed. "Why is it when the rest of the world takes a siesta, you want to write a book to change the world?" He spoke in jest, the expression in his eyes hinting at an element of its truth, in his mind.

"It's not a book to change the world, I'm just sharing my thoughts and experiences in the hope they will help people," Sophia replied. "When it's finished I can take all the siestas that I want."

"Will you be swimming again this evening?" he asked.

"Yes, Alex, at the usual time, if that's okay with you?" she politely replied.

"I have a personal training client at the hotel at four o'clock," he replied. "I will return as soon as the induction is complete."

Respectfully, Alex took his leave.

Sophia watched the handsome figure as he walked away across the marbled hallway and out of the villa, thinking how fortunate she was to have found him. Alex had graduated from the University of Paphos as a physiotherapist, and was working in the hotel gym of the local holiday resort, whilst developing his private practice. He had told her that he was more interested in treating his patients in the remote areas of the mountains, the elderly and infirm who would receive no help if it wasn't for his mobile service. However, working with the tourists in the holiday season also helped to supplement his income. The manager of the villa had passed on his contact details to Sophia and he called around to see her twice, sometimes three times a day, to supervise her swimming rehabilitation.

She was some nine months into her post-surgical recovery period and could do most things for herself, yet she felt happier knowing that there was someone close to keep an eye on her. She had deliberately chosen this villa for its ground-floor accommodation and full-size pool. However, the slippery steps still provoked her anxiety, as her healing spine felt too fragile to withstand any further incidents. Alex's availability to advise on strengthening exercises, and to provide regular muscular relief, in the form of massage, was also greatly appreciated.

Now dressed in a loose linen shirt and white shorts, Sophia picked up her notebook and pen and walked through the open doorway into the garden. Imbued with the vitality of the elements, she sat in the shade of the fig trees, sipping a cocktail of freshly squeezed juices and writing down her thoughts. Since the accident, when she had been forced to stop work, the many hours of silent solitude which marked her recovery had served to facilitate her reflections. With fifteen years' worth of work as a psychotherapist, she had a head full of ideas, experiences and emotions to document. She now felt a compulsion to communicate her knowledge to a wider audience. Over the years, she had spoken with many people about their most paralyzing fears and deepest desires. In this way she had developed a keen insight into the nature of the issues which affected the lives of so many. She wanted to write about her findings in such a way that readers with similar problems would feel in safe company, yet also inspired to make the life choices that were right for them. So far, Sophia had managed to sketch out a loose framework for the book; yet each time she sat down to write something of substance, her mind wandered and she felt that she was losing a grip on her motivation. Life here at the villa was easy; there were no other people with needs to concern her. She received a weekly visit from the local managers who, between them, cleaned the villa and the pool, and for the first time in her life, she was finding her focus forced into a spotlight on her own wellbeing. She had, so far, spent a most relaxing three weeks simply swimming and sitting under the shade of the fig tree. *The publishers might just have to wait a little longer for the final manuscript,* she mused.

Resting her pen on the wooden table in front of her, she sat back, removing her sunglasses and closing her eyes. Turning her face in the direction of the sun, she allowed its muted rays to fall through the branches of the tree, onto her sun-screened face. There was no doubt that the climate was proving favourable for her recovery. The warmth relieved the pain and stiffness of her healing bones and the sunshine lifted her spirits. She was also greatly appreciating the simplicity of life here. There was no clock to watch, a lack of city traffic to negotiate and few raindrops to dodge. She loved the abundance of fresh fish and salads, easily prepared and flavoursome. The days were long and peaceful; she saw only a few faces each week, and actively welcomed the frequent visits from Alex.

Her mind wandered to her next swim and the promised massage. Sophia found herself contemplating her choice of swimming costume. Reluctant to reveal her recently scarred body to the penetrating rays of sun or the eyes of others, she had chosen a selection of one-piece costumes and a tankini. All had some flattering features, such as high-cut legs and accentuated waist detailing. However it was the halter-necked, purple piece that Sophia had in mind. Alex had been perfectly professional in the delivery of his treatment, but she was aware of the mutual spark of attraction between them. A knowing smile spread across her sun-kissed face as she imagined him gently unfastening her. In her mind she set the scene for a romantic encounter between them. Through the bedroom doors which opened out onto the lawn, she imagined them watching the deep red sunset as it hovered over the horizon of the sea. His hands were working their magic, massaging her neck and shoulders with a musk-scented oil. She was feeling loose-limbed and light-headed, each stroke eliciting a deep sensation of pleasure which melted into the core of her being, just as the crimson heat of the scorching sun dissipated into the waves. She imagined his hands working their way lower down her body, when her trance was suddenly broken by the sound of tyres on the loose chippings of the driveway. It was the postman. She turned to see him step out of the van and wave a handful of envelopes in her direction, his manner most relaxed and congenial.

"Hallo, Miss Sophia. How are you today? Are you well? I have mail for you," he said.

"*Yiassou*, Giorgo. It's another beautiful day!" she responded, sitting up and straightening her shirt.

"Yes, June is a great month here. Soon the temperature will get hotter, but here in the mountains you should still get the breeze off the sea." Giorgio looked around, gesturing appreciatively towards the surrounding hillsides.

"I will only be here until the end of the month," she informed the Greek grandfather, as he placed the week's post on the table in front of her.

"You should stay longer," he advised her in his direct manner.

"Thank you, *efharisto*," she spoke in both of their respective languages. "Giorgo, I like the idea of staying longer, perhaps I will make some enquiries of the travel company to see if the villa is available for another couple of weeks."

The respectful, grey-haired man nodded in approval before taking his leave of her. "Enjoy the sunshine, Miss Sophia, for as long as you can!" He waved, walking off towards his parked van. She waved in response and turned her attention to the post. She had entrusted a key to her apartment in England to a friend who had kindly agreed to forward her professional journals, urgent bills and any other important mail to the villa. She was surprised to see a postcard falling out from the pile. The photograph on the front of the card was of a marble bust of a woman's face. Sophia's first thought was that of a classical Greek sculpture. Intrigued by who else might be in the Mediterranean or Aegean regions, she turned over to read:

Dear Sophia,

I hope this finds you well. As you have probably realized from the picture on the front of this card, I am writing from the Greek island of Lesvos. I am currently overlooking the majestic mountains and a beautiful expanse of beach. My transition is now complete and I have come here as I believe it is the best place for me to make a new start. I wanted to thank you once again for all of your help over the past few years with 'finding myself'. I am forever grateful for your help and support.

Warmest wishes always,

Brigit x

Sophia noted that the card had been posted two weeks previously. She recognized the signature as belonging to a one-time client of hers. So Brigit had completed the process and was about to make a new life for herself? This was inspiring news. Reading the message once more before taking a closer look at the photograph on the front, Sophia smiled widely and replaced the card respectfully on the table. She had succeeded! Brigit, one of her longer-term clients, had transformed her existence and freed herself up for a whole new future. It seemed that the woman had finally managed to shake off the ghosts of her past and had chosen to live a life which reflected her true values, wishes, dreams and desires. A wave of satisfaction washed over Sophia. She picked up the card again to read the small print. It informed her that the statue featured on the front of the card was an impression of the ancient Greek lyric poet and muse, Sappho.

Pushing aside the pile of mail, she replaced the sunglasses on her face. As she leant back in her soft, comfortable chair, her mind became occupied with memories of her many hours spent with this former client. At their first meeting, Brigit had explained that she was a pre-operative, transgender woman, born as Brian, into a large Irish family living in the East End of London. Through the early years at school she had encountered many torturous incidents of bullying. At home, whilst her father had spent time training her older brothers in the fine of art of becoming a man's man, her mammy had always seemed preoccupied with the arrival of the latest edition to the clan; the soft-featured, sensitive young lad floundered in a world where there seemed to be no mould for him to fit. The school bullies, so adept at sensing the discomfort of the loner, sniffed him out at every opportunity to create misery for him and in doing so, provide easy enter-tainment for the friends they wished to impress. Sophia now recalled the many emotional outbursts during the early sessions as Brigit recalled and eventually resolved the most painful of her memories of her formative days as Brian.

"Why were they so cruel? I hid away so as not to offend them, in the hope they would just forget about me and leave me alone," Brigit had wept. Although there was little that the therapist could do to ease the pain, she listened, responding always with warm compassion. It was during these sessions that Brigit learned of the link between the rejection by others and the subsequent rejection of herself. She understood that that the cruel acts of kids are often their way of transferring the energy of their own bad feelings to others.

"Looking back, I wasn't the only kid having a hard time at home. I guess it was that my way of dealing with it was different from the rest of the boys," Brigit surmised. She acknowledged the many causes of the bad behaviour of others and learned to accept herself in the process.

Sophia had facilitated her client's empowerment; she had guided her to the realization that she wasn't the worthless person upon whom the bullies heaped endless, hurtful names. She was the innocent person inside, seeking shelter from the negativity of the others around her.

"Even when my father and brothers abused me for not standing up for myself, I suppose it was a sign of strength that I refused to be bullied into their way of dealing with things. I knew I was different from a young age. Everyone told me I was wrong, but I was only being me." Brigit had spoken aloud her insights and when Sophia had suggested to her that she might have internalized the voices of others when young and later mistaken them for her own, the notion made perfect sense to her.

"Yes! I always knew the voice inside me was female. It may have been the voice of my mother, but as I grew up there was never a time when it became masculine." Brigit's expression had become deeply thoughtful as she had expressed the realization, "I guess ultimately, underneath of the other voices, mine was sitting quietly, just waiting for a moment to be heard."

Sophia's recall was accurate and detailed. She also had a file of the most poignant research notes to which she could refer. Inspired by the memories, she reached for her notebook and jotted down some notes, before her ideas withered away once more under the hot, Mediterranean sun. The postcard had elicited an epiphany. She had finally decided on a format for her book; she would use the exact words of anonymous clients to illustrate the turning points in their lives. After all, she had documented the precise phrases they used to describe a realization as it dawned on them; how an important decision was made, or when the way suddenly became clear for them and they were able to commit to a desired change in their lives. She noted the many similarities in peoples' thoughts and hoped that by sharing these insights she could clarify some of the issues affecting a wide range of the population. If nothing else, she could let them know that they weren't alone in their suffering. Her words could act as signposts to help the readers; she could, in theory, help to direct many more people to find happiness and contentment in their lives. She would title her book, *'Moments of Truth'*. Sophia wrote the words in bold capitals and underlined them. Finally, the concept of her book was complete and now she could fill it with authentic and unique material. Stretching her arms into the air, she felt a curious lightness in her shoulders and for the first time in months she was able to move her neck more freely.

* * *

Alex arrived at dusk to find a relaxed Sophia sitting on a chair at the edge of the pool. Removing her wrap she draped it over a nearby sun lounger and took the man's hand to walk down the steps into the pool. He sensed something different about her. Watching her traverse the pool, he asked, "Have you been resting? You seem much more relaxed this evening."

"No, Alex, I have been working," she teased. "As you can see, work is good for me!"

Smiling, he replied, "So is rest. It's all about balance, remember?"

It was Sophia's turn to smile as she continued with her gentle strokes. The water was always at its warmest at this time of day;

the glare of the sun had softened into a golden glow and she managed a few extra lengths. She swam until the sun hovered just over the horizon, and feeling stronger, she took one of Alex's hands to climb confidently out of the pool.

"Are we still on for that massage?" she asked as they walked towards the entrance to the villa.

"Yes, of course," he replied earnestly. Sophia wanted to make him smile. He took his work very seriously and his manner was always respectful. She wished for a sign of humour, some evidence of a sense of fun.

"Where do you need me to sit, or lie?" she asked, emerging from the shower, wrapped in a clean towel and gesturing towards the bedroom door.

"Here will be fine," Alex replied, walking into the kitchen and pulling an upright chair away from the table, its wooden legs scraping the tiled floor. Quickly, Sophia turned the chair to face the direction of the sunset, through the open villa door.

"I will just close this, to keep out the insects," Alex announced somewhat irritably, as he shut out the last rays of sun behind the door and flicked on the bright interior light. Sophia closed her eyes. Covering his hands in a fresh minty gel, the physiotherapist gently warned, "This might feel a little cold at first." She took a deep breath and laughed silently; this was not quite the romantic encounter she had envisaged.

* * *

Sophia awoke at dawn with a head full of memories and ideas for her book, which she needed to commit to paper as soon as possible. Reaching for her file of notes full of the painstaking research she had conducted for the benefit of her many clients, she ventured into the kitchen to flick through her writings whilst brewing a pot of coffee. Opening the villa doors, she greeted the beauty of the day, inhaling the scent of fresh pine. Taking three deep breaths, she envisaged the clean and fragrant air permeating her lungs, and being carried to every cell in her body. For a moment she felt new, clear and flooded with light, and wondered if Brigit was experiencing the same sensation; after all, they were both under the same sun. Sitting at the kitchen table, Sophia now looked closely at the doodling in the margins of her notes. Here she had sketched an image of a castle, surrounded by a moat, and a drawbridge in the process of being lowered. She recalled the moment when she had introduced Brigit to the notion that, although individuals, we are also a mixed bag of our own ideas, those absorbed from our nearest, and not necessarily dearest; and those we discern from the wider, collective unconscious. In response, the young woman had rather poetically described the ensuing revelation as the *'lowering of a drawbridge to the cold castle of her imprisonment.'* Wide-eyed, she had glimpsed the fresh horizons of a new world and realized that all she had to do was to brave the treacherous wooden bridge, to trust and tread carefully, and she would avoid immersion in the perilous waters below. Armoured with a new suit of confidence, Brigit had excitedly announced that it was now her turn to venture out into the world to find out exactly who she was.

Sophia had also scribbled her analysis on the page. She had viewed this realization as a major transition point in her client's life, and together they had continued to explore this new perspective. The therapist knew it was important for Brigit to develop her strengths and to acknowledge her individuality. However, she also felt that her client needed to experience acceptance. As such, they discussed the various traditions in different cultures where the gender divide was not always so apparent. Sophia had introduced her client to the traditions of the Indian Hijra Caste, where emasculation and has been common practice amongst several million transsexual people in India and Bangladesh for hundreds of years. The two had also discussed the comparable 'lady boy' culture in contemporary Thailand.

The therapist now cast her mind back to the session where her client informed her about her chosen name. Searching through her notes, she re-read the nature of the conversation between them and the information that she had imparted to her client.

"It was always there, in the back of my mind," Brigit had explained. "Maybe it had something to do with my Celtic roots, but it definitely had a ring of familiarity to it."

"The name is associated with the fifth-century Irish saint and an earlier Pagan deity," Sophia had explained. "She is viewed, quite eclectically, as a goddess and saint of fire, healing and poetry." At the foot of the page, there was a pencil sketch of the four-armed cross of Brigit, believed to invoke the healing process for the people who symbolically stepped inside it during the Celtic fire festival of Imbolc.

"You know that in some circles she has been represented as a virginal saint, and in others a lesbian?" Sophia had explained, watching in the ensuing silence as Brigit's frown turned slowly into an expression of raised eyebrows and eventually an acknowledging nod, as she tried to make sense of it all. The therapist had savoured such moments, when she openly witnessed the deep engagement of her clients with the thera-peutic process.

Sophia continued to sift through her research notes. She read:

'In 1814, the medieval Book of Lismore was discovered at Lismore Castle, in which it was been recorded that St Brigid was in love with another woman saint, Darlughdach, with whom she shared a bed at the convent.

In Kildare, in 1807 the order of Brigidines, Catholic nuns with a difference, was established. They defied convention by mixing into the community and admitting married woman to the organization.

The current Cathedral of St Brigid is said to stand on the original site of the pagan shrine in the shadow of an ancient oak tree.

It seems that the essence of the woman, or the myth, has changed to survive over time. In many of the many stories written about the figure, she quite often appears to be in-between states, never fully fitting one definition or another.'

Pouring a second cup of coffee, the therapist sat at the kitchen table keen to record her ideas for the book, which had been re-activated by her memories of her work with Brigit. Feeling inspired, she wrote:

'In-between, on the edge, just crossing over...reality is in essence a constant of change. Those terms, whilst appearing mutually exclusive, also convey a fundamental truth. Aren't we all, only, forever in a state of liminality? From the first moment when a single cell becomes a fertilized...from a bundle of cells to a recognized human form...from an amphibious foetus to an oxygen breathing infant...from a toddler to a teenager...a daughter to a mother...from lithe sex kitten to stiff, old crone...we are always one crucial heartbeat away from the state of an electrically-charged being, to one of an inert, decaying, and finally, dead entity. How can our state of being ever be regarded as definitive, when in actuality it is forever changing and adapting? Against that vast backdrop of the human condition, how significant a feature is the reassignment of an individual's gender, breakdown of a relationship or a broken bone?'

"*Kalimera,* Sophia!" Alex arrived at the open door of the villa, interrupting the writer's train of thought.

"*Kalimera,* Alex! Is it that time already?" Sophia snapped her head up in response and grimaced in discomfort at the corresponding pain in her back.

"Take it easy!" Alex's smile dissolved at the sight of Sophia's suffering. "Smooth moves, keep it fluid! How are you this morning, Sophia? Are you ready to swim?" Encouragingly he offered her a helping hand. Sophia closed her book and laid down her pen. Stiffly she walked into her bedroom and struggled into her swimming attire, before venturing outside to the pool. Gently stretching under the morning sun, she slipped off her wrap and took the hand of her handsome assistant to step tentatively into the cool, sparkling water.

"Stretch out your abdomen," Alex instructed from the pool side. "Make sweeping strokes with your arms; take them wide and let them pull you through the water. You need to build up a steady pace." Lurching awkwardly for the first couple of lengths, the woman's muscles soon relaxed under the warmth of the sun and she slipped into a comfortable rhythm. The stiffness melted from her joints and she moved more freely. Looking up to Alex for his approval she saw him removing his T-shirt and shorts, to reveal a close-fitting pair of swimming pants.

"What are you doing?" she asked, blinking in the sunlight and focusing her gaze on his tanned, toned chest.

"I am joining you in the water," he replied, stretching both arms into the air and diving effortlessly into the pool. He surfaced alongside her moments later, brushing his wet, floppy, dark hair out of his face.

"This is good," he announced. "Come, swim with me, Sophia!" Alex encouraged her to make large, elegant movements with her limbs and to immerse her face completely in the cool, fresh water. "Feels good, eh?"

Sophia looked in to the clear eyes of her companion, their white sparkle contrasting with the deep brown hue of his irises, the colour of trust. The warmth of their illumination spread through her; she floated along feeling safe in his company. She loved the sense of weightlessness. Since the surgery, her body had often felt awkward and heavy, and now it seemed as if she was learning how to move in a whole new way. Although quite content to float around, she knew that a little discomfort often signalled a strengthening muscle and keen to please Alex, she dipped her face into the water and gently propelled herself forwards.

"How many lengths have you completed?" Alex asked as they surfaced once more in the shallow end of the pool. He gazed at the diamond drops as they sparkled on the shiny black lashes framing her deep blue eyes.

"I've lost count," she laughed, gently brushing away the water with the back of her hand.

"Are you tiring yet? Please stop if you are. It is important that we take this process slowly and steadily." Alex never failed to impress her with his caring and concerned manner. Sophia, feeling warm and relaxed, smiled and gently bit her bottom lip before turning away from his attentive gaze. Standing face to face in the shallow end of the pool, neither wanted to leave the pool, nor the company of the other. She felt there was something that Alex wanted to say to her but for some reason he was holding back.

An awkward silence ensued, broken only when Alex finally announced, "Sophia, you are doing so well. I am very pleased with your progress." The serious professional was back.

Later, in the shade of the fig tree, Sophia sat once more immersed in thought. She had been largely alone for the past year of her life. Having ended a long-term relationship, she had been persuaded to embark on a holiday with some friends in rural France. Here, the course of events had irrevocably changed her life. Whilst out cycling one late summer afternoon, she had slowed her pace and stopped for a drink, whilst her companions raced ahead, soon disappearing out of her sight. As she stood astride her bicycle, swigging on her water bottle, a tourist, unfamiliar with the roads and unaware of the stiff penalties for injuring cyclists, hurtled around the corner in his rented car, crashing into her. Sophia felt only the rushing of air as the sky appeared to drop beneath her; a thud as her toppled body hit the ground, and the crunch of her bones against the warm tarmac. The cycle landed upside down in the overgrowth at the side of the road, its wheels still spinning in the air. The small Citroën had skidded to a halt a few feet in front of her, as she lay zigzagged in the centre of the road. All she could think of was the possibility of someone else taking the corner in the same manner and crushing her beneath their tyres, as she lay paralysed with shock on the ground. The young driver had jumped out of the car and appeared in shock, running around in circles before coming to his senses and rushing to her aid. Meanwhile, his girlfriend had rushed straight to her side, advising Sophia to hold on whilst they waited for medical assistance, trying desperately to press the keys on her mobile phone despite her wildly shaking hands.

Thankfully, Sophia's recall of the whole incident was hazy. She remained semi-conscious and numbed with shock, until the *vehicule de premiers secours* arrived. She had a faint recollection of the sound of hurried instructions, spoken in French, flying around and above her, until her body was painstakingly placed on to a board and lifted into the rear of the rescue vehicle. She regained consciousness, albeit fleetingly, a few hours later, to find herself in a trauma unit where she was told that she was being prepared for surgery. Sophia had moved her head very slowly when asked if she had a husband or partner to be contacted as next of kin, mouthing the word 'no'.

She was still unsure as to whether the supportive smiles on the faces of her friends, gathered around her bedside at that time, was merely a side-effect of the medication. Although they visited her in hospital in the days following the surgery, they had been unable to stay on in the country at the end of the holiday. Sophia had also received one visit from the driver of the car and his girlfriend, both very relieved that she was still alive. The man had been breathalysed at the scene and co-operated fully with the police investigation. As there was no evidence he was exceeding the speed limit, and the cyclist admitted to foolishly stopping just past a blind bend in the road, the incident was regarded as an unfortunate accident amongst holidaymakers. However, it was out of a sense of guilt that the girlfriend noted down their contact details for Sophia to be in touch with them upon her return to England.

"If there's anything we can do to help..." she had implored the recovering patient in her bed, "please don't hesitate to call." Sophia noted the address as somewhere in the northern counties and knew that she, a southerner, was unlikely to ever see these people again, yet thanked them graciously for the offer.

Having to break one of Sophia's ribs and puncture a lung to reach the spine, the surgeon had finally broken into a sweat on discovering an exposed spinal cord at the site of the injury. When the titanium reinforcement of the broken vertebra at the top of her T-spine was announced a success, it came as a major relief for all concerned. The injuries situated down in the lower lumbar region of her back proved rather more problematic and painful, however, as surgery was not indicated to address the minor nature of the damage. The chipped bones were left untouched to allow for the natural healing process. These continued to cause the woman much discomfort. However, she was fortunate that her strong stomach muscles, contracting fiercely to curl her into a ball as she was propelled through the air, had prevented her unprotected head from smashing on the ground. The clean breaks to her right collar bone and wrist were treated with firm strappings and pain-relieving medication.

For the duration of her hospital stay, Sophia had little else to do but listen intently to the language being spoken around her. Her conversational French soon became littered with medical terminology as she endeavoured to keep advised of her own progress. As soon as she was able to travel, she intended to fly home to England. She was advised to contact a physiotherapist upon her return and to remain gently mobile.

It had a been a bleak winter at home, when the patient had closed her curtains on the dark, cold evenings and retired to bed alone, on more occasions than she cared to remember.

As an only child, having lost both parents in a fatal road traffic accident, Sophia had assumed sole responsibility for herself from the age of twenty-two. Her last boyfriend had left in a fury; telling her that she spent all her time in the minds of others to avoid facing her own problems in life. She conceded that there might be an element of truth in his statement, yet, in her view, he quite clearly could not see the bigger picture. She knew there was no going back to him. That would simply be another example of her taking a seat in the rest-room of her reality. As such, allowing him to assist her with the recovery would only cause further complications and so she refused his repeated offers to return to the apartment to help her through her rehabilitation period. She became reliant on the casual workers of a local business providing home care for the elderly and infirm. Despite their warm manner and best intentions, she was still exposing her broken body and tired mind to strangers and was finally forced to face her own fragility.

However, Sophia believed that the events of the past could never be re-scripted. For her, the future was a gloriously blank page. It was the thought of choosing the words to depict the detail of her own life, that kept her morale high and her attention firmly focused on her recovery. She had been rudely knocked over on her own path and was having to pick herself up and tentatively start out again. The brave woman had accepted that she could no longer travel in the fast lane. However, this had never been her preference; she had always chosen a slower, contemplative pace of life. Now she was determined to claw her way up from the curb. She would approach all future obstructions in a positive manner. As for the possibilities of what could happen upon her from behind, in that she could only place her trust in the innate goodness of human nature.

Now, Sophia smiled as she recalled the conversations with Brigit which formed part of her client's post-surgical recovery. Who would have thought that she, the therapist, listening intently to her client's experiences of medical intervention, would soon find herself gazing at her own scars and working through her own physical pain?

Sophia was a humanist, not easily given to spiritual notions, believing that the answers to most existential questions were to be found by looking inside the self. Believing in the ultimate power of the mind to overcome any social and psychological issues, she was now facing the challenge of harnessing the power of her own mind, to successfully adapt her lifestyle to the unexpected changes to her state of health. After all, she told herself, it wasn't as if she was facing death.

Prompted by this sudden realization, she sat up in the afternoon sun and searched her file for notes of the psychotherapy sessions she had conducted with one such client.

Another young woman had come to her initially for help with accepting the changes to her body caused by a double mastectomy. The therapist soon discerned that the brave woman, whilst asking for help to accept the new version of herself, was actually looking for a way to face her impending death. Ella had been diagnosed with terminal breast cancer at the tender age of thirty-two; cursed with the same cruel fate as her mother. Sophia had identified with her client on so many levels, although her incursion into the realms of life after death was unprecedented. Most of her clientele were looking to solve the problems they were currently experiencing in their life. This unique woman was staring the unknown squarely in the face and was consumed only with courage. The detailed notes served to refresh Sophia's memory of their conversation:

"There is one person that I wronged and if it's the last thing I do I want to make it right between us before I go," Ella had explained to her therapist. "Ed did nothing wrong, it was my own discontent which drove me away from him and into the arms of a man who really had no love for me. I wanted an easy life, nice things and I thought that Ed just wasn't going to be the one who could provide them for me. I was shallow. I had no care for what he wanted in life and if I'd stayed with him, given him more of a chance...who knows...things might have turned out differently."

"What was driving you to seek more?" Sophia had asked.

Ella had explained, "My dad left when I was a baby. All I can remember is my mother struggling to provide for us. As a kid, I was resentful that I couldn't have all of the things I wanted, all of the fashion accessories that my friends wore to school. I just always wanted more; I believed that I deserved to have all that I desired. Now, I don't think anyone would ever have been able to give me enough. I just wasn't thinking like that at the time. I would just like to tell Ed that it wasn't him, he didn't do anything to destroy our marriage; it was me. I take full responsibility for the breakdown of the relationship."

"How do you think Ed would feel if you got in touch now?" Sophia had asked.

"It's been seven years since I left and we got divorced," Ella thought aloud. "We parted on bad terms and have not been in touch at all during that time. I know he moved to the flat above the butcher's shop when the house was repossessed. If he's moved on from there I'm not sure if I will be able to find him. I have just this one last chance."

Concerned that Ella might not have success with this, her final wish, Sophia had asked gently, "So what's the worst thing that could happen...that you can't find him? What if he has moved on and he refuses to meet with you...how might that feel?"

Ella, clearly having considered all possibilities, spoke with conviction, "The worst outcome would be if he refuses to listen to me, but that will be his choice and at least I will have tried."

Sophia had heard nothing further from Ella.

Now, the brave woman's words echoed around in her mind. She scribbled down the words, *'choice'*; *'responsibility'* and *'one last chance.'* Where many people might have felt resentment at their fate, cheated by the cruel events of their lives, Ella's strength lay in her understanding and acceptance of her state. In truth, Sophia realized that the false sense of security of the perpetuation of life as we know it, which afflicts the living, is in fact as much a blank canvas as the advent of death, and she wrote:

'Not one of us can be sure of the shape of our future life.

We have no control over who will feature as important players in the drama of our daily lives; we cannot be sure that our loved ones will choose to stay around or that our precious children will outlive us.

We simply cannot predict with any certainty as to the circumstances in which we will find ourselves, or when unexpected events might crash their way into our lives.

We cannot see into the future in any way and such belief in our ability to do so is clearly an illusion.

We are free to choose our companions and trust our senses; we can pick ourselves up when we stumble, and we have the power of both mind and body to continue the walk.'

Sophia had lost all track of time. Rising from the garden chair she went inside the villa to check the clock. It was nearly four. Alex had failed to show up for her lunchtime swim. Checking her mobile phone she could see no message or missed call from him. She was a little confused. Was it something she had said, or done? No, of course not! She reasoned he had simply been delayed. A slight panic set in as she thought of him driving his moped on the winding mountain roads. What if there had been an accident? Sophia quickly checked and rationalized her thoughts. The chances of such an incident occurring was highly unlikely. However, she was all too aware of the strength of her feelings, at the thought of Alex not arriving at her door. She quickly reassured herself that he would call around later, in time to supervise her evening swim.

* * *

As she stepped out from the pool later that evening, once more feeling tentative and alone, Sophia knew that something unexpected had happened in Alex's world. It was unlike him not to show up and in the silence her fears were sounding louder in her mind. Her only concern was for his wellbeing. Should she call him? Something was stopping her.

Standing in the warm shower, she covered herself generously with the jasmine-scented cream, massaging herself gently and deliberately in a soothing, circular motion. Sophia consciously and carefully moisturized her body, concentrating on the areas of previously broken skin and bone. However her thoughts kept coming back to him.

Stepping out from the shower, she reached out to the rail to find only a towel damp with pool water. She remembered that a fresh supply of towels had been laid on the bed, by the house-keeper, earlier that day. Placing the used towel on the floor, naked, she stepped out of the shower and walked into the adjoining bedroom to select a clean towel from the pile. Something in the mirror on the wall at the foot of the bed caught her eye. It was the reflection of Alex, standing in the hallway, looking into the bedroom through the open doorway. He cast his eyes to the floor and quickly turned away, muttering an apology; whilst Sophia's cheeks flushed red. Quickly she gathered up a clean towel and her clothes and returned to the bathroom. She knew he had seen her, all of her, including the large, unsightly scar which cruelly twisted its way around her torso. It was no longer the original angry shade of red and had even started to fade in places. However, she knew the memory of the accident would forever be etched both in her mind and on her body. Firmly, Sophia reminded herself that any notion of physical perfection was just a powerful illusion and that acceptance was always the first step towards happiness. However, it was the fear of rejection which now pervaded her body and mind.

Once dressed, she garnered the courage to face her fears and found Alex pacing up and down outside the villa.

"I'm sorry," he started to apologize.

"I wasn't expecting you," an awkward Sophia explained, "I thought you weren't coming…"

"I should have called, I am sorry," Alex continued gesturing with both hands, as if asking for forgiveness.

"I was worried…" the words seemed to find their own way out of her mouth as their eyes met.

"I was at the hospital, I could not call earlier," the troubled man started to explain. "There was a client in the gym, he collapsed and I had to go with him to the hospital. It was a heart attack, the doctors said, and they asked me what exercises he was doing and how it happened."

"Oh, Alex," Sophia could now see the fear and sadness in the young man's eyes. "How awful! Was there anyone else with him, a wife, or a girlfriend?"

"He was on holidays with his family. He seemed so healthy, and said he felt well. There were no signs of any problems with his heart. The doctors said they are sure it was not as a result of anything I did. A post-mortem will show exactly what happened. But still, I was there and I saw him in pain and struggling to breathe. By the time his wife and their son arrived it was too late…" Tears welled up in Alex's deep, brown eyes. With outstretched arms Sophia held him gently at the tops of his arms. She was shocked to see him looking so dishevelled. Taking him by the hand, she led him to sit at the garden table.

"You have had a shock, sit here. I'll get you a drink. What will you have?"

"Whatever you may have to offer," he accepted, gratefully. As he sipped on a glass of Metaxa, Alex talked about the events of the day and Sophia was content to slip into listening mode. She acknowledged his fear and nodded supportively at his explanations of his actions.

"I came straight here, as soon as I could," he informed her as his account of the day's events drew to a close.

"What about your family?" asked Sophia. "Have you called them? Will they be worried about you?" She wondered why he had not returned home. Alex explained that during the summer months he worked extra hours and so his absence from the family home this evening would not be unusual.

"I have a large family. Two of my sisters still live at home, with their families. I have four nieces and a baby nephew. Believe me, they will not miss me!" The image of a loud, happy family gathering around a large table appeared in Sophia's mind.

"My brothers also live close by with their families and so the house is always full of people," Alex continued. "When I have enough money from my business I will find a place of my own."

With the image of a family table laden with fresh, colourful food still vibrant in her mind's eye, Sophia spoke her thoughts aloud, "You must be hungry. Can I make you something to eat?"

Seemingly calmer now, Alex explained that he would be happy for some bread and olives to soak up the alcohol. He accompanied her into the kitchen where he also chose some tomatoes, feta cheese and vine leaves to make up a small meze. Sophia lit two candles in the lanterns on the garden table and the two sat down to eat in the warmth of the muted evening light, against the backdrop of the sunset, to the soundtrack of the cicadas in the tree.

As they chatted about their feelings and ideals, Alex joked between mouthfuls of his meal, "Now I am the patient and you are the therapist."

Sophia smiled shyly in response. "I am more than happy to

help you," she replied, pouring herself another glass of wine.

"Did you know that your name, Sophia, means 'wisdom' in Greek?" he asked. "It suits you well. You are very wise. Your parents chose well."

Sophia explained that her parents were no longer alive and that unlike Alex, she had been an only child. "My work has been my life, the clients my family," she explained. "Some people just couldn't understand that."

"Your work is important to you. This is a good thing. It's a service to...man..." For the first time she watched him struggle to find the correct English translation to express his thoughts in her language.

"Humanity?" she volunteered.

"Yes, thank you, a service to humanity," Alex repeated. "It is good to serve, to help. There is no higher purpose than to help our fellow man."

"Or woman," Sophia added.

"Yes, and woman," Alex corrected himself.

"And what is the meaning of your name, Alex?" Sophia asked.

"Alexandros, it means leader, defender of men," he replied.

"Alexander the Great!" she noted.

"I am no conqueror or empire builder," Alex smiled. "I am interested in the people of my own village, the wellbeing of my family and of the local community." Sophia saw the spark in his eyes as he spoke of his passion.

"I can see how proud you are of your heritage. I like that you have such a strong sense of identity," she stated, warmly.

Alex smiled and nodded in acknowledgement of her comment. "What will you do when your recovery is complete?" he asked. "Will you return to work in England?"

"I guess so," replied Sophia. "I have an apartment in Brighton, by the seafront, a psychotherapy practice and some friends there. But I am not yet ready to leave Cyprus. I love the warmth of your beautiful island. I am thinking about staying on for another few weeks. I am going to make enquiries to see if I can rent this villa for another month or so." For the first time that evening Sophia saw a smile spread across Alex's face.

"This is good," he said.

"I'm not saying that I expect you to continue calling around as often," she added hastily, "I think I am finally making good progress."

"Yes you are," he replied, sitting back in his seat. The sun had now set and the moonlight was shining through the leaves of the fig tree overhead. "Your progress is steady and this is good. But I will still need to call around to check up on you." He spoke with a serious expression on his face. "After all, you are the most beautiful of all my clients," he added, with a surprising, moonlight twinkle in his eye.

Sophie's world seemed to stand completely still in the midst of an inexplicable, magical moment. She felt as if another dimension was simply shaping up around her and effortlessly enveloping her being. For the first time Sophia became aware of a sense of existence outside of the human plane. She could not rationalize or explain it. However, she knew it was real.

* * *

"It was at this moment that I realized I had fallen in love with Sophia," Alex announced to the guests at their wedding breakfast, one year later. "That day, we had a meeting of minds and then of our hearts. It was a few weeks later that I returned home and we had a meeting of the family, who of course fell in love with her too."

A ripple of laughter spread amongst the English guests, who had journeyed to the Mediterranean island to join in the celebrations with their friend, now sitting around a large table, in a clearing amidst the olive trees in the grove of Alex's family home. "I just hope that Sophia's love of this place and my people will last, at least for a lifetime," Alex continued, raising his voice for it to be heard above the laughter of the children of the large family, who, already bored with the proceedings, were running around, noisily, whilst their parents sat, animatedly chatting amongst themselves.

In contrast, his comment was met with a respectful silence from the English guests, yet Sophia knew that all eyes were on her. She simply smiled and announced, "I am very happy living and working here, thank you. I am very grateful for all of the kindness shown to me by Alex and his family."

"Of course we have moments of disagreement also," Alex interrupted. "But that is usually when I use the wrong word when trying to speak in English. Sophia's Greek is also much better than mine," he joked. "She has to learn all of the psychological terms to translate her book, '*Moments of Truth*' into the Greek, '*Steegmess tees Aleethsias,*' so that her Cypriot family may now also read it and know how beautiful she really is."

Sophia beamed at this comment, her happiness illuminating the faces of those looking at her. For this one moment in time, in truth, she sensed no need for words.

Goodnight Girl

The dark demons were conspiring to keep Charis awake for the third night in succession. This was proving especially irksome, as she needed to feel fresh the next morning. She wanted to appear enthusiastic at the job interview. In truth, her energy levels were already running on reserve; her job had descended into monotony, her marriage was staid and her husband's ritual snores had become amplified in the dark hours. She just could not close her eyes and calm her bubbling brain. She crept out of bed and crossed the apartment into their home office, intending to read through her CV once more and try to anticipate questions from the board of interviewers. The process was unlikely to throw up any questions. She was a seasoned PA, but it always paid to be prepared. However, after booting up the computer, an unexpected email caught her attention. Scanning through the usual suspects, she focused her gaze on the entry of a message from a sender named 'Nate.' She gasped at the sight of the name. Surely it couldn't be him?

Nathan E. Brandt was someone from her past. At one time they had been very close; a stab of realization reminded her of the distant, yet still painful parting. She rationalized that he could do nothing to hurt her now and that she should merely consign the unopened message to the trash folder. However, her heart was beating like a drum and her brain was refusing to acknowledge reason. She clicked open the message. It read:

'Hey, hello, how are you?

Long-time no see/speak. I know it's been a while but I've just got back online and thought I'd let you hear my side of the story.

Of course the press have gone to town on this one and I just wanted you to know the truth.

It was not as dramatic as they made out and in fact there is no evidence to suggest that it was a deliberate act. However, as usual, everything had spun widely out of control by the time the story of my poisoning hit the headlines.

The woman concerned is already receiving psychiatric care and as I should make a full recovery, I don't see the point in pressing charges. The police are baying for blood but I don't believe in stirring things up out of spite. The poor woman was clearly out of her mind.

As long as she stays away from me I will be happy. Anyway I'll be in the hospital for the rest of this week. Discharge is likely to take place on Friday. I am being asked if there is anyone who can keep a close eye on me for a while. I'm living in Campbell Green Walk these days which, if you're still in the area, is just a few streets away from you. I can walk, although I'm re-learning some of the other functions that got switched off in my brain during the coma. The prognosis is for a full recovery but they are reluctant to release me unless I can demonstrate that there will be someone there for me, in the case of an emergency.

I know it's a big ask, and I won't be offended if you are just not able to help me out on this occasion. The truth is I just couldn't think of anyone, apart from you, that I could trust enough to approach at this time.

I sincerely hope you are well and happy and I would so love to hear from you, if you ever get to read this...

Yours, in love,

Always, Nate x'

Charis realized she was holding her breath and let out a deep sigh.

She had read nothing about Nathan in the press lately. She had no knowledge of the events he was referring to. In fact she had not seen or heard from him for the last ten years. However, his life seemed to have progressed just as she predicted. They had once been very close and their parting had been painful. It appeared, from the events that he described, that he had finally crossed the wrong woman, one who was obviously more danger-ously narcissistic than himself.

Charis' thoughts were not born from jealousy or rejection. She believed that she and Nate had once shared the most intense and complete love, that was until she had discovered a horde of other women who had also experienced such passion with him; each predictably becoming irate upon learning about the existence of their contemporaries. When Charis was with Nate, she thought the two were exclusively in their secret bubble of urgency and excitement. In their time together she felt absorbed into his world and the memories pervaded her mind even when they were apart. She simply could not imagine life without him. However, she was devastated when he faded out of her private life with false promises and curious absences. He had taken a part of her away with him; she became drained of energy and her life became devoid of any joy.

It had been so difficult for her to continue working with him, fielding calls from his ever-increasing harem of faithful, female followers. However, she wanted to prove herself the consummate professional, and so continued in her role as his personal assistant, assuming her responsibilities with dignity and self-respect. From the moment she had learned of his promiscuity she had pulled back from sharing any intimacy with him, despite his repeated attempts to bed her. Some seven years passed in this manner, with Charis biting her lip at his vitriolic outbursts; distancing herself from him emotionally when he was chasing yet another pretty girl and, much to his frustration, disengaging from him on the occasions he endeavoured to seduce her.

The deadlock of this depressing dance was finally broken by the arrival on the scene of one particularly powerful woman. Mylene, the haughty actress and model, took an instant dislike to Charis and persuaded the guru that he no longer had any use for his faithful personal assistant. Her intervention had proved to be a blessing in disguise. Despite the initial blow to her self-esteem and bank account, Charis soon found herself floating in offers of jobs and friendships. She took some time out to reassemble her fragile sense of self and soon found a love with Grant, with whom she felt safe and secure.

However, now he was back in her life and she couldn't deny the burning desire to see him once more. Charis knew she would be playing with fire, but she couldn't stop herself from typing a reply:

'What a surprise to hear from you, Nate. I hadn't read anything in the press and so had no idea of what had happened to you. How long have you been living in this area? I'm surprised we haven't bumped into one another. Which hospital are you in?
Charis x'

She agonized over the 'x', but finally reassured herself that he would only take it as a gesture of friendship. Now, her heart was pounding and conflicting thoughts were ringing around her head. She reassured herself that things were different now; she was a much stronger woman. She feared only that the lack of sleep, coupled with this adrenaline rush was the perfect mixture for a migraine. It was 4:30 a.m. and there was no point in going back to bed. She trod quietly along the polished oak floor and headed into the kitchen for a cup of tea and some analgesics. Watching the sun rise over the city rooftops, she recalled the first time she had met Nate:

"You expect me to go on my own?" Charis had been shocked at the mere thought.

"I'm really sorry but this cold is really heavy, I've got the shivers and aching limbs. I'm so sorry, I so wanted to go to this workshop," her friend Laura had snuffled. "I've been sipping Echinacea and raspberry tea all night. I haven't slept a wink."

Charis had felt unnerved. The workshop had been her friend's idea; Laura her lively, new workmate had taken her to the 'Sunny Souls, Shining Spirits' festival earlier that month and a whole new world had opened up to Charis. She had enjoyed participating in the sample yoga workshop and listening to the lively speeches of the many health and wealth gurus. When Laura had told her she had tickets to a local workshop featuring Nathan E. Brandt, one of the speakers who had caught their attention at the festival, Charis had reminded herself of her promise to be more open to new experiences and she had agreed to go with her friend.

As she recalled his hypnotic presentation, she toyed with the rose quartz pendant she had recently bought. The lady attending the stall selling the crystals had promised that it would bring her love. The young Charis knew she would have to overcome her shyness if she ever had the chance of attracting a boyfriend. A couple of unsatisfactory, drunken encounters with lads during her student days had never amounted to anything nearing a relationship. On becoming a sales assistant in a large fashion house, she was forced to pay more attention to her appearance. Although she refused to adopt some of the more extreme beauty regimes of her colleagues, she had become aware of both her assets and her less attractive traits, and she was rapidly learning how to focus on her strengths. She had asked for promotion which meant she would work behind the scenes, assisting the departmental manager with administrative tasks where she felt that she would be more successful.

Taking a deep breath, she had advised her friend to rest and assured her that she would tell her all about the experience.

Charis had also promised she would ask Nate for a dedication and signature on his newest paperback, *'Love it, leave it and let it be'* on Laura's behalf. After all, she would find it easier to speak to him, if it was on behalf of someone else.

Charis recalled choosing a pair of loose-fitting linen trousers and a plain, white fitted T-shirt. She had worn her shoulder-length, sandy-coloured curls loose, adding a light covering of leave-in conditioner. Despite suggestions from her friends to cut and bleach her hair, to 'make a statement', Charis had believed that her natural softness could speak for itself. It proved to be an enduring belief, as her look, some twenty years later was still very clean and understated. She remembered spraying her wrists and neck with her favourite fruity fragrance before applying a light base of complexion-perfecting cream and some nude lip gloss to her plump lips. The lashes of her large brown eyes were easily brought to life with slightest touch of mascara applied only to their tips. Charis smiled to herself as remembered looking intently in the mirror telling her reflection to relax. She still did it now, under times of stress.

Arriving at the hotel which was hosting the workshop, Charis had nervously asked for the location of the event and was ushered into a large conference room. As the door opened, she saw a carpet covered with cross-legged girls and women, chattering and laughing amongst themselves. She had quickly found a space to sit down. Conscious of her sole status she had fumbled about in her bag for her diary, as not so many people had carried mobile phones in those days. She had flicked through the pages, whilst chewing on the end of her pencil, as if contemplating serious commitments. When a revered silence crept around her, she looked up to see Nate, a man in his prime, striding into the room. Confident and tanned, he beamed a wide, gleaming smile, whilst his sparkling eyes eagerly scanned the adoring faces in the crowd. With a shrug of false modesty, he firstly thanked the crowd for turning up and stated that he hoped to live up to their great expectations of him. As a young woman of just twenty-one, Charis, along with every other young female in the room had already fallen for his act.

When she came to recount the happenings at the event to Laura, she could remember very little of the day. Once their eyes had locked, Charis had been flooded with excitement which appeared to interfere with her memory. At the book signing, she had not considered whether the 'accidental' touching of their hands had actually been intentional on his part. Neither had she questioned that their meeting in the hotel foyer was anything but incidental. The rest of the night was a dreamy blur. Yes, she had agreed to some drinks in the hotel bar, where he had asked about her job and announced that he was looking for a new personal assistant; and then to dinner in a small and intimate Italian restaurant, just a short walk away from the hotel. Here, across the table as he poured her a large glass of Chianti, she had admired his dark glossy waved hair and piercing blue eyes. As he looked into hers, commenting on their deep, velvet, brown beauty, she blushed self-consciously. Although she was sober enough to know it would not be a good idea to accept his invitation to accompany him to his hotel room at the close of the evening, it wasn't her mind making the decisions that night.

Charis felt a familiar stirring and a sudden rush of excitement, as she recalled his strong embrace and ardent desire. He had known exactly how to please her, and in the dark hours, for the first time in her life she had felt like the only girl in his world. Never before had she felt so desired by another and so consumed by the experience. Nate invoked a fundamental awakening in her; life had changed forever as a result of their intimacy. For Charis, there was no looking back. However, the following morning he had seemed irritated at her presence and anxious for her to leave the room. She had given him her home telephone number and, whilst appearing distracted, he had said he would call her about the job. She had thought his manner a little odd, but still enraptured by the evening's events she made an allowance for his busy schedule. As they parted, Charis truly believed that he would call. Late that night, unnerved by the conspicuous lack of communication from him she called the hotel to be told he had checked out.

A week passed and she started to doubt her memory and then her judgement. However, as he had been so vociferous about his workshop tour, she knew the time and place of his next appearance. Without sharing with Laura any account of her intimacy with him, she had bought the tickets for both of them to attend the event.

His cool response to her when they came face to face at the next week's workshop filled her with a sense of shame and self-doubt. She thought that something special had happened between them and yet he treated her as if they strangers. Charis had been so relieved to have Laura at her side. Avoiding his face for the rest of the event, she had busied herself when Laura had ventured up to speak with him, not realizing that her friend had offered up both of their services to help out with unofficial marketing of his appearances and his books at an upcoming festival. When he had shown a romantic interest in her best friend, Charis had advised her to beware of him. However, her words of wisdom had not been heeded and an impulsive Laura had dived straight into bed with him. Charis had tried to hide her jealousy, but when the short-lived affair ended as abruptly as it had started, Laura simply moved on to a new job and a new set of friends. Weakly, Charis had stayed around in the background, helping out with the marketing and administration of her guru's business. An astute Nate soon realized her value and began once more to pay her attention. However, more women came, and when disillusioned with the flawed guru, they left. When her face was the most familiar in his entourage, he asked her to work for him in an official capacity and she accepted. For a few months she was again the centre of his world and she believed she had made the right choice in sticking around. However, she was once again dropped without warning when someone new came on the scene. It was a pattern she recognized after a few months and yet it took years for her to finally overcome.

Now, the sounds of the early morning stirrings of her husband in the house jolted her back into the present. Charis switched into auto pilot and started to prepare breakfast. After the usual coffee and French croissants, Grant had kissed her cheek tenderly and left for the bank. She showered and dressed in readiness for the upcoming interview. However, she could not wash the thoughts of Nate and his plight out of her mind.

* * *

In her pristine white shirt and crisp, stylish suit she looked out of place as she passed the old men in beds on the hospital ward. Most of them looked up briefly on hearing the echoing click of her heels on the polished floor. One solitary, familiar voice called out her name, "Charis? Is that you?"

She turned around and retraced her steps. She looked in the direction of the voice, searching the name cards placed above the beds for a 'Nathan E. Brandt'.

Shocked at the sight of the pale, drawn face weakly smiling up at her, she asked, "Nate?"

She barely recognized the thin, balding man. His once sparkling eyes were now sunken, and he was cloaked in an air of bewilderment. Charis approached his bedside and he beckoned her to take a seat on the sturdy chair placed alongside a trolley on wheels. On which she noticed a compact laptop computer.

"Charis, how wonderful it is to see you! How are you? You look amazing! How kind of you come."

"I'm well, thank you," Charis replied. "How are you doing?" She lowered her voice as she spoke and threw a glance around the room.

"Oh I've been in here for months now. Everyone knows my story. It's just a bit of a joke."

In that moment Charis caught a glimpse of the man she knew; always at the centre of attention.

"So now you're well enough to go home?" Charis' expression betrayed her scepticism.

"I've been on this ward for over a month now. I was unconscious in ITU before here, where they tested to see what was causing the shutdown of my organs. They realized it was the poison in my bloodstream. By the time I came back to consciousness I was akin to a stroke patient. I had to learn to talk and walk again. I have made good progress." Charis' eyes filled up with tears and she bit her lip. Nate noticed and grabbed her hand. "It's okay now, it's over. I'm going to be fine."

"Why?" It was all Charis could manage to say, for fear of bursting into sobs.

Nate took a deep breath. "It's a long story. I first met her on a retreat in Indonesia three years ago. She was a participant, but she stood out as a strong character from the start. I know you won't believe this but I just wasn't interested in having anything other than a professional relationship with her. I had actually been in therapy for sex addiction and I was starting to look at things in a different way." He paused, waiting for her reaction. Charis nodded in acknowledgement and he continued, "She pushed and pushed for it and in the end, well, we got together. I thought it would end when we both left Bali. But she wouldn't let it drop. I told her that I wasn't ready for a relationship, but she just wouldn't go away. She was so aggressive, I swear, she scared me into seeing her again. And I guess there was no one else on the scene. Everyone had gone their own way. It started when you left. Since then, my life gradually fell apart at the seams."

"What about Mylene?" Charis asked. She shivered at the memory of the six-foot blonde who had stamped her way into Nate's life, kicking many of his acquaintances to the side-lines in the process.

"Once she had forced you and everyone else out of my life, she left too..." Nate replied. "After that, my confidence hit an all-time low, the work dried up and after a one night stand with a high-risk partner, I knew I had to get some help."

"You got tested?" Charis failed to conceal her alarm.

"Yeah, I took all sorts of tests, and went into treatment." Nate shrugged.

"So you were healthy and happy until you met this woman?" Charis continued the story.

"Yes, I was, or I thought so, until I got mixed up with her," Nate confirmed. "Things soon spiralled out of control. She was so obsessed with me, paranoid that I would cheat on her. I told her I had been in rehab, but she just couldn't trust me, even though I was really working when I said I was. I just didn't have the time or energy to see anyone else. She just wouldn't believe me and kept accusing me of leaving her. I guess the poisoning was her way of gaining control of the situation, of stopping me going away, making me dependent on her. And if I had managed to leave, I wouldn't have been with anyone else for very long..."

Tears trickled down Charis' face. Nate was just a shadow of his former self. She felt so sad for him. How could it have come to this? What had happened to the handsome, confident man she had fallen so deeply in love with all those years ago? She began to wonder if she had made a mistake in coming here.

"Aren't you going to press charges? She could do the same thing to another person," reasoned Charis.

"She's in hospital. She checked herself in. I don't think she's a danger to anyone now, except herself," Nate replied. He had clearly made up his mind on the subject. "I really don't see the point of dragging it all out in the world's press. Can you imagine it? Just think of the trial coverage for a start..." Charis couldn't see it making the headlines. Nate was not the 'A' list celebrity he had once been. Did he know the truth? Or was he so delusional so as to think the world was still watching him? The truth was that his popularity had peaked over ten years ago. After damning video footage surfaced of a drunken and lascivious Nate, slamming shots at a bar in Mexico with a scantily clad troop of twenty-somethings, the Family Health Food company had pulled its sponsorship. The hotel chain stopped hosting his guru events and the American publishers of his series of 'Love life-Live life' books, who promoted an ethos of 'clean living,' failed to renew his contract.

However, even under these circumstances, he still had the knack of drawing her into his world. On this occasion it was with compassionate love. Charis too had sought counselling to help figure out her time with Nate. She had learned to look at people from an angle of 360 degrees and to break the cycle of interdependence. And now, for the first time, she felt that she had more of a grip on life than the international lifestyle guru Nathan E. Brandt. She had developed an interest in relationship issues and had read much on the subject of attachment theory. It had helped her understand how she viewed the world and some of the reasons why people sometimes chose to behave in a hurtful manner. Telling him that she had, earlier that day, attended an interview for a new job, she explained that she would have to wait to find out whether the position was hers and the hours she would be obliged to work, before she could commit to helping him out. However, she promised that she would try all of her contacts to see if anyone could suggest a suitable carer. Standing up she leaned over to hug her old friend, now looking as if he had lived out in full, each and every second of his fifty-five years.

"I'll come back later in the week," she promised, as he seemed reluctant to release his hold on her.

"Thank you." His gratitude was palpable.

Her mind fired up with a hundred questions as she walked away. *What really happened? And why was he so reluctant to press charges? Has he told me the truth? Was he hiding anything from me?*

Just a couple of emails, one short hospital visit, and Nate was once more occupying the fullness of her mind. Should she tell Grant? Charis justified the fact that there had been no time at breakfast to tell her husband about the emails and the visit to the hospital had been a spur-of-the-moment decision. She would tell him as soon as she got home. He would help her make sense of it all. She had met the well-groomed Grant on the rebound from Nate, and in his calm and controlled manner he had helped her through the difficult times.

Over dinner, Grant commented on Charis' aloof manner and asked if there was anything bothering her.

"I'm just a little anxious about this morning's interview," she tried to dismiss his concern.

"The position is for a personal assistant to the chief executive of 'Soul Awakenings,' a boutique, spiritual publisher recently acquired by a mainstream publishing house. If I got it, I would have to split my time between the London and New York offices."

Charis had advised the interview panel that such a schedule would not be a problem. Although optimistically cautious, she felt she had made an impression at the interview and the panel seemed to have warmed to her. However, she did not want to jinx the outcome. Grant's smooth face became creased. He was sullen. He did not like the idea of her travelling alone.

"It would become second nature," she assured him. "Just like catching a train. And the time apart will allow us the space to appreciate each other and to enjoy what we do have together."

"We already appreciate each other," he had retorted. "We have things sorted. I love our life; so many of my friends are envious of our lifestyle." The truth was that Grant's life was planned out, for the two of them. He liked his weekday routine of bank business meetings over lunch and squash tournaments with his colleagues after work. He was always home for dinner and he expected Charis to be there. Grant had not wanted a family. He liked everything to look and feel new, and that included his home and car. His clothes were perfectly creased, his hair always combed, his complexion moisturized and smooth. Children were messy, expensive and tiring in his view. He liked his workday routine and weekends with his wife in country spa hotels. There was no allocation in the budget for maternity leave or nursery furnishings.

At first Charis had acquiesced. She had been in no hurry to become a mother at the outset of their relationship. However, now aged thirty-nine, she was tiring of the stifling routines and seemed to be surrounded by the constant chatter of childbirth. A recent conversation with Grant about taking a career break to start a family had resulted only in tense silences and sulks. Applying for the new job was the only way she knew how to inject some energy into the drone-throb of her existence; until she had received the email from Nate.

Despite soaking in a lavender-perfumed bath and drinking some camomile tea, Charis found herself unable to sleep again that night. The events described by Nate were playing on her mind. If they had, as he said, made headline news then she was sure their squalid detail would not have passed her by. Typing his name into the website search engine she waited for the various links to appear on screen. She was sure the tabloids would have some lurid coverage of it. There was nothing on the first page, so she clicked on the consecutive pages. The only article she found was a six-month-old entry in an online celebrity gossip magazine 'Buzz!' It read:

'Celebrity health- food chef, Carolyn Carlton, suffering from anxiety and depression according to her agent, checks into rehab after boyfriend Nathaniel Brand alleges domestic abuse. Brand, a one-time lifestyle guru disputes the allegations that his hospital admission followed a drink and drugs binge. He is no longer residing at the chef's Chelsea home.'

So *she*, who he seemed reluctant to identify, was a bigger celebrity than *he*. And the news article couldn't even use his correct name! Charis set to thinking. So he was still twisting the facts to suit his own version of a story. The story contained no reference to allegations of poisoning and there did not seem to be any further coverage. Charis clicked onto the chef's website and checked out her biography. It seems she was a regular feature writer for *'Fruit First'*, a popular magazine for advocates of juicing and smoothie-making. She had also published two recipe books, one for super-food salads and another titled, *'Raw foods: The natural way to spice up your love life.'* Charis could see why Nate would be attracted to her; she had good looks, money and status. No doubt his taking a flat in her own neighbourhood was as a direct result of being thrown out of Carolyn's stylish Chelsea home.

Initially she felt angry at him for telling her a pack of lies. The memories of the many instances of his dishonesty over the years now came flooding back. She fought them with the skills she had developed during her counselling sessions. She could now see quite clearly how his distorted thoughts were reinforced by those around him. She had never heard Nate speak about his early experiences; in fact it often seemed to her as if he was forever reliving his childhood. Charis guessed that his actions were symptomatic of an individual who had not emotionally developed further than his teenage years. Over the seven-year period that she worked with him, she had witnessed his dalliances with pretty girls morphing into an obsession with successful women. It seemed as if he never wanted to grow up. Nate didn't want to take the responsibility for himself, let alone anyone else in his life. She guessed that explained how he had remained alone, unmarried and childless.

Yes, it was obvious that he had not changed, despite his claims to have signed himself up for sex-addiction therapy. Nate was still as self-absorbed as ever, interested only in what and who could him help to further his career. It was clear that he still manipulated people to get whatever he wanted. As she seethed at the computer, an email from him entered her inbox.

Sorely tempted to delete it, she nonetheless still experienced a compulsion to open it. It read:

'Dearest Charis

I was so surprised and so very pleased to see you today. Thank you for taking the time to come and see me. I just wish we'd had longer to talk… You really look great, the years have been kind to you and of course you have always had that timeless, natural look. It's hard to believe that we haven't seen each other nor spoken over the last ten years. I know that is largely my responsibility. As I explained, it was not only you that Mylene pushed out of my life. She wasn't content until I had absolutely no more friends left. She also bullied her way into my business and upset so many of my contacts that no one wanted to work with me. And as for her contacts, well it seems she had already alienated herself from the world of film. I now suspect she over-exaggerated the extent of her 'friends' in the industry. I only ever saw her in a couple of low-budget made-for-TV movies and some of those, quite frankly, bordered on soft porn. When the work dried up she called me a 'loser' and left me for some celebrity fitness trainer. I had always had my suspicions about them. Somehow, I don't think the sweat she worked up was always as a result of pounding the treadmill.

Anyway, enough of that and more about you; how have you been all of this time? We hardly had the chance to chat yesterday. I'm glad that you felt able to come and see me. I was afraid that I had lost you forever. We worked so well together, you really were my rock. No one else has ever come close to understanding me the way you did. I really am so sorry for the way things ended between us. I have regretted it every day of my life.

I'm looking forwards to seeing you later in the week, if your work and home life afford you the time to visit.

Yours, in love,
Always, Nate'

Damn him! Why had he re-appeared now? She had a clear image of him sitting, alone, in his hospital bed; from which he had crept in through one of the cracks in her seemingly smooth life. If she was to be completely honest with herself, she could identify the first time she had questioned whether her marriage and work were fulfilling her. Now the fissures loomed larger than ever, even when she closed her eyes to the realities of her life, the magnifying glass of her conscience was revealing deep crevices.

It was with a heavy heart that Charis attended her second interview. She so wanted this job. She had seen it as an escape route from the stultifying existence. Now she was unsettled; unsure as to her true feelings and annoyed at herself for once more getting caught up in the dramatic world of Nate Brandt. Beneath her polite smiles and composed exterior her emotions were running amok. Memories she believed to have been long buried under her stable marriage and safe job choices were unearthing at the most inappropriate times and in unexpected ways. She even found herself thinking of ways she could help Nate to get back on his feet, if she was offered a position with this publishing house. So caught up in the many possibilities she had floating around in her mind, Charis almost missed the moment that she was tentatively offered the post.

"Of course you will have to be prepared to leave at short notice, but what you're saying, *Charis*, it seems that that won't be a problem for you."

Her full attention was restored at the sound of her own name.

"Of course, I'm really excited about this opportunity," she replied. "Especially because of the travelling involved..."

"Well there's nothing glamorous about arriving, jet-lagged, after a night flight and having to start the day again," the only woman on the board piped up.

Charis flashed a knowing smile. "I'm sure it will have its challenges," she acknowledged. "I'm prepared for them."

The thin-faced, pinched-nose woman nodded as she noted down the comments.

Charis had researched the location of the offices on Park Avenue in New York. She pre-empted the 'raising questions' section of the interview by asking some practical questions.

Such as the transfer times from La Guardia as opposed to Newark airport and the location of the company's apartment. They were basic enquires but at least it showed she had given the venture some thought. The pinched-nose woman curled her thin lips in response. Charis wasn't entirely sure it was in approval. She switched her attention to the others, whilst awaiting a response. It was clear that most of the interview panel had warmed to her.

With the promise of a contract to be emailed to her for signing later that day, Charis agreed a start date of the 23rd September and floated out of the offices on a cloud of *what may come.*

"Congratulations! I am so pleased for you. That is really great news. How wonderful. It's such a great opportunity for you! I'm sure they loved you. I did always say that your name should be Charis-ma!" Nate's tendency to effuse at good news had lost none of its power.

"I still have to sign the contract and the start date is not until 23rd September," she said, curbing his enthusiasm with the facts. "They could always change their minds." Charis could see Nate's mind was churning over the situation. She still recognized his thoughtful expression.

"Either way I'll be around for the next few weeks," she confirmed. "I might not be able to help you out directly, by being at your home, but I'll ask around and see what I can arrange in the way of help for you." She caught the glint in his eyes and a comforting sense of familiarity settled over her.

"I would be so grateful for anything you could arrange." He

spoke slowly and smiled widely, as he looked directly into her eyes. Charis wanted so much to turn away. She knew she was being sucked back into his world and yet she could not find the strength to resist.

"I'll text you," he offered, picking up his mobile phone. "I'm sure you can't keep coming around here like this, taking time out of your busy schedule for me. What's your number?"

* * *

"So that's it? You've accepted the job, without talking it over with me? Well I hope it makes you very happy," Grant shouted. "It will mess things up around here, for sure."

"Perhaps it will improve things," suggested Charis, not wanting to engage in any conflict.

Grant shot her a disproving look and sloped out of the study. Having received an email acknowledging receipt of the signed contract, Charis now felt even more determined to make a success of her new position. However, she passed the next few days under a cloud of resentment. She applied for garden leave from her employer, who was reluctant to see her go. As an assistant, she was sensitive and accommodating. Supporting others was Charis' strength, one skill she had relied on all of her adult life to earn a living. However, now she felt it was time to make her own voice heard. The new position allowed for more than attending to the executive editor's needs. She would also be reading manuscripts and giving her opinion. It was a responsibility that she relished, one that had been withheld by her current CEO and dismissed out of hand by her husband. He continued with his silent protest. The rocky impasse exploded on the arrival of a text message to Charis' mobile, whilst she was in the shower. Unable to contain himself any longer, Grant reached over the breakfast table to read it. As Charis walked into the kitchen, trying to wrap her wet hair in a towel, a red-faced Grant blasted a barrage of accusations into her face.

"How long has this been going on?" he demanded to know. "I should have guessed he would have something to do with this! You have been sneaking around behind my back with that womanizer. Did you not learn your lesson last time? You're going to let him mess you up again? Because he will, you know. Men like him never change their ways. Did you ever love me? Have the last ten years meant nothing? Who was there for you when he dropped you like a stone, when you smashed into a million pieces? It was me. I picked you up and put you back together. And that's the thanks I get; you running around with that jerk behind my back!"

Taking a step back, Charis allowed the reluctant towel to fall to her shoulders. "I don't know what you mean," she tentatively replied.

Grant's face flushed crimson. "Meeting him at his are you? What time this evening? Before I'm due in from the office I guess. Is that what you do when you say you are home?"

"I don't know…" Charis was genuinely confused. Her lack of response served to further enrage him. The ringtone of the mobile on the table focused the attention of each and both made a grab for it. Grant won.

"Give me the phone please," Charis requested.

"Why? Is there something on her I shouldn't read; something secret, or salacious?" Grant was taunting her.

"Don't be so ridiculous!" she replied. "Please just pass me my phone."

"So that you can make arrangements with him?" Grant's face was now twisted into wild and weird contortion.

"What is wrong with you?" Charis was becoming exasperated.

"What is wrong with me?" he hollered. "What is wrong with you? That's the question you need to be asking yourself."

"I got an email from Nathan, Nate, yes. He's in hospital and he's asked me to help him. I've told him there's not much I can do. I promised to ask around to see if anyone can find some home care arrangements for him. That's it. There is no more," Charis explained.

"Then what about this text?" Grant clicked on the offending message. "It reads *'will be so great to see you tomorrow. How does ten o'clock suit you? Text for directions if you need them, love always, Nate, kiss, kiss, kiss.'* And now there's another. Let's open this and see what it says…"

"He's being released from hospital tomorrow morning at ten," Charis blurted out. "He wants me to be there so the hospital can see he has support at home. The occupational therapy department won't let him home otherwise. That's all. He's a sick man, Grant. He needs daily support until he can look after himself again." Grant's demeanour changed, his red face faded into an embarrassed, pink blush.

"This job, these changes, they have nothing to do with him," asserted Charis. "For once, this is about me and not about the man in my life. There is no longer any man in my life."

Nate's messages received no response.

* * *

One month later, in an apartment in the East village of New York city, a reborn Charis looked out over a lively Tompkins Square Park, watching as its visiting inhabitants peacefully soaked up the sunshine or relaxed on picnic blankets under the shade of its trees. She could understand how the place was credited with the birth of the Hare Krishna movement in the United States. This was to be her home for the next six months and she intended to absorb every last drop of its vibrant, autumnal colours and creative energy. Getting ready to meet her new boss, Genevieve, Charis chose an eclectic outfit to suit her mood. No man had ever complimented her when she wore the colour yellow. Now she could dress in a style for comfort and in colours to suit her mood. She had changed more than her location. There was no more dressing or acting to please any man. She was dancing to her own tune and its resonance was exhilarating. For once it seemed that the scales were tipped in her favour and there was no man monopolizing her time or attention. She had refused to communicate further with either her husband or her ex-lover. In her mind she was on a self-imposed sabbatical from her life, and only she could say when, if at all, it would end. She wanted to hit the ground running in her new role and what better a way than to tread the sidewalks before pitching up at her desk. Lunch with Genevieve was a good start. She had a photo safari booked for later on that day to start in Central Park and she intended to catch the twilight in Times Square. She was so looking forward to the sounds of the Charlie Parker Jazz Festival in the park and was curious to watch the spectacle of the outdoor drag-queen festival, 'Wig Stars.' Of course she would have to sample the delights of Broadway and the musical 'Kinky Heels' was the one catching her fancy. The city held the promise of a hundred first dates; just her and the lights, the sights and the sounds.

As she left, the email alert sounded on her computer and in response she simply closed the lid of the old laptop. She no longer needed to stop and check to see if she was needed elsewhere, or required to carry out any additional requests. Charis' New York communications would be exclusive to her new connections. She felt sure that the sole entry of Genevieve's number in the contacts folder of her new cell phone would soon be accompanied by many others. She grabbed her new bag, a tote from the Marc Jacobs' 'Too hot to handle' range and headed out.

A final email from Nate remained momentarily unread on the abandoned machine:

'Hi! Well hello you, Miss New Yorker! How is the Big Apple? Everything it's cracked up to be? I haven't been there for years,

although I'm sure I would still know my way around. I'll dig out some of my own contacts and ask them to look you up, so you won't feel so alone there. I'm hoping to make my way out there soon anyway. It's time to make a change and a new vista will work wonders for my creativity. Did I tell you I had been working on a new book? In fact I'll send it over...it might be the sort of thing your editor might be interested in publishing. Tell me what you think...'

Vanquished

"I sit up, blinking in the darkness, to watch the crack in the bedroom doorway slowly widening. I freeze. I know exactly what is about to happen, but I just cannot do anything to stop it. Silhouetted in the moonlight, framed by the doorway, he is menacing. He crosses the room towards me in slow motion yet, paradoxically, he seems to cover the distance in the fraction of a second. The barrel of his gun is in my face. I close my eyes. I jerk violently at the impact of the shot and wake up shaking, in a cold sweat." Katarina spoke perfect English with a Slavic accent. To the listener, her almost emotionless delivery made it sound as if she was reading aloud a scene from a play.

"So the medication isn't helping? Have you thought any more about the counselling option? Perhaps you now feel able to give it another chance? Perhaps I could refer you to a different therapist? You have been through a traumatic experience." The young doctor was at a loss for what else to suggest to the striking Russian woman on this third visit to his clinic, complaining of insomnia.

"In cases such as yours, where you are still experiencing symptoms a few months after such a shocking event, it can help to talk about the actual incident with someone qualified to deal with these issues," he explained, looking straight into the steely, blue eyes of the enigmatic beauty; so slight in stature and lithe in body, yet ice cold to the core and stalwart in her manner.

"But this has not actually happened. This is a dream. It is my husband who was shot," she coolly responded.

"Nightmares are often a symptom of post-traumatic stress and depression. You have suffered a shock and a loss. Perhaps it might be worth talking to someone about everything?" he implored her.

"The only thing I have lost is my faith in men," the Russian replied tartly.

Katarina was not really one for talking. She had attended one session with a therapist who was, in her opinion, far too interested in her past experiences than her present problems. She was an action-orientated individual.

On discovering that her husband of just one year was involved in an international smuggling ring, comprising of Class A drugs and illegal arms, she had informed the UK police. Whilst they were wasting time doubting the efficacy of her story, he had been taken out in a violent confrontation but the evidence had been snatched away from under the noses of the authorities by a rival gang from the criminal underworld. The police were left with nothing but his bullet-ridden body and a host of unanswered questions.

In an attempt to make good, Katarina had been offered an alternative identity and some funding towards a move across the country. However, she knew that she could trust no one else with her life. She would make her own arrangements. And she knew exactly what she had to do to take back control over her own life.

For the previous 18 months, she had been dragged along like a piece of debris caught up in the tornado of her husband's criminal world. Whilst acknowledging that her suspicions had been aroused on a couple of occasions, Katarina had wanted to believe that the generous and passionate man she had met through the agency funded their lavish lifestyle through legitimate business interests, as he had claimed. As the dream had started to fade, the stark realities of the criminal activities underpinning their existence became all too apparent. After an extensive search of his covert computer files, she had challenged her husband and it was at that moment she learned how little her happiness actually meant to him; she was just another pawn in his twisted games of power and greed.

It was with a broken nose and a badly bruised cheekbone that she had sat in the waiting room of the local police station, refusing to move until they had arrested her husband. Suspecting she was the victim of a domestic abuser who had, until now, remained beneath their radar, the police consigned her vital information to the pile of 'vengeful accusations, most likely to vaporize within 48 hours.'

Whilst she remained steadfast, refusing to speak with the family liaison officer and rejecting offers of safe house accommodation, the emergency call came through, requiring all available officers to attend an incident located on a deserted building site on the edge of the city. Shots had been fired and a number of casualties had been counted. So far, there was one reported death. Katarina knew it was him. She had directed the police to this very location yet they had chosen to disregard her valuable information. Realizing their mistake, they were reluctant to let her go, but had no reason to hold her against her will.

"Can we get you another coffee? It's rather cold here, at the station. Would you like to come through into the interview room at the end of the corridor? It's less draughty than here and I believe it's the only room with an extra radiator," suggested the gruff duty sergeant.

Katarina politely declined the offer. Originating from the North Russian port of Arkhangelsk, where the average temperature in the month of October could fall anywhere between minus two and minus seven degrees, Katarina found the climate of South East England rather mild in comparison.

One rather sharp-nosed officer wanted to question her further. He was suspicious that she was, to some degree, actually involved in the whole business.

"Are you sure there's nothing further you can tell us, love?" he had asked with a hint of contempt to his voice. "If you think a bit harder, you might remember something else that could help us to catch the low life that killed your husband."

What they needed was a reason to search her home and her husband's belongings. However, Katarina had other ideas. She had looked straight into his black, lifeless eyes and stated simply that she had told them everything she knew. Securing her leather Gucci shoulder bag over her right shoulder, the stoic woman had stood up and marched out of the station.

* * *

Stepping out of the clinic into the winter evening, she pulled up the fur-lined hood of her Burberry coat over her long, sleek, brown locks and clasped her arms tightly across her chest as if to cloak herself from the eyes of the approaching night.

Following the death of her husband she had attended the inquest, cleared their bank account and emptied the house, which, she suspected was about to be repossessed by the mortgage company. Selling all of their ostentatious furnishings, she packed up her clothes, jewellery, accessories and the computer her husband had used to conduct his business. She had found a comfortable cottage in a quiet woodland setting, with just one neighbouring home. On the second viewing, the young widow had been approached by the landlady who was also the neighbour; a well-spoken, elderly woman who said she would be grateful for some quiet female occupation of her empty property. The two had signed a cautionary three-month lease agreement for the cottage as Katarina had no idea how long she would stay here. As the weeks had passed, she had tired of both the daytime intrusion of the lonely, old woman and the night-time terrors which had started almost immediately upon her moving in.

Whilst now walking through the late October night in search

of a taxi to take her home, Katarina was haunted by the memories of her time on the streets as a frightened teenager, making her escape from the industrial town on the edge of the Dvina river at the mouth of the White Sea. The sole, illegitimate child of a sailor and a streetwalker, she had spent many nights alone in a cold and sparsely furnished, docklands apartment whilst her mother was out earning money for food and clothes. Abandoned with a kiss and the reassurance that her guardian angel 'Michael' would be looking after her, the child had learnt that solitude was a safe place. When her mother had started to spend her earnings on hard drugs, the thirteen-year-old Katarina found herself abandoned. The morning she failed to return from the streets, Katarina knew her mother was dead and that she would have to leave the apartment. She considered whether to stow away on one of the cargo ships and sail to a foreign land, or head inland to the city of her dreams. She decided to head south for the bright lights in the big city of her homeland. With just one goal in mind, the young girl had used whatever means she had found to hand as she journeyed alone to the city of Moscow.

Embarking on a six-week journey, she hid herself away in the luggage compartments of passenger trains, climbed intrepidly into the cabs of articulated lorries and smiled at the drivers of passing empty buses in the hope they would stop and allow her to travel unseen to the next town. Some days she gratefully shared in the scraps of food and sipped on the coffee offered by kindly souls at roadside cafes. On other occasions, she found herself using all of her strength to fight off the unwelcome advances of inebriated men emerging from the shadows of city doorways, as she waited for another vehicle to turn into the road and rescue her. She had learned how to disappear into the shadows when faced with danger, yet also how the night had arms which held many horrors for an unsuspecting child.

Although she had quite miraculously reached the city of her dreams without sustaining any serious physical injuries,

Katarina had been most cruelly divested of the few remaining vestiges of her childhood. She no longer expected the sun to shine and the people to welcome her with open arms. The girl now understood what happened between the people who ventured out at night. She recognized the sickly sweet taste of alcohol on the breath of old men, the stale smog of cigarette smoke lurking in deserted buildings and the sex-scented trails of discarded condoms left by coupling strangers in dank alleyways.

Katarina knew only of one way in which to earn money for food and the warm clothes at which she stared longingly in the shop windows. As she was approached by strangers on the street, she took a moment to ask her guardian angel to watch over her; as the rough hands of desperate men grappled her young body, delighting in its soft suppleness, she would raise her eyes to heaven and pray.

Four years later, on graduating early from the harsh school of street life having endured countless assaults, survived two abortions and attained the status of never being able to bear children, she gave thanks to her guardian angel for not allowing her to fall victim to murder and for protecting her from contracting a deadly disease. Now a shrewd, self-assured seventeen-year-old, she had signed up with an escort agency with a view to finding one man to whom she could offer herself in return for some semblance of a peaceful life.

As fashion had become of greater importance than food to her, she sported an array of designer clothes and shoes; the props with which she became a confident escort on the arm of more wealthy citizens and visitors to the capital. The bright young thing provided excellent company to middle-aged businessmen and she was quick to learn the necessary phrases and curious sexual predilections of her international clientele.

Whilst waiting around one evening at the brothel for one of her regulars to call, Katarina had sourced a website advertising the opportunity for beautiful women to meet wealthy European and American men looking for a Russian bride. Without a second thought, she had signed up and completed the details for her own profile. She did not have to wait long for a positive response to the alluring photograph she had chosen carefully for the site.

Frankie, her future husband, had bombarded her for weeks with emails and text messages in an attempt to arrange an initial meeting. Wishing to distance herself from both the poverty of her painful past and her current, demanding career, Katarina arranged to meet her man in the neighbouring oblast of Novgorod. It was unlikely that anyone would know her there. She explained that she had recently lost her administrative job in a Moscow hotel and had travelled to the city in search of a similar post. It was some six months later, on her eighteenth birthday, that she was given the gift of a new name and status, signing her first passport application in the name of 'Mrs Katarina Fitch.'

* * *

Now, on the cold streets of Southampton, she finally flagged down a cab and gave the driver directions to her comfortable home in the New Forest. Katarina had no intention of returning to the clinic, or to the therapist. She would work this thing out for herself.

Sinking into the saggy seat of the old Mercedes, trying to avoid the gaze of the driver's eyes as he stared at her in his rear-view mirror, for the first time in her life, the vulnerable, young woman believed that her guardian angel had deserted her. Where was Archangel Michael? He who was with her for all those years in the dark, lonely rooms of her childhood and on the bone-chilling streets of her adolescence, why had he not saved her from the furious fists of her violent husband? Had he deserted her? How could she get him to protect her now, in her dreams? She brooded in the back seat until she arrived at her destination.

As the car turned into the secluded lane, she leaned forward to thank the taxi driver with a fifty-pound note. He switched on the interior light and held up the note to verify its authenticity whilst she focused on the features of his bemused expression, thinking the dim light very unflattering. As the car pulled off into the darkness, she made a mental note of the registration plate. He was one who could now be trusted, she thought to herself. Since childhood, Katarina had learnt to be vigilant with all men and she was finding that all she really could trust were her old habits.

On turning the key in the lock she heard the rattle of her adjoining neighbour's door and counted the footsteps on the loose gravel before the old lady appeared at her side.

"Good evening, my dear! I was getting quite concerned about you. The nights set in so quickly these days. I was hoping you would be home soon. Is everything okay? You're looking very tired."

Katarina knew that the old lady's concern was a mixture of compassion for a sister widow and an antidote to her own loneliness. However, this evening she was just too tired to be polite.

"Ruby, I am fine, thank you," she said with irritation. "I just need to get in the house. I have some things to do, so if you will excuse me," she added firmly as she stepped in front of the old lady, blocking her entry to the cottage. A downcast Ruby turned and shuffled off along the driveway. Katarina felt a slight pang of regret for her cold manner, before reminding herself that she had important things to do. She had to get rid of the interference in her dreams. She could not face another sleepless night.

Inside, she opened the heavy door to the cast-iron stove in the lounge and set some seasoned logs alight. After changing into a cashmere robe, she poured a large glass of Golden Frigate brandy over ice, and curled up on the sofa. Watching the flicker of the flames and the falling of the charred logs in the fire, the frail figure strengthened her resolve not to be consumed by the night-time horrors of her mind. Just past midnight she covered herself with an Afghan Saghari throw, before falling asleep amongst the sofa's velveteen cushions.

As is the way with recurring nightmares, Katarina soon discovered that each evolves in a subtle way, as if to keep the dreamer guessing as to what could happen next. Later that night, on the appearance of her dead husband in the lounge doorway, there was a sinister new development to the scenario. She heard a sadistic laugh emanating from the figure as he crossed the room and, on waking, her whole body not only shook wildly with the ricochet of the shot, but now also with the deep resonance of his voice.

It was four in the morning and the pale, dishevelled young woman's hand was still trembling as she poured herself a mug of lemon tea. Some of the boiling water splashed into the mug but the rest of the kettle's contents covered the tiled work surface. Reaching for a cloth, she soaked up the spillage before sitting at the kitchen table with her cold hands cupped firmly around the mug. However, the more her nerves quietened, the louder the merciless laugh echoed around her brain and body.

Katarina switched on her laptop, virtually her only link with the outside world, and searched the internet for nightmare remedies. As the dark night gave way to the deep, pink hues of the cloud-blurred sunrise over the fields, she found herself immersed in the notions of unresolved issues and symptoms of post-traumatic stress disorder. Having read about the medication, natural remedies and therapies available for relief, her imagination had been caught by the idea of re-scripting her experience. The one principle that the doctor had failed to understand was that this phenomenon was not a figment of her disturbed mind. It was a real-life invasion of her sleep by the ghost of her dead husband. What she needed to do was take control of the experience by writing a different ending, and she had thought of a most appropriate conclusion to this disturbing chapter.

Katarina switched off the light and raised the window blind. Opening the kitchen door she stood for a few moments in the dim winter morning light, breathing in the chilled air. The day had a curiously new feel to it. Perhaps this was the start of better times, she thought. Feeling invigorated and with a tentative sense of liberation, she left the kitchen to stand with her face directly under a hot shower, before choosing her ensemble for the day. Dressing had become much more than a functional act for Katarina who chose her clothes and accessories as if deciding on artefacts for an exhibition. Settling on a pair of skinny jeans and a Betty Jackson silk blouse, she pulled her long hair back into a severe chignon and slipped her narrow feet into a pair of three-inch, snakeskin ankle boots. Looking at her reflection in the mirror, she was pleased with her work. For Katarina there had to be an artistic coherence about her appearance. A specific blend of shape and textures were important to her. Whilst choosing the most figure-revealing clothes, she always opted for luxurious fabrics which were pleasing to the touch, to soften the harsh outline of her frame. The colours she chose were always neutral and her style was low-key and expensive, creating the illusion of wealth.

When she returned to the kitchen, it was to find Ruby leaning in to read the laptop screen which was open on the kitchen table. She looked startled at Katarina's sudden appearance in front of her.

"Oh! Hello, dear, I knocked but there was no answer. When I tried the handle, the door was open and I didn't think you would have gone far this early in the morning." In response, a scowling Katarina snapped the laptop shut. The old woman continued, looking critically at the younger woman's slim figure postured angrily in front of her, "I was worried about you, dear. Last night you looked so tired and you have lost so much weight over the past few weeks."

"You need not worry about me, Ruby, I can look after myself," Katarina huffed. "I would appreciate it if you would in future wait for me to answer the door, rather than just letting yourself in. You startled me."

"Yes, of course, my dear."

For the second time in as many days, the rejected old lady retreated back next door. Katarina reopened the laptop to check the last web page she had been viewing before had she caught her neighbour snooping. It was just the local weather forecast. She closed it back down, relieved that Ruby had not seen anything to incriminate her.

Three days passed with Katarina drinking espresso coffee and shopping online for accessories in an attempt to stay awake through the nights. Her eyes had dark circles and her cheeks were hollowed out. As she checked her profile in the mirror, she could see that her teeth were becoming more prominent and her skin had taken on a new shade of grey. Her reactions were slowing down and her ability to concentrate was waning. However, she was determined to fight on. She could not allow herself to fall asleep again, not yet.

Late afternoon, fearful of slipping into unconsciousness, she stood up from the kitchen table and reached for her coat. A brisk walk across the fields would help to keep her awake. She decided to make the most of the daylight hours left on that late October afternoon, to soak up all of the sun that would fall onto her face, and flood her brain with as much oxygen as she could inhale. The cold stillness had both a calming and an energizing feel as she enjoyed the silence of the open space in the dimming light. Momentarily, Katarina felt as if she had stepped into an alternative reality; one where time and space conspired to create a safe place for her. She revelled in the release, knowing that as soon as the final shaft of winter sunlight disappeared behind a cloud, she would have to turn around and make her way back home.

Crossing the fields at dusk, her breath was now appearing in a cloud before her face and she wrapped her midnight-blue pashmina higher to cover her nose and mouth.

With watering eyes she saw the front door of her cottage illuminated by the security light.

"It may just be a cat or a fox," she told herself.

However, on approached she could see a figure standing under the light. It was Ruby, holding some sort of parcel. Katarina felt panic rattle around in her chest. She knew exactly what the package contained. She needed to take it from the inquisitive old woman before she started asking any questions.

"This was delivered by courier, my dear," she said as Katarina stepped into the light beside her, hastily reaching out for the parcel.

"Thank you," she breathed, taking hold of the handbag-sized box.

But Ruby was not yet prepared to leave the scene. She had questions to ask. "It wasn't the usual delivery van, my dear, just a man in a car..." she ventured, continuing the conversation. "It needed signing for and I was more than happy to help out. I was quite surprised at its weight; it's very heavy for such a small parcel..."

Katarina knew that she could not just dismiss the nosy neighbour for a third time and so she invited her in for a cup of tea as thanks for her kind assistance. The mysterious parcel sat on the table between them. She knew how curious Ruby was to discover its contents but she also realized she could never reveal what had been delivered that day. She was adamant that both the concealed item and its intended purpose remain undiscovered forever. After a second cup of tea and a handful of biscuits which weight-conscious Katarina kept only for her visiting neighbour, Ruby became resigned to the fact that nothing was going to be revealed about the curious parcel and left.

Katarina set to work immediately. Quickly typing a page full of bullet points, she re-read her composition until she knew each off by heart, then she deleted the document. Closing the laptop lid, she secreted it away in the false bottom of a small flight bag which she hid at the bottom of a very full closet of clothes, shoes and other accessories, and then returned to the kitchen. Ensuring that the doors and windows to the cottage were locked and the blinds firmly fastened at the windows, she carefully opened the mystery package. Although no stranger to violence and the presence of weapons around her, this was still the first time that she had held a gun with her own hands; her own gun. Reading the handwritten instructions she had requested, Katarina loaded the weapon and replaced it carefully on the table facing away from her. Feeding the incriminating document to the flames of the fire, she then prepared herself for her first night's sleep that week. Leaving the kitchen door open, she turned the chair to face the front door which was now visible through the porch. Double-checking that the front door was locked and the key was hidden away in a kitchen drawer, she took her place, propped up with cushions in the chair, resting her right arm on the table, holding the gun in her hand.

Bullet-point two of her plan stated that upon seeing or hearing her dead husband, whichever way he intruded into her dreams that night, she would order him to leave and never return, warning that if he did so, she would shoot him.

If she was forced to count to three, she would stand and point the gun directly at him.

Four would see her fire as many shots needed to rid herself of the ghastly spirit.

All she knew was that she had to hold her nerve and not react when he shot at her. He couldn't kill her. He couldn't hurt her unless she allowed him to do so because he was already dead.

* * *

"So, let me get this straight," the police officer said, quickly turning the page of his notebook, eager to record all of Ruby's words, "you heard the firing of shots, gun shots, and you looked out your window to see two characters standing outside your neighbour's door under the security light?" The uniformed man pulled back the lace kitchen curtain and pointed to the area now illuminated by the flashing blue lights of the parked patrol car.

"Yes I saw her, Katarina, pointing a gun at a man. I saw him fall to the ground and I called you straightaway," the old woman replied.

"What happened next?" the officer asked.

"I locked my door and switched off the lights," Ruby whispered. "I didn't want her to know I had seen anything."

"And you can say you had a good look at the man?"

"Yes," Ruby said with confidence. "He was very tall, thickset, about six-foot-four, with fair shoulder-length hair tied in a ponytail. He was wearing dark clothes, jeans I think, and a black leather jacket. You know, the ones men wear for riding motor-bikes."

The officer spoke into his radio, "Sarge, this description of the man sounds very familiar."

"Yes, very much like the suspect's old man, as she's calling him, but he's deceased," was the sergeant's curt response. "There is no body over here, just the traumatized woman and a gun. The back-up team has searched the place from top to bottom. Is your lady absolutely certain she saw a man at the scene?" Ruby heard the conversation and folded her arms in a defiant manner.

"There's nothing wrong with my eyesight and I'm not senile yet, young man," she asserted firmly. "I know what I saw. They were under the light. I could see them both quite clearly."

There was no doubt that shots had been fired and the old lady was sticking to her story. However, the officers had conducted a painstaking search of the scene for a body or some blood and had found only a shaky Katarina. So far, they had failed to elicit any sense from her regarding the events of the evening. Having bagged and tagged the weapon, they had now decided to take the suspect into the local station for questioning. Unsure as to her state of mind, the officers were concerned as to whether she posed a threat to herself or anyone else and had decided that the interview process needed to be reliably recorded.

"What about the handcuffs, Sarge?" The arresting officer was fresh out of training school and keen to follow procedure to the letter.

"I don't think she's an escape risk," replied his seasoned superior. "Let's just get her to the station, caution her again and record the interview properly."

In the silence of the car, interrupted only by intermittent messages on the radio, Katarina volunteered her own version of events. Despite the officers' advice for her to wait until they were at the station, she insisted on giving them her own account of the evening's bizarre happenings.

"I was ready for him. This had to be the last time he did this to me. Whatever happened, I could not let it continue." As usual, she spoke clearly and with a Slavic accent. Without acknowledging her, the officers exchanged quizzical expressions. "When he came in through the door I stood up and told him to leave, that he was not going to hurt me again. Then, for the first time, he spoke to me. He said that I had to pay for selling him out to his enemies. I told him that I had nothing to do with the ambush, indeed that I tried to stop it by informing you guys, the police. I had no wish to see him dead, only in jail where he belonged and where he could no longer hurt me. He refused to leave, saying that I was only getting what I deserved and then he raised a gun to me. I told him that he could not hurt me as he was dead, although he quite clearly had not realized it. I also informed him that, conversely, although I had in fact been dead for most of my life, it was he who had shown me what it was to be alive. Then I raised my gun and shot at his feet. He looked shocked but he did not move, so I took the opportunity to shoot him again. This time I aimed higher and he panicked. I could see the look of horror on his face and I could smell his fear. This is when I felt very brave and moved closer towards him. I was feeling in control now. I took his gun away from him and I told him to back out the door or I would shoot him dead. When we got outside, I fired one more shot. That is the last thing I remember. Then I heard the sound of sirens and you guys arrived at my house."

Later that night at the station, when the interview had been concluded and Katarina had categorically stated that she had tried to shoot the ghost of her dead husband, the keen rookie still had some questions for his supervising officer.

"So what can we do? It's not like she actually shot anyone."

"We can do her for illegal possession of a firearm and the discharging of a firearm. But, although we found all the shells and bullets, there was no blood at the scene and apparently no one else present, so we can't claim intent. We could make her tell us where she got the weapon from, I suppose. Perhaps she's not so innocent after all. Let's see if she has links with her dead husband's colleagues. Other than that, I think what she really needs is some medical, and possibly psychiatric, care."

Both turned to look at the screen through which they were monitoring her behaviour. Katarina was sitting silently in the interview room, perfectly still apart from the hint of a smile which was easily missed on first glance by the officers who focused more closely on her shiny heels and the shape of her nipples showing through her sheer blouse. Feeling only an overwhelming sense of empowerment that even the threat of criminal charges or convictions could not diminish, she had no concern for the thoughts or actions of the officers. She was finally free from her past, from all the grasping hands in the dark shadows. She had faced her innermost fears, embodied in the form of her dead husband; he who had represented all that was bad in her world, all of the unfortunate experiences she had fallen victim to and all of the regrettable choices she had ever made. She had acknowledged the depths of her fears, fashioned them into a target, aimed and vanquished them, forever. For the first time in her life, she felt truly free.

"Are you okay in there, love? We can arrange a room with a bed, if you're getting tired."

The supervisor was conscious that he was in the presence of a trainee. "We can't hold her for more than twenty-four hours without charge," he explained. "The initial six hours are up and now we will have to look in on her from time to time, offer her a cuppa tea, a smoke; things like that."

Katarina shook her head in response. She was quite comfortable here. Used to staying awake through the small, silent hours, she had almost seen this night through. Confident that there was no further evidence to be found, she expected that following a review of events in the cold light of day, she would be released and able to indulge herself in a deep, long and uninterrupted sleep. From within, she detected a curious warmth; a gentle heat which started a thaw. Katarina began to recall how it felt to be alive, feeling as if she had just stepped out of a dark cave and into the warm sunshine. Her guardian angel had returned to protect her. Now she could go back out into the world, safe in the knowledge that Archangel Michael would be with her on her travels.

Upon release, Katarina had a fool-proof plan to execute. Task number one was obtaining a United States visa. This she was confident of securing, with a generous online bank transfer from one of her dead husband's many accounts to the supplier of the gun. Perhaps he realized his client was actually dead, or maybe he just didn't care. Katarina knew it was just a matter of time before the fraud investigators detected and froze all of the accounts. It was imperative that she had all her paperwork in order before that happened. Momentarily, she cursed her neighbour for interfering in her business and calling the police.

She would now have to retrieve the laptop from its hiding place and destroy it as soon as she got home. However, the accompanying scowl darkened her expression for only a few seconds. Very soon she would be released and could enact her disappearance from the little world she had created in this country.

Katarina had her sights firmly set on far-flung shores. With the transfers she had already made to offshore accounts, she should have enough money on which to live comfortably for some time. But if at any point she needed to find another source of income, she would be well-placed to exercise her various skills among the rising middle-classes on the island of Cuba. Originating from a communist country, she felt sure that she would understand the historical mindset of the people. Also, the time she had spent in Western Europe had given her an invaluable insight into the entrepreneurial spirit which fed the capitalist system. She felt sure that now was the time to arrive in the country, to take advantage of its free education and health systems before the newly-created property market took root and corporate business flourished. As soon as she could arrange a visa, she would fly to Miami and maybe holiday in the Quays to enjoy some serious shopping, before moving on to the Caribbean island.

Closing her eyes, Katarina could feel the warmth of the Cuban sun on her face and the smell of expensive perfume on her body. She understood the power of dreams. For the duration of her stay she allowed her mind to drift, envisaging the brightly coloured clothes of the dancers at the Tropicana and the sweet taste of rum on her tongue. She saw herself walking around the streets of Old Havana, feeling the cobbled streets of the colonial city beneath her feet. Yes, she would head straight for the capital and look for opportunities there. Her plan was almost complete and the police detention-time clock was ticking.

"We'll have to let her go," concluded the arresting officer. "The place has been searched and the evidence of the only witness is very dubious. We can't say that this woman is a threat to anyone. We'll inform intelligence and they can keep an eye on her for a while."

On hearing the words, 'You're free to go,' Katarina stood up and stretched out her arms. Without a trace of emotion, she walked out of the interview room and approached the officer behind the desk in the custody suite to request the return of her personal effects. She was happy for them to retain her mobile phone, safe in the knowledge that they would find no evidence in relation to any of her internet activities.

Stepping out into the cold morning air, she wrapped her coat tightly around herself and walked along the streets towards a taxi rank. The cabbies were just starting to line up to wait for their first morning fare. Katarina scanned the line until a short, broad man smoking a fat cigar caught her eye. It was a sign. Watching her approach the driver, the owner of the cab at the head of the queue called out, signalling his availability. Katarina ignored him. She was going to ride with the man and the Cuban cigar.

The Magic Works

"See anything that you like?" asked Gina, appearing alongside the gallery viewer.

"Oh, I'm surprised that it's all portraits!" exclaimed the elderly lady. "Given the name of the gallery, I was expecting something a little more, well, esoteric," she explained, flushing with embarrassment as her eyes alighted on the face of the petite proprietor.

"There are a variety of portrait styles, as I'm sure you've noticed," Gina replied, noticing the ornate gold leaf ring neatly fixing a crimson, silken scarf around the lady's neck. She cast a glance over the generous cut of her calf-length tweed skirt, visible from beneath her mink-collared coat, and clocked the expensive, sturdy shoes. However, it was the blood-red ruby earrings on which she chose to comment.

"Your earrings, are they rubies?" she asked.

"These? Yes, they belonged to my mother," the lady replied. Gina noted the golden sparks of interest in the irises of her rich, hazel eyes.

"Isn't it amazing how a colourless gemstone can be brought to life by way of a chemical reaction, how a piece of common corundum can be transformed by a drop of chromium!" Gina spoke her thoughts aloud.

The lady continued, "My father bought them for her when we were posted to India. Quite unique aren't they? I've yet to see another pair like them." Using the short, blunt nail on her index finger, the she tucked her neatly bobbed, greying hair behind her ear and turned her head to afford Gina a clearer view.

"Exquisite!" Gina said, leaning in closer towards the lady. "Quite clearly handmade, and with such intricate detail." She studied the tiny markings carved into the gold, edging the set of the rubies, reflecting the light onto the contours of the stones and illuminating the crimson heart of each precious gem. The overall effect was one of richly hued warmth with a magical sparkle. The fiery energy of the precious stones flared out at Gina, who took a deep breath and stepped back.

"Is there anything you'd like to ask me about the portraits?" she asked, looking directly at the old lady and extending a hand in friendship. "My name is Gina, this is my gallery and I will be pleased to help you in any way."

"There is one thing…" The lady walked excitedly over to a delicately framed watercolour on the wall. "It's never occurred to me before, but I think I would quite like a portrait of myself in this style. Would it be possible to arrange it with the artist?" She asked. She had chosen a watercolour painting of a younger woman with a carefree expression and long flowing hair. Although the lines faded out towards the edge of the work, the detail in the face was precise; the gentle features of the subject's face were depicted in a soft, yet elegant manner.

"Certainly," Gina responded with a smile. "I am the artist." She knew exactly what this woman wanted from a portrait of herself; she wanted to feel young, beautiful and desirable again. She sensed that the lady had spent her early life in exotic locations but had somehow wandered into unfamiliar territory, into a monotonous place which served to deaden her soul.

"I have been in mourning for my lost husband, my children have grown up and now I'm ready to go out into the world and look for a new love," the lady announced excitedly.

Somewhat taken aback by her candour and pleased at her own insight, Gina asked, "Do you have a favourite photograph I can work from?"

"Ah! Yes, one springs to mind. It's in a frame on the hall table, I'll just have to pop home and I'll bring it in for you, dear," the lady replied before leaving the gallery with a noticeable spring in her step.

Happy thoughts swirled and spiralled in Gina's mind and the lady's words left a taste of succulent peach in her mouth. She was going to be so pleased with the portrait Gina had in mind for her; she could sense it, in so many ways.

As a child, the artist had been surprised to learn that not everyone experienced the world in the same way as she. Once forced to stay behind in class alone with her teacher, awaiting the delayed arrival of her mother, she appeared to stare aimlessly into space, when she should have been committing the twelve times tables to memory. Her teacher had addressed her sharply, asking why she was wasting her time. The dreamy child's reply had only served to irritate the woman further:

"I'm watching how the number three, all shiny and silver, is twinkling in the light," Gina had innocently replied, clearly entertained by her discovery. However, faced with a scowl of disapproval and a sarcastic comment, her joy turned quickly to confusion and a sense of shame settled over her shoulders. Similarly, at home when she referred to the voice of her visiting auntie as tasting of 'hot, milky porridge with honey,' she was reprimanded by her father for being foolish. Despite her mother's attempted soothing with sympathetic smiles, his harsh words had left her with a taste of bitter lemon on her tongue. Realizing that not everyone else experienced such things in same way, Gina became a quiet child; she withdrew, alone with her secret tastes and imagery.

It was during this time of her life that she developed her acute intuition. Just as she was able to sense the texture of colours and taste the meaning of words, she also saw the true intentions of others, as if projected onto an instant drop-down screen, playing out in front of her very eyes. Of course, neither did she speak openly of this ability; the scathing comments relating to her apparent lack of concentration on her school reports having long silenced her. However, she knew the difference between the products of her imagination and the phenomena which played out its existence on a totally different plane.

The ringtone of the office phone called her back behind the scenes of the gallery, where she exchanged some words with her loving wife, Freja.

"What time is it with you?" she asked, never confident about her calculation of the time difference between the continents. The newlyweds were having to live apart until Freja's fellowship at the university in Missouri drew to a close and she moved to England to take up an academic position in Oxford. Her voice sounded so quiet and distant, that for a split second Gina saw an endless spiral of grey space between them. She wanted to reach out and grasp for the reassuring hands of her loved one.

"I have another commission today," she announced, trying to calm her trembling voice.

"So you will be painting for the next few days? That's great news. It will make you happy. It's just a few weeks longer, and I will be there with you." Freja's reassurance warmed Gina and she closed her eyes to say a silent prayer of gratitude.

"I love you." Gina broke the silence.

Freja responded with a shy smile. No words were needed. Despite the distance, the women were clearly tuned into the same frequency.

* * *

As the Morpho butterfly closes it wings to disguise its iridescent beauty from potential predators, so Gina had sat quietly through her years at art school lectures, focusing closely on the elements of the classes which fuelled her imagination. Some lecturers expressed concerns as to whether the vibrant work she was submitting could be attributed to her, such a diminutive, shy creature. She silenced their suspicions with her final installation project, when she displayed the magnificence of her gifts and talents. With a mind naturally immersed in a multi-dimensional arena, she was able to produce a spectacular interactive light show, which evidenced her knowledge and understanding of the medium of colour, extending way beyond the expectations of the course. Gina wanted her audience to share her experiences of creating the energy of colour by heating chemical compounds. She sought to challenge the spectator's perception by demonstrating that the colour of the light, or luminescence, depends on the amount of energy emitted by each electron of the compound, as it returns to its natural state. Although she guessed that most people would expect copper to produce a blue flame, she was correct in assuming that only a few were able to guess that calcium, when heated, produces an orange flame. Therefore she set up an interactive computer display, where footage of her experiments in the laboratory replayed when people answered the questions correctly. The successful spectator witnessed barium burning in a green glow and lithium producing a crimson hue.

To connect this information to the notion of the human body containing centres of energy or *prana* resonated strongly with her, she also constructed a life-sized figurine sitting in a cross-legged position, from sheets of folded metal and strategically coloured LED lights at the points correlating to the Hindu chakras of the body. As the visitor approached the areas, they activated the sensor for the lights. A bright yellow light was placed at the point of the solar plexus; green at the heart chakra above, and a vibrant orange at the sacral chakra below. A deep red throbbed out from the base chakra. She chose the shades of turquoise, violet and purple lights placed at the throat, third eye and crown chakras in the head of the sculpture, which was placed at the centre of the room to facilitate the flow of spectators and to maximize the variety of perspectives available to them.

To further illustrate this concept of chemoluminescence – the chemical creation of colour – she handed glow sticks to the children attending her exhibition so that they could safely experiment with colour in the darkened room.

Her final piece proved a success with the visitors, their children and the university examination board. Gina was invited to stay on and study further at the university. However, the wider world was beckoning and she was far too restless to stay in one place for any length of time. Gina, the artist, took direction from one source only, her own fascination.

* * *

For the next decade she wandered through the US, seeking colour and inspiration in its vibrant cities. With a reference detailing high regard from her school of art, she escaped her humdrum, hometown existence in the English countryside and travelled on the ticket of 'voluntary artist in residence', at whichever charitable or educational institution would accept her. To feed and clothe herself, she participated in paid experiments offered by university departments, often finding herself involved in psychological research. Intrigued by investigations into the creative process, she was happy to answer any questions and engage with the myriad of experiments designed to shed light on the nature of human processes.

For inspiration she visited all of the art galleries and museums that she could find.

In California she was spellbound by the array of abstract works on display at the Museum of Contemporary Art. Despite the negative critique, she could quite clearly see the magic of the universe in Pollock's Reflections of the Big Dipper. She floated out of Chicago on Kapoor's Cloudgate and finally found herself amongst the abstract artists of the 1980s in the Times Square Gallery.

Although the multi-sensory work of Hockney, an artist who perceived music through the medium of colour and shape, caused strangely familiar stirrings within her, it was the earlier imagery of Kandinsky that whispered directly to her soul. Like him, she too was concerned with the spiritual aspects of art. Whatever its form, she felt that its purpose was to enrich the soul. Kandinsky had believed in the resonant power of colour; that its energy could permeate the core of the individual. Like Goethe, he was concerned with the human experience of colour, in sharp contrast to Newton's scientific measurement of the frequency of individual hues. Goethe associated aesthetic qualities with specific colours; he ascribed the term useful to the colour green and regarded the colour orange as having noble qualities. Gina wondered if the notion of synaesthesia had been apparent in eighteenth-century Germany. If so, she felt sure that his abilities would have been recognized.

It was as she was passing through the state of Missouri that Gina happened upon her own, personal diagnosis. Replying to an advertisement looking for participants in research being conducted at the university, she found herself signing up for an experiment with the drug psilocybin, which was believed to induce the same cross-sensory state of cognition in the brain as the condition of synaesthesia. However, she did not progress to the stage of imbibing the drug, due to the fact that the preliminary test results identified her as naturally demonstrating a variety of aspects of the condition.

For the first time in her life, Gina was able to explain openly how loud, brash words spoken by others tasted hot and spicy in her mouth and how quiet compliments were sweet and juicy. Without fear of ridicule or repercussion, she elucidated on the sour taste she experienced on hearing nasty words, some of which could burn her tongue like acid. In response to the genuine questions and supportive smiles from the beautiful, blonde student conducting the research, Gina was happy for the first time in her life to explain how the sad words she heard spoken by others were flavourless, like decaying fruit, and that she found it hard to be free of their trace, like the fibres that get caught in the teeth.

The following day the two young women met at the university's Museum of Religious and Spiritual Art to continue their dialogue. As she walked through the exhibition stands alongside Freja, Gina felt drawn into the eclectic realm of the artefacts, magnetized by the power of their energy. In contrast, when she looked at her companion, she felt a pervasive sense of calm. This was to be the case whenever the two were together. Often they were to find that words weren't necessary for them to reach a mutual understanding.

Freja, a philosophy graduate from Sweden, had found herself at the intersection of her specialist subject and the fast-moving highway of cognitive science. Plato had claimed that humans learn universal truths by lifting the veil covering their physical reality; Freja believed that the human mind had the capacity to experience a much more complex existence. Her curiosity had led her to cross-Atlantic travel and involvement in a graduate research programme in the state of Missouri. She had spent the previous two years observing and recording the effects of hallucinatory substances on the functioning of the brain. She believed that the chemically induced spike in the level of serotonin served to change the cognitive functioning of the brain, facilitating a similar experience to the naturally occurring phenomenon of synaesthesia.

At dinner that night, as Gina gazed across the table at the Riverfront restaurant into the sparkling blue eyes of her pale-skinned companion, a perfectly composed vision of beauty, she felt a hot, sweet, sticky sensation wash over her and realized she was falling in love.

For the summer break, she found herself disinclined to focus inwardly in order to work and instead she turned her face to take in the sun. Restless, she found herself visiting the open spaces of the city. She lay in the sun on the grass in Forest Park, her eyes closed, listening to the splash of egrets and herons, as their beaks broke the surface of the water in the Angel Fountain Lake. Wandering through the art-deco Jewel Box greenhouse, she gently squeezed the juicy leaves of the trees and plants between her thumb and fingers and stopped to inhale the delicate fragrance of the exotic flowers. From the World's Fair Pavilion she stood, silently surveying the breeze-brushed pickerel weed and white hollyhocks lining the banks of the waterways. And from the Grand Basin Bridge she watched a painted lady butterfly land on a sunlit water lily, as it meandered downstream.

As soon she was able to escape from the psychology laboratory, Freja joined her new love in an exploration of all that the city and the state had to offer. The young women camped out at Cherokee Springs Festival of Culture, joining the ring around the fire to absorb the rhythm of the Native American drummers and listening respectfully to the elder voices telling traditional tales.

They trailed through the heat in the Ozark Mountains, following the flow of the White River, stopping to cool off in the cavernous cellars of Herman's Hillside Winery, before sipping and savouring the rich, fruity nectar. Sitting on the riverbank, Gina felt the cool, fresh water of the mountain springs as they cascaded over the rocks. The empty expanse of the spaces between the mountain ranges soothed her soul, as she stepped out of the tent to drink in the pure, early morning air. As if she was frightened of forgetting the beauty, she finally picked up a pencil and started to sketch the detail of her surroundings. Freja watched quietly, with a satisfied smile on her soft-featured face.

At night as she lay awake in the gentle arms of her love, Gina struggled to banish the fearful thoughts and painful memories of past relationships. All too prominent in her mind's eye were the grey monitors, blurred with the sound of conflicting voices, before they finally gave way to the silent opacity of a blank screen. Having experienced only troubled relationships in her life, she was only too aware of her tendency to fall deeply into love with the wrong people. Highly sensitized to the emotions of others, she had often lost herself in someone else's life, only to find that she couldn't stay indefinitely.

It was different with Freja. Gina felt grounded by the woman's inner calm. Her cool detachment was warmed with kindness and she was the first person with a true insight into Gina's interior world. She had felt relaxed, from the first moment of meeting with Freja, and able to reveal the many facets of her full self, without apology. To speak about her secret, internal world had given Gina a new sense of freedom. Paradoxically, she also felt a deeper level of intimacy with her new lover. However, she could not bring herself to truly believe that timeless happiness in a relationship was possible. The following morning Freja asked her directly what was on her mind. Unfamiliar with such openness, Gina struggled to harness her thoughts to provide a coherent explanation. She managed some vague statements about the expiry of her visa and having to return home in the autumn, when what she really wanted to express was her fear at the thought of living without Freja by her side.

"You know that I am already looking for another research post, to continue my work?" Freja asked. "When the tender for my current research runs out, this time next year, I will be free to leave this place. I have a choice of applying to one of our affiliated universities to continue with my work. I could apply to Oxford…" she suggested.

A rush of relief gladdened Gina's heart. *There might be a way,* she thought.

* * *

As she travelled home alone, Gina delved deep into intro-spection. On the overnight crowded Greyhound bus, she closed her eyes to block out the sounds of muffled coughs and hushed conversations and found her mind filled with the vivid detail of people's faces. The light, crinkly lines at the corner of Freja's eyes which appeared when she laughed; the lined brow and dignified expression on the face of the storytelling chief, illuminated by the flames of the camp-side fire; her mother's nervous bite of her lips, in response to the loud voice of her father; and the curve of the downturned mouth and disapproving sneer of her primary-school teacher. Unable to block this new imagery from her mind, Gina took out a pencil and sketch pad and committed the contents of her memory to paper. The act served to release the emotional pressure from the young woman. She saw herself reaching into a deep, cold, body of murky water, her fingers feeling around for the plug chain. The weight of the water was bearing down on the back of her hand; the force resisting her attempts at lifting the chain and pulling the plug. Once she committed to the action and pulled the plug, lifting her hand back up towards the surface of the water, so its resistance acqui-esced.

Gina learned that just as art could speak to the spirit, so it could release the tension from the soul. This insight and experience would prove to serve her well.

Just as her body travelled miles over land and sea; so the journey inwards continued deep into her consciousness. Peeling back the overlay of contemporary and abstract art through which she had interacted with the world for all of her adult life, Gina was now facing her own, innate humanity, along with the essential humanity of others. The love and acceptance demon-strated by Freja had somehow acted as a catalyst to enable her to look deep into her own core and acknowledge the truth of the person, behind the colours, tastes and emotions that had shaped her existence. For the first time in her life, Gina attempted a self-portrait. Flicking through the photographs of her taken by her lover, she looked closely at the shapes and shadows of her facial features and attempted a work which represented the truth of the photographic images. In each sketch she was discovering new aspects that the world might have seen etched on her face, and yet of which she had been unaware. Never having been one to spend hours looking in the mirror tending to her appearance, Gina now found herself considering each crease and contour of her own face. Gradually there was a reconciliation of the perspectives through which she perceived the world and the face she presented to others. It seemed that Freja's love and understanding had served to acknowledge every facet of her being, in effect, her acceptance had served to holding up a mirror; so allowing Gina to see herself through the eyes of the rest of the world.

Whereas few people outside the art world were able to converse about the motivation for some of the most abstract art, Gina found that even a two-dimensional representation of the human face appeared to offer up so many stories and opportunities for conversation. The aeroplane passenger in the seat next to her kept snatching glances at her drawings, finally summing up the confidence to comment as the seatbelt sign lit and the air steward passed asking for trays to be stowed.

"Excuse me," said the young, Chinese man as he removed his earphones, "I couldn't help but notice your art work. It is amazing! Do you get asked for lots of portraits?"

Gina found herself at a loss for words. No one had ever asked her to paint a portrait. Following an awkward silence, the plane descended onto the runway in London and she replied, "It will be a new beginning for me."

Apart from the odd university holiday at Christmas, Gina had spent very little time at home with her family for the past thirteen years, choosing to visit other countries when her visa limit expired. During a few Thanksgiving celebrations that she had attended in America with friends and lovers, she had felt little nostalgia about her own family life in England. In her parents' eyes she had left home as a child. Now she would return as a woman. From the airport she called to explain that she would catch the national bus to her home town. Her mother's voice sounded excited and Gina also detected her anticipation. She was informed that her father would drive to the station, pick her up in his car and bring her home, that they would all be so pleased to see her and have her stay for a while.

On the bus, a sense of restlessness over took her. Old images of past events seeped into her mind and she reasoned that it was normal to feel a little apprehensive. Communication with her family had been sparse and polite during her time away from home. She had been informed of the various trials and tribulations befalling family members over the years and duly reported back her newest job and the fact that she was well and happy. For her, now, the notion of re-entering the family womb was starting to feel a little suffocating. She tried to tell herself it would be different this time; her strong memories continuing to vividly illustrate their poignancy. There was only one way for her to survive this challenge and it was to face it in truth and with acceptance.

It was a white-haired man who waved to her from an unfamiliar car, as she stood watching and waiting at the bus station. He parked up and got out of the car, Gina recognizing his familiar gait as he beckoned to her and called her name. They embraced. As he loaded her luggage into the boot of the car, her father commented on how grown up she looked and announced how pleased her mother and her auntie, both waiting patiently at home, would be to see her. In the car, Gina struggled to offer any meaningful conversation and so perfunctorily outlined the route and duration of her journey. As they travelled through the town, she began to recognize some of the other places which had featured in her childhood. She noted the primary school and the adjacent park through which she had often made the walk home, alone. Some of her classmates had picked up on the negativity displayed by the teachers and regarded her as weird. As such she was often excluded from playtime games. Gina now recalled how she had entertained herself at such times; often tuning in to the energy of the flowers and trees surrounding her. She felt no fear when sitting high on a branch listening to the bird sounds and watching the children at play beneath her, waiting until the last one had finally sloped off home for dinner.

She stepped over the threshold into her childhood home, to find her shrunken mother standing with outstretched arms. Her brown curly hair was streaked with grey and she had a tired look in her eyes. However, her beautiful smile retained its reassurance and warmth. To Gina it seemed as if roles had been reversed and she was now the beneficent adult. As her auntie called out her name from the lounge, she experienced the familiar taste in her mouth of milky porridge with honey. The two women hugged and as she stepped back out of the embrace, her auntie exclaimed on how well Gina looked, despite the many hours of travelling. The prodigal daughter was being carried aloft on the coursing of excited energy from her family.

"I am fine," she offered in response. "I am tired, but it is such a good feeling to see you all again and to be home."

"Here you go," her father appeared in the hallway with the luggage. "Shall I take it straight up to your room?" Gina helped him up the stairs with the bags and stepped into her old bedroom, which she found to have remained just as she had left it. The bedsheets were starched clean and there was the smell of fresh furniture polish, but the same wooden bed, chest and wardrobe stood on the green close-piled carpet. Gina instantly recognized the childhood photographs which still adorned the walls, and the familiar, flowery curtains which framed the window looking out over the neatly kept garden. In one way it seemed as if the years that had passed since she was last here had been played out on some distant plane, in another world. She could recognize still frames from it, but the whole experience now felt like a dream, a work of fiction. This was now her reality. She had finally returned to the scene of her childhood to find that the time passed and the distance endured had served to sweeten the relationship with her family. The once powerful element of fear and disapproval seemed absent. Knowing that this situation was unlikely to last, Gina relished the sweetness of the moment. When she closed her eyes she could see an overflowing cup of cinema popcorn and a she could taste the sugary sweets from a bag of pick-and-mix candies. She paused a while to suck in the sweetness, before unpacking her case. Finally, she took out the images she had sketched in readiness to show her family, after dinner.

* * *

The atmosphere hovering over the table formed a curious cloud of anticipation and excitement. Its electric charge left a metallic taste on Gina's tongue, killing her appetite. There was chatter about the mainly banal events in the lives of relations whom Gina had long forgotten, in the form of an update newsletter, before the questions started to flow in her direction.

Where had she been? Which places had she enjoyed visiting the most? Hadn't she ever been scared all alone in big cities? And finally, was there anyone special in her life? Surely she had found love along the way?

Gina knew she would have to tackle this subject eventually, as she would be staying in the country for the foreseeable future. Reaching for her portfolio book, she chose a careful selection of sketched portraits to show. Affording each a narrative, she presented a pictorial account of the most beautiful places she had visited and the intriguing people she had met. Her audience reciprocated with questions and comments and the story of Gina's journey unfolded before their eyes. Lastly she brought out a sketch of Freja. Whilst her auntie responded with a smile and complimented Gina on her skills, Gina detected the aftertaste of sour cream in the atmosphere. She looked at her father. His expression was dour. Swiftly looking to her mother for support, she saw only disappointment in her eyes. No one asked any more questions and the silent freeze slowly iced a grip on Gina's heart.

"And this," she announced with pinched breath, "this is Freja. She is my love, my lover, and we are going to be married."

* * *

"Yes, this is exactly what I'm looking for!" exclaimed Gina; much to the surprise of the estate agent who was accompanying her on the viewing of the empty, old, high street shop. "This space will make a great gallery and I can utilize the backroom as my workshop."

The agent tried, but was clearly not sharing her vision. "If you can accompany me back to the office, you can sign the lease today," he suggested, keen to seal the deal. The place had been empty for over a year and this was the first sniff of interest. Although the square footage was considerable, the amenities consisted only of an ancient toilet and a stained old washbasin in the back room. The landlord had recently agreed to a reduction in the price and Gina, who had been eagerly scanning the column of property lets in the local, free newspaper, had spotted it immediately. Now, busily texting the news to Freja, she looked up and nodded in agreement with the agent. The shop front was a blank canvas and she had already imagined how to arrange partitions in the space to display her work. The scant furnishing of the damp, rear room of this lock-up unit did not discourage her. She intended to move in and start work as soon as the papers were signed.

* * *

Six months later, the space had been truly transformed. Gina's sign over the door, 'The Magic Works', had intrigued many a passer-by; most of whom had entered out of sheer curiosity and had left feeling surprised to have commissioned a portrait of themselves. Not fully aware of how she enchanted her clients, Gina had grown to believe in her own, unique perceptions of the world and had bravely channelled them into her work. No longer needing to hide her exceptional insights, she was now free to express her talents in the alchemic atmosphere of this sacred space. Nearly every visitor commented on the name of the gallery and, without exception, all clients were delighted with their paintings of themselves. Although working on the facial details from photographs submitted by her clients, Gina had actually gleaned the most important information she needed for the work in the instant the clients stepped over the threshold. She could tell by the taste of their words whether or not they were happy, contented people; their auras told the story of their lives and denoted the particular space they were trying to fill. Since becoming aware of the potency of the portrait, Gina knew that most people were looking for an affirmation of their own worth, their unique beauty; their personal truth. Just as Freja's love for her had served to hold a mirror up to Gina's face, affirming and encouraging her, she was now able to use her gifts to help others.

Now she set to work on her latest commission, sketching out the shape of the face of the lady who had just left the gallery. Before she returned with the requested photograph, Gina had begun work on a bold and vibrant painting, the deep colours suggesting the re-invigorated passion of the woman; the ornate and intricate edging representing her deep-rooted complexities. She had seen right through the respectable, middle-class clothing and glimpsed a view of the subject as a sensuous young woman, with a passion for life. She drew out the exotic heat at the core of this woman; with bold curves and sensual sweeps, she created a rich and powerful image, capturing the quality of her essence, before marriage and motherhood had dulled her passion and muted her soul. Bearing no resemblance to the safe style of portrait requested by the client, Gina had no doubt that once her eyes alighted on this glorious, ornate depiction of her, framed in spirals of red and gold, the lady would instantly fall in love with the work. She had a one hundred per cent success rate in this respect. To date, each client had returned to view their commission and they were all thrilled with the offering. A curious practice had started, one where the clients would appear to fall in love with the work, declare their delight and request that the painting stay on display at the gallery. They would return from time to time as if to check on or their image, and as Gina regarded it, to recharge their sense of self-satisfaction. For once, Gina felt that she had created some unique magic. When looking into the soul of her client, the energy of her own soul magically entered into the mix before morphing into a person-alized portrait of the individual. One which reflected back to the subject the aspects of themselves that they feared lost or destroyed. Gina's artwork restored their sense of self, and in doing so, during the process, she also healed herself. Her once-smothered soul had finally broken through into a space where it could breathe and grow. Gina knew that her family's inability to love her for who she truly was, had served only to block their own search for happiness. No longer did their discontent taste so sourly on her tongue. She was free to connect with anyone who crossed her path and she had learned the true meaning of love. In allowing Gina to be exactly who she was, from the core of her being, Freja had simultaneously released the woman from her self-imposed prison and taught her to turn her face to the sun. In return Freja received a love that was boundless and unique.

Ophiuchus

"So the last time you saw Annaliese Shewring, she was in her office?" asked the investigating officer, Tom Watson. "What day was that? And what time did she leave? You're sure you haven't seen her since?"

"No. I told you, I haven't seen her since November 29th. It was a Friday. She was here, writing her column. It was a normal working day. The only difference was that a guy, I assume it's the same one, he called himself 'Oliver', no surname, he kept calling her and she kept asking me to take a message. Eventually she took his call. I have no idea what it was all about. She did not discuss it with me. She left the column and the replies to the readers' questions on the system, for me to check and submit to the editor, as usual, and said goodbye. It was about five o'clock and no, I haven't seen her since. I've called her home about a dozen times over the past month, but she's never returned my calls." Mary Pryce looked drained; she felt deflated. This was the third time she had been questioned by the police and she really had nothing else to add. Annaliese's sudden disappearance was as much of a shock to her, as it was to everyone else.

Mary was Annaliese's trusted assistant. She made sure the writer's work for the online magazine news site, 'Signs of the Times' was received and prepared on time for submission to editorial. They spoke most days, even when the writer was working from home. She submitted a weekly astrology column and provided answers to readers' problems, under a pseudonym, as the resident agony aunt. The paperwork aside, Mary knew that Annaliese was also working on a book and provided private astrological chart readings by email. She admired the writer's imagination and often marvelled at the imagery she seemingly conjured out of nothingness, words appearing from out of nowhere and leading you on a magical journey. However, their relationship was strictly professional and Mary was speaking truthfully when she told the policeman that she actually knew very little about the woman's private life. She was aware that Annaliese had just left a previous relationship when she started working with her, but she had not heard her speak of another beau since.

"What about that email sent from her home computer on Monday 8th December?" Detective Watson pushed once more.

"I've told you. I received no such email. If I had, I would have told you, I would have replied to Annaliese." Mary's irritation was turning to frustration.

"Did anyone else have access to your email folder?" the questioning continued. "Would it have been possible for it to have been read and deleted by someone else?" The investigator was holding fast onto this issue.

"I guess so," Mary replied. "If there was someone watching and waiting for me to leave so they could come in and access my emails in the three minutes before the timed screen-lock prohibited access, except by password."

"And you are the only one who knows the password?" Tom checked. Mary rolled her eyes in response.

"Okay, what about remote access?" Tom asked.

"Well now you're out of my league," sighed Mary. "You'll need to speak to the techies department to get an answer to that one." Tom failed to mention the phone call from Annaliese's home number to the office on the 11th December. He would keep that to himself for the moment. After all, the call only lasted 90 seconds and was possibly not answered. He wondered why she had hung up so quickly.

"One last thing," the detective said tentatively. "Do you have any other photos of her, other than the one on her readers' questions column? We need more for our appeal."

Mary stifled a smirk. "No, there is just that one."

She knew damn well that the column image was not a photograph of Annaliese.

There had been no recorded sighting of the woman since the 29th November and it appeared her apartment had been vacated somewhere between the 16th and 21st of December. Her landlord had reported her missing when he showed up with a skeleton key to find the place deserted. She had failed to make her monthly rent payment on 30th of November and had not answered his calls, emails or the door when he had visited her in early December. It was the leatherbound, handwritten diary entries found at the property by the police, which chronicled the events of the next eighteen days, therefore providing the only insight into the events leading up to her disappearance.

* * *

It was a bleak; late January morning and Detective Sergeant Tom Watson rubbed his frozen hands vigorously as he walked away from the office of the *'Signs of the Times'*, feeling a disquieting resistance to the 'missing persons' case that had been recently offloaded onto him. For some reason, no one else wanted to touch it. He couldn't find anyone in the department who could help; apparently they were all far too busy. There was an uneasy air about this story. Relatives of the woman, an aunt and a cousin now living in Limousin, France, had told the police that she had planned to visit them over the Christmas and New Year period. She had not contacted them to say she had changed her mind and when she failed to show up, they had been unable to contact her. They had been able to supply only a childhood photograph of the young woman. Her employers said that the woman's actions were totally out of character. She had been a reliable employee for over seven years, with a clean sick record, and she had only ever taken holidays which were scheduled in advance. Her landlord had found her single, missed rent payment most unusual and he was concerned about his trusted tenant. However, there were absolutely no leads in this case. Some argued that as there were no suspicious circumstances, such as a break-in at her flat, signs of a struggle, or anything questionable on her computer entries, that she just might have decided to take time out from her own life; she had no dependents. She left no personal documents or photographs at her home.

So far, no one who had interrogated the journal had been seen to make any apparent progress on the identification of the man named Oliver. The writings had now been passed by shaky hands to detective Watson and no one else wanted their name to be associated with this investigation. The detective now needed to read the damn thing himself in the hope of making any progress. He had a gut feeling that this diary had been deliberately left behind. He felt sure that it was the key to this whole mystery; one that some people might want to remain unsolved. Venturing into a quiet corner of a café, he ordered himself a large Americano and a slice of almond pastry to enjoy whilst he read the first journal entry:

'Friday, November 29th:
I finally finished this month's column. I don't know why it was such a struggle. Maybe it was down to Jupiter opposing Pluto, or my personal Saturn return. It's been a strange week and I am so tired. I'm finding it hard to concentrate and clarity is eluding me. Perhaps I'm sickening for something. The most bizarre of all things turned out to be that phone call. I'm still not sure about it all. It sounds so far-fetched and implausible, and I was a bit spooked when he told me that he had sought me out specifically for his purpose. At

first he sounded as if he had an interesting story to tell, but I told him that I'm not a ghost writer. He kept on, saying that it was an amazing tale which really needed to be told and if I just listened to him for a short time I might change my mind. Rather stupidly I gave him my landline number as I intended to be home all weekend. He said that he would be happier speaking to me on a private line and that he would call me at 10 a.m. tomorrow. Just as I was about to end the call he asked me not to mention his name or the contents of this call to anyone else, which freaked me out a little bit. If he does call and turns out to be some weirdo, I'll just have to change my number again. It's not as if I gave him my address... It's no big deal. I'll sleep on it and hopefully things will look clearer in the morning'

'Saturday, 30th November:

He phoned, on the dot, exactly as he said he would. I was anxious. I wanted some answers but he wasn't listening to any of my questions. He warned about recording any of our conversation on any computer, hence me writing about it here. He said he had withheld his number when calling the office so his number would not be easy to trace, and if I agreed to help him, he would in future call from random public phones to prevent his location being identified. He repeated it was crucial that I did not share any of this information with anyone else. He just wanted me to write down what he told me, saying that the events of the story would speak for themselves. He made me promise not to post it anywhere online, not to send by email and not even to store any of it locally in the word-processing programme on my computer. He said that unless I was willing to handwrite his story that he would look for someone else to help him. However, he also said that time was running short and it was important for him to get as much of his story written as possible. I asked him again 'why me?' He told me that he had been following my column for some months and that he knew I was also the 'Sign of the Times' agony aunt. He said that it was clear from the way I wrote, the language I used. He complimented me on my writing style and said that I reminded him of his mother. We used similar terminology, he said, we seemed to have the same take on things. As a child he had been fascinated by his mother's astrological stories and predictions. He told me that she had been the first and greatest influence on his life. He still resented being sent away from home at such a young and tender age and he treasured his early memories of his early childhood in Africa. I asked how many words he had to write, how much time he thought it would take to transcribe his memories. He said he would call me later and that I should be ready to start writing down his words. He refused when I asked if I could record him, for the benefit of my future reference. He was clearly angry at that point and I wavered. I wondered what exactly I was getting involved in...

When he hung up, I plotted my transits for the coming year, to see if they indicated anything untoward, or any time I should exercise caution. I have avoided doing this for the last couple of years, as I don't seem to have the same clarity when reading my own chart. For some reason I find it easier to narrate the astrological influences on the lives of others. This time was no exception. I am highly frustrated.

I will be here if he calls back, as I really need to do some work on my novel this weekend. It's been weeks since I last had the chance. If he does call back, I'll make sure he answers a few of my questions before I agree to spend any more of my time on this weird man.'

'2pm, Saturday 30th November:

"I was born in Dakar on 29th November 1963, just three years after Senegal gained independence from French rule. My mother had hoped to fly home before my birth so I would be born in England. However, she was taken ill and admitted to hospital in the capital. I was born with a fever and the doctors didn't hold out much hope for my survival. Against the odds, we both survived and my mother called me her miracle child. It was the start of a very unusual childhood. My mother was a nurse, my father a doctor at *the hospital in which I was born. They had travelled to West Africa under the auspices of the church. They were pioneers, furthering the Christian cause by bringing medical knowledge and skills to the godforsaken, 'dark' continent. That's the sceptical slant. I can't remember much about my father. He would often arrive home after I had gone to bed and left for work before I had woken up. We had to live within close proximity to the capital's hospital, but when I was born my mother gave up her job and stayed at home to raise me. I was the eldest of five children, from whom I was separated, for most of my childhood. However, the very early years were the happy times. We lived in a small village, further along the coast from Dakar and I remember spending lots of time on the beach, splashing in the surf and digging in the sand. My mother struggled in the heat, especially when she fell pregnant with my brother, and she craved the fresh, Atlantic breeze. At night, when we were the only two people on the beach, we lay on our backs on the sand, listening to the sound of the waves and looking at the stars. My mother showed me the constellations and told me stories about the characters in the skies. I could see them all quite clearly in my imagination and so I believed that they were real. Located opposite Orion, she showed me the constellation of Ophiuchus, the serpent-holder, and told me that I was born under a special star, one that meant I would have magic powers and that I must use them carefully in life. She said I had been born to do good in the world and I needed to listen carefully to what the important people told me. I grew up to respect to my elders and heed authority.*

However, I learned that life was not always quite as it seemed.

Things changed for me when I was sent away to school. I was seven years old, my brother Charlie was four, and my mother was pregnant with her third child. The church school was situated much further inland. I remember arriving at the whitewashed buildings in a clearing in the bush, having cried for the duration of the journey. I did not want to leave my home and my mother. She had cried at our parting, as I was tugged out of her embrace. She did not want to send me away, but both my father and the church expected me to attend the school. It seemed so cruel at the time, yet I was reminded to listen to the teachers and be a good boy.

You can imagine the trauma at being ripped out of your loving mother's arms at that tender age and being taken to live with savages. Yes, that's what they were, the white 'Christian' teachers at the school were little better than beasts. They berated the natives on the basis of their beliefs; however, some of these men were inhuman in their treatment of us children, who were ritually humiliated. That was the truth, the reality, the legacy of the church. We were beaten when we showed any signs of insubordination. But that's not really what this is all about and so I won't name people or places, but those who are interested will be able to work out the important details.

This is about is an occurrence which saw me sent away from the school and back to England, away from my home and my family. I was nine years of age and had been at the school for just over two years. I had become familiar with the ways in which it was run and the people whom to avoid if you wanted to stay out of trouble."

At this stage of the phone call, his voice cracked and I instinctively, and stupidly, told him that 'it was okay'. I didn't know what else to say. I had no doubt that what he was telling me was of huge emotional significance to him. It was in the intonation of his voice and the detail of his recall. No one could fake that. I was as also apprehensive of what he was about to tell me. I wasn't sure I wanted to hear it. At the same time I felt locked in. It just seemed inevitable that he was going to tell me more. The silence seemed to last for hours and eventually we both spoke at the same time. I started to offer him a way out by saying

"Do you want to leave it there…?" He cut across me with "I'm ready to go on now, if you are." I wiggled my fingers and shook out the stiffness in my right hand. It had been a long time since I had written so much by hand. He must have heard my deep breath as he offered to take a short break, if I needed it. I asked for half an hour, to use the toilet and make a cup of tea and he said he would call back at five from a different number.'

'5pm Saturday 30th November:

He asked how I am feeling and if I want to continue. Although tired and unsure as to what he's about to drop on me, I reasoned with myself that I could withdraw at any time. He is clearly emotional and impatient but I believe he is genuine and there seems a pressing need for me to record his story. (Although I have no idea what he wants me to do with it). I said I was happy to continue and so he continued with his story, he spilled out the details whilst I silently recorded his words. He told me:

"We often had visiting foreign officials and members of the church. Most of them came to lecture us on how to go out into the world and become upstanding citizens. One particular man stands out. He was a diplomat, I believe, a very tall man with a domineering attitude. He visited a couple of times a year. He seemed to be very friendly with the headmaster, more so than the other visitors. Looking back now I can see that they were obviously friends. He did not always stand before us, lecturing us as a group, sometimes he would interview individual boys in the headmaster's study. No one ever spoke about what was said, or done in the study, but everyone feared being called to attend there, and those who may have had a tale to tell, often hung their heads in shame. Some research I conducted later, after being sent back to England, confirmed that the headmaster and this man were themselves at school together. It wasn't until I reached adulthood that I fully appreciated the mutual basis of their association. I believe the headmaster is now dead. I heard he had a massive heart attack and died in the grounds of the school.

The other man has been a member of the cabinet, a notable Conservative MP and is about to be honoured in the Queen's New Year List. He will be granted a life peerage and will shortly take up a place in the House of Lords. He is known for his right-wing politics. He opposed the motion to allow women priests in the church, is anti-gay marriage and became fanatical about immigration issues. And he was involved in the incident which got me exiled from my home and family at the age of nine.

I saw my mother for the last time, at the Christmas holiday following my ninth birthday. I was home from school, and was jealous at how close my mother and Charlie had become. It would be another year before Charlie would be joining me at school. My youngest brother, Michael, had just started to walk and talk and there was yet another baby on the way. My mother looked tired and was a bit irritable with us, but she had enough energy to ask me how I was enjoying school. As a child, I told the truth, about the beatings, the isolation and the boys who turned bad and started to bully the younger ones. I had been lucky, so far, none of them had targeted me. She was horrified. I still remember the wide-eyed, fearful look on her face. I assured her I was okay, although we never knew who was going to be selected for the interview in the headmaster's study. I believe she managed to contact the school during the holidays, as I was called into the headmaster's study upon my return. I was shaking as I entered the lion's den. I stood before both men, red-faced and angry. They demanded to know what I had been saying and warned me that I had better stop spreading heinous lies about the school, else I faced expulsion. I was quite pleased at the thought of being told to leave the school. However, I was very naïve to think I could interfere in the lives of these dangerous men and defeat them.

For the rest of the term, I kept my head down and my wits on high alert. I can't recall hearing of any other boys being subject to the insidious interview technique. However, just before the Easter celebrations the diplomat showed up once again at the school. I kept my eyes peeled.

It was whilst the school was busy with preparations for the service and celebrations that I saw him talking to Jonathan, one of the native boys, just a couple of years older than me, who worked in *the school kitchen. Although we met every day, each of us acknowledging the other with our eyes, our lips had never exchanged a word as conversation between staff and pupils was strictly prohibited. As I poked my head around the door, hoping to swipe one of the cakes that had been baking in the school oven, the diplomat stood with his back to me, towering over Jonathan. The young boy shot me a beseeching look, but fearful of being caught in the wrong place by this man, I retreated from the kitchen building and ran away through the cloistered hallway. It was then, through the window, that I saw Jonathan leaving the kitchen, head down, walking away from the back door; the diplomat was marching swiftly behind. I watched as they left the compound and headed out into the bush. I asked myself where they were going, and for what reason? I soon found out the answer.*

We were summoned to assemble before lunch the following day and informed that one of the native staff members, Jonathan, had disappeared without permission. If any of us were to catch sight of him in or around the school buildings, we were to report immediately to our form master or the nearest member of teaching staff. This was not an unusual occurrence. At least one native boy worker ran away each year. Most were picked up after dark, lost in the bush, scared senseless and returned to face their fierce punishment – the lash.

However, another twenty-four hours transpired before we were once again gathered together. A subdued headmaster announced that the boy had still not been found, and it was now unlikely that he would return, alive. It appeared that he had run away and into the jaws of nature. We were all advised to stay safely within the school compound, and not to venture near any of the boundaries whilst the beast was being sought. We would of course be informed once the creature had been captured. The solemn-faced diplomat patted the headmaster supportively on the back as he left the stage, and cast a muted glance around the room before leaving the stage himself.

I knew I had to act.

That night when everyone was in bed I took a piece of paper and pen I had secreted under my pillow and scrawled a note. My own handwriting was quite small and neat and I needed to disguise it, so I cultivated a large spidery form for my letters and wrote:

'Jonathan was in the kitchen with Howard Wentworth-Staines just before he disappeared.'

I hurriedly folded up the paper and shoved it into the top pocket of my pyjamas. Then I sat up in bed to see if any of the other boys in the dormitory had stirred. Convinced they were all fast asleep, I crept, barefoot, over the polished wooden floors of the dormitory and out onto the cold stone floor of the hallway. I was heading for the headmaster's study, using the light of the waxing moon to light my way through the dark and threatening halls. In the silence I caught my own breath, fearful that the slightest noise might alert someone and my transgression would be discovered. Certain that the study would be empty at that time of night, I bent down to slide the paper under the closed door. However, I panicked on hearing voices in the room. I ran as fast as my legs would carry me back into the stone-arched hallway and across to hallway and back into the dormitory. The boy in the next bed turned over as I settled back under the covers and waited to be apprehended. Exhausted by fear, I fell into a deep sleep and woke with at start at dawn. Breakfast was heavy, more subdued than usual; each of us in silent contemplation of the fate of Jonathan, and me also fearful for the consequences of our actions. I wondered why the headmaster had not come searching for the author of the note that night. On reflection I guessed that the less people who knew about its contents the better, their search for the culprit would be carried out by more devious means. The silent conspiracy was electrically charged and I found the burden of my knowledge very onerous. I knew we were all being scrutinized and I kept my own counsel. There was only one way that my subversion could have been uncovered. My letter home was intercepted and I was called before the headmaster. He told me to close the study door behind me and offered me a seat. I politely declined and stood staring at the floor.

'Oliver,' he said, 'I've received a letter from your mother. She is concerned at your wellbeing. She does not think you are thriving here.' My heart soared, I was free! She had read the letter and had told them to send me home. I was ecstatic.

'She is concerned that this environment is causing you to be, how shall we say, a little unbalanced in your thoughts.' A stab of fear caused me to suck in breath.

'We have made arrangements for you to leave here. You are to be looked after by a relative of your mother, in England."

I was stunned. I was being sent to England. I had never been outside of Senegal. I had only seen photographs of England in books. I was nine and half years old and I would be travelling alone over the continents and the ocean. I asked if I could speak with my parents.

I was told my mother was currently in hospital due to complications with her fourth pregnancy and that my father was too busy to speak with me. I was told I could write them a letter when I arrived in England."

At this point Oliver fell silent and I used the opportunity to speak up. I asked him why he was telling me this. Did he believe that this man, Howard Wentworth-Staines was responsible for the death of the young boy?

"Yes," he replied. "I have no doubt. I had many hours to mull over the events as I was escorted overseas by a government aide. When I arrived in England I told my aunt and uncle, my mother's brother, what I knew. They were at first unsure if I was telling the truth. But they were surprised at the trouble and expense to which the school and the Commonwealth government office had gone to appease a 'troubled' child. After all, I was not from a high-profile family. Whereas my paternal grandfather, Edward Taylor-North had been a notable army major, the Blundells were gentleman farmers. My mother had been raised on a peaceful English farmstead. I now found myself the youngest of the family, with one brother and two older sisters. I was cared for and I felt safe and enjoyed discovering a new existences. Kids adapt, much better than adults realize at times. I asked if I could write to my mother and I was very gently told of her death, some three weeks previously. The baby girl had survived, but my dear mother had lost her life during childbirth. I was devastated. The only consolation was that I was told the rest of the family would be joining me, in England, very soon. I was most happy to know that my brother Charlie had escaped the evil of that school.

Some years later I was told that the school had closed. The body of a young black boy had been found in the bush. Listening in to adult conversations I discovered that the victim had wounds to his head and some form of internal haemorrhage, evident from the blood covering his buttocks and thighs. Instantly I knew. This poor boy was another victim of the deplorable diplomat."

'Sunday 1st December:

After a heavy session yesterday, I asked for a little time to reflect on this information. The phone has remained silent for most of the day and I spent the time finding out as much as I could about Oliver, his family and Howard Wentworth-Staines. The latter, being a public figure had lots of information in the public domain. I confirmed his entry in the New Year's Honours list and his MP's profile confirmed that early in his career he was employed in the diplomatic service in Africa. I ascertained that that he currently sat on numerous, cross-party select committees within the House of Commons.

I struggled to find any information in relation to the church school described in the account and resolved to put that search on hold whilst I scoured the internet for any information on Oliver Blundell himself.

I found just one entry. It was part of a conversation forming a thread posted on some obscure website forum dated two years previously. It appeared to be a discussion about sustainable architecture in West Africa. The entries by Oliver appeared to be defending the work of a charity building a village school out of clay. He stated that the project had the backing of the Royal institute of British Architects and the techniques being used were a fusion of traditional materials and modern innovations. Oliver's name was underscored with the professional title of 'sustainable architectural consultant.' This led me to verify his membership of the RIBA. Not on the roll as a current licensed architect, a search through the previous years revealed the last entry of his name dated two years previously.

I wondered where this would all lead. I had an increasing sense of anxiety and was concerned as to whether he would call again. I tried to put the images of the young boy, Jonathan, out of my mind, but my heart was crying out for a sense of closure, an instalment to tell me that justice was served and there were no more victims. I need some answers.'

'8pm call from a subdued Oliver. He apologized for his tone and explained that talking about the events from his childhood always made him morose. I asked why he was telling me this story and what he expected me to do with it. He told me that things would become clearer. However, he wasn't getting away with that line again. He had already monopolized my weekend and I needed to try and wrap this weirdness up and get ready for the week ahead. I had made no progress on my novel, had two charts to create for private clients and had not even looked ahead at the letters for the following week's advice column.

I asked him outright what he did for a living. He replied that he had previously worked as an architect. I asked if he had any family, a wife, or children of his own. He confided that his father had died of malaria about four years after he himself had been sent to England. He explained:

"I had no relationship with my father. He was from a military family who believed that children should be seen and not heard. Looking back I can see that he and my mother were mismatched. She *was a nurturer, a carer. I learned far more about her when I was taken in by her brother and his family. I was surrounded by photographs of her as a child and as my uncle Peter still lived in the family home, there were some of my mother's childhood toys still sitting on the shelving in the nursery. Peter Blundell was the nearest thing I had to a father. That's why I took his surname. I have always found relationships with women very difficult. I was once engaged to a woman who accused me of comparing her to my deceased mother. She left me, saying that she could never match up to such a romantic and idealized vision of womanhood. I remember her accusation so clearly, still; that temper, those flashing eyes and scathing expression on her face."*

There was a heavy silence. He was clearly emotional. I spoke a little more gently to encourage him to volunteer further. Oliver cleared his throat and described to me his years at university studying architecture and his enduring love for the environment:

"I guess that growing up in Africa made me aware of nature and the fragilities of existence. I still prefer open countryside and the shoreline to inner-city landscapes. I often travelled alone, during the university recesses and sketched the unusual or unfamiliar forms, both natural and manmade that I happened across. This was reflected in my work. Of course, this was decades before the green revolution and the search for sustainable sources of power. I made the connection between the traditional building and power-sourcing skills of the West African people and believed that a fusion of the traditional with the Western innovations could be married to optimize the benefits of both."

Oliver explained how, in his capacity as a sustainable architectural consultant, he attended a select committee meeting in the House of Commons to advise on policy making. Here he came face to face with Wentworth-Staines, who was also member of the committee:

"I recognized him immediately. Still tall but less imposing; he was approaching the age of seventy, his hair had thinned and

whitened and his once muscular frame was wasted and withered. From his demeanour and wry comments he appeared very resistant to any notion of change or progress. In an irritated manner he questioned the reasoning behind my recommendations. When I expanded on the differing methods required for buildings in countries like Britain which experience four seasons, as opposed to the hotter, wet climates, I referred directly to my project in Senegal, and then he became noticeably more agitated."

I asked Oliver if he thought that Staines recognized his name. He replied that as a child, he had been known by his father's surname of Taylor-North. And as far as he knew, the Blundells and the Wentworth-Staines did not mix in the same social circles. He continued:

"During the debate I started to feel his burning stare. I became restless, hot and uncomfortable. I'm sure he was also feeling the discomfort and was trying to work out the reasons for it. It took all of my courage to look him in the eye and confirm his worst fears. Using the name of the school I had attended as a child I stared him in the eyes and talked about the inappropriate aspects of its construction, given its location. I explained how the natural temperature of the environment was absorbed by the concrete, causing its stifling atmosphere indoors. I referred to the excess mud that accumulated around the circumference of the buildings in the rainy season and how the whole place was plagued with pestilence when the pools in the bush surrounding the school stagnated. His face became thunderous and I knew that I had him in my sights. I delivered my final comment directly to his despicable soul. I stated that the environment had served as a haven for a myriad of hidden threats for the children of the establishment; and the sad deaths of some of the school's children finally culminated in the early demise of its headmaster and the destruction of the buildings. Staines spluttered and choked at this point; a concerned colleague poured and passed him a glass of water, as he continued to cough."

"How did that feel?" I asked Oliver. "Did you feel any sense of triumph? Were you hoping that his past would be raked up and his heinous crimes uncovered?" Oliver remained silent for a few moments.

"I don't really know what I was hoping to achieve. I think the hurt child within me wanted revenge, but it is the fifty-year-old man who is facing the consequences of those actions."

It was my turn to become silent. With a creeping sense of fear I quietly asked him, "And what are those consequences?"

"Wentworth-Staines is a powerful man, he has friends everywhere and he's on to me. I fear for my life."

We were now deep into dangerous territory; I could feel it, with every nerve ending in my body. My imagination was aflame with the possibilities; my body was on fire with fear.'

'Tuesday, December 3rd:

I'm feeling a little more together today, things are a little clearer. I have to admit I was spooked. I haven't been outside the door, switched on the computer, or answered the phone for two days. I don't know if he will call again. I don't know where this is all heading. I said I would have to speak to Mary very soon and he said to do nothing for the next couple of days, until he is sure that no one is watching or listening in to us.'

'Wednesday, December 4th:

I have run out of fresh milk and bread. There's not much food in the freezer and I will need to breathe some fresh air soon. He's even made me afraid of opening the windows.'

'Thursday, December 5th:

He called. Said he's been moving around to make sure he's not being followed. Is this all for real or have I got caught up in the world of a mad man? How would I know? Why am I listening to him? I have been watching all of the news channels, as he suggested, but have heard nothing. The weather forecast says there will be a frost and a light covering of snow is forecast for the weekend. I told him that I need to buy some food. He said not to worry, he would arrange something.'

'Friday, 6th December:

Still avoiding calls from the office. My answerphone is full of messages and I only pick up the call if he signals as arranged. Three rings. I answer the immediate call following. He has my number on automatic redial so as to ensure that no other calls can get through in-between.

There was a quick call today only to confirm my address. He said that he had arranged a food parcel delivery and to expect a caller between 2 and 4pm. Feeling brave I ventured to the window and looked at the street below. A plain white van arrived at 3:30 and I watched as a man opened the back doors and lifted out a plain brown box. He approached the building and pressed my buzzer.

"A delivery for Annaliese Shewring," announced a male voice. I pressed the intercom button and released the door to my first floor apartment.

"It's me," he said quietly as I opened the door. I froze; more with excitement than fear.

"Can I come in?" he asked. I was transfixed by the intensity in his eyes. It was him, Oliver.

I knew by his aura, the energy that had imbued his words and fashioned his distinctive voice. He had the air of a distinguished man, an open, intelligent face with hair greying at the temples.

"Yes, do," I came to my senses.

"I can't stay long," he explained in a muted voice. "I paid cash but I had to rent the van with my driving licence and so the agreement is in my own name. I will have to return it today and get a train or bus to another destination. I have a friend who is getting me a false passport."

I closed the door behind him and felt a rush of exhilaration. He was real. He was enigmatic, but he was human. I could sense his anxiety and I wanted to help him. He held out the box of provisions and I came to my senses.

"You don't look anything like your column photograph," he noted.

"It's not me," I confided in him and thanked him for the box, taking it through to the kitchen, unloading its contents on to the table. I looked back at him to see him standing awkwardly and nervously looking around.

"Have you got time to drink a cup of tea?" I asked. He sat down for a while and I had to stop myself from staring at him. It felt bizarre. There was nothing false or threatening about him. Here he was, a complete stranger sitting on my sofa, and yet I knew so much about him. I asked him how much he knew about me and he confided that he had been searching for a ghost writer for some time. Although he was not the typical purveyor of agony aunt columns and astrological forecasts, he said that there was something familiar about my writings. He loved the gentle way in which I responded to people's insecurities and issues. He explained that I reminded him of things long forgotten, things his mother had told him when he was a small child, and he felt comforted by that. I believe he was speaking the truth.

He impressed upon me once again that Wentworth-Staines was a powerful and influential man.

"He has friends in government agencies, the police, parliament and the church. He has innumerable business and media contacts. It's getting harder to hide from him. I believe he will do anything to stop my story coming to light. It is the only thing between him and his peerage."

'Monday, 8th December:

No word for two whole days. This is torture. He left on Friday, saying he would be in touch as soon as he could. I've been online searching for more information about him and his 'situation'. I don't know if he's just laying low or if anything untoward has

223

happened, but I can't allow myself to think like that. He is a warm, charming man one minute, then he's shy and awkward the next. There is such an intensity about him. It's alluring. I tried to concentrate on writing the column but my mind is clouded, and I'm unsure about my judgement. Perhaps it's because the sky is full of snow waiting to blanket the world white. I emailed the office earlier today to say I have been poorly and will be back to work as soon as possible. So far there has been no response.'

'Tuesday 9th December:

I was woken at 7am by a frantic call. It was Oliver speaking so quickly that I could hardly understand his words.

"I'm running out of phone credit and I have no more cash, can you call me back?" He sounded highly stressed.

"Isn't the number withheld?" I asked, sure that he hadn't forgotten to do so.

"Fuck! Fuck, yes," he spoke through gritted teeth.

"Do you have the option of reversing the charges?" I asked.

The line went dead.'

'Wednesday 10th December:

I had a sleepless night. I spent the silent hours watching the snowflakes gently falling, illuminated by the golden glow of the streetlight. I don't know what to do. Should I go to the police? What if they have already got to him? He told me that Wentworth-Staines had managed to influence his bank manager to foreclose on his business loan and pressured the building society to repossess his home after just one month's missed mortgage payment. What if they traced him by way of his driving licence and the hire car agreement? I checked my email and there was still no response from the office. I wonder what's happened to Mary. I really want to call her. Is this just paranoia? I've lost six pounds in weight. Perhaps I should talk to someone outside of this situation. I'll see what transpires today.'

'*Thursday, 11th December:*

I dreamt of him last night. I could feel him, smell him. We were close, he was warm and loving. I awoke with an inner smile and a sense of closeness with him. Then I remembered that I haven't seen or heard from him for forty-eight hours and my heart hit the pit of my empty stomach. I can't go on like this. I have to speak to someone, to get out of this place today. I called the office but no one answered and I got a call-waiting signal. I switched lines but it was too late, the caller had rung off. I took a long hot shower and he rang, leaving a message.

"Pick up the phone, it's me. Annaliese, are you there? Pick up the phone if you can hear me. Oh God I hope they haven't got to you. If you pick up this message, I'll call tonight at 10:30. Make sure you delete this message."

I wasn't sure if he meant call on the telephone, or in person. Was it safe for him to come here? Is it safe for me to me to be here?'

'*Friday, 12th December:*

My buzzer sounded at exactly 10:30 last night. It was him. I let him in and he trod soft, wet snow up the staircase, kicking off the remnants from his boots before he entered my wooden-floored hallway. I was so relieved to see him. I hugged him and he seemed a little taken aback. He said the flat was warm and welcoming after a two-hour trudge through the snow. No buses were running and the trains were on a reduced service. He opened his rucksack and offered me more supplies of coffee, milk and bread. I made up a bed for him on the sofa. We sat talking into the early hours amidst the lamplight. He told me more about his childhood, how much he missed Africa and his mother. His biggest fear is disappearing and his family not knowing the reasons why. He has told them about his childhood experiences, but he has deliberately not kept them informed as to the events of the last two years, since that fateful committee meeting with his old adversary. They have no idea how he has been hounded by the powerful and influential figure. He says it's not fair to implicate them as he is sure the ruthless man will stop at nothing. They believe that his business has failed and he has lost his house, as he is having a mid-life crisis. He believes it is safer for them to think this than to know the truth. Hopefully, with my help the truth will out and they will not suffer in any way.'

'Saturday, 13th December:

I awoke to the sound of a man speaking in a strange language. It was Oliver, speaking to someone using a mobile phone. I reached for my wrap and headed into the lounge. He acknowledged me and curtailed the call.

"Pay as you go, disposable phone," he explained. I felt uneasy.

"What language were you speaking?" I asked him.

"Mandinka," he replied. "It is one of the African languages spoken in parts of West Africa, such as Senegal. French is also widely spoken there," he explained.

"Are you fluent in French too?" I asked him and he nodded, yes. He asked if he could use the shower and I showed him through the bedroom to the bathroom. I couldn't help but check the contents of his rucksack whilst he was washing. I had to know if there was something he was hiding from me. I found nothing.'

'Sunday, 14th December:

He's like a caged animal, pacing from room to room, waiting for a phone call.

I don't think he slept much last night – I didn't, as I could hear him moving around in the lounge and kitchen. I can feel his tension; it's becoming unbearable.'

'Monday, 15th December:

The pressure got the best of both of us yesterday and we argued for the first time. I shouted that I hadn't asked to be involved in his shit and I needed my life back. He hugged me and apologized.

"I'll be gone soon, I promise. I'll take what you've written and

make sure it gets into the right hands before I go. I'm sorry, but you were the only one who could, who would help me," he said.

"And it's messing up my life," I told him. "If I don't show my face in work soon, I'll have no job. Then I'll lose my home too. Then I'll hold you responsible."

He grabbed my arms at that point and drew me towards him. "Please don't shout, don't be angry." He looked at me beseechingly. I started to cry. He pulled me in close to his chest and wrapped his arms around me. "I didn't mean for this to happen. I never should have come here. I didn't mean to implicate you, but once we started talking I couldn't help but tell you the whole story. I never meant for you to be drawn like this. I just wanted someone to write the story. I thought you would be able to remain detached and anonymous. I thought you would be safe."

"You thought I'd have no feelings, no empathy with you? Is that why you picked me? I thought it was because I reminded you of your mother and your childhood," I spluttered.

"Yes, but I didn't think we would ever meet. I hadn't bargained for how things turned out. I just hadn't thought it through, how it might affect the feelings of someone else, someone like you." He tried to explain, each time digging himself in deeper.

"And what happens when you leave? Am I expected to forget all about you?" I asked through my tears.

We reached an understanding and made a decision. Oliver took a photograph of me and messaged it to his contact. They held another conversation in Mandinka. I asked if I could use the phone to make one final phone call.'

'Tuesday, 16th December:

This is a story that needs to be told. All of the necessary details are contained within this journal and whoever discovers it has the responsibility to make its contents public and to ensure that justice is done.

By the time anyone reads this, Oliver Blundell will be in a place *where the twisted law of Howard Wentworth-Staines has no juris-diction.*

After a lifetime of fear, he will finally be free.'

Tom Watson raised his eyebrows and whistled as he closed the diary pages.

Looking around, he knew he had to act swiftly. He needed to check that no other police force had issued a missing-persons report. The café was empty apart from the sullen waitress sitting behind the counter with a bored expression on her young face. He called in to central records and asked for a check to be run on one 'Oliver Blundell.' He waited just a few minutes for a call back assuring him that there were no outstanding warrants, charges or investigations involving someone with that name. Relieved, he asked one more favour of the operative on the other end of the line. She sighed, but processed his request. Tom thanked her genuinely when she came back with another clear result.

He now had a full understanding of the situation. He guessed that both Oliver and Annaliese were in Senegal. The photograph sent by phone would have been for her fake passport. The arrangements being finalized in Mandinka were for travel. Finding them in Africa would be an expensive and unlikely prospect. Besides, all the evidence pointed to her willingness to travel, he thought to himself. Neither of them had committed any crime, except perhaps for travelling under fraudulent documents. She believed that if she stayed behind and produced the diary entries to the authorities, her own life would be in danger; and perhaps she was right. His mind switched to her assistant Mary Pryce. She knew. She had failed to tell him that the column photograph was not a true likeness of the woman. She had allowed it to be used for police purposes, knowing full well it wouldn't assist them with their enquiries. That last phone call referred to on the penultimate entry in the diary; it must have been to her, Tom reasoned. She knew full well where her colleague was, hence her reluctance to help with the enquiries. But still, she hadn't reported the woman missing. The only people who needed to know about the woman's whereabouts, perhaps, were her relatives in France. Perhaps they would receive a call from a French-speaking Englishman resident in Senegal, explaining the events?

Asking the young, expressionless waitress for the bill, he rose, placing the diary in the inside pocket of his thick, woollen overcoat. Pocketing the change, he pulled his coat closed and wrapped his grey woollen scarf around his neck. As he walked out of the café and along the riverside, he dropped his hands into his pockets and his chin into his scarf to avoid the ice-cold wind catching his lips. He hated having dry, cracked hands or chapped lips. He wondered what the temperature was in West Africa at this time of year. Probably too hot for him, he reasoned. He wasn't one for extreme temperatures. Heading across the bridge, he battled the cross wind from the gushing river below and stopped to re-arrange the jacket he was wearing under his heavy winter coat. He wondered if Mr Shaky Hands had signed out the diary out under his own name. Tom certainly hadn't signed for it. Pieces of evidence went missing all the time. He couldn't think of anyone who wanted to pursue this case and he certainly didn't want anyone like Wentworth-Staines interfering in his life. Why should the responsibility fall to him? He'd never even heard of the guy and was certainly not aware of any current investigation involving him.

As he leaned on the railings and opened his coat to button his suit jacket against the wind, ever so slowly and deliberately, the small pocket diary slipped out from his inside pocket and slid through the railings, into the fast-flowing river below. He watched purposefully to ensure it quickly submerged, before walking briskly on.

Lady Magpie

"I salute you! Now stop frightening me and fly away!"

The solitary magpie was back, his claws scuffling at the edge of the open window. He had been annoying Jude with his daily presence for over a week now and she was tired of it. Just into her thirty-sixth week of pregnancy, the pre-natal depression had set in and she was feeling heavy and tired. She irritably snapped the window shut and the bird flew off the ledge, leaving her with a sense of unease. What did he want with her? She could not shake off a sense of impending doom: what if she had made a huge mistake? Well, only time would tell. One for sorrow, two for joy... Why couldn't the magpies just let her know if she was a having a girl or a boy? She found a sense of comfort in repeating the verse that she recalled from the childhood recesses of her mind.

It was time she got herself downstairs and into the kitchen where she was to start preparing the lunchtime specials. Since she had fallen pregnant, her husband Ed had virtually taken over the running of the pub. They had employed a bright and cheerful young assistant, named Maya, who seemed keen to learn and eager to please her new employers. Her presence served to both lighten the workload and spark up the atmosphere of the place in this curious seasonal lull between Bonfire Night and Christmas. Ed insisted that Jude rested as much as possible; yet she knew it was important to keep her hands busy and her mind occupied for as long as she could. However, she was struggling at this stage in the pregnancy. Usually so svelte in appearance, she had begun to feel a little dowdy and less inclined to spend so much time socializing with customers in the bar. With Maya's waitressing assistance, it now suited her to remain behind the scenes in the kitchen where she could concentrate on the secret ingredients for her magical recipes which had proven so popular with the diners. As Jude reached the bottom stair, which led from the cosy nest shared by the couple, she smiled as she stepped into the lounge of the country pub that they had so lovingly recreated as a welcoming place for travellers, families and local customers alike. She was greeted by her husband with a loving peck on the cheek.

"And how is my beautiful wife feeling this morning? I must say, you're looking radiant!"

Ed knew that Jude's resources were running low. The rich, autumn glow had faded from her cheeks and he knew that she would soon need to spend the winter weeks of her pregnancy with her feet up. She had battled through the morning sickness of the early stages, but had blossomed in the middle trimester. However, now in the final weeks, her face was tired and Ed saw how slowly she hoisted her heavy frame up and down the stairs. During the six years of their ownership, the Juggler's Arms had grown into a thriving business and the couple had decided it might be a good time to bring a child into the world. Until they had met, neither Ed nor Jude had considered the possibility of having children. However, the synergy of their creative natures had resulted in a deeply loving relationship and to raise a family together felt perfectly natural for the both of them. The arrival of this lucky child was excitedly anticipated by the most warm and loving of parents-to-be.

Today was the weekly lunchtime meeting of the local Ladies' Circle members. Jude was familiar with their favourite orders and always ensured that their personal specials were on the board. From the kitchen she could hear Maya chatting with the ladies and she turned her attention to the fresh ingredients with which she would magically create the most delicious of meals. As the Ladies' Circle members scraped the creamy vanilla custard from the rims of their dessert bowls, Jude stepped in to serve their freshly ground coffee and drew a sharp breath at the sight of a thin woman, wearing a brightly coloured turban, walking into the bar. Approaching Jude, she asked if it would be possible to order a bowl of hearty winter soup, a side salad and a cup of green tea. Jude agreed and asked her to take a seat, saying that she could have the meal ready in just a few minutes.

In the kitchen, Jude closed her eyes and imagined the foods this customer's body was crying out for. In her mind's eye, she saw slices of creamy avocado and ripe blueberries amongst the leaves of baby spinach and felt the soft crunch of walnuts between her teeth and the crumble of some blue cheese between her fingertips. Arranging the rich foods on the plate, she also shredded some carrots and beetroot mixed in with raisins before lightly sprinkling a few drops of olive oil and a pinch of linseeds over the surface of the lovingly adorned plate. Jude then turned her attention to the hot tomato soup, which was gently spiced with radish and celery, waiting on the hob. She ladled some into a bowl and placed a warmed rye baguette on a plate. Reaching for a serving tray, she carefully arranged everything atop to ensure it would balance and carried it out to the waiting customer.

Ed watched curiously from the bar. The lady wasn't a regular customer but there was something familiar about her. She chose a seat in a quiet corner of the room from where she could look through the window into the pub garden. The evergreens planted by Jude and Ed some six years previously had now started to flourish prominently on the edges of the lawn so elegantly lined by beautiful deciduous trees.

"That was absolutely delicious, as always, my dear," said one satisfied customer as Maya approached to clear away her bowl of sherry trifle. Overhearing the expression of gratitude, the thin young woman smiled and swung her attention back to the interior of the bar. Her eyes connected with Ed's, who had been staring at the back of her head.

"Ella?" he mouthed. The frail-looking woman smiled back in acknowledgement.

"Ella?" Ed repeated, out of shock and a sense of disbelief. Looking around with a bemused expression, he wondered to himself if this was this some kind of weird dream. He had not seen or heard from his ex-wife for over seven years, except through their respective solicitors when submitting their divorce papers. The woman who had left him and disappeared to Spain to live with her lover now appeared before him as a shadow of her former, glamorous self. No long, glossy hair or nail extensions and no revealing clothes or stylish shoes. The same woman now wore loose fitting, comfortable clothes over her wasted frame, and a colourful bandana around her head. Bare lashes, which used to be heavily coated with mascara, made her blue eyes now appear larger than her pale, bare face. Ed was unsure whether he should go over to speak with her. What was she doing here? What did she want? Had she come here to see him? What had happened for her to appear so different now? What would Jude think of her coming here?

At that moment, his wife appeared from the kitchen and walked over to the customer carrying a large plate of salad. Ed watched the two women chat as Jude put the item on the table. Then he saw his wife nod her head, smile and stroke her large, pregnant abdomen. Sensing his gaze, she turned to face him but he quickly busied himself by moving clean glasses around on the shelf behind the bar. Jude walked over towards the bar, where the Qualita Vittoria coffee machine was situated.

"The lady sitting by the window has ordered some green tea," she informed Ed. "Can you fill a pot with hot water for me, please?" Ed obliged and handed a stainless-steel pot to his wife and she returned to the kitchen to brew up the healing tea. Once again, he cast his glance in the direction of their most unexpected guest. Part of him wanted to rush right over and look into her familiar face. He was torn between maintaining a respectable distance and releasing the pressure of the many questions burning in his mind. However, Jude returned with a tray bearing the pot of tea and a large cup and resumed her conversation with Ella, so Ed stayed behind the bar.

As the afternoon drew to a close, the last two jolly women from the Ladies' Circle emerged from the toilets to be accompanied out of the front door by an obliging Maya.

"Yes, I'm off now too," the smiling girl explained as she swung her scarf around her neck and pulled on her woollen mittens. "It's the end of the lunchtime shift for me, but I'll be back tomorrow. I'll see you ladies next week!"

Jude stood up and walked across the room to bolt the door behind them. Ed looked up at her and she beckoned him to join her in the lounge at the sole remaining customer's table. Ed thought that his heart was beating so loudly that he was sure that Jude would hear it.

"Come and join us for a cup of tea," she mouthed, whilst the juddering from within worked its way through to his shaking hands. Wide eyed, he took the seat across the table from his ex-wife.

"It's good to see you, Ed," Ella said quietly as she reached over the table to quieten his trembling hands. She calmly explained, "I spoke with Jude, your lovely wife, a few days ago and she said it would be okay for me to call around today to see you. I haven't come to make any trouble, Ed. I just wanted a chance to put right some past wrongs."

Ed flashed a look of amazement at his wife. So they already knew each other? He managed just a few words, "What's happened, Ella? You look...so...different."

"I have breast cancer," Ella said calmly and then hastened to soothe the shocking announcement, gently rubbing the back of

Ed's hand with her skeletal thumb. "I was diagnosed five years ago. Do you remember that my mother died from the disease some ten years ago? Well, I had surgery in Spain. They removed both breasts and then I had chemotherapy. Then I had to wait. After further tests, they said there was nothing more they could do for me as I never really went into remission. The cancer had already spread. I came back home a year ago and have tried every sort of alternative treatment, from Reiki to nutritional therapy." She cast a grateful glance at the remnants of the salad on the plate then continued, "I've even had psychotherapy to help me to understand all that has happened to me and I've finally learnt to accept my impending death." The room fell silent. Ed's gaze dropped to the table top where his and Ella's hands were resting.

"I haven't come to cause any trouble or spoil your happiness, Ed. I'm really happy that you found love after I left. And now you're going to be a dad!" Ella clasped his hands within her own and Ed looked up to see a faint sparkle in her eyes.

"I'm so pleased for you, for you both. You're having a Christmas baby!" She turned to smile at Jude, who nodded serenely in response. Looking back at Ed, she concluded, "I just wanted to say sorry for the way that I treated you when we were married, and to ask for your forgiveness. I don't want to leave unresolved issues behind for others to deal with when I'm...gone."

"What about Alan?" Ed tentatively broached the subject of Ella's lover.

"It's been all over between us since I discovered my illness," Ella explained. "In the beginning, he vowed to stick by me but soon after the surgery he started to spend more time away from home and when I was going through chemotherapy he just couldn't handle it and walked out. I can't blame him. It must have been hard for him to just helplessly stand by and watch. You know Alan, he's a macho man. He's remarried now, I heard.

He finally divorced Aimee and settled down with some young Spanish girl. Anyway, it's all history and I have forgiven him. I've also made things up with Aimee. She refused to speak to me for years and I can't say I blame her. After all, I ran off with her husband when their baby was only a few months old. Some friend, huh? I don't know if she's really forgiven either of us, but at least she now knows I'm truly sorry for the sadness I caused her with my selfish actions."

Ed leaned back in his chair and took stock of the situation. Ella looked and sounded so different. Had she really changed? Catching a glimpse of her protruding collar bones, he felt a pang of guilt at his fleeting doubt. Sensing the momentary discomfort, she rearranged the loose scarf draped across her shoulders to cover her exposed bones.

"So, are you here for more treatment?" Ed asked. He was confused.

"No, there is no more treatment. It's just palliative care now. There is nothing more anyone can do for me. It's just a matter of time."

Realization dawning, Ed whispered, "How much time?"

Jude shifted uncomfortably in her seat before announcing, "I've invited Ella to stay with us for a couple of weeks."

Ed sat up sharply in his chair. "What, here with us?" he asked.

"I've been staying at the flat above the butcher's shop but Alan's found a buyer for it and I'm not yet ready for the hospice..." explained Ella.

"She has daily assistance from the Macmillan nurses, Ed," added Jude. "It's just like she'll be renting the spare room from us for a while, if it's okay with you?"

"What about the baby? I thought you wanted me to decorate the room in readiness, for a nursery?" Ed's mind was awash with confusion.

"The baby will be in the bedroom with us for the first couple of months for night feeds. He, or she, won't need the room until we're into the New Year and…" Jude's voice trailed off.

"…And if I'm still around, I'll probably be in the hospice," Ella said, finishing the sentence for her. "Ed, I'll understand if you want to say no to the idea. It's a big ask. I would never have dreamt of asking but when Jude suggested it, I had a lovely, warm feeling. The idea of spending my last days somewhere like this, with friends like you, well, I couldn't really ask for more."

"And she has no one else to turn to," Jude added, feeling that it had to be said.

Ed was constantly amazed by his wife's creative business ideas and her general upbeat attitude to life. However, he was doubtful of her judgement in this instance. Perhaps it had become clouded by her condition. He had read somewhere that women's brains function differently when they were pregnant. Biting his lip, he turned to look at Jude, "Perhaps we need to speak about this, in private? I'm sorry, Ella. This whole situation has come as something of a shock to me. I really don't know what to think, or what to say. I just don't know."

"I understand," Ella responded instantly. "It was just an idea, a most kind thought on the part of your lovely wife. It's okay to say no. You don't owe me anything and, anyway, I've had my wish granted. All I wanted was to have an opportunity to apologize for the hurt I caused you. That was my aim. I never expected to be greeted with open arms and taken back into your life. Thank you for speaking to me, for taking the time to listen to me." Ella stood up.

"Now, if you let me know how much, I'd like to settle the lunch bill with you."

Ed also stood up and walked over to the till behind the bar. Turning his back to the room he mechanically typed in the codes for Ella's order and totalled the cost. Turning back to announce the price of her meal, his eyes once more rested on the forlorn figure of his ex-wife, now shrunken to a fraction of her former size. He saw the tired face of an old lady, from which peered the scared eyes of a lonely child. Flooded with emotion, Ed realized that this woman could not cause any harm to him or his family. She was crying out for some human warmth and comfort in the last days of her life. How could he have feared her?

From her seat across the bar, Jude recognized the expression on his face. She knew how deeply her husband's feelings ran and she saw this as a moment of great healing for both him and his unfortunate ex-wife. Although she was taking a risk in allowing Ella back into her husband's life, she was confident of his love for her and their unborn child. And besides, this brave lady was not going to be around much longer.

* * *

Early December witnessed the Christmas decorations adorning the walls of the Jugglers Arms. Ella had some great designs in mind and both Ed and Jude were grateful for her sharing her ideas.

As she sat quietly in front of the log fire, describing a decorative centrepiece for the bar consisting of an arrangement of three purple, one pink and one white candle, Ed remarked, "You always did have an artistic eye for detail."

Ella explained, "Since I have been ill I have found a faith. I believe that God has decided it's time for me to go and that he is waiting for me. This is one way I can show him that I too am counting down the days. Tomorrow, I will light the first purple candle: the prophesy candle. Its purpose is to remind us how Jesus's coming was foretold long before his arrival. Next Sunday I will light the second purple one: the Bethlehem candle. On the third Sunday of Advent it will be the turn of the rose-coloured candle: the candle of love. The fourth candle is the angel candle and we light that on Christmas Day. Promise me that if I become too ill you will remember to light them on my behalf."

Ed had come to appreciate how much Ella had changed over

the seven years since she had left him. It was clear that she had spent much time alone, soul searching and now seemed to be a much happier and contented person. During their marriage, she had appeared a very frustrated and discontented young woman and she could now explain how she had come to gain some insight into the reasons for her past behaviour.

"I was so impatient, so frustrated with everyone. There was so much I felt that I deserved in life, stuff to make up for my crappy childhood, and that it was the role of the man, or men, in my life to make me happy. My therapist helped me to realize that this was probably due to the anger I felt when my father walked out on us. All I can remember is my mother struggling to provide for us. I discovered that I had become intent on having all the things in life that I couldn't have as a child; all the material things I thought would make me happy, and that it was the man's job to provide them for me. But it was never enough. I was always left wanting more. Even when Alan took me to live on his yacht in Spain, it didn't seem to satisfy me. Alan called me an ungrateful bitch when I got tired of the partying and said I wanted to move off the boat to live in a villa. I guess he was right."

Ed started to protest that it wasn't true but was silenced by Jude's gentle, restraining hand as she lightly squeezed his thigh beneath the table.

"She needs to come to terms with everything, Ed," she explained later when they were alone together. "Just let her say everything she wants to; she's not looking for compliments. Our role is to witness her redemption. That is the kindness we are offering."

Aware that Ella's newfound faith was not shared by Jude, whose beliefs were rooted in the African practices taught to her by her grandparents, Ed held his remarkable wife close and whispered in her ear, "I am so lucky to have you. I love you." Then, gently rubbing her bulging belly, he added, "And I love you, too."

As the weeks passed and the days became shorter, Jude found herself spending more time with Ella. Both were physically and emotional tired, albeit for different reasons.

"I never wanted kids," Ella confided one late afternoon as they sat by the fire, waiting for Ed to refresh the tea in their shared pot. "They never figured in my grand plan." She laughed at her own words. "Not that anything really figured, except for having lots of clothes and all the latest beauty products. If only I knew then…"

"Yes, priorities change," agreed Jude. "I think that's the case for most people. Accepting the changes is where people struggle." With a smile she emphasized the expanse that was once her trim waistline. "It sounds ungrateful, but I am so tired of this pregnancy. I just want it to be over so that I can at least have my own body back."

In the moments of sharing, both women felt temporarily relieved of their respective burdens. Ed watched them chat, a warmth permeating his chest at the sight of the smiles spreading over their faces.

"One thing I want is for Ed to know that, despite the way I treated him, I really did love him," Ella confided. "I was on a crash course to self-destruction and no one else in the whole world could have succeeded in making me feel happy with my life."

"I think he's got that message, loud and clear," assured Jude. "I believe that Ed just wants everyone to be happy. He too had a tough childhood. His father wasn't around much and, when he was, Ed never seemed to be able to match up to his expectations. From what he's told me, that's how he developed his drive to succeed. He doesn't seem to hold onto grudges. And now he's so excited about this baby, about becoming a father himself."

Ella smiled through her tears, "He will make a great father, of that I'm sure."

* * *

On the third Sunday of Advent, Ella asked Ed if he would be so kind as to light the rose-coloured candle on her behalf as she was not feeling strong enough to make it down the stairs.

"I might be coming down with a cold, so I'd better rest up," she explained.

Jude too seemed out of sorts that day and later that evening a call to the local maternity unit resulted in her admission to hospital.

"Her blood pressure is slightly raised and she had protein in her water sample," explained the on-call midwife. "I'm not overly worried but as it's her first pregnancy, and the unit is quiet for once, we'll admit her for observation."

Ed found it very strange driving home to the pub without his wife. It was to be the first night that they would be spending apart in over six years. His memory transported him back to the day he had first stepped over the threshold of the place, keenly following the attractive Jude. He had been strongly drawn to the place from that first moment and neither had spent a night away from the place since they had moved in. Neither had been able to drag themselves away, even for a honeymoon, for which they had simply locked the front door, hung up a 'just married' sign and celebrated at home.

On the stairs he crossed paths with Margaret, the Macmillan nurse who was now attending her charge twice daily.

"How is she?" he whispered.

"She's very weak," the nurse responded. "I have increased her daily dose of morphine and so she will probably spend more time asleep from now on. But she shouldn't be in any more pain. If you see she is distressed, don't hesitate to call me. I'll be back early in the morning to check on her."

Ed's heart sank. He knew that this was not a good development. "I thought she might have more time...I mean, she still seems quite cheerful in herself although she has lost more weight over the past few days," he thought aloud.

Margaret shrugged her shoulders and forced out a kindly smile, "It could be weeks or days; we really have no way of knowing."

When Ed called the hospital early the next morning, he was informed that Jude's blood pressure had increased and she was unlikely to be coming home for a few days. Panic emanated from deep within his midriff.

"What about Ella?" he asked Margaret upon her arrival to attend to her daily needs.

The nurse explained that she had brought some equipment which meant that Ella would no longer need to leave the bedroom to use the bathroom and that her visits were to be increased to four each day.

"In-between visits, she will probably remain asleep," Margaret explained.

"Yes, but I can't just leave her alone whilst I'm visiting the maternity unit, can I?"

Ed was tense. Margaret suggested that as long as he stuck to the arranged visiting times she could arrange for a sitting service to take over from him.

"We'll do all we can to keep her out of the hospice," she assured the fraught man.

* * *

Ed crept through the pub in the midnight silence, consumed by exhaustion that had accumulated over the past few days. He had been oscillating between Jude's bedside in the hospital's maternity unit and Ella who was dying at home; his thoughts always, and most annoyingly, wandering in the direction of the empty chair. If there was any way of being in two places at once, this was exactly the moment he would have chosen to utilize the skill. However, as the contractions of induced labour had once more died away, he had been advised that both he and Jude were in need of some sleep and he had left his heavily pregnant wife in the hands of the night shift staff at the hospital, returning home to relieve the Macmillan nurse of her evening sitting duty. Peering around the edge of the open door to Ella's room, he caught sight of her restful face eerily lit by the moonlight in the still night. For one horrible moment he feared she was not breathing. Just a few steps into the room his fears were allayed as she sighed, nestling her head further into the soft feather pillows surrounding her. It was the only time she would be without her head covering.

For the first time, Ed saw the smooth skin of her scalp, bald except for a few scattered tufts of soft downy hair looking for life. It was his turn to sigh. He smiled gratefully and looked lovingly at her familiar face. He had repeatedly reassured her that she didn't need the false eyelashes, hair extensions, nails or make-up to improve the way she looked. She had always dismissed his comments with a tut; a sharp stare from those sparkling blue eyes, and a toss of her pretty head. Now the inner beauty showed through her bare face, which wore the expression of the sleeping child within; her shrunken, wasted body occupying only a small space beneath the bed clothes.

The brave woman's strength showed in her acceptance. She had long stopped fighting against all of the aspects of her life with which she was unhappy, discovering a sense of inner peace which blanketed all of her previous discontent. In her mind, she had tucked in all of the frayed edges of her life and smoothed over the surface of her mistakes. Gently cosseted in the soft, loving care of her closest friends, she dreamed only of the happiness of the magical couple and their family and, for herself, a future without pain.

Ed backed away from the bed, not wishing to disturb her further. Leaving the door ajar, he took himself across the hallway to his room. Within minutes, he lay partially clothed and deeply unconscious atop the duvet on his bed. His sleep was heavy, his limbs leaden from the weight of his duties of care. He collapsed into a seemingly soundless vacuum of enervation, featureless and black.

* * *

The alert of an incoming text message startled him some seven hours later as he started to surface from the depths of his sleep. Reaching out to the bedside cabinet for his phone, he squinted in the strange, winter-morning light to read, *'preparing for emergency caesarean section, come now!'* He noted the time as 7:10. Instantly he leapt up off the bed. Bending over the bathroom hand basin he splashed his face with cold water, momentarily pausing at the reflection of his heavy-lidded face in the mirror as he lifted his head from the sink.

Ella! It was her face he could see in the mirror. She would be alone if he left for the hospital straightaway as the nurse was not due to arrive until seven o'clock. Yet if he delayed his departure, he might well miss the birth of his child. Pulling on a clean shirt over his crumpled jeans, he stopped for a moment, brushed his hair out of his face with his hands, and took a deep breath to try to clear his mind. Drawing back the bedroom curtains, the sight of the full moon standing proud in the cloud-strewn sky caused him to catch his breath.

"Ella, I'm so sorry to disturb you but I just got word that the birth is imminent and I wanted to say…" Ed faltered before finishing the sentence. The word goodbye was looming large in his mind's eye. He became unsteady on his feet in response to the stark realization. Regaining his composure, he attempted to mask the reality of the situation, "I just wanted to say that Margaret will be in at eight o'clock. That's just half an hour from now. Do you think you'll be all right on your own until then?"

The truth was reflected in Ella's eyes. She also knew that this was the last time they would be together. She nodded gently and whispered, "Go!"

Ed knew that his place was with Jude and their newborn child, and he was deeply grateful. He leaned over to kiss her fragile cheek and tasted a tear. Gulping down his choking emotions, he straightened up and walked over to the window. Lifting aside the curtain he motioned to the full moon, majestic in the winter-morning sky. He spoke of the clarity of the icy atmosphere and for a moment Ella thought she could once more feel the cold air on her lips. She inhaled the pure chill and a shiver ran through her body, despite the fact that she was wrapped warmly in several layers of soft, clean bedding. She felt the icy grip pinch the tips of her fingers and toes. Both looked at the grey and pink streaks of clouds strewn across the sky, momentarily entranced by the simple beauty of the serenity. Never before had Ed stopped to watch the sunrise whilst the moon was still highly visible in the sky. Neither felt the need to speak. There were no words to describe the exquisite beauty of the slow dance as the sun started its glorious ascent into the sky as the moon faded away gracefully.

As Ella slipped back into a peaceful sleep Ed quietly left the room, glancing back just once to see a silvery trace of tranquillity on her face. Silently, he gave thanks for the moment of peace, before a deadly shiver ripped its way through his body. Taking a moment to compose himself in the car before setting off on his journey to the hospital, Ed forwarded the text from Jude to Margaret, adding to the message that he was leaving the house at 7:30 a.m. and would be in touch further as soon as there was any more news about the impending birth.

Driving through the sleeping streets in the space between the close of night and the opening hours of a new day, time now took on a curious dimension for him. He had witnessed the tireless cycle of nature. He was in a curious place; a lonely platform from which he was viewing a life nearing its end, yet also from the unique, if uncertain, vantage point of waiting for another to begin. Very grateful for Ella's return, he had found the peace to heal the pain of his discontented wife's sudden departure from his life.

Arriving at the hospital, all of his senses switched to high alert. He was immediately informed that there was grave concern for the safety of the baby and the wellbeing of the mother, and surgery to deliver the baby was imminent. With the baby's heart rate dramatically dropping below a safe level, it had been too late in the labour for anything other than emergency intervention. He was ordered to wash his hands and wear protective clothing and ushered behind a glass screen from where he could see his beloved Jude lying unconscious on the operating table. This was not how he had expected things to be. Ed felt alienated and helpless. After a blurred week of bedside waiting he was now expected to just stand and watch as the medical team worked quickly and methodically; almost mechanically, he thought.

However, he had little time for reflection. Within minutes, he was watching as his child was lifted from his wife's body and taken away from the table for observation. As the sound of his daughter's first cry resonated at the core of his soul, so his unrestrained shriek of delight emanated loudly through the surgical mask. His heart pounded to the point where he was sure it would overheat and melt into his chest. His thoughts evaporated into the void where his head once sat atop his shoulders. As Jude lay unconscious from the anaesthetic, the surgeon tended his postnatal stitching duties and the midwife took the baby for observation. Ed became overwhelmingly sad that his wife had missed this moment. He watched intently for the reaction of the medical and nursing staff as they noted changes in the monitoring equipment and wrapped the tiny newborn to keep her warm. Ed knew it was a girl. As his wide grin refused to leave his aching face, tears of both sadness and joy streamed from his eyes. Seeing the overwhelming tide of his emotions, the midwife joined him to hand over the carefully wrapped, precious bundle to her father, offering congratulations before turning away to record the details of birth.

On the chart, she wrote, 'Date: 23/12/2012; time: 07:59 hours; sex: female; weight: 3.23 kilos.'

"What are you naming her?" she asked, looking up from the page with a warm, knowing smile spreading across her face as she watched the besotted father, awestruck at the sight of his newly born child.

"Ellie, Ellie Grace," Ed managed to mumble, mesmerized by the sparkling, blue eyes of the baby. "In memory of a close friend," he added. Unsure as to how long he held his daughter in his arms, it was in those uniquely precious moments that he learned of only one truth: that of the all-embracing power of love. He knew that love could wrench your heart, painstakingly draining every last drop of energy from your body. Yet it could effortlessly flood you with warmth and lightness. Ed learned that there was no greater force in life than love.

An hour later, when Jude had regained consciousness and was able to sit up in bed to cradle their beautiful daughter in her arms, Ed lovingly kissed his smiling wife and reached for his coat. Leaving the hospital ward, he stood outside the main hospital entrance breathing in the fresh morning air. The fading moon was now retreating as thicker grey clouds had arrived to take centre stage in the sky. He looked at his watch. It was nearly nine o'clock. Reaching into his jacket pocket, he switched on his mobile phone and clicked on the entry for 'home' in his contacts folder. Before he could choose the 'call home' option he heard the familiar notification alerts. There were three unread text message symbols flashing for his attention. Each one was from Margaret and marked up as urgent. Ed opened the most recently sent message. It read, *'Have tried calling and left 3 voicemail messages; sorry to have to tell you this way, Ella passed away just before 8 this morning. I found her at peace on arrival.'*

* * *

As he waited for the last coat of paint to dry on the nursery walls, Ed remembered the Advent arrangement on the bar and dutifully lit the fourth candle. Better late than never, he thought to himself. His attention had been otherwise occupied that week with both the funeral arrangements and the preparations for the baby's homecoming. Both events were scheduled to happen on the same day. Jude had insisted that she and the baby attend the cremation and Ed knew better than to argue the point. Ella's instructions had been short and straightforward and the hospice had been very happy to offer their assistance. All that remained was to find a suitable resting place at the Juggler's Arms for the urn containing her ashes.

Next, his attention was drawn to the last remaining white candle. The 25th December had passed, but Ed knew it was the intention behind the act that really mattered. As he lit the wick and watched the flame dance, he whispered a final goodbye to Ella and uttered heartfelt thanks for the safe arrival of his precious daughter and the wellbeing of his beautiful wife. In that moment, Ed learned what it meant to feel truly blessed. His trance was broken by a tapping sound on the garden door of the pub. He saw the movement of a shadow, but couldn't make out a figure at the door. As far as he knew there was no one in the walled rear garden, accessible only through the bar. Unlocking the door he looked out to see two magpies engaged in a playful scuffle on the garden path. As he stepped out of the door, the birds ceased their activity and flew away. *Two for joy,* he thought, smiling to himself as he stepped back inside and closed the door, surprisingly comforted by his belief in that old superstition.

The Glass Cliff

Location: The State of Kind (formerly the United Kingdom)
Date: 2060 AD

'We are on the edge of the abyss. We can no longer continue in the ways of the past. The future lies ahead; and the way forward is sparklingly clear from the brink of this glass cliff. There is nothing for us to return to, no limit on the possibilities and no one to stop us making the leap.

The days of patriarchal, capitalist, hell-on-earth are behind us and the way to prosper is to restructure our communities, our economies and our lives, in the way that only we women know how.

Love will replace lust; care will replace cost; compassion will reign supreme over personal wealth and profit margins, and passion for war will burn out, giving way to the flaming, ardent passion for peace.

We will build a framework of support and a network of encouragement. Our leaders will listen and enable; our people will be heard and assisted to help to build healthy and rewarding lives for themselves and their loved ones. Together we will provide an invaluable, humanitarian service for ourselves, our families, our friends and our communities.

When the men lay down their arms, the women will pick up their alms to treat the sick and the wounded. We will bury our dead, and in honour of their memory we will create the future they believed they were fighting for.

However, it is time that we followed our feminine vision and implemented our own, divine methods.'

Forty years on, Kalista's words now seemed so altruistic and naïve. With the benefit of hindsight she knew she should have spoken in stronger terms. If she'd had any idea of the intensity of the struggle ahead she would have prepared her people for conflict. Yes, it was crucial to build on the solid foundations of knowledge gleaned from the past, but as The Kind were entering a new era; there was also a great demand for innovation and creation. It was these aspects which had called for bravery and fortitude. She sighed and began to write:

'The transition had been a long, arduous stretch of awakening, on the philosophical front; accompanied by a struggle for power on the political front. The male-dominated government members had held on until each was systematically uprooted by the revelations of the investigators. Axed by the self-defeating slices of their own hypocrisy, the politicians fell from glory, leaving their lies scattered around them like rotten leaves.

Each was replaced by a woman of values; vetted and verified by The Kind, until it was believed that the balance of fairness and justice had been adequately adjusted. Family name and money were no longer the prerequisites for power. The Kind looked for people with altruistic passion, a track record of charitable, environmental or humanitarian works and who truly spoke from the heart. Yes, they were mainly women; however the age also witnessed the flourishing of heart-centred men. Once the dictatorial aggressors had 'warred' themselves out, the passives, poets and conscientious objectors picked their way through the piles of bodies of needless slaughter to stand at the front and be counted. The poppies from the killing fields finally stood tall and proud to speak openly of the power of nature and wisdom of the universe.

As the macho world system of money-powered madness fell into dysfunction and disrepair, it lay dormant, in positive disregard by society. It seemed that to completely destroy some things would not bode well for the structures intended to replace them. The new would *merely be sucked into the vacuum left by the old. As such, the situation dictated that it was better to allow the negative things to dwindle, and die a natural death, than to engage in the dirty work of wilful destruction. To have done so would have made us no better than any of our predecessors.'*

Kalista's long-awaited memoirs were finally being written. The great leader's wisdom was eagerly anticipated by a people keen to celebrate their successes and show the world how they had achieved such greatness. Marianna, her close confidante of many years, knocked gently on the open door, before walking across the room, bringing with her a fresh glass of water. She smiled supportively as she placed the item on the desk. Kalista gratefully acknowledged the refreshment.

"Is it just me, or is everyone else experiencing this lull in energy?"

The two women surveyed the mountainside scene from the large window in front of the desk. Usually Kalista drew inspiration from the rugged landscape surrounding her exclusive home. Now the deep green forests appeared pale and withered, the thin atmosphere constricting her chest. Pensively she sipped the sparkling water. Marianna drew a deep breath, her chest expanding until she stood in her full Amazonian glory; a woman of compassion, a warrior of wisdom.

"If anything, there is an uncomfortable restlessness amongst the young people. I believe they are looking for change," she explained with a cool pragmatism.

"Perhaps they sense my tiredness, and are eager to move on with a new leader, one who has the energy to drive forward their change," Kalista mused.

"All the more reason for you to complete your memoir," Marianna assured her.

The original members of the inner circle of The Kind still held their treasured positions. The twelve women knew that their individual strength was greatly enhanced by the support of the others. There was no hierarchy to speak of within the group as each valued and respected the contribution of the others. Whilst each woman held responsibility for one particular aspect of the interior governance of the state, Kalista who had sacrificed her personal life and any chance of motherhood to lead the changes had been selected as the figurehead by her colleagues. The people could only listen to one voice at a time and hers was recognized as the tone to which most people were likely to attune. However, each member of the inner circle also knew that Kalista always spoke their truths. Still gazing at the mountains she thought aloud, "It's time for you to seek a replacement for me; make some enquiries and see if any names surface. I can't think of anyone of the inner circle wishes to replace me, but we don't want to be taken by surprise. We also need to look further afield for new circle members and of course we need to know their inside story so that we can choose wisely."

Marianna nodded in silent agreement and left.

Her leader continued to write:

'We picked up the pieces, the bits that still functioned, and we fixed them. We fashioned our economic structures with symmetry and clarity. Our benchmark was fairness; our quality controls the smiles of satisfaction at the smooth workings of the system. Our transactions were based on mutual trust, our currency was kindness. We rebuilt the health and educational infrastructures and we promoted sustainable methods of production of the necessary domestic goods.

Changes in the habits of consumption were quick to follow. With a different rewards system we found that values were quick to adapt, and gratefulness became a popular feature of daily interactions. Quality replaced quantity and we were living proof that with less, we actually had more – more time, more energy, and more appreciation of the wonder of our existence.

As our communities flourished, more people were keen to join *with The Kind and so we devised a system whereby a representative would venture into another community and teach the workings of our ways. As people internalized the vicissitudes, so the subsequent changes became evident in their surroundings. It was as miraculous as flowers blossoming from tight buds into layers of soft, gentle beauty.'*

It was very important to Kalista that she clearly imparted the concepts on which her great nation was founded; that she detailed the principles which had enabled its successful, sustainable growth. She knew it was not the time to sit back and rest on her successes. Now it was crucial for her insight to be sharper than ever, her research to keep her ahead of the game and her working knowledge of the world to allow her to both walk amongst her people in warmth and admiration; and to stand aloft, to speak to them, and for them when the occasion arose.

One of her most successful achievements had been in the sphere of education, where ability was viewed on an individual basis and opportunities provided to fill the needs of the society, which fluctuated over the years. When there was a good fit between the micro needs, the accurately measured strengths and abilities of individuals and the macro requirements of society, progress was firm and new frontiers were forged. When any aspect appeared to be failing, there was immediate intervention and where necessary, the appropriate changes were swiftly made. Stagnation was viewed as an early sign of decay and never tolerated. As such, the constant theme of change became part of the narrative of The Kind. This ensured the dissemination of a proactive consciousness amongst its people and accordingly, education became another self-directed facet of life.

Kalista felt that she needed to explain in detail how her compulsory programme for teenagers, which included both studies and hands-on experience in international disaster management, helped them through the tetchy, transitional years; whilst also affording them a wider perspective on life, and a breathing space from any family tensions.

She would speak at length of the selflessness of the women at the heart of communities who, in addition to raising their own families, chose to take care of the less able amongst them. She wanted to explain that the true heroines were not the strategists, nor the policymakers, like herself, but those who spent their days looking after their families and their nights looking after the members of the wider community: the children of sick parents, those injured, the hurt and often those who had somehow become lost along the way.

These women were the ones who made the whole system work. They gravitated together in an organic fashion and determined what their communities needed. They organized their people and skills in a manner most suited to the issues at hand. These women walked tall, earned the respect of their peers and were awarded the responsibility of the wellbeing of others. They were leaders who further facilitated and empowered those in need. Recognizing that the true measure of any society is the manner in which it treats its unfortunates, The Kind strove to provide for the weakest. The strong knew that there would always be the weak to be carried and this aspect was regarded as of equal importance as to the other successes of life.

As a result, the skills that encompassed empathy, patience, acceptance and intuition pervaded society, through familial, educational, social and vocational layers. These skills were valued as highly as the rational, the deductive and the scientific had been in the previous system. Results were gauged on a wider, inclusive continuum, where financial success and profit held no greater value that generosity, integrity and gratefulness. The concept of GDP had been refashioned to include the value added to society in the form of happy, functional individuals creating a rewarding world for everyone. Where the incidence of poverty and loneliness was negligible, there was a discernible correlation in the form of a greater output of creativity. Quite simply it was proven that happier people created more art, music, theatre and film for others to engage with, and enjoy.

At this thought, Kalista lay down her pen and sat back, releasing her knot of long, greying-black hair, which tumbled down the back of the cushioned, wicker chair. As she relaxed with a sigh, the wrinkles softened out of her olive complexion and she gently rubbed her dark-circled eyes. At the start of this adventure, she had been a woman in her prime, gifted in the ability to cast her gaze around her and know what her contemporaries were feeling. Now, the needs of a whole new generation lay before her. These were the children of the evolution; the ones who had known only The Kind system of living. Yet they were already looking at ways to change and improve their world. In her society where equality reigned, where intelligence was rewarded with responsibility and the once menial jobs of caring for children and for the sick, infirm or elderly had been elevated to the positions of high priority there was still an undercurrent of discord, a restless need for challenge and change.

She knew that amongst her people there were individuals who had resentfully chosen their position in the new society, rather than languish in the ruins of the old system. Now she wondered as to the efficacy of their activity. Perhaps she had underestimated their influence, or maybe they were now regarded as the rebels of society, the romantic heroes so appealing to the younger generation. Kalista called for Marianna, "Can you send through the latest monitoring report on the movements of the masculine underground?" she asked. "This is concerning me and I really need to know that the situation is not out of hand."

* * *

The Kind system had established a wide range of genetic testing for individual predisposition to life-threatening illness and a widespread health education system. Intertwined with psychological and academic learning, it had ensured that the current generation suffered no prejudice as a result of ill-health. The emphasis was on encouraging the wisdom of self-responsibility, as opposed to penalizing those who had appeared to cause their own health-related misfortune. Research into the neurological rewiring effect of the applied practice of empathy was still inconclusive, however there was evidence that the practices had resulted in a significant shift in social attitudes and consciousness. Kalista was hopeful, that in addition to the growth in self–responsibility that the propensity for deep levels of empathy would proliferate in future generations of The Kind. Contemporary biological research had a higher regard for the effect of intention on the individual memory cells of the body and was constantly expanding in the realms of unlocking all of the types of information encoded within the human body. As such, people's average lifespan was increasing and insight into the nature of human existence was revealing a wealth of information. The multi-layered workings of the mind were gradually being peeled back to reveal the pervasive nature of the power of thought at a cellular level.

However, there were still influential members of the society for whom this information proved problematic. These were the die-hards who denied the intrinsic, peaceful nature of humankind. They were intent on preventing any challenge to the precedent of mankind as natural warriors with innate aggression. Kalista and her followers had to tread most warily on this front. With hindsight, it was this perilous boundary that had demanded so much of her time and attention. Having ceased with open attacks, the secret, extreme, masculine movements had gone underground and she had been obliged to plant various sources to monitor their activities. If they now returned evidence of an increase in support for the movements, or a growth in their strength, she would have to act immediately; and she knew exactly what she would have to do.

There was a single blight in Kalista's existence, as those of the inner circle were fully aware. One personal issue with which she had wrestled, for many decades. If The Kind were looking for a new leader, she would need clean hands with which to pass over the reins.

Experiments had started in the adult, male prison system in 2020. Although the society created by The Kind had largely eradicated the phenomenon of crime, the existing prison UK population of ninety thousand adult males at that date, had largely remained within the confines of the existing prison walls. The compendium of research into the nature of offending had revealed that by 2018, some eighty per cent of the population were recidivists. As such, each individual was afforded a final opportunity to engage with the prescribed rehabilitation methods. Further efforts at rehabilitation under The State of Kind were concentrated towards the eight women previously imprisoned for lesser offences such as those related to drug use and petty theft, and all young people held in juvenile penal institutions between the ages of seventeen and twenty-one. The new age of criminal responsibility was set at sixteen and anyone displaying antisocial behaviour below that age was subject to compulsory therapy, with the funds previously used to prop up the criminal justice system now being reassigned into education, social support programmes and therapeutic research. Using the statistics as a precedent for a change of legal status, all remaining adult inmates who refused to engage with rehabilitation programmes, were regarded as invalid residents of the state, and commonly referred to as the 'Un-Kind.' It was envisaged that although in the early years there may be some additions to the numbers, over time the size of the population would level off and start to diminish. As such, the programme of prison closures had commenced within the first ten years of the inauguration, and an annual report documenting the changes was published. In a society where openness and transparency was crucial, Kalista's challenge was to allow enough access to the system to dispel any urban myths which might otherwise spring up, whilst ensuring that prison was seen as a last resort. The system was one of containment, rather than punishment, as it had long been accepted that inhuman treatment only resulted in a further deterioration of antisocial behaviour. By virtue of their new legal status, the 'Un-Kind' were not entitled to the same specific rights as compliant citizens, such as freedom of movement and freedom of speech. Although detached from society, in which they refused pro-social participation, Kalista could not sanction dehumanization of the inmates. It was not her way to order destruction; she believed that contained negativity would dwindle and finally turn in on itself. Meanwhile, the prisoners were still afforded the appropriate care for their health and wellbeing. For followers of the old regime the changes were confusing. They had been used to acting on the precedent that prisoners were fair game for their own, subliminal antisocial behaviour. They viewed the attention of medics, behaviourist professionals and teachers as 'luxuries', of which the prisoners were not worthy. Kalista knew that merely suspending criminals in an unchanging state would only serve to reinforce their thought patterns and problematic behaviour. She saw it as a necessary way of both discerning further insight into the causes of the condition of deviancy, and a way of disempowering the phenomenon. Those prisoners who demonstrated compliance and progressed through the system were rewarded with a move to the 'research facility', where they believed that life was easier and perks would be more forthcoming. To counter any resistance from the personnel involved in the system, who were actively encouraged to act on their positive emotions in every other aspect of their lives in The State of Kind, Kalista had suggested that they treated the negativity of criminal activity in the same way that scientists regarded the 'dark matter' of the cosmos, and continued in the same, tireless search for enlightenment.

Additionally, for the leader, the problems of state prisoners were surprisingly close to home. Despite the serenity of her public face, and her seemingly uncluttered demeanour, there was one secret that consumed her private thoughts and feelings. It was about him; her estranged husband of fifty years, who had disappeared from public life on her inauguration as head of The Kind State. It was no secret that he had earned his millions on the old money markets, screwing every last penny out of immoral mergers and secreting his acquisitions where the tainted tax men never shined their torches. It was an undeniable fact that when his rebellious wife had succeeded in creating a system with no place for him, he had taken his money and fled. However, it was knowledge to only a few as to where he found shelter. Kalista had taken pity on him and couldn't forget the support he had afforded her during their marriage, despite their ideological differences. She had helped him fly beneath the radar when others were calling him to account. She couldn't forget that she had once loved him. The survival of The Kind was of greater importance to her and she had sacrificed her life with him for the greater good. They had communicated infrequently and in a covert manner, and when his health had taken a turn for the worse in the later years, Kalista had ensured only the best healthcare for him. Her good health and wellbeing was, in part, a testament to her sensible life choices. However, they were both now in their seventh decade and she knew that time was of a premium, to both of them. It was time she visited to consult him, before taking the next step.

* * *

To any member of the public or visiting official from overseas, the drive along the sweeping, tree-lined avenue was a surprising first impression of The Kind State's *Antisocial Behaviour Research Facility;* a stark contrast to the penitentiary-style super-prisons built by the UK authorities during the last years of their rule. The grounds were immaculately groomed and the building a contemporary structure. Expanses of glass had been designed to optimize the benefits of the natural surroundings, whilst retaining the necessary safety features to preserve the integrity of an impenetrable facility. Once through the security lasers which verified the DNA of all visitors, Kalista was afforded maximum clearance to attend all areas of the facility, including the private rooms of prisoners. When the 'Un-Kind' agreed to transfer to this facility they automatically relinquished all privacy rights. As such, their behaviour was perpetually observed, recorded and analysed. By nature, the inmates in the facility actually enjoyed the attention, most enthusiastically engaging with the enduring 'game of outwit', as they perceived it. In return, the researchers were able to monitor and experiment with the more intelligent psychopaths. Those with strong narcissistic tendencies particularly enjoyed life at the centre, and were able to provide state researchers with an invaluable insight and experience of the condition. It was here that significant medical and surgical inroads were made into the functioning of the human brain. In the belief that they were the most important subjects for the researchers, many participants allowed extensive MRI scanning of their brains over many years. Others volunteered for chemical research by testing for the long-term effects of excessive use of psycho-active medication and neurotransmitters. Older prisoners, who knew their use was more limited, often resorted to the donation of their brain tissue for stem-cell experiments and cloning purposes. In short, the male brain became the most deeply explored region in the science of The Kind.

It was to the hospital wing that Kalista now headed. The director of the facility accompanied her along the corridor and showed her into the room of her estranged husband, Aeron Flood. His health had degenerated over the past few weeks and he was now in isolation, hooked up to a heart monitor, with an intravenous drip which fed and medicated him with morphine. Kalista could see from the sanitary objects placed around the room that he must now be largely bed-bound. Once a powerful and charismatic man, Aeron now lay prostrate with a single sheet covering his naked body. His eyes were closed and an oxygen mask covered his nose and mouth. The doctor assured Kalista that he was still alive, despite his repeated requests that they release him from his miserable condition. A stroke had left him paralysed on his right side, and in the later stages of diabetes he had significant impairment of his sight. He had recently been diagnosed with oesophageal cancer and she was advised that it would not be advisable to stay for any length at his bedside, as he was weak and cantankerous.

"Aeron... Aeron, it's me, Kalista," she gently tapped his arm as she spoke. Slowly he opened his eyes and squinted to try and focus on her face.

"Kali?" he mouthed.

"Can we remove his oxygen mask?" she asked the doctor. He nodded and once more reminded Kalista to limit her stay.

"You have only this window," he advised. "Just ten minutes. Remember to replace the mask and press the call button if you need any assistance." He pointed out the wall-mounted alarm switch, and turned to leave the couple alone in the room, throwing the catch so that the door did not automatically lock behind him. It was the one reminder that this was a prison hospital. Leaning over the bed, she reached for the Perspex mask and gently removed it from his face. Aeron's eyes widened, as if to take in more light and he tried once more to focus on Kalista's face.

"You are looking old," were the first words out of his dry mouth.

"Do you need some water?" she asked on hearing his hoarse voice. Aeron nodded. She filled a glass from the jug on a bedside cabinet. "Okay, I'm going to raise the head of the bed," she said as she looked about for the foot pedal, to allow him to sit up. As she lifted the glass to his lips, Kalista took in the sharp lines of his bony, thin face, once so handsome it had left her feeling weak. Now his lips were thin and cruel, his face contorted into a lopsided sneer. The last long strands of thin, silver hair fell from the top of his head to land beside his face on the pillow. Aeron had taken up his post of director of the facility on its opening. It was the only place that Kalista had believed he would be both safe and subject to supervision. She also believed that it was a useful employment of his skills. She knew that he would only be able to function in an environment where he felt challenged. In the past, as a financier, he had achieved great wealth and status due to his high level of intelligence and his lack of empathy for the suffering of other people. Admired by many, he was also loathed and feared amongst those who made sacrifices for him. He took from many and rewarded few. He accumulated power and distanced himself from anyone who could harm him, with the exception of his own wife. They met around a boardroom table where she sat in her role as legal advisor to the chairman when Aeron had dazzled her with his charismatic charm. Over time, the effect had diminished, and she found herself rebuked, isolated and often lonely, Aeron preferring to have his ego massaged at endless conferences, both at home and abroad, or wheeling and dealing with prominent financiers on the world stage. However, a brave new world had also opened up to the impressionable young woman. Their relationship afforded her insight into the workings of the international monetary mechanism and corporate politics, and also to the nature of the powerful people responsible for the decisions. Young and impressionable, her initial distaste on discovering a world of corruption and greed had nevertheless soon turned to disgust at the reality of the consequences for the innocent, whose lives were adversely affected by the workings of the rotten institutions.

When she could no longer stomach it in silence, Kalista had started to seek out like-minded people and form alliances with others within the system: those who saw through the fading glitter to the dusty, bare floors of the empty warehouses, disused office blocks and abandoned industrial units. She had worked tirelessly, behind the scenes, with those who shared her vision, to create a real alternative to the system. But she acknowledged that without a rich and powerful husband to support her, she would not have been able to leave her career and spend her time and money on fulfilling her dreams and creating an alternative reality. His fearful cold-heartedness and cruelty served only to spur her on.

Since his demise, he had been installed in the facility, allegedly working for The State; although Kalista knew that he would never have conceded defeat. As his psychological make-up matched that of the inmates, he knew how to hook their interest and manipulate their attention. The interplay between them proved fascinating for the supervising psychologists. Whilst Aeron's sense of social importance was maintained, the less able amongst the psychopathic community learned the skills that would help them succeed, without having to resort to violence. They developed into a community where the more subtle skills of manipulation and negotiation now served to assuage their pulsating egos. Power was still the currency, yet it was achieved in different ways. As in any isolated group, the weakest member was always subject to the actions of the strongest; those who could no longer control their situation chose the only available option for getting out by committing suicide. As the inmates grew older, so the nature of the dynamics between them changed, and it became an unwritten rule that this was the only way in which the inmates could maintain any self-respect. To take one's own life was the ultimate act of control. It proved that not even God could get one up on you.

"Aeron, I need some information from you, and some advice," Kalista said as she pulled up a visitor's chair to the bedside. "You still have your finger on the pulse. I know. I get reports of who visits you and how long they stay. It's all on the record. I need to know what's happening on the underside."

"You give me what I want, and you'll get what you want," the old man retorted weakly.

"I want names, just the key players, those with the power in here and the contacts out there."

"I want your promise," Aeron demanded, swallowing uncomfortably between his words.

"How many names can you give me?" Kalista had no time to waste.

"Five names, but first you must find the isolating switch in this room." Aeron had thought through this moment on many occasions. Even in death he needed to feel in complete control. Kalista knew the drill. If she simply unplugged the machines they would raise alarms. She needed to cut the room's supply to the main circuit. As promised, the camera in the room had already been disabled and the electronic record of her arrival had been erased from the system. She had been briefed as to the route and function of the machines in the room and the order in which they should be removed from the body.

"One name, before I take the first step," she bargained. After that there would be no going back, and they both knew it. She glanced at the clock on the wall. Aeron sensed that the power was finally within his grasp.

"Flick the switch," he ordered.

"Tell me the name of the man in here with the contacts on the outside," Kalista contended. "Give me him and his contacts, and you'll get your wish." Her voice shook a little as the realization of the situation sunk to the bottom of her stomach. She had already crossed the line. The act went against every principle of her personal integrity, and every nerve ending in her body was on high alert. She wanted nothing more than to be free of this man and his slow, poisoning presence. With the population of the facility declining with the progression of years, to lose its leadership would render it weak and ripe for new leadership. It was imperative that she disempowered this dangerous community by extinguishing its links with the outside, before the pressing evolution of The Kind was unleashed. As the current leader, the facility was her only Achilles heel. Although every cell in her body informed her it was illegal, immoral and unforgivable to take the life of another, she took heart only in the notion that she was releasing this man from his pain and anguish, at his own request. Once more she asked herself if she was truly serving the interests of The Kind, and she was reassured that this sacrifice was the only way forward from this point. The slate would be clean and the foundations she had built would stand clear, untainted and proud. After this one final act as Head of State she could retire, relax and allow the responsibility to be borne by the new Kind. For the last time she had to play Aeron's game. Walking over to the door, she turned back and shook her head.

"You've missed your last chance," she announced to the dying man. "I'm leaving and there will be strict instructions to let you die naturally, however long it takes." Aeron mouthed a name. She asked him to repeat it. It was a name she recognized. She walked over to the morphine drip and increased the dosage. Aeron's chest heaved in relief.

"Who are they and how can I make contact with them?" His lips hardly moved but she was sure she could hear a whisper from the fast-fading voice. She repeated her request. He obliged with the required information. Kalista clarified a few further details with him before once more increasing the level of medication. Aeron's eyes were now closed, his breathing more shallow. She had minutes to incapacitate the machines and leave the room before the sabotage was discovered. Aeron was unconscious and would probably die from organ failure due to the overdose of morphine alone. Kalista could take solace in the knowledge that his last moments of life were painless. She removed the line feeding him insulin and dropped it to the side of his hand, to make it look as if he had pulled it out himself. Next she had to cut the electricity supply to the heart monitor before he flat-lined and automatically raised the alarm. Opening the drawer of the bedside cabinet, she retrieved the screwdriver which had been left there for the purpose, gently moved the unit aside and quickly unscrewed the plastic cover to the electricity supply of the machine, positioned on the wall behind the cabinet. Carefully removing the wires from the contact, she checked that the power to the heart monitor had failed before hastily re-affixing the cover and replacing the cabinet. She slipped the screwdriver into her pocket and leaned over the bed to check to see if Aeron was still breathing. Her heart was pounding as she replaced the oxygen mask, her shaking hand accidentally brushed his cheek. Cool to the touch, Kalista knew that his body was failing fast and he would never again open his eyes and look coldly at her. She stood silently and closed her eyes. She asked for forgiveness and wished him a safe journey. Then she opened her eyes and took a step back. This was the end of an era. She felt a need for some mark of respect, yet in truth the only emotion she felt was relief. She turned and walked away. Without a final look back, she left the room, resetting the catch and locking the door behind her. As she hurried along the corridor, someone stepped out from an office doorway. She froze. It was the director. He looked into her face. She breathed.

"Mission completed?" he asked in low tones from beneath raised eyebrows. She nodded and handed over the screwdriver. He stuffed it into his pocket and accompanied her to the exit, opening each door by way of his own DNA screening. If people looked close enough they would be able to discern that she had been present at some point that day. Her fingerprints would be all over the place. However, only a handful of people were privy to the relationship between her and the deceased and so at its best the link was tenuous. The director would be able to amend the records accordingly and provide her with an alibi. Who would dispute the facts as presented by the Head of State and director of the facility?

"It had to be done and you can be assured that all records of your attendance here today will be erased," he reminded her. Neither of them knew what might happen next, whether or not Aeron's death would be questioned by the staff and inmates. Kalista had the names she needed to make arrangements for the systematic disempowering of the individuals and the organizations concerned. The problem had been identified and now she could implement a solution. The information would be filtered down to the necessary people and the required changes would be implemented. No one would know the true reason for the sudden changes in their lives and by the time that the next leadership election had been fought and won, enough time would have elapsed for any suspicion to fade; no one would make any connection with the retired leader and the death of an elderly member of staff at the facility. She could now stand down safe in the knowledge that she had served her State. Kalista and the director had played their part in securing the future existence of The Kind, and the director would be rewarded by an offer of early retirement, once the new regime was inaugurated and the smooth transition completed. However, both knew that there were no assurances and Kalista found herself once more on the edge of the glass cliff, preparing to take a further leap of faith.

Secret Powers of the Silence

With the ivory, silken knickers wrapped tightly around her stubby fingers, Rose Westwood lifted them to her face and rubbed her fat cheek. She revelled in the feel of the soft, creamy texture of the luxurious garment on her pallid skin, and felt a hot throb in her groin. Covering her nose and mouth with the delicate piece, she closed her eyes and inhaled the familiar scent. Next she lifted the matching bra out of the bedside drawer, and toyed with the pearl on the centrepiece before holding it up to her own chest and looking at herself in the mirror. Turning for a side view of the delicate, lace garment she checked the label and decided to shop for one of her own, if the range included larger sizes.

She turned her attention to the wardrobe, opening the glass-fronted doors to reveal a large selection of clothes and shoes. Rose went straight for the patent-leather evening stilettos. She had never seen her neighbour wearing this glamorous footwear. As a landscape designer, Jade was usually seen in old jeans, faded T-shirts and grass-stained training shoes. Rose ran her fingers along the three-inch metal heel, pressing the spike into the palm of her hand. A shot of jealousy permeated her to the core.

Incensed, she rifled through the dress collection, fingering the luxurious garments, noting the names of the designers and checking the sizes on the labels. Rose's irate imagination added another fictitious chapter to the little-known history of her enigmatic new neighbour. She rubbed the velvet of a long evening dress between her fingers and imagined Jade's long, tanned legs underneath. She saw her dancing with an adoring male companion, his hands firm on the svelte torso beneath the satin bustier; Rose scowled at the thought of her neighbour smiling and laughing; her partner leaning in to whisper in her ear and kiss her neck. However, secretly she would be high on the thrill of these forbidden acts for hours.

Rose's heart had skipped a beat on receiving a request to watch over Jade's home and office, whilst she went away for a couple of days. Recently she had been shut out of her neighbour's life, without explanation, and so had seized the golden opportunity to crawl back under the woman's skin.

Perspiring in excitement, she turned her attention to the top of the dressing table. It may have been a while since she was last here, but she was confident that things were much the same. She searched through the bottles and lotions to see if there was anything new. Squeezing a blob of self-tanning body crème onto the palm of her hand, she reached into her blouse to rub it onto the roll of fat on her midriff, sagging out beneath her greying, nylon ill-fitting bra. If it worked, she would buy some for herself. Spraying an unfamiliar fragrance in the air, she was undecided as to whether or not she liked the scent, but made a mental note of its unfamiliar Japanese name to ensure she bought the same product.

Next, it was the turn of the jewellery box. Rose was about to release the lock when, with her clumsy, ungainly stance, she knocked a loose key out from the lock of the dressing-table drawer. A deep sense of discovery now flooded her. This was new territory. The contents of this drawer had, until now, remained hidden from her sight. It had always been locked and the key stored in a location which had, most frustratingly, eluded her many attempts to find it. She bent over to pick up the key from the carpet, and with shaking hands, placed it in the lock.

The shallow, wooden drawer opened to reveal a passport, a bank statement, two separate credit-card statements detailing recent purchases and three handwritten letters. Scanning the bank statements she noted the healthy balance. Next she scoured the bills and scrutinized the recent purchases made by Jade.

With hot, sweaty hands she lifted the letters from the unsealed envelopes and read the private contents. Rose relished the graphic, personal descriptions of Jade's breasts in the text, licking her lips at the thought of the sensual activities the couple had engaged in. Skimming through the pages, she focused in on the salacious details in the third letter, denying her own arousal by expressing a faked sense of disgust. When her eyes alighted on the word 'affair' on the last page, her heart raced. This was the information she had been seeking! The revelation brought a glint to her dead fish eyes; an insidious smirk spread across her bloated face. *Jade Morrigan has been having an affair! That is why her marriage ended!* Rose concluded.

She had found more than she could have hoped for. Thrilled at the thought of drip-feeding this information around the village, she began to imagine the initial look of shock on the faces of her friends, and then the wry smiles of secret knowing which were bound to follow. She would whisper the news in the ears of the schoolyard mothers as they congregated at the gate, on her way to work the next morning. She could email the working women from the computer on her office desk. By the end of the day, everyone in the village would know of the marital transgressions of its newest settler, Jade Morrigan.

The feeling of self-righteousness was one of Rose's deepest addictions; rubbishing the reputation of someone else was the quickest way for her to receive her fix. In a final search at the rear of the drawer her intrusive, fat fingers retrieved a golden locket. Inscribed on the back were the words, '*For Jade, for whom my love will never die, ever yours, Will.*' An intense jealousy burned through Rose's body. Why should Jade have all this: good looks, nice clothes, jewellery, money and men? She didn't deserve it. In Rose's mind her neighbour was a stuck-up bitch and now also a slut. Rose raged. She stuffed the locket it into her pocket and replaced the documents inside the drawer. She rammed the drawer closed and roughly replaced the key in the lock. Walking back through the hallway of the house, she cast a sly glance at the empty, wicker dog-basket, complete with its grubby blanket and half-chewed teddy, and grinned.

Leaving the house she glowered at two young boys riding their bicycles in the dusk and stomped back behind her own gate. She was greeted by a fat, black and white cat with a large scab on its nose, which she roughly kicked aside as it competed with her to enter the front door. In the lair of her own bedroom, she took out the locket, a red mist lowered around her head and she raged in her heart. The mere existence of the locket had inflamed her levels of jealousy to previously unknown heights. She incubated her twisted emotions until it seeped, as poison, out of her pores.

Later that night in bed whilst replaying the sensation, scents and scandalous descriptions in her mind, she furiously manipulated herself for that elusive sense of pleasure; with her unconscious husband snoring beside her. In her frequent fantasies, Rose imagined her own, lithe, tanned body being subject to sexual worship, usually by the husbands of her colleagues and neighbours. She longed for their attention, and whilst feeling entitled to receive it, she also knew that revealing the true pale, dimpled flab covering both her thighs, her pendulous, sagging breasts and the overhang of her stretch-marked skin of her stomach over her mount of Venus, would never get her the attention she craved. Mr Westwood had never satisfied the needs of his younger wife. Oblivious to her internal world of envy, jealousy and resentment of the bodies, houses and husbands of other women, he dutifully placed his meagre salary in their joint bank account each month and listened passively to the barked instructions of the discontented woman. From the outset of their convenient marriage, Rose had taken care of the family accounts, ensuring that only half of her wages went into the communal pot. The rest she spent on whatever she believed would bring her personal happiness. She watched others closely for ideas of what clothes, shoes and jewellery to buy. She frequently changed her hair colour and style, and dieted to imitate the look someone of she envied, seeking to emulate all aspects of their behaviour and lifestyle. When Rose believed that things were going well in her life, she would spend more time out of the house, ingratiating herself into the lives of others, in the hope of escaping her own miserable, mediocre, little world. Her husband and son simply did not feature in this fictional version of her life that she continually replayed in her head. On these occasions she viewed of her own family and her dreary home, as a necessary evil, an albatross, but one that necessarily afforded her a steady income and cheap accommodation, when there was nothing better on the horizon. Inevitably things soon turned sour in Rose's latest fantasy world. Some months into the new friendship, she would view the innocent actions of a close friend as deliberate slight to her, or accuse them of finding favour in the company of another, and a darker side of Rose would rise to the surface. Her home then became a prison, where she would malignantly linger, planning her spiteful revenge. Her heavy presence and poisonous outbursts at these times sent both her husband and son into the outside workshop to repair yet another broken tool or tinker with a faulty engine. With no one else to bully, she would load up her plate with pork pies and sweet pastries and sit for hours on her already-ample backside, surfing the internet to see where she could plant lies about her latest frenemy, soiling some innocent woman's reputation to assuage her own pain. She would seethe in secret, whilst still smiling to the face of her imaginary nemesis, as they passed in the street, the local shop or in the office; all the while indulging in distorted dreams of ways in which she could destroy the unfortunate victim's life.

When the neighbouring house became occupied some three months previously, Rose's frequent offers of help were just a devious way of gaining access to all areas of the unsuspecting woman's life. In the guise of a friend, she was forever calling around, usually at inconvenient times, late at night or early in the morning, in the hope of catching a glimpse into the private life of her latest victim. However, Jarvis the cocker spaniel never failed to alert his mistress as to the arrival of the intruder. When sure that no one was around to witness the act, Rose often delivered a swift kick to the ribs of the lively, liver-coloured young dog. Volunteering to assist with her ironing and other household tasks, Rose often let herself into the house, when she knew that Jade would be at work, in her garden office. As such she had familiarized herself with the layout and knew where Jade kept her personal effects. She monitored every new item that appeared in the house, from coffee maker to new pieces of linen and even checked the log on Jade's telephone to find out to whom she had been speaking; whilst simultaneously smiling and waving through the window to the landscape artist at work in her summer house.

She had summoned the courage to persuade Jade to attend an aqua-aerobics class with her; such was her desire to catch a glimpse of her neighbour's bare skin. Secretly thrilled when they had been forced to share a cubicle in the busy changing room, she became consumed with jealousy as the slim woman bent over to dry her toes, revealing her neat, naked rear and slim, toned thighs. In a rage, Rose had neglected to dry the extremities of her own body, driving home with the fat of her thighs uncomfortably chaffing and her bulbous wet feet squelching inside her sad, downtrodden training shoes. Such was the depth of her dissatisfaction with her own body and life, that Rose's thinking about the people around her had become painfully twisted out of the realms of reason. She was able, in her mind, to ascribe any behaviour of others to the category of unacceptable, whilst constantly justifying her own, demented notions. When she managed to get so close to someone, their initially envied attributes suddenly became contentious issues, and their actions interpreted as personal attacks on Rose. The deeper her envy for the person concerned, the more vile her outpouring of venom amongst the unfortunate woman's friends, colleagues or neighbours as the friendship dissolved. Rose had a long history of such behaviour. If anyone had bothered to piece together her actions over the previous decade or so, and spoken to her variety of acquaintances, they might discern the distinct and rather disturbing pattern in her life.

In the early months of her move into the village, Jade had trusted her neighbour with a key to her house and Rose had spoken openly about her interactions with other villagers. Believing she had the innocent ear of the newest village member, she sought to win Jade over by revealing denigrating information about key members of the community, with a vindictive glint in her eyes. Jade had listened in silence as her neighbour had so inappropriately divulged financial information about the housebound old lady she so charitably drove to the local bingo hall twice weekly. She was shocked by the reckless revelations of the mental-health issues faced by another shy, struggling neighbour. She recoiled at Rose's gleeful announcement at the failure of the marriage of the local schoolteacher; appalled at the unhealthy display of interest in the rumoured impotence of the woman's husband.

As Jade maintained her silent listening and refused to be caught up into the malign dramas, so Rose's intensity deepened. She stared hard at Jade, as if trying to fathom her thoughts. Rose was used to the easy manipulation of others around her; she felt frustrated on sensing resistance from her latest intended victim, on her failure to ensnare them in her venal world, with her savage spite.

In the quiet moments, Jade reflected on Rose's comments and became increasingly fearful of the woman's true intentions. Despite Rose's low, soft tone of voice, Jade had heard her heaping harsh and cruel words onto her husband and son, her shrieks emanating from the open lounge window of her house and disturbing the quiet stillness of the garden. Jade was chilled by the woman's ability to adopt the same sly smile when she was speaking ill of people, as on the odd occasions that she spoke well of her family or friends. She wondered what juicy gossip Rose hoped to glean from her and spread so dishonourably around the small-minded members of the community. As a childless divorcee, she had resolved to make a fresh start on moving to the quiet countryside village alone, with only her trusted pet, Jarvis, for company. She was determined not to fill up her neat cottage with the baggage of the past. As such, she had spoken sparingly of her personal situation. However, Rose's persistence had paid off when Jade wearily explained that her marriage had broken down as result of clashing shift-work patterns.

As she ventured further afield in her new surroundings, Jade started to learn of some disturbing family history concerning Rose Westwood. From snippets of local gossip picked up at the bar of the village inn, she began to piece together a rather unsavoury picture of the childhood of her next-door neighbour. She unearthed a shocking rumour concerning the scalding of a puppy belonging to Rose's younger brother, Edward Dalton. According to Carrie, the friendly barmaid, the reporting of the incident by ten-year-old Rose was simply not believed by the vet responsible for putting the poor creature out of its misery.

"He asked Rose's parents if anyone could verify the child's story, as the facts did not add up. In his mind there were too many unanswered questions," Carrie said with raised eyebrows, before describing how poor Edward had been traumatized by the suffering of his beloved Christmas pet.

"Rose had failed to even shed a tear at the sight and sound of the whimpering pup, as it lay on the passenger seat of the family car, on the drive to its death at the vet's surgery," she vented. "Edward told us that himself."

Jade ordered a round of drinks for her companions and asked further after Edward. Where was he? Did he still live in the village? She was informed that he had moved away from home at the first opportunity.

"At eighteen he left for university and never returned, except when summoned to the odd family celebration, such as Rose's wedding to Cecil," explained Carrie. "Rose and Edward had clashed throughout their childhood. The young girl had a vile temper and Edward had sported many a black eye in the schoolyard. Yet it was Rose who constantly won her parents' backing and attention." So it had seemed to Carrie. The barmaid had also shared the common village knowledge that Edward had instructed a solicitor to challenge his deceased parents' will, suspecting it had been subject to unauthorized amendment in their last days.

"The new will left the family home solely to Rose and the parents' life savings to Edward. On receipt of the shocking balance in the account, Edward had raised a challenge claiming that the change was made without his knowledge, and stating that his parents had always made clear their desire that the house and savings should be shared equally between the children.

"Of course, Rose accused him of dishonouring the family name by discussing the finances in public and refused to speak about the matter any further with him," Carrie confirmed.

Then, in the village inn, she described how Rose had publicly announced that her brother was a 'malcontent' who refused to have anything to do with the family and now had the audacity to think he was due something from the family estate. It was rumoured that Rose had instructed the family doctor to enter a description of the death of each as being from 'natural causes' on their certificates. And during their joint funeral, she had melodramatically announced that her poor father died of a broken heart, following the death of his beloved wife and her dear mother.

"Only days later, Rose had been seen waltzing about the village in her shiny new car and matching blue coat." Carrie lowered her voice and opened her eyes widely as she imparted this damning piece of information. With hindsight, the seasoned barmaid noted that it did seem suspicious that Rose had been so stubborn in her refusal to allow any services for the elderly into her parents' home in their later years. People had commended her for her commitment to their comfort and wellbeing as she spoke about the meals she cooked for them and how well she coped with their developing incontinence, whilst also holding down a part-time job as a legal secretary in the probate department of a local firm of solicitors.

Rose had been heard to say that she despised any selfish person who put their elderly parents into a care home. And more recently, the local gossips had questioned why she was now involving herself in the lives and business of other elderly and lonely residents of the village; those whose spouses had died and children had grown up and moved away.

Logging in to the village network, Jade had found a whole host of voices waiting for a new ear willing to listen to their historical gripes and current moans. It made sense to her that a small amount of people, most interrelated, and all living in such close proximity, would, after time, inevitably turn on each other and a darker picture of Rose's motivation was being pieced together in Jade's mind. She became aware of just how dangerous this seemingly innocuous woman could be, and deliberately created some distance between them. She grew increasingly concerned at the woman's real reasons for offering up her services, almost exclusively, to the elderly and infirm village residents.

However, as Jade had started to refuse all of Rose's offers of help, and invitations to attend social and recreational events with her, her neighbour's obsessional behaviour had heightened. She could be seen more openly gossiping on the village green, whispering aside when Jade walked past. She couldn't be sure of the cause, but Jade seemed to detect a sudden coldness in the attitude from the lady in the village grocery shop. Previously keen to engage with her in conversation, her manner had recently become distant. People who she habitually passed on her morning dog walk now crossed the street to avoid acknowledging her, and from one old man with whom she had hardly exchanged a word, she now found herself on the receiving end of a series of menacing, hard stares. Despite this unpleasant atmosphere, Jade had persisted with her routine activities and to secretly scratch beneath the surface of her neighbour's falsehoods and façades.

One afternoon Jade received a phone call from Mrs Parsons, who lived in the Rectory off Church Lane.

"Is that Jade, the gardening lady?" she asked.

"Yes, I'm a landscape designer," Jade replied, not sure the difference would be appreciated by the old lady.

"I was wondering if you could come and mow the lawn for me, dear. The usual chap has not turned up this week and I have guests arriving this afternoon for Bridge Club."

"Well, I don't usually do that sort of garden work..." Jade started to explain.

The old lady interrupted, "I picked up your details from the card in the garden centre and I remember that Rose recommended you. She said you would be more than happy to oblige."

"Oh, well, if Rose recommended me then I'm sure I can fit you in," Jade seized the opportunity. She was in no doubt that if Rose was involved with this lady, she would have an underlying motive. "What size is the lawn?" She asked.

An hour later, Jade loaded her home gardening equipment

into the boot of her trusty old Volvo estate car and pulled out of her driveway, her every move monitored by Rose who watched through her kitchen window. She drove slowly through the narrow, winding roads of the sleepy village and turned into Church Lane. Once the main thoroughfare to the hub of the village, the overgrown lane now led only to the Old Rectory and the long-abandoned twelfth-century church, which, despite its restoration in the 1800s, had lost its congregation to the village pub. Originally an illegal poteen den, the pub had opened its doors in the late 1920s. The occupants of the village were largely descendants of Cornish mine workers, with a strong drinking culture, who had come to seek work and settled in the area in the thirteenth and fourteenth centuries. As more people became part of the fabric of the alcoholic habit, so the church abandoned its outpost in the village and sold off the property. Mrs Parsons lived alone in the Old Rectory, which she and her husband had bought in the early 1960s. As Jade approached she could see the old lady standing in the doorway. Mrs Parsons was petite with a haughty demeanour. Jade recalled how Rose had once referred to her as 'a dried-up old witch'. Despite having moved into the village over half a century ago, she had never been accepted into the bosom of the locals, as they did not like her accent. Her children had attended the local schools but had moved away to find employment, upon graduating from university. Mrs Parsons had watched their contemporaries grow into adulthood and prematurely become parents themselves. She was saddened to watch once-promising young lives stifled by the village naysayers, sinking to the low level of expectations by the embittered older generation. Financial investment and education had failed to gain a foothold in the village and as the population fell, so one by one, all of the amenities which had once promised hope for the future of its inhabitants fell into disuse or a state of disrepair. The homes of people began to look tired and their faces wore a defeated expression. In stark contrast, Mrs Parsons was a proud lady and her immaculate home and garden were clearly cared for. She greeted Jade as she opened the rear door of her car to lift out the petrol mower and garden strimmer.

"Good morning, you must be Jade, Jade Morgan? What a beautiful March day, very mild with a nice cool breeze, ideal for gardening!"

"Jade Morrigan, actually," the younger woman replied. "Yes, it feels as if spring has arrived. I'm here to cut your grass and trim the borders."

Mrs Parsons looked her up and down. "Just in the nick of time, my dear," the old lady responded. "My guests are arriving later this afternoon. Will you be done before two o'clock?"

Jade looked around. "Is it just this front lawn or do you have more ground?" she asked.

"Oh yes, my dear, there's much more around the back," she motioned to the side gate of the house.

"Can I take a look?" Jade asked.

"Certainly!" Mrs Parsons replied, stepping over the threshold to her home and walking along the gravel path leading to the side gate. Jade followed. The rear garden was enclosed by a high wall and climbing plants. There were a number of fruit trees, a riotous border of flowering shrubs and a carefully positioned swinging seat.

"I like to call it my secret garden," Mrs Parsons explained. "Not many people know about it. I only entertain a few friends here and of course, none of the villagers have ever been here."

"It's beautiful!" exclaimed Jade. "I'll unpack my equipment and make a start."

As Jade completed the mowing of the gently sloping lawn, Mrs Parsons appeared on the patio with a tray.

"Tea or coffee, dear?" she asked, setting the tray down on the wooden garden table. Jade opted for a cup of coffee. It was clear that the old lady was keen to chat. "So, how long have you been in the village?" she asked.

Secret Powers of the Silence

Jade replied, "Just a few months or so, I'm still finding my way around and learning who's who and what's what, so to speak." She was being deliberately vague.

"And have you always been a gardener?" the old lady continued.

"I had another job before this, but I wanted a healthier and more relaxed pace of life, and so I studied landscape design and set up this business," Jade replied. "I enjoy working outdoors. I find it quite therapeutic on occasions. It gives me time to mull things over and I find that I can attune my intuition to the plants. I just seem to know where certain trees and plants will grow more easily."

"Well, you certainly do a good clean-up job and I hope we can come to some arrangement. Can I rely on you? I'm afraid the old chap has just become too unreliable, and I have standards to maintain. Could you come by weekly, just to keep up with the grass and weeding?" she asked.

"Yes, weekly visits should be sufficient for the season," Jade replied. "Where did you say you heard about me?" She was hoping to glean a little more information about her neighbour.

"Rose Westwood," Mrs Parsons replied. "Your neighbour I believe?"

"Oh Rose, yes, of course." Jade nodded.

"She mentioned you a few months back but I saw your card in the window of the local shop and it reminded me. The old chap who used to look after the gardens has been quiet ill, so it seems. I didn't think he would be able to keep up this job and when he failed to turn up again yesterday I rang him to say that his services would no longer be required. Then I called you."

"So you are a friend of Rose?" Jade asked.

"She's a very helpful girl," Mrs Parsons replied. "She calls around weekly to take my washing to the laundrette for me. I pay her of course. She is very reliable and was most helpful to me when my husband was very ill, just before he died, a little over

281

two years ago. He had been ill for quite some time and I had become quite worn out caring for him. Rose would sit with him so that I could get some rest and respite. I'm not too well myself, you see. And when he passed away, she saw to it that the solicitor that she works for sorted out all the probate business for me. I didn't have to leave home to make visits to his office. She explained that I was poorly too and he very kindly let her bring the paperwork home for me. It's the diabetes, you see. My eyesight is getting worse. She explained all of the paperwork to me and showed me where to sign. She's a dear girl."

That's not what she thinks, or says, about you, Jade thought to herself, whilst maintaining her silent listening.

The following week, when Jade was next working in the secret garden, she noticed two figures watching her from the window. It was Rose. She was inside the house with Mrs Parsons. Jade continued working in the flower beds until Mrs Parsons arrived on the patio with the refreshments. This time she placed a pot of coffee and a plate of home-baked fairy cakes on the table and invited Jade to help herself.

"These were so kindly provided by Rose," Mrs Parsons informed her. "She called in to collect the laundry and presented me with these. Of course, I can't eat them, there's far too much sugar in them for me. She meant well, of course, dear girl."

Jade politely refused a cake. "Not for me thank you. I have to stay fit and healthy for this job," she explained. She couldn't help but think that Rose had watched her leaving home and worked out that she was maintaining the garden of the Rectory. But why had she chosen to turn up now? Was she checking up on Jade or did she have another motive?

On returning from the Rectory, a sense of unease weighed heavily in the pit of Jade's stomach. As she pulled up on her driveway, she felt sure that something was wrong. As she turned the key in the lock she became aware of an eerie silence. There was no greeting bark from Jarvis and no sight of him through the glass pane, jumping up and scratching the wooden panelling of the door. Jade felt nauseous. As she rushed through the entrance hall, she was relieved to see him in his basket. But as he slowly lifted his head, she could see the sorry look in his eyes. Her precious boy was poorly. As she stepped through into the kitchen she was greeted by a large mound of some noxious smelling, waste material. Jade was unsure from which dog orifice the mound had presented itself and gagged as she leaned over to clean it up. There were patches of fresh blood in amongst the fibrous tissue. It did not resemble anything like the food she had placed in his bowl earlier that day. She checked the bowl to find it still full of the biscuits she had placed there. She looked at Jarvis and saw some blood smeared over his jowls. She knew that she needed to get him to the vet's surgery.

* * *

"So you think he's eaten something which has made him ill?" asked Billy Arthur, the veterinary surgeon, who had agreed to examine Jarvis at short notice. "They are scavengers by nature. Have you any idea where he has been to eat this garbage?"

Jade told him that there had been blood in the vomit and that Jarvis had been at home all morning, as she had been out working.

"And you didn't see any evidence that he had destroyed any of the household items?" asked Billy.

"No, I couldn't see anything out of the ordinary." Jade started to wonder if she had missed something. Billy advised her that he would be a couple of hours and was happy to phone her later that day with a progress report.

However, Jade wanted to stay close. "Is it okay if I wait whilst you sedate him and pump his stomach?" she asked. In the reception area she filled out the insurance details and handed the form to the lady behind the desk.

"Jarvis Morrigan, 8 Meadow Side Close?" The receptionist checked the details. "So you're Rose's new neighbour," she commented.

"Is Rose a client of the practice?" Jade asked irritably. The world seemed to be closing in on her. Everyone else's business seemed to be the local currency. The receptionist lowered her voice and explained that she had been born in the village and went to school with Rose Dalton, but she had moved out when she got married. With a weird look on her face she said that Rose and Mr Arthur, the vet, had fallen out years ago and would have nothing to do with each other.

"I'm not sure but I think it was something to do with a family pet," she whispered, and then offered Jade a cup of tea as she would be in for a long wait. Jade gratefully accepted and sat back to watch and listen to the conversations of the other clients as they arrived and left with their pets.

"Were you good friends with Rose?" she asked during a lull in the appointment schedule.

"Not really," the receptionist replied. "I can't remember now who her friends were."

"So she wasn't a popular girl then," Jade attempted to lighten the tone of the conversation. "It's just that she's been quite kind to me..." she added provocatively.

"Oh she will be, at first," the receptionist took the bait. "Until she decides to take against you, that is, and then she can make your life hell."

"Did she do something to you?" Jade asked a little too quickly and the receptionist, unsure if Jade was friend of Rose, tried to back track.

"Oh we were just kids really. You know how young girls can be, bitchy and cruel sometimes." Jade just nodded her head in acknowledgement, whilst thoughts of Rose's childhood bullying loomed large in her mind. It was true that the school bully often grew into the malicious village gossip.

"I expect she's very different now, married with a family of her own." The receptionist tried to fill the awkward silence. Jade sipped silently on her tea. Two hours later, the surgery door opened and the vet stepped out in to waiting room. A stiff-backed Jade stood slowly to receive the news.

"I'm so sorry," he started. "There was broken glass in Jarvis's intestines, small, ground pieces mixed in with a lamb chop, but still very sharp. I didn't realize until I had emptied the contents of his stomach. He has internal bleeding for a while and septi-caemia has set in. I'd say that this wasn't his first and only ingestion of glass. His organs had started to fail. I have decided it would be kinder to make him comfortable and let him slip away peacefully. Do you want to come and be with him in his last moments?"

* * *

With bleary, red eyes, Jade woke the following morning to face the stark realization that her beloved dog was dead. Snatches of the conversation with the vet and the receptionist were replaying in her head. Through her tears, Jade had returned home to search frantically for any broken items which might have caught Jarvis' attention. There was no sign of anything. She had slept on it and now knew what she had to do.

"And the vet said that the glass had been consumed by the dog over a period of time? The house was secure, and you say there was only one person with a key?" asked the desk officer at the police station.

"It can mean only one thing," Jade was sure.

"Is there any other evidence?" the frowning sergeant inter-vened. Jade shook her head.

"Well, there isn't enough to go on to make an arrest, you know that," the sergeant reminded her firmly.

"What about fingerprints?" Jade knew she was clutching at

straws.

"Unless she has a record then it's a pointless exercise and we would have no authority to retain them on file. You know that, Jade. Look, if we could help you we would. All we can say is keep your ear to the ground and if you come up with something else let us know."

* * *

The following Saturday as Jade pulled up onto the Rectory driveway, Mrs Parsons greeted her at the door. "Good morning! Is everything alright, my dear?" she asked. Jade explained what had happened to Jarvis. She made no mention of her suspicions of Rose.

"Oh dear," the old lady replied. "How dreadful; poor animal!" She could sense that Jade was in no mood for heavy manual labour that morning.

"How about we start with a cup of tea, and if you feel better you can do the garden later on?" she suggested. At first Jade protested, saying she would rather get straight on with the job. However, she succumbed to the old lady's gentle persuasion. Sitting at the kitchen table with a pot of tea and some homemade scones, courtesy of Rose, Jade asked Mrs Parsons about the passing of her husband.

"It was a strange thing, you know," the old lady started thoughtfully. "He had a heart condition and I was trying to get him to eat more healthily. His cholesterol levels were sky high and as he had been forced to give up smoking, he was becoming very cranky with me. He was a large man and I was trying to get some help with looking after him as I was struggling. I asked Rose if she knew which department of the social services I should contact. She had looked after her own elderly parents and I thought she would know. But she offered to help me out. She was quite happy to spend the weekend here with Mr Parsons, so I could go and visit my sister. I was very grateful to her. After that she would come to spend a few hours with him every week, just so I could get out to lunch with my friends for an hour or two. It was very kind of her, although he wasn't very pleased with the arrangement. There seemed to be no pleasing him at that stage. One day, when I returned, she was very concerned about him. She took me to one side and said she had noticed blood in his urine and stools and that I should call the doctor." The old lady's eyes filled up with tears at this point and Jade gently took her hand. "And that was it. The doctor admitted him to hospital and he was gone the next day. Multiple organ failure, they said. I still don't understand it. Internal bleeding had turned toxic, they said. His spleen, liver, kidneys and finally his heart packed in. Looking back, he went downhill so very quickly."

Jade's hackles rose and shiver shot along her spine. She thought to herself, *Internal bleeding; an injury inflicted by Rose, or just a coincidence?*

Mrs Parson pushed the plate of scones towards her, "Do help yourself, dear," she said. "I have told Rose that this sort of thing is no good for my sugar levels, but she insists that she has followed a diabetic recipe. I tried one and they still taste very sweet to me."

"Would it be okay if I took them home with me?" Jade requested.

"Of course," Mrs Parsons replied. "I would be delighted."

Jade rose to start the gardening and Mrs Parsons wrapped the plate in foil in readiness for taking away.

Later that afternoon, Jade called the police sergeant. "I may have something. Would it be possible for you to get something analysed?" she asked and proceeded to relate the details of her conversation with Mrs Parsons. "I have a suspicion that a crime is being perpetrated. Yes, I know I left the force over two years ago, but I can't help it if I've stumbled across something. I can't ignore a copper's hunch." The sergeant reluctantly agreed and asked her to deliver the sample of scones to the station. Rose was watching through the kitchen blinds as Jade loaded the covered plate onto the passenger seat of her car. Sensing she was being watched, Jade swung around quickly to see her neighbour step back from the window and straighten out the blinds. She hoped that she had not recognized the covered item. The last thing she wanted to do was to arouse the woman's suspicion.

It was as she was driving home from the police station that Jade came up with a plan. She would set a trap, provide Rose with an opportunity to commit some incriminating act which would allow the police to search her home. Jade felt sure that they would find all sorts of interesting evidence. She created a false excuse to be away from home for a few days, before knocking at her neighbour's door, an hour or so later, to ask of her a favour. A very surprised Rose answered and said she would be delighted to help out by keeping an eye on the empty house whilst she was away.

"You still have a key?" Jade asked.

"Oh, yes I think so, let me check..." Rose replied and reached over to the hall dresser to rummage in a drawer.

"Is this the one?" she asked, holding up a key, knowing full well that it was the key to her neighbour's front door.

"What about the dog?" she asked slyly. "You know I don't like the way he barks and jumps up at me when I walk in."

Jade bristled, the hairs on the back of her neck prickling at her collar. She shivered lightly but managed to keep her overall composure. "He won't be there to trouble you," she said stiffly and backed away from the door. "I'll be leaving early in the morning and I'll be back on Tuesday evening," she informed her neighbour, before turning and walking away. The scabby-nosed cat hissed at her as she stepped over it on the path

Before leaving the village, Jade called in on Mrs Parsons. For some reason the old lady was playing on her mind. She was very glad that she had listened to her inner voice telling her to check up on her. She came to the door in her pastel-coloured housecoat and slippers, looking pale and drawn.

"I'm not sure what's wrong with me, my dear," she tried to explain. "I have some sharp pains in my chest and my stomach and…" She started to cough and as she took a handkerchief out of her pocket to cover her mouth, Jade could see it was stained with specks of blood.

"You need to see the doctor. Do you want me to make the call?" She asked.

"Oh it's not that bad, dear," Mrs Parsons backtracked. "Just a virus, I'm sure."

"Have you had anything to eat today?" Jade asked, knowing it was important for the woman to keep her blood-sugar levels stable.

"I had a drop of lamb stew for supper last night, dear. Rose kindly brought it around for me. But I had a dreadful night's sleep and I haven't been able to eat anything since."

"Where's the stew?" asked Jade. "Is there any left?"

"I finished the lot!" Mrs Parsons proudly announced.

Damn! Jade thought to herself.

"But don't worry, there's more in the freezer," she added. Jade made a mental note.

"Well, I think you should call the doctor," she said. "I'd like to stay until I'm sure you're okay, if that's alright with you."

"Oh no, you go on. You have some place to be," replied Mrs Parsons. "It's Sunday and the doctors won't want to be bothered with me. I'll be fine. If I need anything I'll just call Rose." Jade wanted to say something else, but she knew it would be a waste of time. She told the old lady that she would be returning on Tuesday, but that she feared leaving her. Giving her mobile phone number, she instructed Mrs Parsons that if she needed help, she must call immediately.

Jade drove just thirty minutes out of the countryside and headed for the small motel located at the end of the motorway.

Here she would be far enough away not to be spotted, yet close enough to promptly return to the village if needed. She made herself a cup of instant coffee from a damp, complimentary sachet and unpacked a magazine on permaculture. Sitting atop the rough-worn cover on the bed, she tried to close her mind to thoughts of what could be happening in the village, but images of Mrs Parsons kept creeping into her consciousness.

Just as she suspected, Rose had taken the bait. Waiting until the fall of evening when her husband and son were busy working in the garage, she had walked around to her neighbour's house, where she had discovered the letters and pocketed the gold locket planted there by Jade; who knew that Rose would not be able to resist the temptation.

As Rose had lain awake, that night, tortured by her spiteful thoughts and overwhelmed by a sense of jealousy and discontent, so Jade had also spent a sleepless night in the noisy, uncomfortable motel. Bleary-eyed, she had shared an early breakfast with the long-distance lorry drivers at the motel, before heading back to the village. En route, her mobile received a call and she pulled off the road as soon as she happened upon a lay-by. A very shaky Mrs Parsons had left a garbled message. Jade could just make out the words, 'throat' and 'hospital' and she tried in vain to call the old lady's home. There was no answer. Jade drove straight back home. Rose was standing in the street talking to another neighbour as she pulled up.

"You're home early," she remarked as Jade parked up and got up of the car. "I was just going to check on your house. I didn't get round to it yesterday, but I thought you'd be away until tomorrow. Now I won't need to bother." She could not contain her smugness.

"No worries," Jade replied. "Thanks anyway." She wondered if Rose was aware that Mrs Parsons was in the hospital. Inside the house, she headed straight for her bedroom and the dressing-table drawer. The locket had gone. She was right. Now she needed to inform the police and get Rose's house searched before she could dispose of the incriminating item.

Next she rang the geriatric ward of the local hospital and asked after Mrs Parsons. The hospital would only confirm that she was on the ward and requested that if Jade was planning to visit, that she attended between the hours of two and three or six and seven – p.m. Jade confirmed that she would be visiting that afternoon. Inside the house she paced up and down, before picking up the phone to report the theft. Rose had blatantly lied outside, saying she had not been inside the house, and if the locket was found in her possession she would have a hard time explaining it.

Later, at the hospital bedside of Mrs Parsons, Jade asked if Rose knew she had been admitted and whether she had eaten any food made by her. The weak, old lady, who was very pleased to see Jade, said she hadn't seen anything of Rose since the Saturday night that she had delivered the lamb stew. She was now on nil by mouth until they stabilized her sugar levels and discovered the cause of her oesophageal haemorrhage. Reassured that the lady was now in good hands, Jade asked her for permission to enter her house and retrieve the container holding the frozen stew. Mrs Parsons was happy to oblige and handing over her house key, she asked if Jade would also pick up the milk from the doorstep and the mail from the hallway mat. Jade knew she was playing for time. It was only a matter of hours before the news of Mrs Parson's hospitalization was bandied around the village by its bored occupants. She drove back to the Rectory and headed for the kitchen. She retrieved the freezer container and hurried back out of the village. At the police station she asked for the sergeant and offered over the evidence. She was informed that the analysis report on the scones was not yet back from the lab.

"You're looking for ground glass," Jade spoke with confidence. "There's an old lady in hospital at the moment with oesophageal bleeding, who has been eating food provided by the same woman who killed my dog," she stated. "If you call the hospital, I'm sure they will report a finding of internal bleeding. Rose Westwood had a hold over Mrs Parsons. Her husband died unexpectedly on her watch, and she is privy to the details of the woman's estate. If you search her house you will find some sort of glass-grinding machinery, maybe more food containing the deadly ingredient and you will find a stolen, gold heart-shaped locket with the inscription '*For Jade, for whom my love will never die, ever yours, Will.*'

In the early hours of Wednesday morning, a police car containing one male and one female officer pulled up into a sleepy Meadow Side Close. An unsuspecting Cecil Westwood opened the door to number seven and at their request, he let the uniformed police into the house. One golden locket, a number of items from the freezer and a multi-purpose sander were confiscated from the property, and a shocked Rose Westwood was seen climbing into the back of the police car, flanked by the female officer. She had been asked to attend at the police station for questioning and her initial refusal had not pleased the officers. Under the threat of arrest, she had finally obliged, much to the confusion of her husband.

Jade opened the door of the Rectory to allow another pair of officers to look for further evidence.

* * *

A month later, Jade was walking her newly rescued Irish wolfhound, Marvin, along the village green, and past the grocery shop, when a group of women stopped to stroke the friendly animal.

"Have you heard the news about Rose Westwood?" one asked, adjusting her volume to ensure she was within Jade's earshot.

"Out on bail I heard, but under strict instructions not to come back to the village. It looks as if she's been falsifying the contents of clients' wills at work, and got found out," piped up another.

"I heard she was up on attempted-murder charges," chimed the voice of a tall, thin woman, excitedly leaning in to join the conversation. "Apparently she was caught trying to poison her husband and son!"

"Well, the house is empty," added a fourth. "But I was told that she was planning to murder a neighbour." The women shot a collective look in Jade's direction; her failure to respond clearly proving irksome to them. Jade maintained a resolute silence, simply refusing to acknowledge the charged speculation.

"Come along, Marvin, Mrs Parsons is waiting to meet you." She addressed only the dog and proceeded to cross the road, turning her back on the village gossips, leaving an uneasy silence in her wake. In this village, where innuendo and lies fuelled the sad lives of its desperate inhabitants; where people fed off each other's misery, glorying in the failures of others and creating a feast of fictional successes for themselves, Jade knew that her silence was both her only defence and key to her survival. Despite their hungriest endeavours, they simply could not swallow her up, nor spit her out. She would remain a most elusive taste, yet a tantalizing tease on the tireless, tattling tongues.

Soul Rocks is a fresh list that takes the search for soul and spirit mainstream. Chick-lit, young adult, cult, fashionable fiction & non-fiction with a fierce twist